POINTE, SHOOTS, AND SCORES

CAROLYN MILLER

CHAPTER 1

Winnipeg, Manitoba
June

Words were sly things. So often meaningless and mundane, a day could be filled with innocuous words, then *bam*. Four little words could change her whole world.

"You cannot keep going."

Bailey Donovan stared at the bank manager, struggling to comprehend. "What do you mean? My classes are full, and I have waiting lists, and I'm getting good views on my YouTube channel." And at just over seven hundred subscribers, she was getting closer to the earning mark.

Mr. Mitsom sighed, and she knew it was way worse than she'd dared imagine. "You don't earn enough money, Bailey. Your classes might be full, but you're charging too little."

"But you know I wanted to keep the dance classes affordable and accessible to all. That was always part of the plan." Ever since she'd been forced to pivot to a new dream. Her grandmother had understood, even if others, like her dad, had always questioned why she'd do such a thing. "I just don't understand. I thought we were doing okay."

Mr. Mitsom tapped the papers on his desk. "The accounting seems up to date. But with the refurbishments you've done, it looks like you've eaten into your safety net. And considering your loan is with this bank, I need to advise that you consider alternative sources of revenue immediately."

"But I've applied for every grant there is."

His lips rolled in, and he shook his head. "I'm sorry. I know this is important to you."

Try *everything* to her. No. She couldn't have failed. She refused to believe it. Was her sister-in-law right in claiming she'd wasted her grandmother's money?

"We need to see substantial increases in your repayments, otherwise we will need to call in our loan in two months."

"Two months? But it's summer, and class numbers always take a hit when school is out."

"I'm sorry. But that's the way it is."

No. She couldn't lose her dream. Not again. Losing her career a second time was unthinkable, especially when everything that had been said suggested it was her own mismanagement that had killed things this time, and not just her broken body.

She peeked up at him, catching a trace of smugness in the pity-smile he offered her, something that drew memories of previous ballet masters who used to regard her with that same sneer hidden behind a mask of caring. Something that drew fresh determination to prove him wrong.

She rose, eyed him firmly. She might look delicate, but there was no need to make the man think she was soft. Only a fool underestimated ballet dancers, who were some of the toughest athletes out there. "You'll have your money in two months, then."

"I hope so. For your sake."

Challenge accepted.

She offered a nod, then left, before the shuddering inside made its way to her limbs. She opened the brass-handled glass door and escaped to the pavement and the rush of cars.

Bright sunshine beat down on her as she walked the blocks back to the studio, her black leather bag bouncing on her hip. Maybe she should've shown she meant business and dressed in a suit and not, well, in a floaty floral dress. Maybe she should've followed other people's advice instead of her heart and what she'd thought was a God-given inclination to keep her fees low and classes open to all, regardless of their background or body shape. The temptation grew to wonder about the what-ifs: what would've happened if she'd never left professional ballet? Would she be living out her dreams, dancing on stages across the world, instead of now living her second-best life, with her shadowy one-day hopes forced into substance and airtime? No. She couldn't afford to indulge in thoughts like that. Pity parties only led to the dark vortex of despair, and she had no time for that. Not anymore.

"Lord, what do I do?"

Her thoughts twisted and turned, never landing solidly enough to give answer. She could work more shifts at the Coffee Haus. She could shut up shop. She could end the lease and take a cheaper place in the suburbs. She could increase her fees. But increasing fees and moving locations wouldn't help some of the students who lived nearer the studio, whose parents already struggled. At the moment, with her apartment within walking distance of both the studio and coffee shop, she barely needed her car. Maybe she could sell it…

Her insides knotted with an instant protest. Sell her grandmother's car? Mom would have a fit. Her sister-in-law would have even more reason to hate her. No, for all kinds of reasons —not least the fact she loved the vintage vibes of the older-make Mercedes—she wouldn't do that.

A weighty breath escaped, her shoulders slumping in a posture she'd instantly take exception to should one of her students do it. But right now she barely could stand upright. What should she do?

The pale pink sign of the Donovan Dance Studio slowed her steps. It was hard to believe she and Poppy James had started this from scratch just four years ago, before Poppy had returned to Calgary last year, when the business couldn't quite support them both. Was Mr. Mitsom right? Had this been a giant mistake? Poppy's absence meant Bailey had needed to drop classes, and not taking much of a wage herself meant she had been living on her savings, meager as they were. Yet having another teacher meant they could offer more classes again, and increase revenue that way. But she couldn't ask Poppy to return. Could she?

She opened the door, turned on the lights, and made her way into the studio. The long, mirrored room with wooden barre was as neat as ever, a faint scent of disinfectant hanging in the air. Little kids were notorious for sharing germs, which was one of the reasons she was fanatical about cleaning, and didn't babysit these days. After battling too many colds, she'd suffered pneumonia when her body couldn't keep fighting it anymore, the week off work something a sole business owner could ill afford. Poppy had been here then, which meant she'd covered Bailey's classes. And while Bailey loved kids, and babysitting could lead to good money, illness wasn't something she could risk again. Especially when she now needed to be focused and earning as much as she could. Heaviness propelled her to slump over, her spine stretching as she touched the floor and closed her eyes.

What should she do? Her days were already filled with

everything from her personal passion, classical ballet, to tap, modern, jazz, even ballroom. She ran classes for all ages, from tiny tots to seniors, who ranged from those needing refresher tips on how to waltz to more basic movements. She might've once felt forced into this career, but now felt like it was her calling. She loved to teach, and showing the least confident or coordinated person how to find and move to the rhythms of music was always a joy. But was offering more classes the answer?

She moved into a side stretch. Maybe she should just do more shifts at the coffee shop. She had less classes over summer. She could possibly combine a few, swap some students around to allow more time to earn. Or did she need to get more creative with how she advertised and marketed the studio? Maybe she could ask Poppy, whose brother Franklin James was a famous NHL player, or so Bailey's brother said. She didn't follow hockey—such a rough, uncouth sport—but Poppy had been excited about Franklin's recent wedding to a sports broadcaster. Surely his new wife Hannah would know a thing or two about how to garner interest.

Her eyes opened, her nose wrinkling. But she'd never liked exploiting connections to push ahead. Using people wasn't her scene. Maybe she was too soft to run a business, but there had to be another way rather than piggybacking on someone else's success. But what was it? What could she do?

The questions kept circling, pecking at her like seagulls after crumbs, like she remembered when she'd danced in England and had visited Brighton's seashore. The cheeky birds had crept closer, wanting a sample of her hot chips and mushy peas, getting closer and closer until Mark, her English ballet friend, had chased them away with a series of grand jetés. Dance had an answer to everything. Which reminded her...

She moved to switch on the speakers, and pressed play on her phone's playlist. The quiet oboe of *Swan Lake* filled the space, crowding out the fears as she closed her eyes, swaying, then stepping into an arabesque, elevating her right leg behind in derrière.

Dance—and God—had always combined to calm her soul. She figured dance, like any of the creative arts, was an expression that the Creator God fully understood, as much as people who made music or poetry or painted. Dance was an expression of the soul.

She spun her way across the room in manèges, a series of pirouettes that brought release and a smile, and reminded her that just as she'd relearned these movements and could now trust her body to do manèges, so she could trust God for her future. It was just a matter of pausing, waiting, sensing what God wanted her to do.

The music ended, the room filling with silence again. She drew in a deep breath, then slowly released, pausing, stilling her heart to listen.

"Lord, I need a miracle. What do You think I should do?"

LORD, what should I do?

On the heels of Luc's prayer, his heart filled with peace.

It was an easy yes. This was something he'd barely dared dream about. But first, he had to make sure he was actually awake and that this wasn't just a dream. "Are you sure?"

Winnipeg's coach and general manager nodded. "We've been watching you for a long time now, Luc, and been impressed by the way you've really stepped up in recent years. And now with Linzey's retirement, it seems the right time to reward someone who's been a part of the organization for these many years and helped carry the team, and been a face for the franchise in recent times."

"You really want me to be the captain?"

More nods. "It seems most fitting that it falls on you."

Wow. Luc Blanchard leaned back in his chair, excitement popping in his veins like microwaved popcorn. His parents would be so proud. The other guys too. He'd never dared imagine that his love for the game would result in this huge honor. Captain of a Canadian pro hockey team? If he'd been a weaker dude, he might've shed a tear. Instead he grinned and nodded. "I don't really know what to say, except thank you. And I'm really honored to have this opportunity."

Coach Frantzen smiled. "I'm sure you'll be a popular choice with the guys."

Luc exhaled. He sure hoped so. Not everyone was a fan of his—apparently his Christian values were a little extreme, according to some, like ex-teammate Sean Hart, who'd been one of the pros caught up in a betting scandal last year and been booted out of the NHL. Not that he cared. Speaking up and being vocal about what was right, as well as being someone who occasionally dropped the gloves to stand up for his teammates, was likely what had helped tip him over the captain-worthy line as far as the coach was concerned.

"There's just one thing." The GM glanced at Coach Frantzen who nodded.

Okay…

"We'd like to keep this on the down low for the moment, then make an announcement at training camp."

"My lips are sealed."

"And while most locals know who you are, your name isn't as widely known across the NHL as some."

Luc placed both palms up. "Hey, I know I'm no Brent Karlsson or Zac Parotti." He didn't have the national profile or endorsements those two did.

"We don't need you to be a Karlsson or a Parotti. You being a Luc Blanchard is fine with us. But we figured there was room to grow your profile a little."

"Sure. Whatever you like. I'm your man."

Coach Frantzen chuckled. "Well, I sure hope you're going to be so agreeable when you hear this."

"If it's visiting more hospitals or media opps, I'm in. You know I love doing that kind of thing."

"We do, hence why we've tapped you for this." Another glance passed between Coach and the GM.

Uh oh. But he'd made a habit of speaking before letting fear sneak in, and that wasn't about to change now. "So what is it? Like I said, I'm happy to do whatever it takes."

"Your media profile needs lifting."

"You want me posting on Instagram and TikTok?" He hoped his face hadn't given away his dismay. "I think it's only fair that you know I've never been real great at that kind of thing."

"Oh, we know." The GM glanced at the papers on the desk, and tapped one. "Our social media team have sent through your numbers, and there's definitely room to improve."

He winced internally. He hadn't posted on Instagram in over a year. "Um, well, I'm happy to do whatever it takes to see that improve. But hey, if we're talking TikTok, I gotta admit I'm not on it. And anyway, I'm not great at dancing or any of that kind of stuff."

The GM's eyes gleamed. "But if you were asked to?"

"To dance?" His nose wrinkled, as his words from Franklin and Hannah's recent wedding wiggled back to memory. "I really feel like that's a sight better left unseen."

Coach grinned.

No. They didn't want him to dance. Did they? "Look, I really hope being captain isn't dependent on this, because I am terrible. I have two left feet. And I'm sorry, but I think everyone who's trying to look cool by doing those dumb dance moves just because everyone else is doing it, well, I think that looks cheesy and unprofessional."

The GM laughed.

Luc's stomach fell. Man. He really should've checked into

this. Was the GM a secret TikTok star or something? "Sir, I'm sorry if that sounds offensive or something, but—"

"One of the things we like about you, Luc, is that you say what you think. But we want you to hear us out for a moment longer. And don't worry, we don't need you dancing on TikTok or anything quite like that."

Phew. He wiped his brow in an exaggerated movement. "For a minute there I thought you were wanting me to dance, and..."

His words faded as both men crossed their arms, their faces blanking. Years of working with both men told him this was news he really didn't want to hear.

The GM cleared his throat. "How's your mom's health these days?"

"Mom?" He blinked at the sudden change of topic. "Um, she's good. Been in remission for four years now. Thanks for asking."

"We know you've been a big supporter of charities that fight cancer, and we wanted to present another opportunity for you."

"Sure, I'm in. What is it?" Thank goodness it wouldn't involve dancing. He wouldn't wish that on his worst enemy.

The GM smiled. "We've had a television show reach out and offer fifty thousand dollars as the initial sign-up fee, plus another twenty-five grand to the charity of the person's choice, with another twenty-five if they reach the final."

"A TV show?" His gut moved uneasily. "What kind of TV show?"

They exchanged another glance between them. "A, er, celebrity-type show."

"And I'm guessing you're wanting me to be the celebrity?"

They nodded.

His nose wrinkled. "You mean a reality show?" More nods. "What type of reality show?"

Coach Frantzen's teeth glinted as he smiled. "Before you say no, just remember, that's potentially fifty K that could go to a good cause. Plus, it would definitely help boost your profile and name recognition. Show that you're a little more nuanced than just a skilled truck on skates."

Nuanced? He wasn't exactly sure he knew what that meant, but figured that didn't matter so much as the more important thing that had crystallized in his brain. "What type of reality show?" Luc repeated.

"One your mom would probably approve of," Coach Frantzen said.

Uh-oh. "We're not talking cooking, are we? I'm not great at that. I mean, I love to eat, but I really only cook basic stuff."

"Yeah, it's not cooking." The GM cleared his throat. "It's called *Dance Off Canada.*"

Luc closed his eyes, fighting the temptation to swear. If he wasn't trying to shine a light for Jesus he probably would've dropped a word others often used in the locker room after a loss. "Are you kidding?"

"Nope."

"Come on, just think about it as a good cause, good promotion, and a great opportunity to learn a new skill," Coach Frantzen said. "What do we like to say around here about great opportunities?"

"Great moments are born from great opportunities," he mumbled. How many times had those words tumbled from his own mouth? "I just don't think this'll result in any great moments. It'll only show everyone how bad I am."

"I seem to remember a few quotes about that too. Something Eric Lindros once said about how 'it's not necessarily the amount of time you spend at practice that counts'…"

"'It's what you put into the practice.'" Man. They really weren't letting him off easily. "But if I fail and I'm a laughing-stock, then the other teams will treat me like a joke."

"You don't have to do it. But it *is* for a good cause. We got the phone call today, and they're eager to put a new celeb into place as soon as possible."

"I'm not even that much of a celebrity."

"Something that can change after national TV exposure."

Dear God, no. *Lord? You're not really feeling this, are You? Please say no...*

But the peace from earlier seemed to have fled, which led him to suspect that maybe God had something up His heavenly sleeve.

"Aren't you worried about my conditioning?" he asked Coach Frantzen.

"Look, can I be frank? If you're as bad as you think you are, you won't be there for long. Just long enough to get your name out there, and to get twenty-five grand for your charity."

"I need to think about this, talk to my agent." He sighed. "How long until you need an answer?"

"Tomorrow."

Another word begged to tumble from his mouth. "You're kidding."

The GM shook his head. "They've already started filming promotional material. They'd need you later this week."

"Where?"

"Toronto."

"No way. I can't drop everything."

"Do you have plans?"

Well, no. Now he'd gotten his trip to his MPFG sponsor kids in the Philippines and Franklin's wedding out of the way, summer had stretched before him, blissfully empty. He swallowed. "Are you saying I'd have to move there?"

The GM shook his head. "That's the best part. Normally they'd be filming all of it in Toronto, but I checked, and they can actually film most of your rehearsals here in Winnipeg."

"Why?"

The GM shrugged. "With the Royal Winnipeg Ballet based here apparently it's known as a dance town."

Huh. First time he'd heard the Peg called that.

"Which is why it could work well for you. You don't need to fly to TO except for the weekend filming, and if you're as bad as you think, it doesn't sound like you'd have to do that for long."

"Man."

"Is it doable?" the GM asked.

Luc's nose wrinkled. "It's doable, but not wantable," he admitted.

"What if I said the club is prepared to match the charity earnings as incentive?"

That'd be fifty grand to Hockey Fights Cancer or a similar charity. Fifty grand to help those who had helped his mom beat that vile disease, and support those struggling with it, and those looking for a cure. He exhaled. "You really want me to do this?"

"We think it'd be good for your profile, and good to get people thinking about hockey in Winnipeg for a change, instead of associating it with the other major cities." Like Toronto, Montreal, Vancouver, Calgary, and the big E. "Show them some of your natural charm—"

Luc snorted.

"—and have fun. You could boost your social media numbers at the same time too."

Or maybe get on some of those platforms, at least. That wasn't exactly the way to sell it to him. He liked his privacy. Although being captain would mean having to give a lot of that up, anyway. He bit back another sigh.

"Come on. It's a dancing competition. How hard can it be? And don't forget, it's for a good cause. You can always spin it that way if you're embarrassed about what people might think of you."

He winced internally. He'd had a lifetime of not bothering about what other people thought. Embarrassment was only another name for fear, after all. He shook his head. "I can't believe I'm even considering this."

The GM straightened, his ever-subtle signal for drawing the

meeting to a close. "Talk it over, with your agent, your family, and your mom." He winked. "It could be a lot better than you think."

Or it could be the worst thing ever.

Lord, this can't be from You. Help me out. Please!

The guys in both his team and online Bible study crew would never let him live it down. Just like he'd mock the heck out of them if their roles were swapped.

Man. He pitied the poor woman he'd be paired with. *If* he agreed to do it. But how could he say no?

Lord? Help!

CHAPTER 2

The sound of coffee beans grinding shrieked off the tiles lining the store. Despite the name, the Coffee Haus café had been designed to not encourage its customers to linger and treat the space as a home, its demographic more the busy office workers who were employed around here. There was only one comfy couch, the rest of the place consisting of stainless-steel tables and chairs that were lighter than they looked, and a narrow wooden bar with steel-and-wood stools where some intrepids liked to work. Bailey didn't understand it. She much preferred the soft pastels and vintage wannabe French vibes of those cafes that longed to evoke Paris, but held little actual resemblance to those she'd seen when she'd lived in France five years ago. But a job was a job, and with her money worries she'd be jumping at any extra shifts she could take, hence this one, different from her usual, which meant a different array of customers.

And while she served customers, made coffee, wiped tables, she kept a smile on her dial, hiding the consternation within. The questions from yesterday continued. What should she do? God was with her, she knew that, and Jehovah Jireh was her provider, so she knew she'd have to trust Him to open a door.

Her parents and brother had all reminded her of that in the group messenger chat when she'd asked for prayer. Cindy, her brother's wife, hadn't acknowledged her comment, even though Bailey knew she'd seen it, thanks to the little face next to the chat. Her sister-in-law had never understood the close relationship the rest of them shared, and Bailey suspected Cindy was jealous. Whatever. She just had to keep turning the other cheek.

"Bailey, can you wipe down those tables?" Max, the non-binary manager, pointed to the corner from behind their spot at the coffee machine.

"Sure."

She grabbed the cleaning products and stepped to the section, stacking empty cups on a tray then wiping it down. Her backside buzzed, but she didn't answer. Phone calls were for break times only, and Max didn't like it when people ignored the rules. And while this new world was hard to navigate as a Christian sometimes, and she knew her father would never understand, showing Max respect had to be something Jesus would do, right? Regardless of how Max chose to identify, God still knew Max's name, and Bailey had determined to show Max God's love however she could. It wasn't like she hadn't had to work with people dealing with similar issues before. The ballet world was full of people who needed God's love more than being pigeonholed.

So she cleared and cleaned, and returned behind the counter to Max's nod.

"Surprised to see you working today," Max said.

She shrugged. "I'm after any extra shifts I can get."

"Don't you have classes?"

"Now it's summer, there are less kids, and I still need to pay rent." She smiled. "Hence you get the pleasure of my company."

Max's mouth flickered into a micro-smile. "I'll remember."

A new customer entered, a shadowed silhouette filling the doorway, and Bailey paused, taking him in. The man, who looked to be around thirty, was big, broad-shouldered and obviously muscled, according to the T-shirt straining across his chest. His hair was a dirty dark brown, flowing beneath a Jets cap in a style she just knew was her all-time least favorite on a guy: the mullet. But from his tattoos and very presence, she sensed he didn't care what she or anyone else thought about him. She noticed the way others had paused too, subtly or not-so-subtly watching as he moved to the counter. He seemed aware of but not embarrassed by the attention, like he was used to it, even though he didn't acknowledge anyone else. Instead, his eyes were firmly fixed on her. She shivered.

He reached the counter, nodded to her, unsmiling, just like Max. But unlike Max, there was no questioning the gender of this man, who was very much the embodiment of masculinity, at least in her limited experience. Muscled, strong jawline, thick dark eyebrows, a spray of fine whiskers on his jaw, with intense dark eyes. Not exactly handsome, but strong-featured. Just very... strong. The epitome of a tough guy. "Hey."

Even his voice was deep, seeming to splay through her. She blinked, suddenly conscious of her petite height and frame and long hair pulled up in a high ponytail, and lifted her chin and lips. "Hi. What can I get you?"

"It's okay, Bailey," Max said, glancing at the new customer. "Usual?"

"Thanks."

So Mister Intimidating was a regular. He tapped his card, then moved to the serving center, eyes on his phone, leaving her feeling weirdly short-changed. Which was dumb. She didn't know the guy, had no desire to know the guy, but there'd been something in the way he looked at her which sent a ripple through her soul, almost like he was someone she was supposed to know. Which made no sense at all. *Lord? This is dumb. I don't know what's going on, but please stop the weirdness.*

She served another customer, a woman who nudged her friend as they glanced at the big dude, still on his phone. She peeked across. He was now pivoting away as he answered a call, his shoulders sagging, like this call was bad news.

Maybe it was because she was recently familiar with bad news that she felt a new ping of interest, but she kept sneaking glances at him, noting when he inched closer to the door, like he'd forgotten his coffee order.

Max eyed her, then called out, "Luke!"

The man didn't turn, obviously listening to the call as he shook his head, his voice too low and rumbly to hear. Not that she'd ever listen to café customers' conversations or anything.

"Can you—?" Max gestured to the coffee. Tall black, no sugar, according to the plastic lid.

"Um, sure."

She picked it up, then moved to the man whose back was to her, time seeming to slow like she was being drawn by an indefinable, inescapable force. She lifted a hand to tap him on the back when he suddenly pivoted, and his elbow bumped the coffee she held. Her hand jerked, the lid popped off, and hot liquid sloshed on him and her.

She squeaked as the coffee splashed her neck, he muttered something, and seemed to almost snarl, which forced her to take a step back. "I'm so sorry."

He grimaced as he pulled his stained shirt away from where it had been sculpting his impressive chest, then glanced at where she'd been doing the same. Not that her chest was impressive. At least the coffee had mostly fallen on her apron. His expression softened. "That was my fault, huh? Sorry. I should've been paying attention."

"We'll get you another one. On the house."

He shrugged. "Forget it. I've got things to do."

"But—" She placed a hand on his arm and froze.

Her mouth dried. Muscles lay there, stealing her words. What was she *doing*?

He seemed to think that too, eyeing her hand, then her, then shifting so she suddenly clasped air. Her hand dropped. He stepped back, studying her with another of those deep looks before whoever was on the phone squawked loud enough to be heard.

He snapped to attention, nodded, then pivoted and walked away.

Leaving her feeling foolish. But also feeling like something seismic had just occurred. Which was stupid. She didn't believe in instant attraction. And this definitely *wasn't* attraction. It was just instant… weirdness.

"Bailey," Max called.

Her phone buzzed another notification, and she hurried back, conscious of smirks and muffled laughter, and a few phones held upright that seemed to be tracking her walk of shame. Unlike the man monster, she was very aware of people watching her. She might've danced on stages across Europe and North America, but knew people watched to criticize, not just to applaud. She faked a smile, pushing down the nerves.

"Sorry, Max. He said he had to leave, and couldn't stay for a do-over."

Max nodded. "No worries. He's a regular. He'll be back."

"Phew." She grimaced. "I really didn't mean to do that. I hope I haven't scared him away."

"Yeah, I suspect you gotta be a lot scarier than that to throw Luc Blanchard off his game."

"Who?"

Max smirked. "I love that you're so dance-focused you don't recognize his name."

"I've got no idea who he is."

"That's apparent. He plays hockey, is a bit of a big deal around here."

Her nose wrinkled. She didn't like hockey, or people who considered themselves big deals.

"Now, go clean up."

She hurried to the back room, quickly exchanging her white tee and apron for clean ones. Her phone buzzed again. Seriously. Who *was* this?

She drew it out, saw her friend's name flash on the screen. What did Coco want? She hadn't called in forever. Ever since Bailey had returned to Winnipeg it seemed Coco's dancing career had gone on to stratospheric heights, while Bailey's felt like it had floundered. They still messaged regularly, though. But Coco had tried to call at least three times today now. It must be important. She peeked around. The café was quiet, and even Max was drinking a coffee and chatting idly to one of the customers. She pressed Return call.

"Coco?"

"Bailey! Oh thank goodness. Look, I don't have long, but I have an amazing opportunity for you."

"I'm at work—"

"At that café? Honey, that's caretaking, not work."

"Can we talk later?"

"No, there's no time. I've just pulled the most amazing opportunity for you."

Bailey huddled behind a stack of boxes labelled arabica coffee beans. "What is it?"

"You're about to get a call from a producer, and look, just say yes, okay?"

"A producer? For what?"

"Just say yes, okay? If you don't do this, someone else will, and I'll never talk to you again."

"What?"

"Just jokes. But not really. So say yes. Oops! Gotta go."

The call ended, and she stared at her phone. The weirdness today was in overdrive. "God," she whisper-prayed, "I don't know what's going on, but You do. Open the right doors, close the wrong ones, and—"

"Bailey!" Max called.

She tucked her phone away and returned, only to have her phone buzz again. She winced. Was this the producer? If so, what kind of producer? Coco knew a lot of people, and had danced in Broadway and on TV. Was the producer connected to one of those things? Was that them on the phone now?

She tugged out her phone, saw an unknown number. Glanced at Max who was looking at her askance. "Can I please take this? It's important."

Max sighed, then nodded, and she returned to her hidey-hole, and pressed answer.

"Hello, is this Bailey Donovan?" an unknown female voice asked.

"Yes. With whom am I speaking?"

"My name is Joanne Mascieski, and I'm a producer with a television show called *Dance Off Canada*. We've had a little snafu with our upcoming season, and I was told by Coco Flintoff that you were available to step in as one of our dancers."

Bailey's mouth fell open. Thank goodness this was a phone call and not video. "Um, I'm afraid I don't understand."

"We're a celebrity dancing competition, like *Dancing with the Stars*, but on a smaller scale."

"I know the program." She watched it when work permitted, thanks to Coco's performances. She'd been one of the pro dancers these past three seasons. "I just don't understand what you mean about me being a dancer."

"We pair our celebrities with professional dancers, and—"

As Joanne continued explaining the obvious, Bailey's heart picked up in pace. Had Coco seriously put her name forward as a professional dancer? Was Coco crazy? Bailey was a professional, and yes, even taught ballroom, but this was on a whole other level.

"—and thanks to their affair being exposed, we now need another couple pronto, and we have the man, just need the dancing partner. Coco was sure you'd agree, especially as you're local."

"I'm sorry, when is this supposed to start?"

"We're shooting promotions in two days, so you'd need to fly to Toronto tomorrow."

"Tomorrow? Are you kidding?"

"Look, I know it's short notice, but we're desperate."

Way to go to make a girl feel valued.

"And because we know it's short notice we're prepared to offer you five grand upfront if you sign up today."

Breath hitched. "Five grand?" Five thousand dollars would go a good way to paying off the bank loan.

"Plus all expenses, plus another five if you make it to week three, and another ten if you make the final."

She closed her eyes. Twenty thousand meant she'd almost be in the clear. "How long is the time commitment?"

"Five weeks, plus this next week of promotions and rehearsals before the premiere the following weekend. You'd be starting behind the others, which is why we're desperate to get this happening now."

"But where? Are you talking Toronto?"

"We're shooting the weekends in TO but the weekday rehearsals are in Winnipeg, which is where he's based. You're there too, aren't you?"

"Are you saying I could use my studio here for rehearsal?"

"Absolutely. And that'd be some nice exposure for you, too."

Yes, it would.

But how could she just up and leave her students, her commitments, for something that seemed little better than a dream?

Just say yes, Coco had said. *Lord? What are You saying?*

Seconds ticked away.

Then, "I understand. Never mind. We'll find someone else—"

"No, I'm interested," Bailey's words spurted. "But I'll need to see a contract."

"We sent one already. Coco gave us your email address."

"What?" She switched to her email app, and sure enough, an email with a bunch of attachments sat there from one Joanne Mascieski, producer with *Dance Off Canada*.

Oh my goodness. Oh my stars. Her chest tightened. This really was real.

"So, can I lock you in?" Joanne's voice was tinny.

Bailey lifted the phone to her ear. "Um, I need to check the contract, and I'd need to figure out my dance school schedule, but I think so."

"Oh, thank goodness!" Joanne exclaimed. "Look, I know it's short notice, so if you need us to reimburse you, just say the word."

"I will need to reschedule classes, and get another teacher in." Maybe Poppy would be okay to return. Especially if she could count as an "expense".

"Like I said, we're willing to negotiate."

And now would be the time to negotiate, while they were so eager for her to join up. "I'll need to send you my projected expenses," she dared.

"Send it. If it's within reason, we'll pay it straightaway. We need this to happen now."

What would they consider reasonable? Canada's premier TV network wasn't likely as flush as some US networks, although they seemed to find enough money to pay big time for sports like hockey. She rolled her eyes. "I'll check over the contract as soon as possible."

"Look, can you do it now?"

"I'm at work," she protested. And there was no reason to let this woman think she was a pushover.

"I'll need an answer by two, otherwise I have to call someone else. In fact, I might just do that anyway, as we can't afford to delay any longer."

"But…" She bit her lip. She really needed the money. And God hadn't exactly put a check in her spirit to say no, had He? What if this opportunity was actually from Him?

"I'm going to read through the contract now, and I'll get back to you immediately."

"Thank you. I'll hold off calling anyone else until two PM."

"I'd appreciate it."

"Good."

"Oh, one more thing. Who would be my celebrity?"

"Well, we wouldn't normally tell you, but seeing you're behind the others by a week I suppose I can." Joanne whistled softly. "And oh, you got the cream of the crop, Bailey."

The way she said that, Bailey wasn't sure if she was being sarcastic or not.

"He's an athlete. You might've heard of him. He plays for Winnipeg's hockey team. Luc Blanchard."

CHAPTER 3

$\mathcal{U}$nbelievable.

What a difference forty-eight hours could make. Two days ago, he'd been sitting in the GM's office, being talked up as the next captain. Today, he was standing in an airport, waiting for his flight to Toronto, trepidation eating him like he was a new kid on the first day of school. He hated feeling insecure. Hated it. And he had a funny feeling that this whole experience he'd just said yes to was going to be one massive ride on the insecurity train. Starting with meeting the perky person who was going to be his dance partner. Ugh.

He glanced around, but nobody fitted the image of the woman's picture he'd been sent. Bailey Donovan was super pretty, but the ballerina costume made her look so fragile, like a breath of wind could blow her away. And here he was, built like a truck, he'd probably scare her into next year with a single exhale. Why had he said yes?

A silent groan escaped. Because the team wanted it. Because his agent had pushed him to do it, saying it'd be great for future endorsements. Mostly because his mom had been excited, sounding more excited about the thought of him dancing than being captain, actually. Which was disconcerting, but whatever. His dad had laughed, but said as long as he didn't get cut from the show first that it couldn't hurt. That hadn't exactly filled him with confidence, so he hadn't dared tell the online Bible study guys, only asking them to pray for him for wisdom for "a new opportunity" as he'd casually phrased it. Yeah, a new opportunity to be publicly humiliated. He just hoped this Bailey chick knew a thing or two about helping prime movers actually move.

The announcement for his flight was made, and he picked up his bag, moving to the business line, where he flashed his phone to have his ticket scanned. The airline steward's smile widened, as if recognizing his name, and he half-smiled then walked down the airbridge. He didn't mind fans, and as captain, he'd need to get used to being in the spotlight more. But still, this little break in Toronto, before returning to face the media and do team stuff, felt like his last chance to be anonymous before the proverbial hit the fan. He wouldn't be anonymous after the TV promo aired this Friday.

He was greeted at the plane door, then guided to his seat, a comfy big-sized seat for a taller-than-average man, complete with view out the window. He stowed his stuff, then got his phone out, as the chat from two days ago filled the screen.

Mike Vaughan from Calgary had asked what people were doing for the national holiday, which had met with various responses ranging from picnics with friends and family, to big city fireworks, to a tropical sunset picture from the newly-married Franklin James. Yeah, he wasn't going to think about Franklin and Hannah on their honeymoon. He sent a shrugging emoji, more because he needed to put something in the chat to show he wasn't avoiding them, than because he didn't know.

His nose wrinkled. Dancing on TV. What would the others say? What would sports reporter Hannah say? He hated to think what people would say behind his back, or on national TV, especially when they saw how bad he'd be. At least Hannah was nice, and unlikely to mock him. She was a real deal kind of woman he could trust, even if she wasn't his type. Real deal women were scarce, although he'd met a few as more of the Bible study group's single guys had fallen into relationships. Holly Karlsson was a no-bull woman. Neither was the girlfriend of the latest of the Bible study group's single guys to fall, Ryan's Goth-like girlfriend, Sylvie, whose relationship with their Edmonton friend had sparked concern earlier this year. But it was all good now, even if she was sometimes a little too direct and blunt for his liking.

He hadn't had a girlfriend for years, not since he'd found Jesus and realized celibacy was supposed to be the name of the game until he was married, and as he had zero interest in marriage or a relationship until his hockey career was done, he was prepared to wait. Which was why there was zero chance of him failing to adhere to the "family-friendly" clause in his *Dance Off* contract about avoiding relationships until the end of filming with his—or any other—dance partner or contestants on the show. He rolled his eyes. As if.

Nope. As much as he found this Bailey person pretty, she looked way too delicate to suit him. Now if she'd been like the girl in the café yesterday, he might've been interested, with her girl-next-door looks and sunny smile everything he liked, even if she was clumsier than him. But she wasn't, so he was safe. Except for wondering what Bailey would be like, and how on earth he'd manage to still be cool enough after this experience and not be teased mercilessly by the guys.

By now the seats behind him were filling, and he wondered if maybe Bailey was on a different flight. *Dance Off*'s email last night had contained this ticket to Toronto, apparently for interviews and "promotion" which scared him silly. At least he'd not had anything else to organize. Which made him wonder again about this Bailey chick and how desperate she had to be to agree to do this last minute. Which only resulted in him realizing that much the same could be said about him. At least he could talk about this as being for charity. Bailey must be doing this for the dollars, or to boost her social media profile. He rolled his eyes.

"Excuse me."

The feminine voice drew his gaze up, and his jaw sagged.

It was her. Coffee girl.

Her head tilted. "I think you're in my seat."

He blinked. "What? No. This is mine."

Her eyebrows rose, as the people behind complained about being forced to wait.

He pulled out his phone, checked the seat allocation, and—man, she was right. "Sorry. I'll move."

The protests behind grew louder, as he stood and shifted to the aisle with a ducked head. Heaven forbid the locals got annoyed with their new hockey captain before it was even officially announced—there'd be plenty of time for that later. He brushed past her, and she slipped into the seat he'd just vacated. He plopped down next to her, head still averted to avoid recognition from their fellow passengers. He cleared his throat, glanced at his seatmate. "Um, hey."

Seriously? That was the best he could do? But the realization that the pretty coffee woman from yesterday was sitting next to him, would be sitting beside him for the next two and a half hours, had filled his mouth and lungs with rocks. His brain, too, as he was lost for words, breath, and any coherent thoughts. How—? Who—? Why—? *Lord?*

He cleared his throat again—by now she probably thought he had a problem with phlegm—and tried to smile. He didn't smile much—his teeth weren't great, thanks to too many pucks and sticks over the years—and he knew he often got cast as the serious one in team pics. Sure, he could paste on a version of charm the GM seemed to appreciate, but it was something he'd had to work at, as it didn't come naturally. "I'm Luc."

She studied him, her cheeks pinking a little, before nodding. "I know."

Huh. Had she recognized him yesterday? Plenty of other fans seemed to have, including the two women who'd been ordering and non-subtly checking him out. Which was exactly why he didn't do relationships. Life was cruising along very well without complications like a woman. Even if this particular chick, the only one to pique his interest in recent years, was one he'd never thought he'd meet again. Until he returned for more coffee, maybe.

Conscious that they'd be seated next to each other for the next few hours, and that he needed to keep the conversation going, his thoughts tipped back to their exchange. "Well, uh, I hope you've heard good things."

Her delicate eyebrows lifted, and he heard the arrogance in that statement. "Not that I only do good things. I mean..." Judging from that squinty gaze she was leveling him, he should probably stop talking. He exhaled heavily. "Do you have a name?" Yep. That wasn't much better.

"Of course I do." She turned to clip her belt on.

"And are you going to tell me?"

She peered back at him. "Don't you recognize me?"

"Of course I do. You're the girl who spilled coffee on me yesterday."

She sighed, and something about the lines of her face drew a tug of memory, but what it was he didn't know. "I'm Bailey."

"Bailey?" Where had he heard that name recently?

As she continued to stare at him, like he was the world's biggest idiot, the fogginess in his brain lifted. His heart hitched. No. No way. It couldn't be. "Not—"

"Your dance partner? Yes."

Whoa. "But..." His words failed. Was she kidding? She

couldn't even maneuver a coffee cup let alone teach him moves on the dance floor. This had to be a joke. "You're a dancer?"

"Do you need references?"

As her head tilted, more memories clicked into place. Something about her throat suddenly looked like the picture he'd been sent, when she'd been stretched into a ballerina pose of beauty and elegance that seemed far too delicate for him. His gaze trickled down, and just as he'd suspected, she was about half the size of him. Not in height, but definitely in width. How could this tiny fairy-like creature teach him?

"Look, I don't understand this at all. You're too little."

"Excuse me?"

"Like, I'd squash you." Panic rose. "I can't—I shouldn't—"

"Whoa. Hold on, big guy. You don't need to be scared."

"Scared? I don't do scared. Especially of little girls. No offense."

Her eyes narrowed. "Why do people think they can say offensive things then tack on a 'no offense,'" she said that phrase in a lower, sullen guy tone, "and act like they're off the hook for being offensive? That *is* offensive. But do I point that out to you?"

His jaw sagged. Whoa. Don't hold back, lady. "Except I think you just did."

"Well, I guess that makes us even then."

Her smile thumped him in the heart, just as it had yesterday. He'd never met anyone with her brand of daintiness and fire. She moved to adjust her seatbelt, then peeked across at him before the cabin crew announcement about emergencies stole her attention.

He watched her instead of the safety demonstration. With all the travel hockey demanded, it felt like he'd spent half his life in planes. Now she was up close, he could see the clear skin, the proud tilt of head, the honey gold hair swept high like yesterday, that only seemed to emphasize her cheekbones and delicate features.

She glanced back at him. "You should be paying attention."

"I am."

She huffed out a breath, but he thought he caught a tiny smile before she smothered it with a yawn.

The vibrations of the plane shuddered as it slowly rolled, then picked up speed then lifted from the runway. He noticed how she clasped the seat arm, her little hands looking fragile, like he could accidentally lean on her and her bones might snap. This wasn't a good idea. It felt like all kinds of things could go wrong.

The plane leveled out, her hands released and she stretched out her fingers, before covering her mouth as she yawned again.

"Big night, huh?"

Her lashes lowered. "Like you wouldn't believe."

"Try me."

She pressed her lips together. Then sighed. "How long have you known about this for?"

"Since Monday. You?"

"Yesterday."

"Wow."

"Exactly. So I'm sorry I'm a bit snippy. I was blindsided yesterday at lunch, then basically had to read the contract and rearrange all my classes and get a teacher in to cover everything from today."

"You're still working?"

Her lips twisted. "Not everyone gets paid big bucks. Some of us have to earn a living and pay the bills."

Bingo. He settled back in his seat. "So you're doing this for money."

"I love to dance, but I can't afford to work for free." She shrugged. "I get that five grand isn't much for you, but it'll help get the bank off my case, and means I'm not in debt as much, so this was the quickest way to repay it that I could see."

"Five grand?" He frowned. He was being paid ten times as much. Adding his charity contribution, he was getting seventy-five, maybe even a hundred. How wrong was that?

She winced. "Sorry. I shouldn't have mentioned that, should I? That was part of the non-disclosure agreement, wasn't it?"

The non-disclosure about their involvement and payments. Due to the tight time frame Luc had been granted an exemption, although only his agent, parents, and senior club management knew. He shrugged. "I don't know if it counts when you're sharing with your dance partner." It was a lie. It totally counted. But he wanted to know more about her reasons for doing this, and just what this meant to her. "So, um, you needed some cash in a hurry, huh?"

"You make it sound like a drug deal."

"I didn't mean that. I'm just trying to understand why you're doing this."

"Like I said, I run a dance studio, and I need to pay the bills. This came along out of the blue, thanks to Coco, a friend of mine. She's one of the show's regular dancers, and it seemed like an answer to prayer, and it will help lift my studio's profile. Now we just need to get to round three so I can earn another five grand, then reach the finals so I can earn another ten, that'll be enough to pay off my debts."

Her debts? Was that bad business management or something else? His dad was a financial consultant in Quebec, and Luc had grown up hearing tales about the inexperience of people with starry-eyed dreams of running their own small business who'd gone bust. His dad's cautionary stories had never held identifying details, but had been enough that Luc had learned to save and invest wisely, even as some of his teammates splurged in businesses he knew were doomed to fail.

She rubbed her eyes. "I had to call in a favor from a friend in Alberta to come help."

"Alberta? That's two provinces away."

"No kidding."

Clearly any attraction from yesterday was one-sided.

"Sorry, I didn't mean to sound sarcastic." Her smile held apology. "I had a friend who I used to work with, and thank God, she's able to come help for a bit. I was up until late last night contacting parents about classes, and it's been a little crazy." She sighed. "To be honest, as exciting as this is, and as grateful as I am for the cash, this has really thrown me for a loop."

"It was definitely unexpected," he agreed. But that was the second time she'd mentioned God or prayer. She wasn't a—? No. He must be dreaming.

"So, how about you?" She shifted to face him. "Why would a hockey guy like you do something like this?"

He shrugged. "Probably like you, I had to raise my profile." He lowered his voice. "Don't tell anyone this, but my team basically told me that the only way I'm up for captaincy is if I do this. Apparently they want me to be more relatable, and help the fan base." He snorted. "Whatever. At least the money goes to charity."

She glanced at him, her brows pinching like she wasn't sure five thousand going to charity was much to boast about. Not that he was boasting. Not that he'd tell her how much he was being paid, either.

She kept studying him, with an eyebrow aloft like she was taking his measure. Which made him nervous. "What?"

"Is that all?"

"About why I'm doing this? Like I said, I'm doing it for charity. My mom had breast cancer, so I'm all about trying to promote the profile of charities that raise money to support cancer sufferers."

Her face softened. "How is she now?"

"She's been in remission for four years."

"I'm glad." She touched his arm again, and again he felt that frisson of connection.

She seemed to feel it too because her hand jerked away. "Sorry. I shouldn't have done that."

"Touch me?" He snickered. "I kinda get the feeling that's gonna have to happen if we're supposed to be dancing together."

Her nose crinkled.

Ouch. Good to know she didn't find him attractive at all.

She glanced at her phone, tucked in the back pocket of the plane seat, then put it back, sighing. "Okay, if we're going to shoot promo tomorrow and we've got another two hours or so until we land, then you better start telling me about your dancing experience."

"That's easy. I have none."

She arched a brow.

"Seriously, I have none. I didn't even dance at my friend's wedding last weekend."

She mock-gasped. "Shocking."

"No, me dancing would've been shocking." He shook his head. "This is gonna be so embarrassing, because I'm pretty sure everyone there heard me say I don't dance, and then to do this and prove it will be awkward."

"Come on. Aren't you the tiniest bit excited about learning a new skill? You sound defeated before you've even set foot on the floor."

Her challenge punched him in the chest. He didn't do defeated. Well, not by choice, so he hated sounding that way. "I just don't want to look like a fool."

"Well, thanks a lot."

"Huh? What do you mean?"

"For saying you have no faith in me."

He stared at her. Then realized what his words implied.

"Wait, I don't mean you're going to look dumb, it's just that I don't want to embarrass myself, or hurt you."

"You're not going to hurt me. And I happen to be an excellent teacher."

"I'm sure you are. It's just that I'm like a zero at dancing. Less than. Like a minus one hundred."

"I repeat: I'm an excellent teacher, and I've taught a few men how to dance before."

"None like me, though, I bet." He held up his hands. "And no, I don't mean that to sound arrogant. I just mean that I've been called a truck more than a few times in my life, and I don't want to run you over."

"I'm tougher than I look."

"Sorry to say this, but you're a ballet dancer, right?" He shook his head. "I'm not doing fancy ballet moves."

"Neither am I. This is ballroom, Luc. Have you ever seen ballroom dancing?"

He shook his head. Heard her quiet "Oh dear".

Yep. Exactly as he'd feared. He should've pushed the club to triple the charity donation for this to be worth his humiliation. "Look, I don't want my hockey rep to suffer because I look like an idiot. I've built a career on being tough, so I want to look tough, not the wussy flappy shirt guy."

She laughed, and he almost smiled as her amusement rippled through his chest. She had a pretty laugh, like bells or birds or something, even if it was at his expense.

At his expense. His stomach fell, and he shook his head at himself. See? He couldn't afford to be too honest with her, as she'd just laugh at him.

"Anything else I need to be aware of?" she asked gently.

"I'm great on the ice, but sometimes I have two left feet, so you'll probably need steel-capped boots."

"Noted. Anything more?"

He shrugged. "I don't know who makes the decisions about

what we wear, but I really don't want to lose my Samson strength by having my hair cut off."

She studied him a long moment, eyeing his hair like she thought a haircut really wouldn't be a loss. But it would be. He liked his flow, the lettuce, as some called great heads of hair. It was about the only nice quality he had, apart from his muscles, and there was no way in heaven or the other place he'd go shirtless on national TV.

"Are you a player?" she finally asked.

"What? No. Why would you say that?"

"Samson had a problem with women, and—"

"Hey, I don't have a problem with women."

She eyed him. "As in too many of them. Samson was a bit of a lusty burger who—"

"Wait—a what?"

"A lusty burger," she repeated, "who had a series of women and then got played by Delilah because he couldn't keep it in his pants."

Wow. No tiptoeing around things with her. "I'm not like that at all." Then it struck him. "You know about Samson?"

"I'm a Christian, okay?"

Oh. Okay.

Oh! Okay…

He snuck another look at her. She was staring at her pink nails, like she wasn't sure what to do with him. Which made two of them. He wasn't sure what to do with her. For despite that clause in the contract, and the knowledge that the only reason the two of them were even in this mess was because the previous celebrity and pro dancer had engaged in an affair, he couldn't help but wonder if maybe God Himself had brought them together for a different reason. That was, if she was single.

He eyed her hand. Nope. No ring. She hadn't mentioned a boyfriend or anything. Would it—could it—be possible? Like, after the five weeks or whatever this took? Enough so she could earn her money and he could escape back into pre-season training. He rubbed a hand over his forehead. What the heck was he doing, thinking like this? He wasn't looking for a woman to distract him. He needed to focus. Do this dumb dance thing, then get back to manly stuff like hockey, leading Winnipeg to the postseason, and one day, Lord Stanley's Cup.

She glanced up at him, her blue eyes piercing, then her expression softened. "Hey, you don't need to worry."

"I'm not worried," he lied. Now she'd talked up her teaching, he wasn't so worried about his dancing—a man could only go up from having rock-bottom skills, right? But maybe he was just a smidge concerned about protecting his heart.

"You'll be fine. I promise."

He nodded. He sure hoped so. *God, You better help me out here.*

CHAPTER 4

*B*ailey was wrong. Luc was not fine. She didn't know what she was expecting, but it sure wasn't this. The guy hadn't been kidding. He was as stiff as a board, the sample dance moves they were supposed to do for the *Dance Off* in-studio film crew and photographers revealing the man likely hadn't wiggled his hips for maybe two decades.

The assistant producer groaned. "Come on. Luc, can you try one more time?"

Bailey stifled a giggle at the expression on the bear man's face, exactly like Mikey, the four-year-old she'd been teaching hip-hop, when he couldn't remember a step.

She stepped forward, grabbed Luc's hand. He twitched, like her touch was hot. "How about we do this together?" she suggested.

"It's supposed to be just him," the producer complained.

"And once he's relaxed a little more, then he'll be able to do it, okay?"

She lifted Luc's hand—his paw, really, because the man was like a bear—and swiveled her hips as she held up his arm and danced and spun beneath it.

He stared at her, just like he had since she'd sashayed from the changerooms in her little silver fringed outfit. She was pretty sure his gulp would've been heard on the cameras. "Is that what you're wearing?" he'd murmured.

"Yep." She'd smiled, loving the way the lights hit the silver and made the tassels glimmer and sparkle. She sure wasn't wearing traditional ballet leotards anymore. This outfit wasn't as formfitting as a leotard, but wasn't tame by any means. Good thing her dad wasn't here. He'd be having kittens.

"Come on." She spun into his chest, his silver jacket and black T-shirt-covered, very broad chest, and whispered, "You need to look alive now, and not like a stunned fish."

He blinked, the overhead studio lights glaring into him, then seemed to shake himself as he nodded, and visibly relaxed and gritted out a smile. "Better?"

"Nope." Clearly she had her work cut out with this one. She tugged his head down. "You should look like you're having fun. What do you do to have fun?"

"Put pucks in the net?"

She sighed.

"How about you pick her up?" the producer called.

Luc's eyes widened, his expression so deer-in-headlights she fought another urge to giggle. "Come on. It's not hard. You're supposed to be strong, right?"

"I am, but I, uh, just don't know how to, um, pick you up in a way that's not inappropriate."

"He's not asking you to do weights with me. Just put your arm around me and lift me up against your side."

His hand tentatively moved to her back, and she grabbed it and placed it on her hip. "You're gonna have to get used to touching me, remember?" She placed a hand on his shoulder. "Now catch me."

She jumped up, her hand slipping around his neck, then his

hand slid from her hip down to behind her knees as she smiled at the cameras.

The flashes of cameras popped, as the wind machine blew back her hair, and she smiled at the video camera.

"Come on, Luc. Look like you're having fun!"

She leaned her head closer to his, grinning wider, one hand outstretched, as the camera guy called, "Put your arm out, like you're super strong."

"I am super strong," Luc mumbled.

She laughed, and he instantly relaxed, the tension in his body easing.

Good to know. He needed to laugh, to find ways to make this fun if he was going to relax and find ways to engage with others in a real way.

"Okay, let's try that again."

Luc gently lowered her to the floor, and she placed a hand on her dress to make sure it didn't ride up. "You're so light," he murmured, as she held up her hands in a double high five which he gently slapped, like he was scared to hurt her. And maybe he could, with that big solid build. There was a reason she had thought to not do the swivel and hip check. He'd probably bounce her into the next room.

"I told you not to worry." She squeezed his bicep, conscious the cameras were still rolling. Even this part had to look fun and not awkward, like they were comfortable with each other, and not like they'd met only two days ago and had arrived in TO yesterday.

Members of the production team had met them at the airport, before their luggage—her number of bags had raised Luc's eyebrows—had been deposited at the hotel and they'd been whisked off to a fancy restaurant for a "Welcome to *Dance Off Canada*" cocktail party.

She'd met Coco and her celebrity, actor Jason Streetley, and a bunch of others, who instantly welcomed her, and did their best to welcome Luc too. She'd noticed the way he'd switched from frozen fish and instantly morphed into someone affable and nice, shaking hands, doing backslap hugs, acting like he was thrilled to be here.

"Oh my gosh, girl," Coco had fanned herself. "He's built."

Yes, he was. It had been evident he was the most built man of the group, even while wearing the most subdued outfit of jeans and a tee and plaid shirt.

Coco had squeezed her. "This will be so fun dancing with you again."

"Thanks so much for mentioning me to Joanne." Her bank balance was especially grateful. "I still can't get over the whirlwind this has been."

"Hey, they needed someone fast, preferably based near Winnipeg, and when the next troupe member announced she was pregnant, and the others lacked, ah, personality, I suggested to Joanne she call you." Another hug. "I'm so glad you said yes."

Bailey had nodded, relaxing a little more. She would be too, eventually.

She'd been glad when the money had shown up in her account. Glad that Luc had made an effort last night, even if he was still looking stiff today. He'd relax more, and they'd look as easy as the other couples who had already been rehearsing together for the past week. It would simply take some time.

"And one more," a photographer called.

"Ready?" She glanced up at Luc.

His chin dipped, and she smiled, and caught the faintest smile in his expression as she jumped, her arm around his neck.

This time his hand was slightly higher, nearly mid hamstring, and she pointed one leg across his body and curled the other behind her, like a heel flick, lifting her chin and tossing her hair as the wind machine blew strands across her face.

"That's perfect! That's a cut."

"Whew." Luc gently lowered her, one hand on her knee as she landed back on the ground. "How do you manage to balance on those?" he said, pointing to her heels.

"Probably the same way you manage to balance on skates."

His lips pulled to one side.

"Okay, Luc, let's get some shots of you on your own now."

Luc shot her a look, and she gave him a double thumbs-up to encourage him. There were still cameras here, and who knew what they'd be filming?

She pointed to him, then pointed to her smile, and did a shimmy.

He half-laughed, his stiff posture relaxing, as he pointed back at her, his feet moving in an awkward shuffle. She laughed some more, and beckoned him to come closer.

"That's it," the producer called. "Like you're having fun."

Luc shook his head, then spun in a circle, elbows lifted, his silver jacket flying out, his black T-shirt lifting higher to reveal a glimpse of abs. She blinked.

Apparently she wasn't the only one who noticed, either.

"Well, hello! Hey, now try the strut without the shirt."

Luc glanced at the producer and shrugged from his jacket, then commenced the walk, holding the jacket over his shoulder, like he was auditioning for a runway.

"No, take your shirt off, and put the jacket on."

"Uh." He glanced at her, that panicked look from earlier back.

She shrugged. What was his problem? Surely hockey players were used to dressing rooms and moments of shirtlessness. Ballet dressing rooms meant all kinds of things could be—had been—witnessed, but bodies were bodies. She had a feeling having watched similar shows that he'd probably be expected to do a shirtless number—which would likely require a spray tan. Not that she'd freak him out by saying that just yet.

Already the list of things she was expected to know was lengthy, with everything from the premiere's first dance and song to the costumes and styling options emailed to her by the producers. Then there was all the stuff they were supposed to post on social media—after the announcement this Friday—which would no doubt bring a hefty upswing in the dance studio's social media numbers. Who knew—maybe she'd finally hit enough subscribers on her YouTube channel to start earning! She'd been buzzing with new information, immensely grateful to Coco for answering all her messages and texts. How glad she was that Poppy had been happy to take the studio's classes, leaving Bailey free to concentrate on this. She was so conscious they were already behind the other couples, judging from what she'd seen the others do in their to-camera pieces today.

"Luc?" the producer called. "Can you take off your shirt please?"

Luc straightened his shoulders, shook his head. "Sorry. I don't think you guys are ready for that yet."

There came a round of laughter, the moment of tension eased as the producer called her back in and they did more poses for still photographs, like what might be seen in magazines and news articles online.

"Now, Bailey, move beside him, and Luc, you grab her leg," the producer called.

Bailey leaned close, her right knee up and Luc tentatively grabbed her knee, his other hand behind her waist, as she wrapped her hand around his neck, her other hand on his chest as she smiled.

She could feel his heart thudding faster, and the thought he might still be nervous enlarged her smile. How funny to think something like this freaked him out, and she felt more comfortable.

"And one last one. I want to see you up on his hip, okay?"

"Man," Luc muttered.

She stifled a chuckle. If he thought this was bad, wait until he'd be expected to do some pull-throughs and split-overs like she was already planning for their first dance.

"How do we do this?" Luc asked, facing her.

"Okay, you need to brace with your right leg, while I put my knee up here," she demonstrated, "then I'm going to hoist myself up and you won't drop me. Got it?"

"I don't know that I do, but I'll try not to drop you."

"I'd appreciate that."

He half-smiled again, then followed her instructions as she placed a hand around his neck, her right hand in his left, as she jumped up and tucked herself into his side, all while smiling at the camera.

Sure enough he caught her, his hand on the bare skin at her waist.

"Tuck those legs together, Bailey," the producer called.

Right. Because nobody wanted to flash anyone. Dad was already heading for a heart attack judging from some of the costumes she'd seen. She pushed her knees together, bracing with her core as Luc held her for one beat, two beats, three.

Then, "That's good. Okay, I think we've got enough."

"Thank goodness," Luc murmured.

"Now, Bailey, we need you to join the other pros for rehearsals for the opening number, and Luc, you're going to makeup for your interview."

He blew out a breath. "Man. Somebody should've told me about the makeup."

"Look, you haven't died yet," she murmured. "You're still a real man."

"You've noticed, huh?"

"Go." She pushed him away, her heart fluttering. Which was

dumb. She'd never liked people making comments like that, but with Luc, she wasn't sure if it was his natural cocky swagger, or whether it was a way to assert himself after something that clearly had been a little intimidating and uncomfortable.

"See you soon?" he called, as she pivoted away.

She peeked over her shoulder. He really looked a little anxious. "We've got lots to work on, so yes. Now don't make them run late for your interview, okay?"

"Yes, ma'am."

She smiled. Maybe if he treated her like that she'd have a hope of getting out of this alive.

IF THE GUYS could see him now…

He'd thought joining his first pro training camp was hard. This topped that times ten. Wearing makeup, being dressed by a man, having to touch, to hold a woman he barely knew, which was made even worse by the fact he found her attractive. He should've said no. He should've pushed to see what the consequences would be for his captaincy if he'd declined this opportunity. Already he could feel this was a runaway train that he was holding onto for dear life, knowing the bridge was out and he was destined to crash.

His phone flashed, and he glanced at it. Ryan. *Hey dude, where are you?*

He exhaled, and shoved it away. He couldn't answer. Not with anything that wouldn't be a lie. And already this place felt filled with so much fakery he'd need an ice bath to slew off the untruths.

Last night's meet and greet with the other cast members and judges had been cringe city. He recognized some people, even as he was recognized by more than a few. They'd told him that they hadn't had a hockey player on the show for a while, not since a retired Hall of Famer from three seasons ago. It was enough to make him wonder why his club and agent thought this such a great idea, but there it was. He'd committed now, had signed his autograph on a contract that he couldn't break. He'd just have to hope he did badly enough to get eliminated in the first couple of rounds. At least this didn't go for three months as some other shows like this did.

"Luc Blanchard?" An assistant appeared at the door. "They're waiting for you."

"Am I pretty enough?" he asked the makeup artist.

"You'll do."

"It's okay. I know you did the best you could." He pointed to his face. "It's hard when you've not got much to work with."

"Don't talk like that. You're a handsome guy."

Yeah, if a woman was blind, maybe. But self-deprecation wasn't a quality admired around here. Some of the peeps from last night seemed to live in self-adulation land, and he'd never been too good with that. Sure, he could talk up a big game, and knew how to inspire others to win, but this was a whole other level. He'd not realized the level of competitiveness that existed in the TV ballroom scene. And he didn't think Bailey had realized that either.

"This way, Luc."

He followed down a rabbit warren of halls, then out where the bright lights hit his face. He'd done interviews before, plenty of them, and he knew he'd need to channel some of the personality that viewers might think was fun, and yet wouldn't seem too cheesy.

"Hey Luc, are you ready?"

"Born ready," he lied, settling in his seat, while the makeup girl dusted powder on his nose, and tweaked his hair. It was unbelievable how crazy intense this was, and he hadn't even danced a step yet. How on earth was he going to keep it together?

"Okay, I want you to look in this camera when we're rolling, okay?"

He nodded, as the magnitude of what he was doing hit him like a tsunami. His mouth dried, just like it had when he'd first seen Bailey in that tiny silver dress. She'd looked way too hot for someone like him, and he'd barely known where was safe to look, let alone place any part of him near. But she'd guided him like a boss, which he supposed she was, and he was grateful that at least her Christian status meant they'd likely not get too hot and heavy. *Dear Lord, no.*

The interviewer grinned at him, as his microphone was fed through his shirt and adjusted. "Just relax. It's okay."

His words reminded him of Bailey, how she calmed him with her words or with her smile or laugh. He might not have known her long, but she seemed a real deal chick, for sure.

"Okay, are you ready?"

Luc nodded. "Let's do this." He smiled at the camera and gave a thumbs-up, adopting the fun and bouncy personality of that actor dude Bailey and her friend had hung out with a bit last night.

"And here I am with Luc Blanchard, a man known more for his forecheck than his dance moves. Luc, tell us why you agreed to do this show."

Hit them with the truth, or a version of it? He'd choose option B. "It's always good to learn a new skill, and when the opportunity came, I was sure they'd picked the wrong guy, because I have two left feet, so I guess we'll see how that flies."

"Cut." The producer called. "Luc, I'm sorry, but we need a little more snap and crackle."

"Excuse me?"

"You need to sound a little more positive. You know, like you're excited to be here?"

Man, he wished Bailey was around. She seemed to have enough snap and crackle and sparkle for the two of them. "Uh, sure. Let's do it again." *Lord? You need to help me here. I've got nothing.*

"In three, two, one."

The interviewer nodded. "And here I am with Luc Blanchard, a man known more for his mean forecheck than his dance moves. Luc, can you tell us why you agreed to come on *Dance Off?*"

He made an effort to smile harder this time. That seemed to work for Bailey. "I found this was an opportunity too good to pass up. Who doesn't want the chance to learn a new skill, and make a fool of oneself, all in the name of charity?"

"Cut." The producer eyed him. "A fool? Seriously?"

"I'm just keeping it real."

The man sighed. "Could you try that answer again, this time without the fool part?"

"How real did you want this to be? I didn't realize I should be giving scripted answers."

"We don't need you to have rehearsed answers, and look, I do understand this was a last-minute thing, so perhaps you haven't had the chance to get your head around everything yet—"

That was for sure.

"—but we need positive energy from you, Luc. This interview shapes how you'll be seen by the viewing public, and how long you'll last. Nobody wants to see a downer on TV."

"I'm not being a downer. I'm keeping it real, that's all."

"Maybe just a little less real, this time?"

Wow. "Okay."

Third time lucky. This time, when the interviewer paused, Luc grinned like a fool, and said, "I know my being here will surprise a lot of people, but this was an awesome opportunity to learn a new skill. And when it's all in the name of good fun and raising money for one of my favorite charities, I knew I had to say yes."

"Cut." The producer beamed. "That's perfect."

Nope. That was insane.

He wondered how much more of this fakery his signature meant that he'd agreed to do.

THREE MORE INTERVIEWS LATER, where he'd basically repeated the same false enthusiasm, he finally found Bailey in the green room. She was talking with her friend Coco again, and he slumped into a seat next to her.

Coco glanced at him, arching an eyebrow, which he met with a look of his own. She was Bailey's friend, and he didn't want to interrupt, but his stomach had felt queasy all day, and he really needed to talk to Bailey and find out exactly what all of this meant.

"I think somebody wants to talk to you," Coco finally said, before air-kissing Bailey a goodbye.

Good to know his death glare still worked.

"Hey you." Bailey smiled at him. "How did all your interviews go?"

"I did not realize just what would be involved." He groaned. "This is crazy."

Her nose wrinkled. "Yeah, I know it's a lot, but it's only for a little while."

That's right. A notch of peace edged his heart. Only another day or so then he'd be done.

"Then we'll be back in Winnipeg and the real work begins."

"What?"

Her forehead furrowed. "This is the easy part. It's learning the dancing that's going to be the harder thing."

No. He really wanted to whine like a little kid. "It's too late to pull out now, isn't it?"

"Come on. You'll manage. You're not scared of a little challenge, are you?"

When she put it like that… "No."

"Good."

Her smile arrowed straight through him, giving him courage for the next part of the day. "So, what's happening now?"

"Didn't you check your schedule?"

Clearly not. He'd gotten so many emails from the producers in the past forty-eight hours it'd take a year to read through them all.

"We've got one more interview together, then it's a night off, then we're back early for the morning show tomorrow, then it's a meet and greet but with all the cast and crew, and then we'll fly home."

He sighed. "I didn't realize just how much would be involved."

"I don't think anyone did. Coco has been great in giving me some advice, but I'm looking forward to going back and actually getting the headspace to get this process started."

"What do you have to do?"

"Apart from figure out the choreo—"

"Corrie?"

"The choreography, the dance movements, for the music we've been given."

"They give us music? We don't get to pick?"

"We get given the dance we're supposed to do, whether it's a waltz or foxtrot or jive—"

He groaned.

"What?"

"I've only heard of one of those," he confessed.

"Well, by the time I'm done with you, you'll be able to do them all."

Huh. He leaned back in his chair. "You might look all sweet and innocent, but you're a bit of a spitfire, aren't you?"

Her head tilted. "Is that a good thing?"

"It's a great thing."

She bit her lip, then nodded and slowly smiled. "Well, Luc Blanchard, we better find someone around here who can get that on tape, because I think you'll need to remember that."

"Is this you getting sassy, huh?"

"Oh, Luc, you've got no idea."

CHAPTER 5

Friday started far too early with hair and makeup, which meant they had to leave the hotel by five. She gathered Luc wasn't an early bird, not like she'd learned to be, anyway. But appearing on morning TV would finally let the cat out of the bag. Nobody knew about her involvement in this, not even Bailey's family, as per their contract. Even Poppy only knew that Bailey had received an unexpected dancing opportunity which meant she needed to fly east immediately. Dancers knew such opportunities were rare, and as they often resulted from injury or illness to another dancer, they needed chasing down immediately. A fresh swell of appreciation rose for her friend for being so quick to say yes to covering her classes, few questions asked. She couldn't wait to return to her apartment, where Poppy was staying, and finally spill the beans.

The rush of the morning saw them share a taxi with Coco and Jason, and they arrived at the studios in front of an audience.

Hair and makeup were done, costumes were tweaked—another blingy number for her, hot pink this time—and they were microphoned up and sent to take their seats on the stage.

She sat in the row behind Luc, and she watched him roll his shoulders as if trying to release the tension. After this morning's national broadcast, there'd be no hiding anymore. She leaned forward and patted his shoulder. "It's gonna be fine," she murmured.

He exhaled. "I sure hope so."

Miguel, one of the male pro dancers, smirked and shook his head as she settled back in her seat, saying in an undertone, "He does not seem like he wants to be here."

"It's been a little sudden, and I think it's taking time to sink in."

He nodded, his voice still low. "You two took the place of Carlos and Lesley, didn't you?" He whistled. "They got too hot too quick, if you know what I mean."

Oh, she knew. Coco had spilled the tea last night. Lesley had been part of the pros for years, even marrying a dancer who competed on a US version of this show, and Carlos was a married celebrity comedian known for having thousands of YouTube subscribers. They'd met, their first dance quickly flaming into more which the producers had noted and raised the alarm bells. Then the media had rushed in, rumor-mongering over their relationship after they'd been spotted together at a dance studio, which had led to negative whispers about the show. To avoid being cancelled, the show's executive producers had needed to hurry the release date, and replace the celebrity and pro, hence the rush to get things done this week, then begin the live performances next weekend. Knowing that had helped with understanding the haste with which all had been arranged.

"Well, it's good to have you here, kid. Break a leg." Miguel gently patted her arm, in a way like her friend Mark used to do. She smiled, returning to face the front, catching the way Luc seemed to notice as he shifted too, his heavily tattooed arms now crossed.

The heat of the lights and instructions from the warm-up guy to smile and give big energy put paid to further reflections, and she did her best to look happy while she prayed Luc would do the same. From what Coco had said, Bailey needed to capitalize on her relative youth and looks, and play up her work with the underprivileged dancers in her community. Luc also needed to appear amiable, not surly or cocky, and she hoped he'd find the right balance of endearing clumsiness and have-a-go confidence to win audience votes. They needed to get to round three, if not further, in order for her to get the money she needed.

She glanced at the other members of the cast. There were a couple of actors, an ex-football player she'd noticed Luc had gravitated to that first night at the cocktail party, two singers, and an author. She bet they could take the author and the eighties one-hit wonder singer, at least.

Francesca McLinty, one of the *Good Morning, Canada* breakfast TV anchors, walked onto the set, waved to the seated guests as an assistant spoke to her, then took her spot on the sound stage. A producer counted down, silence fell, then the intro music was piped across the room.

Francesca beamed. "Welcome back, and we're so excited to be introducing you to this year's cast of *Dance off Canada!*"

Cue cheering and applause. Bailey grinned and clapped. This was actually kind of fun. More fun because she strongly suspected she'd not have to say too much, and could sit here in the second row and smile while the spotlight was on the celebrities seated in front.

"We're so excited to have this next season starting next weekend, and there's no one more excited than *Dance Off*'s host, Jenna Bellameade."

More cheering. Jenna was a ballroom legend, having won world titles back-to-back a decade ago. She'd been hosting the show for all five seasons, alongside Peter Drewe, another former dance pro.

The morning show hosts interviewed Jenna, then the judges, Marco, John and Cynthia, each of whom were legendary dancers of their day. Marco was a flamboyant European, John was an intense choreographer, and Cynthia was the "rose between two thorns" as she often liked to say, and the one who always sandwiched critiques between compliments.

Bailey had been learning what they liked, listening to Coco, and watching videos of previous seasons to learn how they were likely to judge. Marco wanted passion, John was the technical guru, while Cynthia was all about how well the celebrity sold the story. Bailey glanced at Luc. She wasn't sure how much story he'd be up for telling, and she was pretty sure his technical skills were close to zero. She hoped the passion he brought to hockey would somehow translate to the dance floor.

"And we're so excited to see all these fabulous celebrities! Wow." Francesca, the morning host, glanced around. "Put up your hand if you're just a little nervous about dancing on national television."

Bailey raised hers, while Luc raised both of his.

"I'm a little concerned about the dancers who are pros who are raising their hands," Marco said, as everyone laughed.

Francesca drew her microphone over to where they sat. "Now I'm here with Booker Prize winning author, Kate Fortescue. Kate, tell us, why do something like this?"

Kate leaned forward, as Miguel straightened. "I'm at an age when I want to try new things, and dancing is something I've always enjoyed watching others do but have never had the confidence to do myself. I'm hopeful that after this experience I'll be more confident."

"You will be, baby," Miguel called, to a general round of laughter.

Francesca smiled. "You're partnered with Miguel, who won two seasons ago, so you're in with a good chance."

"I hope so."

Bailey's stomach tensed as Francesca moved to Luc. "Now, seated beside Kate, we have a treat."

"Yes, we do," Marco called, with a solid lip smack.

Bailey kept her smile pasted on, as she internally cringed over what Luc must be thinking.

Francesca laughed. "Known for dodging defensemen and scoring fast goals, can hockey star Luc Blanchard shake it on the dance floor as well as he can skate on ice? Luc Blanchard, welcome. Tell us, how are you feeling?"

Bailey held her breath.

Luc cleared his throat and leaned forward. "When I got the call I kind of freaked out, but I'm always glad for the opportunity to shine a light on those charities that support people with cancer, even if it means I have to look like a fool."

"Oh, I'm sure you'll be great," Francesca soothed. "And I'm sure being a top athlete you'll bring some advantages to the dance floor."

Luc shrugged. "Maybe. It's cool that it's live, because I'm used to that pressure-filled environment and I love feeding off the energy in the room. I've been training in the offseason, so my cardio will be good. I just need to work on my rhythm—and everything else."

"I'm sure your partner will help with that. Let's give it up for our newest dance pro Bailey Donovan."

Bailey's stomach tensed, but she pushed past it and waved, grinning wider.

"How are you feeling Bailey?" Francesca asked. "I noticed you put up your hand before."

Bailey nodded. "I love dance, and I'm a bit nervous about doing this for the first time, but I'm also really excited to be here. I think it's wonderful to see people step into something they thought was too hard and end up feeling like they've learned a new skill."

"What did you know about Luc before you took this gig?"

Her smile faltered. She hitched it up. "If I'm completely honest, I didn't know too much. We might live in the same city but," she leaned forward, cupping her mouth, "don't tell anyone, but I'm actually not a huge hockey fan."

"Whoa!" Francesca mock-gasped, as Luc swiveled in his seat with a fake scowl.

"Don't hate me!" Bailey said, hands palms up in surrender.

"Well, it seems most of us know that Luc has some skills on the ice, but you'll be teaching him some new moves, too, huh?"

"Exactly!" She grinned and waved again.

"Anything else to say, Luc?" Francesca asked.

He glanced back at Bailey. "I think I've got the perfect partner. She looks sweet, but she's tough, and we're gonna do our best to crush the competition," Luc said, pointing at the camera. "As long as I don't crush her first."

"Them's fighting words," Miguel murmured, as the studio erupted in more laughter.

But even as they smiled, she knew that was the key to getting Luc engaged. He was competitive, and so was she. She'd need to find a way to flick that switch and get him focused on winning, and not all the obstacles surrounding them.

Her shoulders straightened. She couldn't wait to get home and finally start teaching the bear man she'd been partnered with.

WHY HAD he bothered to answer the group's video call? Luc sighed, as the murmurs of the airport lounge faded as his friends' mockery continued.

"Dude. No way."

Ryan hadn't stopped laughing since Luc had joined the group video chat five minutes ago.

"Stop it. You're embarrassing yourself."

Ryan pointed to himself. "I'm not the one who's going to be embarrassed. What the heck?"

"Yeah, come on, Lukey baby, you gotta admit, this is a shock," Vancouver's Chris Thomas said. "Weren't you the one sitting at a table only a week or so ago saying you didn't dance? You been keeping this a secret, huh?"

"No." Luc winced. "It's still true. I can't dance."

"Then why on earth agree to do a dance show?"

Luc sighed, and shook his head. "Nothing has been officially announced yet but the club tapped me for being captain."

"They did?" Mike Vaughan, Calgary's captain asked. "That's fantastic."

"That's awesome," Jai Mullins, the alternate captain for San Jose, said. "Congrats."

Chris applauded. "About time. You're the best they've got, especially now Linzey has left."

"Gee, thanks."

"You're welcome," Chris grinned.

"So, what's that got to do with dancing?" Ryan asked.

Luc shrugged. "They wanted me to raise my profile."

This sent Ryan off in another peal of laughter.

"What?"

"I don't think you can get a higher profile than announcing that. Everyone is talking about it. Have you seen what they're saying on TSN?"

He sighed. No, he hadn't, and he had every intention of keeping it that way. He'd posted on Instagram like the team and show wanted, careful to keep the focus on the cancer fundraising part, but hadn't read any of the comments. He didn't dare. And now he needed to get the heat off him and turn this conversation's focus onto Ryan. "Anyone else think Ryan is a little too happy these days?"

"Don't think you can try and change the subject, man."

Huh. Ryan was getting entirely too feisty since going out with Sylvie. She was good for him.

"I personally am loving the fact that Mister I'm Never Doing Anything Girly is going to be dancing on national TV." Mike grinned. "I can't wait to see what he has to wear."

"My vote is for pirate sleeves," Chris said. "Hey, I bet they'll make you do a bare-chested one."

"They better not," he growled.

"Come on. Don't you think that'll get your socials moving?"

"The wrong direction, maybe."

"Do you have to wear makeup?" Jai asked.

Man. He groaned.

"I'm taking that as a yes," Jai said, which earned another round of laughter from Ryan.

"You guys are not exactly being supportive right now," he grumbled.

"Your partner is pretty," Chris said. He waggled his eyebrows.

"Don't go there, man. She is, but we can't do anything."

"Now that sounds like a man who wants to do something," Jai teased.

"Yeah, the very man who said he's not doing relationships until he's quit hockey." Ryan grinned.

"And I'm not," he snapped. "There's nothing there. She's a professional, and so am I. And anyway, I don't want a relationship with her."

Judging from the new round of jeers he shouldn't have bitten. This was such a mistake. He was gonna get slaughtered, crucified, his rep would never be the same. As soon as he'd finished this morning's interview, his phone had blown up with all kinds of mocking tease. He'd thought answering the video call from his friends would be the easiest way to explain what was going on, but clearly this was a mistake. If his friends were treating him like this, what would his teammates say? What would all the opposition teams say? They'd think he'd gone softer than soft, couldn't play hard or fight anymore, and the reputation he'd built up these past ten years would be blown to smithereens.

"If it makes you feel any better, I can't wait to see you dance, man," Mike said.

"So proud of you," Bree Vaughan called from the background. "Don't listen to them, Luc, you'll be great!"

He exhaled heavily, then glanced across at where Bailey sat frowning at her phone, headphones in. He hoped she hadn't heard what he'd said about her. Even if it was true. Well, kinda true. He could be a professional—*would* be a professional about this. Just because they were spending lots of time together, and he was noticing all kinds of things about her, like how soft her skin was, or how light lived in her hair, or how good she smelled, didn't mean anything had to happen. It couldn't. They had a clause in their contract forbidding it.

"Is she there?" Ryan asked.

"No," he fibbed.

"She is, isn't she?" Bree said again.

Luc sighed. "Haven't we had a conversation or two about how these chats are supposed to only be for us guys? No offense, Bree."

"None taken," she said. "So, is she? I want to meet her if she is."

"No. She's busy, and anyway, I want to change the topic. You know I'd much prefer to talk about manly things."

"Too late for that, Mister Dancing King," Mike teased.

"Yeah, put her on," Chris said.

He sighed, and nudged Bailey. She took off her headphones and looked at him. "Hey, do you mind talking to the guys?"

"And me," Bree's voice called.

He winced. "And Bree Vaughan?"

"Who are they?"

Laughter fell from his phone. "I loved she didn't know who he was," Ryan said.

"What else was it she said?" Jai said. "She didn't know much about hockey? Luc's ego must've sunk to a new low."

Just wait until they saw him dance. Ugh.

"Sounds like she doesn't know who any of us are."

"So we got a clean slate to work with here, fellas," Chris said. "Time to spill all the juice on our Luc here."

Man. "Just say hi." Luc shoved the phone at her.

Bailey instantly grinned and waved at the screen. "Hi."

Then, in a boss move, she handed it back. He fist-bumped his appreciation. Well, tried to, but she looked at his clenched fist as if not sure what to do with it, so he dropped his hand. Clearly they were from different worlds.

"She's pretty," Bree said.

"And she can still hear you."

"Good! Then tell her I'm happy to tell her anything she needs to know." Bree smirked.

"You don't know as much as we do, babe," Mike said, wrapping an arm around his wife.

Bailey laughed, and gestured for Luc's phone. He shook his head. No way was this getting out of control any more than it already had.

"Tell her I've just followed her on Instagram," Bree yelled.

Bailey tapped her screen and held up her own phone. "Tell her I've just done it back."

"No, you can't," Luc protested. "They're my friends, not yours."

"Too bad, so sad," she retorted, snatching his phone back. "I'm all about making new friends. Hi there!" She waved at the screen again, then shot him a smirk.

He fought a grin. She was ridiculously pretty, and he kind of loved how she took charge like that. She might look sweet and innocent, but she was tough, too.

"So, what do you guys want to know?" Bailey grinned at the screen. "Do we need to start a private group chat for behind-the-scenes Luc dance talk?"

"Yeah!" came a variety of voices.

"Look, don't tell them," he begged, reaching across to grab the phone, his arms tangling around her, as his friends' faces bobbed away.

"Whoa, it's Luc Blanchard!"

Luc stilled, as a teenager held up his phone. His hands inched away from where his arms had been around Bailey. She pulled away, straightening, and handed Luc's phone back. Luc ended the call, then faced the teen. "It's not what you think."

"Uh-huh."

Man. He couldn't afford to have scandal follow him. Not when he hadn't even been officially announced as the captain. He peeked at Bailey, who still wore her own wide eyes, and murmured, "I'm sorry."

"We're on show now, aren't we?" she whispered.

He nodded. Truth be told, he'd always been on show. That was why the club insisted on players wearing suits to game days, to show they were professional. He couldn't afford to be caught in any compromising position—or any position that could be misunderstood or misconstrued—especially now.

She glanced at the boy, who was still filming them. "Excuse me, but you know you're supposed to ask before filming someone, don't you? Otherwise it's a breach of privacy, and you could get charged."

The teen lowered his phone. "I thought you and him were just on national TV."

She nodded. "We were. After agreeing to that. And now we're here as private citizens. And I don't consent to you filming me without my permission. Would you like me to film you without asking your permission?" She retrieved her phone, and started recording.

"Bailey," Luc murmured.

She shrugged. "I just think it's rude to do that. And I don't know that this young man has ever thought about what an invasion of privacy that kind of behavior can be. Or," she added in a louder voice, "whether it's something that needs to be reported to the police."

"Bailey," he hissed, as the kid swore and moved away.

"What?"

The team had plenty of media training to deal with similar things. "You can't go rogue on the public like that."

"Even though he'd just gone rogue on you and me?"

"But what if he gets ticked, and finds out where you live, or where your studio is? I don't want anything bad to happen to you." Like people trashing her apartment, or her business. Or hurting her. His stomach clenched.

"What do you think could happen?"

Man. If she really didn't know, he wasn't about to tell her. "I just want you to be safe, that's all."

"Look, I'm sorry if that was uncomfortable for you, and I get that you've got a reputation to protect. But I've looked into this. I'm used to having to get all kinds of permission for parents to film when we have ballet concerts, so he needs to know this is wrong." She held up her phone. "And now I've got proof of who he is."

A reluctant wave of admiration swept through him. She was a lot tougher than she looked. Which meant there was no way she could connect with his friends, who would only tease him more and probably tell her all kinds of things he really didn't want her to know. Especially since he had lied before about not wanting any kind of relationship with her.

CHAPTER 6

He didn't want a relationship with her.

Well, that was great. That was wonderful. That was fantastic, because she felt exactly the same. *Exactly* the same.

She closed her eyes, the memories of yesterday's airport lounge encounter floating through her brain as she ignored the camera crew setting up in the corner of the studio. They'd arrived not five minutes after she'd opened the studio today. She'd missed the chance to do her personal unwind after returning home yesterday, then staying up far too late with Poppy and filling her in on all the goss, and trying to get her head around all that was involved.

She had to choreograph the routine they would be dancing live next Sunday. Next *Sunday*. She had a week—no, not even that, only five days or so—before they had to fly back to Toronto, and prepare for everything from costume fittings to rehearsing the pro dancers' group routine. Then it was camera blocking—in front of the producers, which meant Luc needed to know the routine by then—and the dress rehearsal, before a full day Sunday doing hair, makeup, and costumes, then filming in front of the live audience that evening. Then they'd jump back on a plane, and start rehearsing the next dance, before returning on Thursday to do it all again.

Maybe they were crazy with all this travel by returning to Winnipeg instead of staying in Toronto like most of the other couples. Staying in TO would allow them more rehearsal time. She might have to suggest that to Luc. Except he had hockey commitments here, which meant he'd scheduled four hours a day for dance rehearsal, giving him more time for hockey, although she was willing to bet he'd need more than four hours.

Lord, help me! And him! Her body wanted to shake with the intensity of it all. She'd give anything to release the crazy nerves in a dance-off of her own.

She peeked across at where Ella, the producer, and Ben and Tony, the camera guys, were setting up. Maybe she still had a few minutes to get her nerves under control.

She moved closer, smiled. "Hi there."

"Hey Bailey. You all good?" Ella asked.

She nodded. She had to play nice seeing they would be her and Luc's own little production crew for the duration of the series. And while they might be here filming for four hours to find sixty seconds of footage, she wanted that footage to be of the more positive variety, rather than focus on the stuff people didn't need to see. Like picking a dance thong from her butt. "I just wanted to take a moment to dance if that's okay."

"Honey, that's why we're here. You do you, and forget we're here." Ella smiled. "Most of them do."

Another nod.

"Just don't go forgetting too much, if you know what I mean." Ella winked, then tapped her ring finger.

Bailey winced. Like the pro and contestant she and Luc were replacing. "Understood."

She turned her back on them, and retrieved her phone, and found the music she'd been given this week. Harry Connick

Junior's song, "It Had to be You" was a standard for the foxtrot, the dance they'd been given. She was grateful for the slower pace, even if the foxtrot was a complex dance, but she wanted to remember how this went and move through it as she'd imagined last night. To have one more chance to do so before Luc got here, before his physical bigness and breadth of personality stole her concentration, was necessary.

The elegant swing of the orchestra blared from her phone, and she swayed to the music, imagining the opening scene according to the style and props that had been given her. She had stairs to walk down in her heels, then she'd tap him on the shoulder, he'd take her hand, she'd spin, her long feathery dress swirling out, as per the costume suggested to her, then they'd begin the actual foxtrot. John, the stickler for technical dancing, would be expecting to see the slow, slow, quick, quick steps of the foxtrot, so she needed to make sure Luc could do the basic movements and set pieces, as well as adding in the drama and elegance that Cynthia and Marco always liked to see.

She positioned her arms, holding the phone in front of her as she imagined dancing with him. One line down to the corner of the room, then a pause, before a spin in the middle, then a moment to arch away, then come back together. Foxtrot meant they were holding each other for most of the time, which she knew could get a little dull for the audience, so she would have to include some dips and add a split-over lift, if Luc was ready for that. He should be. His muscles and frame would be perfect for all kinds of lifts sure to please crowds and get votes, if he was prepared to trust her.

His words from their initial plane trip crossed her mind again. His doubts, his concerns about her size compared to his. Well, she was going to have to use that to her advantage, even if that meant resorting to, to borrow the words from her ultimate favorite movie of all time, "flashy, crowd-pleasing steps". She was glad the producers had made it clear that, unlike on the US show, lifts on *Dance Off* were perfectly okay.

She finished, arching backwards, arm outstretched, as she envisaged their routine would end, only to hear a slow clap come from the door. She glanced across, straightening as Luc entered.

"Wow."

She swallowed, thinking the same. He'd dressed as she requested, comfortably in shorts and a tee, a far cry from the tux he'd wear on Sunday, but she wanted him to relax into things today. Even if she bet he'd kick up a fuss at the shoes he'd be expected to wear. His shorts showed his muscular legs, where even his calves seemed twice the size of her thighs, and his shirt was doing his chest and arms plenty of favors. She blinked, snapping into professional mode, as she gestured to the film crew who were already filming.

Whoa. She hadn't been expecting that. She hoped they hadn't caught any expression from her that looked like ogling. She winced, wiping her hands down the sheer flowy dance skirt over tights she'd worn with her basic leotard.

"Hey, Luc." Ella moved closer. "We met briefly at the meet and greet, but I'm Ella, and this is Ben and Tony. We're going to be here for the next few hours."

"Few hours?"

"Yeah. Your contract was four hours rehearsal minimum per day, remember?"

"Yeah, but I didn't think we'd be filmed for all that. I thought you'd be here to film the fake introduction, then a few clips of Bailey trying to teach me to dance."

"Those clips only come about from us getting the right amount of footage," Ella explained. "So, we're going to stay here the whole time, do a few little interviews for the package as well. Don't worry, as I explained to Bailey, you won't even notice we're here after a little while."

"We need to microphone you both now," Ben said, handing them both battery packs.

Bailey attached it onto her dance skirt while Ella adjusted the tiny microphone. She smiled at Luc. "You'll need to be careful what you say now."

He shrugged. "I keep my mouth clean."

"Well, speaking of mouths, look, we have snacks." Bailey pointed to the table where *Dance Off* had provided a variety of granola bars, fruit, and some less healthy options positioned next to a tray of bottled waters.

Luc cut her a look. "I have a feeling I'll need DoorDash. Like, I'm always hungry and eat five meals a day."

Good to know. Bailey turned to Ella. "Okay, so you were saying you wanted us to do the fake 'oh, it's you' scene?"

Ella nodded. "Normally it isn't faked, as the dance pros don't know who they're matched up with until that moment. Obviously, especially given the circumstances we didn't have time for that with you two, but the viewing audience doesn't need to know that. So we're going to film a sequence with Luc outside, all excited or nervous, and then have him coming inside and 'meeting' you. Okay?"

"And um, how do you want us to 'meet'?" Bailey asked, rabbit-earing those last words like Ella seemed fond of doing.

"A hug, a squeal, a handshake, whatever feels natural."

Hmm. Nothing felt natural as far as this man was concerned.

"Ready?"

"Sure."

Ben followed Ella and Luc back outside, leaving Tony with Bailey, and she did her best to relax, to pray, to calm down. She returned to her music, listening as she envisaged the steps once again, and swayed and stretched. *Lord, have Your way. I don't know what Your purpose is in all this, but I'm trusting that it's for my good.*

The door opened. She glanced up. And beamed. Totally naturally. "It's you!"

"Hey, I'm Luc," Luc said.

The fact he was introducing himself drew her laugh, and she dashed across the dance floor and hugged him, like he was her friend. Then paused, as his arms automatically went around her. Oh. This felt a little close. Which was dumb. He'd have to hold her, and her him. Maybe he was just treating her as a friend too. Regardless, this hug was going on too long, and she needed to pull away. Now. So she did.

"And cut. Hey, that was great," Ella said. "You get that down okay, guys?"

Ben was squinting at his camera's playback, nodding. "Yep, looks good." Tony said the same.

Bailey pushed a smile back on her dial, looking at Ella for instruction.

"Okay, just act natural."

"Sorry, this is all so new to me."

"I know. And it will get easier. The first day is always the hardest. Now, you might want to ask how he's feeling, tell him what the dance is."

She nodded. Turned back to Luc, then glanced back at the camera guys. "Do I need to wait for a count in?"

"For this part, yes. For the rest, just do what you need to do. The guys have done this long enough they'll know when to tell you to pause, but they won't interrupt you very often."

Bailey fanned her face. "I don't know why I feel so nervous."

"You'll be great," Luc said. "I, on the other hand..." He made a face.

She laughed, and saw how his expression instantly eased. "Hey, it's okay. You'll be fine."

"Because you're an excellent teacher, or so someone told me."

He remembered that? Huh. "Well, it *is* true."

"Guys, we haven't started yet," Ella complained, with an upheld hand. "Now, let's run that again, then keep going. Ask Luc how's he's feeling, then tell him what you're dancing this week, then get into it. Okay?"

Bailey nodded, Luc muttered a "yeah".

Ben counted them in. "Three, two, one…"

Bailey clapped her hands together. "So, Luc, tell me how you're feeling about dancing." She did a little wiggle, which seemed to draw his reluctant smile.

Luc shoved a hand through his hair, and grinned awkwardly. "I gotta admit, this is something I never thought I'd do, and I'm trying not to freak out about it."

She nodded, her heart filling with empathy. She could appreciate a man admitting to feeling vulnerable. "I think stepping out of your comfort zone for the sake of a good cause is a wonderful thing to do."

His shoulders dropped a little. "My charity supports those fighting cancer, which is what my mom faced several years ago, so I'm prepared to look like a fool if it means we raise money for a good cause."

She grasped his arm. "I'm sure your mom is very proud of you. And I promise that you won't look like a fool. I think anyone should be impressed by the courage it takes to try something so different, so let's go with that."

He nodded, and she released her hand.

"As for looking like a fool, well, if you don't want to look like a laughingstock, you're going to have to prove everyone wrong and you'll do that by following my instructions. To the *letter*. Got it?"

His face screwed up, as if in pain, then he nodded. "Deal." He held out his hand.

She grasped it. Large, calloused, slightly sweaty. He was nervous. Her heart softened. For all his bluster and hugeness, the poor man really was anxious. What could she say to ease his nerves?

She squeezed his hand then let go. "Are you competitive?"

"I play pro hockey, so yeah."

Her nose wrinkled. "I have to admit, I'm not familiar with hockey, and I don't really know much about what you do. Actually, I don't know anything about what you do at all."

He slapped a hand on his big chest. "That cuts deep."

She laughed. "But I guess if you're a pro, you've had to fight your way to the top, right?"

"Absolutely. Peewee, Juniors, minor league, even training camp, it's all about wanting to be the best."

"Then I want you to think of this like training camp for dance. And we're going to train you so you can smoke the opposition."

He chuckled. "Did you say smoke?"

"Yes. Is that not the right word?"

"It's totally the right word."

She smiled at him, and he smiled back, then a cleared throat reminded her they weren't alone.

Ella did a "cut" gesture, then turned to them. "Okay, the chemistry here is undeniable, so that's going to shoot really well."

"The what?" Luc asked.

"You two. You seem to have a thing, but don't go having a 'thing', if you know what I mean."

Oh my gosh. "You don't need to worry about that," Bailey rushed to assure. "We're just friends. Not even that really. More like recent acquaintances."

"Sure you are." Ella did a "get on with it" gesture. "Now, back to the dancing. What is it you're teaching him this week?"

Bailey placed cool hands on her hot cheeks, willing them to calm. "Um, okay." She glanced at the cameras. They were still recording. Oh goodness. How flustered did she appear? "Um, right."

"The dance," Luc said, his deep voice focusing her.

She nodded, taking in a deep breath. Then straightened her shoulders and looked at him again. Luc now wore a small smile tucked up in the corner of his mouth. Cute. She blinked, refocused. "Okay." She clapped her hands, just like she did for her tiny tots. Refocus time. "So, this week, we're very lucky to be doing the foxtrot, which is one of ballroom's most beautiful dances, and you'll be pleased to know it's not too hard." A bit of a fib, but there was no need to further scare the man.

"Phew." He wiped his brow in an exaggerated movement, no doubt for the sake of the cameras. "This is all hard enough as it is."

She laughed.

"What?"

She pointed to a box sitting in the corner. "You say that now, but just wait until you get to wear your shoes."

"My shoes?"

She nodded. "Dance shoes. You have to wear a heel."

"My shoes have heels," he protested.

"Yeah, that's not what you're going to be wearing on Sunday."

"Are you kidding?" That panicked look was back in his eyes.

"Lucky Luc gets to wear a tux *and* special dance shoes with a heel."

"But I don't want to be any taller than you than I already am."

"Too bad."

"Oh my..." His last word was muffled as he hid his face behind his hands. "Remind me why I'm doing this again?"

"Your mom. Cancer patients." She patted his arm. "Look, if it makes you feel any better, we can start today with the basic movements and do those with bare feet."

"You do *not* want to see my feet."

She crossed her arms. "It's bare feet or dance shoes."

He groaned, then toed off his sneakers, then tugged off his socks. She frowned, looking at his feet. They were huge, and a little hairy, which wouldn't film well. She glanced at Ella, but she just made a "keep going" gesture, so she did.

"Alright then."

"What about you? Are you going barefoot too?" he asked, pointing to her dance shoes.

"Are you worried I'm going to stab you with my heels?"

"Super worried," he drawled.

She laughed. "Come on." She grabbed his hands and drew him closer. "Now, this Sunday we're doing the foxtrot, and like I said, it's fairly easy. It's all about the hold, the slow and quick steps, and the rise and fall. Have you waltzed?"

He shook his head. "I've never really danced before," he mumbled.

"Could you repeat that?" Ella asked.

Luc sighed, and nodded, saying in a louder voice, "I've never really danced before."

Bailey knew this already but still felt her smile fade. She pushed it back into megawatt territory. "Well, that's awesome."

"It is?"

She nodded. "It means we don't have to unlearn any bad habits." She rubbed her hands together. "I've got you now, and you're mine, all mine."

He snickered. "You're weird."

"I know. Just imagine how weird you're going to be at the end of this."

He gave a burst of rumbly laughter. "Come on then, Miss Dance Pro. Let's see what you got. Hit me."

HE FELT like he'd been hit by a ten-ton truck. Bailey had transformed from Miss Sparkly into Ms. No-Nonsense as she guided him into the movements, explaining all kinds of things he barely grasped, too focused on the way she touched him, maneuvering his body as she pushed him around, seemingly unconscious of what such movements must look like to the camera crew. Sure, he'd had a vague idea of what would be involved, but this awareness of just how physical it would be, how close they would get, to the point he could see a sweat bead sliding along her collarbone, he hadn't expected that.

She was studying his hips now, tapping his right, as he tentatively held her left hip. He'd been worried about touching her, feeling like a moose trying to hold hands with a butterfly, but then she'd just slapped his hand there, and grasped his left hand, and now seemed none too shy about pushing and prodding him to move the way she wanted.

"Now put your right foot back."

He put a foot back.

She shook her head. "No, your right foot."

He did the same movement.

She laughed. "The other right foot." She tapped his right hip again.

Oh.

"Now, put it back, then bring it in."

He obeyed.

"Okay, now let's look at your arms. Lift them out, then…" She stood behind him and pushed his right arm forward, slightly down. "You're going to grab my back so hold your hand like this." She demonstrated. "Remember, it's all about the frame, and they want to see you upright, not hunched over, so keep your shoulders set, locked in place, and don't lean forward. There needs to be space between us." She shifted to the front, clasping his right hand he hadn't dared move.

She spread her fingers between his, and drew him into the movements.

He tried to follow, but he was clumsy, nearly tripping over her feet in his attempts to not do that very thing. "Man."

"It's okay. You're gonna get there."

Yeah. Sure he was.

"Just smoke the opposition, okay?"

He smiled, but it was like her words clicked his brain into gear. He needed to concentrate. She was doing her best to help him. He needed to do his best to hold up his side of the bargain and try too.

"You don't need to frown," she said, pushing a finger between his eyebrows.

"That's my thinking face."

She nodded. "Well, you don't want to show the judges you're thinking so hard. So just relax. You'll get this."

He didn't think so, but... "Okay." He exhaled. "It's just dancing, right? How hard can this be?"

MAN. Why hadn't anybody ever told him how hard dancing could be? Luc wobbled like an old man to his tan leather couch then crashed on it. He heard a splintering sound, that just may have been a leg crumbling—a couch leg, not his own, though they felt just as likely to.

Every single muscle screamed for an ice bath. He hadn't known four hours of dance—more like five, because Bailey was being a drill sergeant, keeping him on his toes until his toes couldn't handle it anymore—could hurt so much. Who would've thought he'd ache more from dance than hockey? He needed a massage, stat.

Yet Bailey barely sweated. He'd thought his fitness was good, but hers was next-level, which made him all the more amazed.

Bailey really was amazing. She was so patient with him, so encouraging. She really knew her stuff, not being shy about pushing him around simply because he was twice the size of her. Well, not in height, because that would've been dumb. With her heels on she came to his chin, which wasn't too bad, he supposed. The mirrors in her studio suggested that wouldn't look too ridiculous, anyway.

He eased his leg out, toeing off his shoes, that fell with a soft *thud, thud* to the floor. She'd warned him she'd go soft on him today, his first day. If this was soft he'd hate to see what tough was.

His phone rang. He was tempted to ignore it. He'd gotten way too many crazy messages from people in recent days. He glanced at the screen anyway, then pressed answer.

"Hey Mom."

"Lucas. How did you go today?"

He closed his eyes and groaned.

His mother chuckled. "That good, eh?"

"She's a little warhorse. Like, worse than Coach Frantzen."

"But she looks so sweet and pretty."

"She is. I mean," he cleared his throat, "she looks sweet, but she's really mean, Ma. Always picking on me." He smiled.

"Uh-oh."

"What?"

"You like her, huh?"

"No." He winced. He sounded like a little kid.

"I saw the way you two were yesterday morning on that breakfast show. You like her."

"Mom, she's fun, and yes, she's pretty, but she's a pro and so am I. Nothing can happen." If he said it enough, his brain might send the message to his senses to stop noticing her so much. Like that moment earlier when Bailey had looked at him, then tapped his bicep and said, "How strong are you feeling?"

He'd flexed, then said "Plenty strong", kinda hoping that

would make it onto the camera, as long as it didn't make him look like a tool.

Then she said, "I didn't think I'd do a lift on the first day, but because you're so big and strong I feel like we can do this."

She'd then proceeded to instruct him on how to lift her, and he'd grabbed her under her arms and spun her. And somehow, in that moment, he could understand what the fuss was about, why the male dancers on the show owned their dancing prowess without a hint of embarrassment or apology. Because dancing like this, with her, her hair flying out, her absolute trust in him, felt good. More than good, he felt strong and powerful, but also, for the first time in his life, he'd felt sexy too.

Maybe that had been the result of the way she'd looked at him after, eyes wide. "You do have some strength to you, don't you?"

"I try," he'd said, as modestly as he could.

"I bet you could bench press two of me."

"How much do you weigh?"

She told him.

He nodded. "Yeah, I probably could." He'd then glanced at where the cameras kept rolling. "Want to try now?"

She'd laughed, declined, then winked. "You gotta give them something for tomorrow."

He smiled at that now, then became aware that his mom had asked him something and he hadn't noticed. "Sorry, Ma, what did you say?"

"I want to know about tickets. How do your father and I get tickets to watch you perform on Sunday?"

"Oh no, you do *not* want to come."

"You'll be in Toronto, not Winnipeg for a change. Do you know how much easier it is to drive there than Manitoba?"

His parents didn't like to fly. Well, Mom didn't, and their home in Mercier, Quebec meant they didn't see him play too often, except when he played Montreal or Ottawa. "I don't know if I want anyone I know there seeing me."

"Lucas, are you telling me you're happy to be seen by millions on TV and not your own family?"

He wasn't saying that anymore.

"Besides, I want to meet her."

"Meet who?"

"Your dance girlfriend."

"She's not my girlfriend, Ma. She's my dance partner."

"Potato, potata, I don't care. I want to meet her."

He held back a sigh, feeling this was perhaps only fair considering he'd forced Bailey to meet his friends. Via video chat, but whatever. "I'll see what I can do," he finally said. "If not this week, we'll try for next."

"Good. Now make me proud."

"Always, Ma."

The call ended, and he prayed for his folks. They might not know Jesus yet, but they were on the journey. Which got him wondering about the girl his mom was so desperate to meet.

What would she say when she met his folks? He blinked. And did her parents want to meet him? Oh man.

CHAPTER 7

Not even dancing for the first time in *The Nutcracker* had drained her so much as four, no, five hours training with Luc Blanchard. She'd never been so exhausted as when she'd returned to the apartment and crashed on the cream floral couch.

"How did he go?" Poppy asked.

"Oh my gosh, Poppy."

"That bad, huh?"

Bailey sighed. "He's trying. But honestly, I don't know how we're going to get past this first elimination let alone reach the third round."

"That's when you get your second five grand, right?"

She nodded. She probably shouldn't have said anything to Poppy about her payment, especially when she'd gathered from Coco that Bailey had been getting paid a bonus rate for stepping in as an emergency dance pro. But Poppy understood the pressing financial concerns of the dance studio, and the meager earnings of dancers. And while the network was helping subsidize things, and she was giving all the teacher fees to Poppy while she looked after the studio's classes, and giving her free rent while she stayed here, she still felt like Poppy was probably being shortchanged.

"So, you have to get to the third round."

"I don't know how committed he is to the cause, either. I mean, he's competitive—"

"All hockey players are."

"That's right." She sat up, studied Poppy. "I keep forgetting that Franklin plays."

Poppy laughed. "I love that about you. You've always been oblivious to much beyond dance."

"Not oblivious, just not exactly… aware."

"Yeah, I'm pretty sure that's the same thing."

Bailey threw a cushion at her, and Poppy threw it back.

"So, tell me more. Is he as serious as he looks? Funny? Charming?"

"Sometimes." To all three.

Poppy studied her. "You like him, huh?"

"No."

"Come on. He's all big and brooding, and I know you've always had a thing for broody guys."

"No, I haven't." Bailey threw another cushion at her, just missing a china teacup that had belonged to her grandmother.

"You need to be careful," Poppy said, with a schoolmarm finger.

She winced. "Yeah, I'd hate to break that."

"No, I mean with Luc Blanchard."

Bailey rolled her eyes. "He's not my type." Even if the memory of him holding her, his scent of musk and manliness, had caused her to inhale a little deeper than was decent. She really hoped the cameras hadn't picked up on *that*.

"And what exactly is your type? You're not still pining over Mark, are you?"

She sighed. Mark Drummond had been everything she'd thought handsome, with his chiseled good looks, lean build, and floppy brown hair. Some had said he was beautiful, and his accent had certainly been. And while he could dance like an angel, his personal life wasn't quite the same, and while she didn't like to judge, a Christian girl had to have standards about the man she might wish to have as a romantic partner. Even if she couldn't always be so choosy about partners in the world of dance.

"You still like him?" Poppy crinkled her nose.

"No. Not like that."

"Luc is a Christian, at least."

"Is he?"

"Oh my gosh, Bailey. He and Franklin are in the same online Bible study group. You know, along with people like Mike Vaughan, and Ryan Guillemette, and Chris Thomas."

She frowned. Those names were vaguely familiar…

"Please tell me you know who those guys are."

"Look, I'm sorry, but I've been so busy that I seriously can't put a face to those names. Although I might've talked to some of them yesterday."

"What? And you didn't tell me?"

"There's been a lot going on."

"As soon as Franklin gets back from his honeymoon, I'm going to get him to call you and fill you in on everything you need to know about Luc."

"Please don't. I'm getting the feeling that everyone is trying to ship us, or something, and I don't need that kind of pressure in my life."

Poppy stared at her. "Maybe you do."

"What do you mean?"

"Well, if he's really as bad at dancing as you think he is, maybe giving the public something to wonder about would be a good reason for them to keep you two around."

"I'm sorry. I'm so tired I'm not following."

Poppy smiled. "Look, if the audience are supposed to vote

for you, and people think you and Luc are an item, then they'll want to see what's going to happen. You see it all the time with the couples who have chemistry. People always wonder if they're a thing—"

"But we're not. We have contracts that forbid it."

"But the audience don't know that. And they'll be wanting you two to be a thing. You're so cute and pretty, and he's so big and tough-looking, they'll think it's classic opposites attract and want to see you dance in some of the sexy numbers."

"Oh my gosh." A wave of… something rolled over her. Sexy numbers? With Luc? She swallowed.

"Now don't pretend that doesn't interest you. I know you, Bailey Donovan. You've always had a thing for those Latin numbers, haven't you?"

"Ugh." She closed her eyes and covered her face. She might've enjoyed the energy of Latin dances, but her dad had never been a fan. What would he think seeing his daughter dance like that on TV? "To be honest, I'm struggling to imagine Luc doing any form of ballroom dancing, let alone the Latin numbers."

The samba. The salsa. The rumba. The tango. All of them were about creating visuals that were hinting at a particular activity she'd never participated in. She'd always had to act those roles, projecting a sexiness she didn't necessarily feel, when asked to teach those classes. The thought of having to own that sensual swagger and perform that kind of role with Luc was… disconcerting. To say the least.

"Have they told you what next week's dance is supposed to be?"

She sighed. "I haven't dared look. It's been enough to get through everything this week."

"You should find out. See if it's something that might get the crowd going. And if so, then you're in with a better shot of staying around."

"Are you seriously suggesting I pretend I'm in a relationship with Luc so people vote for us?"

"In a nutshell, yes."

"Oh my gosh, Poppy James, I didn't realize you were so devious."

"It's not devious, it's called strategy. And you need the money, right?"

"Well, yes. It's helpful to have the network pay for the studio hire, that was an unexpected bonus, but I don't like the thought I might be deceiving people just to get another five grand."

"You're not deceiving. It's all part of the entertainment industry. It's a show, it's *pretend*. Just give the people what they want. And you and Luc Blanchard being a couple is what they want."

"He won't though. He doesn't want to be on the show a second longer than he has to."

"I thought he wanted to raise money for his mom's cancer charity?"

"I think he wants to get back to hockey as quick as he can. This is just a momentary aberration in his life, not something long term."

"Or maybe it's a God-given opportunity for two Christians to meet and spend time together, in a way they might not normally do. For goodness' sake, Bails, he's a millionaire, he's an athlete, he's not bad to look at—"

"Have you seen his hair?"

"Details, details." Poppy clicked her fingers. "You can ask wardrobe to cut it off, say that's necessary for costume styling or something."

Bailey's mouth sagged. "Poppy!"

"I'm just saying that hair is an easy fix and doesn't have to be a deal-breaker."

"Oh my gosh! I can't believe you're talking like this. Anyway, there is a deal which can't be broken called a contract, remember? Even if I did want. Which I definitely *don't.*"

"Look, if you don't want him, I can help you out." Poppy winked.

"No. He's—*no.* Stop talking about him like that. He's a nice guy. I'm not going to manipulate him or anyone else just so I can make enough money to save the studio."

"This could be a God thing. Just sayin'."

"And it could be a distraction."

Poppy smiled. "Then feel free to send the distraction my way."

Hmm.

DAY two of dance rehearsal saw a later start time, as Luc had insisted he needed a delayed beginning, thanks to a prior commitment. He didn't elaborate, and she supposed it was hockey-related. Seeing it was Sunday and the city in summer seemed to slow down, she was happy to have a few extra hours to attend early church with her parents, then put what she'd learned yesterday, and some of what Poppy had said too, into some sort of order.

Luc needed to do lifts. Everyone knew that lifts were a crowd-pleaser, and something he'd seemed to enjoy doing yesterday too. Most of these shows had the male celebrities as the tree trunks to the dancing branches of the female dance pros. As long as they could move a little, and look graceful enough, attention usually focused on the woman and her dress and kicks and dazzle. She had to bring that, and do her best to cover his mistakes.

He needed to work on his frame. On his arms. Even keeping upright, chin up, "heart up" as she liked to say, so he could dominate the dance floor with his big body and not hunch over.

She'd followed Poppy's advice and looked ahead, seen next

week was a change in pace and was the jive. She thought he'd enjoy that more, if they made it through. The jive wasn't a sexy dance, which was just as well, but the upbeat music would be fun and they could do some cool lifts. But first they had to get through this week.

The studio doors opened, and she smiled at Ella and the crew. "Good morning."

"Barely. It's nearly noon."

"So still morning then."

Ella glanced around. "Luc isn't here yet?"

"I'm sure he's on his way. We said twelve, and it's not quite that yet."

Ella sighed, as Tony helped Bailey get microphoned up. "We really don't need him being late as it sets—"

"Hey."

The deep voice drew a sigh of relief. And another swallow of appreciation. Today Luc wore long track pants and a white singlet, and was channeling a vibe not dissimilar to Paul Mercurio in *Strictly Ballroom*. Oh, she was so due to watch that again. The white top showcased Luc's muscular arms with their intricate tattoos, his powerful chest and abs, and made her think —

"Oh, hello." Ella turned to Ben. "You filming?" At his nod she refocused on Luc, and helped him get microphoned for the day. "Now we're talking. The ladies are going to eat you up."

He frowned. "Excuse me?"

Aw, bless. Did he not know that muscly arms were a turn-on for some women? Bailey hurried over to him, and grasped his hand and dragged him to the mirror. "Put your stuff down there, and let's get started."

"Yes ma'am."

"That's what I like to hear." She grinned at him. "Now, are you ready? You got done all you needed to do this morning?"

He nodded.

"Okay then. Let's see how much you remember from yesterday. We're going to add some more of the routine, and I thought we could tweak it with an extra lift or two, so I hope you're feeling strong."

He flexed. "Always."

She laughed. "So full of confidence, aren't you?"

"The only way to be."

"Okay, let's see how that translates to the dance floor, shall we?"

He nodded, and she ran through the movements again.

He seemed stiffer today, which was completely understandable after yesterday's efforts when his muscles must be sore, and she had to demonstrate in front of the mirror the rise and fall of the movement.

"Now it's slow, slow, quick, quick. See what I'm doing there with my feet?"

"You're wearing sneakers today."

"As are you. I figured we could try your dance shoes at the end." She nodded to Ella. "They might want to film that moment, so brace yourself."

"Man. I didn't realize they'd be filming everything."

"Be thankful they're not filming you pee."

He chuckled. "You know, you're not exactly the dainty chick everyone thinks you are, are you?"

She grinned. "I don't know what you're talking about. Now, no more nonsense from you otherwise you'll need to drop and give me twenty."

He dropped to the floor and did five quick push-ups, which instantly drew a squeal from Ella. "Oh my gosh! Okay, I don't know what just happened, but we need to record it. So Luc, can you get back up, then you two go through that interaction again, then you do the push-ups, okay?"

Luc's nose wrinkled, but he obeyed, and stood close as Bailey tried to remember what she'd said before. Hmm, talking about using the toilet wasn't the vibe she was going for…

"I said, 'You're not as dainty as everyone thinks you are, are you?'"

That's right. She smiled. "You know it. Now don't forget, I'm your drill sergeant, so you better behave otherwise you'll need to drop and give me twenty."

He winked and dropped to the floor and did a series of quick push-ups, as Ben drew close to film.

Then Ella gestured for Bailey to get closer. "Hey Luc, would you mind if Bailey sat on you? That'd be a fun visual."

"No! I don't—"

"Sure."

Bailey peered down at him. "Are you sure?"

"Come on, Bailey. It'd be like a flea sitting on an elephant."

"Are you calling me a flea?"

"A butterfly then."

Oh. She smiled, and perched herself precariously on his back as Ben filmed. Then Luc lowered, drawing her gasp, which made him chuckle as he pushed higher, then lowered and completed another push-up again.

"See? I'm not feeling a thing. Are you sure you're even sitting there?" he teased.

She laughed, but couldn't help notice how his muscles were sculpted, his sleeveless top revealing some of his back muscles as well. He was… built. She bet wardrobe would have a field day showcasing his body in those costumes.

He did another drop, and she slid off, laughing. He glanced at her quickly, but she waved off concern as she got to her feet. "Okay, enough messing around. We need to get focused if we're going to nail this routine."

Bailey held out a hand and he grasped it and she pulled him up. He was standing close to her, so she gently pushed him back. There was something rather intoxicating about being a small skinny woman who could order around a big man and have him do her bidding.

She blinked, refocused. "Now, let's talk about that lift from yesterday."

She demonstrated again, saying this time she wanted to add in a new lift, an extension on the twirl that would see her lifted onto his back then onto his shoulder.

His eyes enlarged. "I don't want to drop you."

"I don't want that either. And that's what practice is about." Although a crash mat might not be a bad idea… "Let's start with what we did yesterday. Remember the plié?"

He nodded. "That's when you bend your knees, right?"

She demonstrated, he copied her. She nodded and turned. "Now, grab me here." She moved, her back to his front, and gestured in the mirror to her armpits.

His hands moved, his fingers brushing the side of her chest, which saw him instantly withdraw, the mirror reflecting his shocked expression. "Sorry. I didn't mean to do that."

She glanced across, saw the cameras were still rolling, then switched off her microphone pack and gestured he do the same.

"What are you doing?" Ella called.

"I'm sorry. I just need to have a word with Luc about something and I'd rather it not be on film."

"About what?"

"About an accidental boob brush."

"Oh my gosh," Luc muttered behind her. "It really was an accident."

"Exactly." Bailey turned to face him. "And you know what? It'll likely happen again. Just as I might accidentally kick you, or hit you in the face, or you might drop me. Accidents happen, but if you're going to get all hung up about it, then you won't try, and I need you to try."

His lips twisted. "You're not saying you want me to accidentally touch your, um—"

"No. Nor intentionally either."

He went red.

"But stuff happens in dance. Just like I'm sure it happens in hockey. I've had partners in dance where I've accidentally kicked them in the privates and they've had to keep on dancing. Stuff happens. So I need you to know that this," she gestured to her body, "is just a body. You're not hung up on the fact I've been touching your hips and legs, are you?"

His lips pressed together. Then he muttered "No".

Hmm. Did that hesitation mean he was? Still, he couldn't afford to think like that. And neither could she. "If we make it through this round, then there will be dances that could get a lot more up close and personal, if you know what I mean. And you've got to be okay with that."

He exhaled heavily, and threw his hands in his hair. "Look, I just don't, ah, do that kind of thing with anyone. Not anymore. And I'm trying to be careful, to, um," he glanced over at where Ella and the crew were watching, but not filming, praise the Lord, "to not do anything that disrespects a woman, or stirs up things in me anymore."

Oh. The fact that this bothered him and he didn't get handsy with women showed he wasn't a player. She'd known Christian guys before who didn't mind getting handsy. Clearly Luc wasn't one of them.

She moved back into his line of vision, and gently moved his jaw to look at her. "I appreciate that. That's a rare thing these days, and honorable."

He stared into her eyes, his lips flat, then he nodded.

"I want you to know that as far as I'm concerned, we're cool." She gestured between them. "I don't want to do anything that stirs up anything in you, so if I do, you need to tell me, okay?"

A smaller nod this time.

"And I also need you to know that I view my body as a tool for my craft, which is dance. Sometimes I forget that, but I have trained my whole life to dance, and that's why it doesn't bother me."

"I'm just not used to working so closely with a woman," he muttered.

She smiled. "Don't worry. I'll go easy on you."

SHE DID NOT GO easy on him. She had no idea just how tough she was to work with. Not in her personality, she was as shiny and happy as ever, but in the way she obviously didn't feel the same way as he did.

He'd never felt quite so mortified as when he'd accidentally touched her before. She'd tried to explain it away, saying it didn't matter, but it did. All these years of celibacy, of trying to live God's way after several years of making the most of his hockey and NHL status and fame, meant she had no idea how tough it was to not want more. Even if it had been completely accidental. In some ways, he'd like her to punch him in the nuts and call it even. But just that thought made his lips twitch, and made her up the ante in her military decisiveness.

"Come on." She clicked her fingers, no doubt conscious that the cameras were back on after her boss-move of requesting they stop filming earlier. "I need you to commit, and look like you want to be here."

He nodded to the cameras.

She shrugged. "If you don't do what I ask, then I'm going to call it out."

"You're tougher than some coaches I've worked with."

"Maybe it's time you had someone whup your backside into line."

Ella laughed. "That's gold."

No, it wasn't. If that comment was broadcast he'd no doubt

be scoring some scathing comments from the team's coaching staff.

"So, come on, Luc. Get your head into the game."

"Look who's coming out with the sporting clichés." Her eyes narrowed, and he muttered, "Sorry."

"Not as sorry as you're going to be. Now move."

He tried to get into the pose, but he still couldn't help wondering about what this would look like on TV.

She sighed. "What is it now?

"I just…" He glanced across at Ella.

She nodded. "I know. How about when we break and get a coffee, you tell me then."

"Okay."

That proved motivation enough for him to fill the next hour, then they were de-microphoned, and released for a ten-minute break.

But he didn't get a chance to talk, because as soon as they exited the building he was recognized.

"Hey, it's Luc Blanchard!"

She eyed him, then turned back inside the studio. "Bailey, wait."

"You've got eight minutes then we're starting again."

Why did it feel like he'd failed her again? He managed to keep up the requisite small talk with the fan, get his coffee from Max and one he hoped Bailey would like, and determined they'd order in from now on. And that he'd try to talk to her after this next session. Two hours to go, then he could explain a little more. And maybe see if she'd regard this as an apology date.

He returned with coffee, and she accepted his apology cup with thanks, they drank, got re-microphoned up, then resumed practice.

Fortunately the coffee had sparked further energy and concentration, and he was able to pick up the steps and moves a lot easier than before, which she appeared to notice. "Well, look whose love language is coffee, huh?"

"Anytime you need more, I'm your man."

She smiled, and his heart filled with sunshine.

But the good vibes were soon tested as she drew him closer to the box that still held his dance shoes. "Now look, I know you don't want to do this, but it's necessary. And now your feet have been working, you'll find they probably feel a little tight, but that's good. It's always best to buy shoes in the afternoon so you're getting the right size. Just remember there's some give in them. Now, please try them on."

He grabbed a seat, unlidded the box, then stared at the tissue paper-wrapped shoes, and, conscious of the cameras filming, tried not to wrinkle his nose.

"Go on. Try them on."

He pulled them out, black, with a slight heel, not nearly as high as he'd dreaded. "They don't look like normal shoes."

"Because they're dance shoes," she said, like he was an idiot. "They have grip, but are designed to move across waxed floors, and allow for dance moves. The heels are to improve your posture."

He took off his sneakers, and he caught her muffled laughter.

"I like your socks."

His socks with jets on them. Yep, branded by the team, that was him. "I'm doing what I can to get the word out."

"That you are. You should put that on your socials."

Maybe he should. He'd take a pic and post it on Insta later.

"Now try them on."

He pulled on the first shoe, laced it up. Winced. "Is it supposed to be that tight?"

"Try the other. Remember, it's going to feel tight because you've been on your feet all day."

He did, then took a tentative walk across the dance floor,

trying not to look like a wuss as his toes pinched. Tough guy he would not appear if he complained too much.

"If you wear them at home, you'll find they'll fit better. And put them on first thing in the day."

"I go for a run first thing in the day." When he prayed, and listened to the Bible and his Northwest Ice playlist or various Christian podcasts.

"Then after that." She eyed him. "You're wearing them on Sunday's show, so you need to get used to it now."

He blew out a breath. Sunday? How on earth would they be ready for the show? Another question he'd have to ask her on their non-date after rehearsals today.

"Look, I just wanted to apologize for earlier again."

"For what?"

Did the woman not hold grudges? Had she forgotten that quick? "I mean with, um…" He motioned to his pec.

She gestured to her chest. "That? Please forget it. I've moved on. You need to as well. And I mean that. And I'd really rather know what was bothering you after."

He winced, trying to remember. That's right. How this would look like on TV. How *he'd* look on TV. But saying that aloud would make him look like a vain tool, and he had no desire to do that.

He glanced around the studio. Ella and the camera crew had left, it was just them. He'd wanted to go to a café or restaurant, but Bailey had shot him down, saying that would look too much like a date, which wouldn't work for the "no-relationship" clause in their contract. So they were still here, having told Ella they were running through more rehearsals. Even if he was wishing they could be anywhere else. Maybe they could go to a park, go running together. He'd have to find out if she enjoyed running too.

"I don't have secret microphones installed if that's what you're afraid of."

He managed a nervous laugh, then sighed. "Look, I don't want to sound arrogant or anything, but I just don't want my reputation as a tough guy on the ice being affected by looking too soft on the dance floor."

"You think my routine is too soft?"

"It's not the choreography," look at him using dance terms, "it's the music."

She nodded. "I wondered. But it's Harry Connick Junior, and he's a legend, and the music for foxtrot does tend to be softer, and you know it's what they sent me. And I didn't figure I could argue about song selection on my very first dance."

"Do you know what's next?"

"The next dance? It's a jive. It's a lot faster, and you can look tougher, if that's what you're afraid of."

"I don't need to look tough, but I can't afford to look too soft."

She nodded. "But you do know this is all edited, right? That the show will want to portray you a certain way. And you're known for being big and tough and intimidating, and someone somewhere thought it would be fun to show a different side to you, show you're a man who cares about his mom and is willing to do this for her. You show that on Sunday and suddenly you're more nuanced than the big man on skates."

Huh. Like the GM had said not even a week ago.

"You don't need to worry about Sunday, Luc. You'll be great. People will love you."

"Are you sure? I'm trying, but I just don't think my body was designed to move the way you think it is."

"It's called training, just like you've had to do with hockey. Were you able to stand up on skates the first time you put them on?"

He shrugged. "I can't remember that long ago."

"Most people wouldn't manage skating well first try, and the audience will understand you're not a dancing pro and that they shouldn't expect perfection from you. Luc, you need to remember it's a show, an entertainment show, and it's about giving the viewers what they want. And they always want stories, don't they? Someone to cheer for, a villain, a hero, an underdog. You understand that, right?"

He nodded. He understood the concept of that, anyway.

She smiled. "Call me crazy, but I guess in some ways hockey can be like that too."

Hockey was life, but whatever. "There's definitely some villains," like Sean Hart, "and some heroes." He winked.

"I wonder who you could possibly mean?"

He chuckled. "I think you need to come to a game sometime."

"Maybe."

Definitely. He could just imagine her, with all the team's WAGs, meeting him after a game and hugging him hello, kissing —whoa.

Her head tilted, exposing those long lines of her neck he'd had the pleasure of seeing up close, yet not too personal. Not yet, anyway. "Are you okay?"

He nodded. He would be. After an ice bath, and maybe a cold shower on top of that.

CHAPTER 8

Toronto
Saturday

This was going to be terrible. Sunday's performance might be tomorrow, but today's dress rehearsal, after yesterday's camera blocking day, was not fueling hope of a good performance. At all.

Coco had watched their performance and offered some tips in what was apparently known as a "show-and-tell", when the couples would dance in front of the others to both gain an idea about what their rivals were doing, and gain the sense of a live audience. Luc kept forgetting his steps and missing his cues, even though he'd been improving. Until now they'd only danced in front of Ella and the crew, and one time when Poppy had "dropped" in, so it must be his nerves. She prayed he'd remember the routine tomorrow night.

The past few days had been insanely busy. Thursday's flight back to TO had been followed by costume fittings, then another meal with their fellow castmates. Friday had seen a fresh wax and spray tan, then camera blocking, then she'd gone back to rehearsals for the opening number with the other pros while Luc did more interviews, and caught up with his friend Dan Walton, who played pro hockey for Toronto. Luc had invited her, but she'd refused, citing too many commitments for any conversation with a new acquaintance to make sense. She was so immersed in the dance that Harry's vocals had started wafting through her dreams, where she imagined the big white dress she was wearing to be one she might wear on her wedding day. Crazy dreams. They needed to move onto the jive ASAP so the crazy dreams would stop.

But today's dress rehearsal was not going well, and as the camera guys chatted among themselves, and the producer spoke to someone else before gesturing for them to begin again, she couldn't help but worry about what this would mean for tomorrow.

Sunday

The day had started early with makeup, hair, then trying on their costumes. This was followed by another rehearsal before a light meal, more photos, interviews, then a meeting with the cast members for a final run-through. Now they were waiting backstage as the clock ticked down before tonight's performance. She was wearing a special spangled number, all silver and short, like what she'd worn in their promotion piece. Luc was looking debonair in his suit, even if he looked like he might be sick at any moment.

She nudged him with her hip. He glanced down, his eyes widening, then he swallowed. "Hey Bails."

Her lips lifted. "Careful. You talk like that and people will think you're from a farm."

He frowned, as if thinking about what he'd said, then laughed.

Good. He needed to relax. She leaned closer. "That smile

you're wearing now? That's what you need to wear the rest of the day. I don't want you looking like you're about to throw up or like you're bored or want to be anywhere else. You need to look excited and bring the energy, okay?"

"Yes, ma'am."

"That's Sergeant Ma'am to you."

He snickered.

"What's got this guy laughing?" Miguel asked. He looked at Luc. "I swear, a minute ago you looked like you wanted to puke, and now you're all happy again."

Luc wrapped an arm around Bailey's shoulders. "She's good stress relief."

"Mm-hmm." Miguel raised an eyebrow.

"Whoa." Luc released his hold. "Not in any inappropriate way, of course."

"I don't know what you mean," Miguel said, before giving Bailey a wink.

Bailey stepped away. No. She didn't need anyone here getting the wrong idea. Dancers did tend to be more touchy-feely than others, but she was pretty sure Luc's need to be near her was simply for his own peace of mind. She was like a child's comfort toy. Nothing else. And she definitely didn't appreciate Miguel's attempt to seed Luc's insecurities right before they were due to go on.

"Okay, places, people. Let's get this show ready."

By now they could hear the audience filing in, and she moved to her spot for the dance pros' opening routine. They'd do this number then it was back to change for her floaty white gown, then she'd need to calm her own nerves before their number started. They were due to perform third, after Miguel's author, with Coco's actor going after the other dancers at the very end.

The beats from Jason Mraz's song filled the studio, and she peeked at the camera standing nearby, ready to record her first action. Thirty seconds in and it was her turn to shake her leg, nod her head, walk two steps then pirouette, then move into a soul train move, smiling at the camera as she held her left hand out and swung her right up and down in a whip motion, then joined the other dancers in a long line as they pivoted and each person shook their tush.

How fun was this? The joy of dance took hold, and as they'd practiced to precision sharpness—no way did the producers want the pro dancers looking sloppy—she knew she could count on everyone hitting their beats. Her role, as this season's newbie pro, was to show everyone she was fun and talented and totally deserved to be here.

She went through the choreography, smiling with her hips, knowing her tiny skirt would shimmer and sparkle, that she had to look perky and sassy and fun. So she tossed her hair and threw a flirtatious wink over her shoulder. Then it was time to partner up, to demonstrate some of the moves viewers would see during the series. She did a quick waltz move with Miguel, arching into a tango stretch before Miguel and the other male dancers glided off the stage, and the female dance pros could do some freestyle moves. She, of course, did her ballet steps, including the rond de jambe leading into développé, the Bournonville variation of the grand jeté, a move that always looked impressive and would film well. Oh, she *loved* to dance.

The men returned, and they continued with their choreography, using light wooden chairs for a series of jazz-like moves, before the routine concluded with a sharp pose.

Hold for three beats, then relax, keeping on smiling. Then, "Cut!"

They were released, and grabbing her chair, she scampered away backstage, glimpsing Luc's dropped jaw before he gave her two thumbs-up, and mouthed "You were hot!"

But there was no time for that. She had to change into her white dress and get her hair quickly restyled before reentering very soon, arm in arm with Luc. She hurried to the dressing room as the hosts, Jenna and Peter, were being welcomed onstage with cheers and applause, then the camera focus would shift to introducing the judges. Even though the dance part was "live" in that they didn't get to do a redo, it was being filmed out of "real" time. While this section beforehand wasn't filmed live, she still only had a few minutes to get changed and have her hair blown out into the big soft curls her costume needed.

Five minutes later she found Luc in the wings, and grabbed his hand.

He glanced down at her, the stiffness in his face easing away. "You're back."

"How are you feeling?"

He shook his head. "I'm trying not to throw up."

"You'll be fine."

"You were more than fine. You were smokin' out there."

She grinned up at him. "I just love to dance, and it was so freeing to do that performance."

"One down, and one to go, huh?"

She patted his cheek. "You've got this. Just remember, it's a show, and you're an actor playing a role to tell the story. Fake it 'til you make it, they say."

"I've never been great at pretending," he mumbled.

"Well, dig deep and try to find something about this to enjoy, okay?"

"Quiet!" an assistant hissed. "Now, you're going on, so let's see big smiles, people. Big smiles."

Luc pasted on a smile, and she grabbed his hand and squeezed. It was almost their turn to be introduced.

The first couple entered past the curtains, and she drew in a breath, caught Luc's eyes on her, and she glanced up and gave a reassuring smile. Miguel and Kate, his author partner, entered, to more applause. Then it was their turn.

"You got this," she murmured, and his grip tightened as they went out, the bright lights hot and glaring.

"And now, please welcome a man known more for giving hits on the ice than for his moves on the dance floor, give it up for Winnipeg's own Luc Blanchard and his partner Bailey Donovan."

This was it. She pasted on a brighter smile and waved as they went down the steps and found their mark, Luc's height meaning they'd been placed on the floor to not overshadow the other, shorter couples. She smiled, he waved, his grip clammy. Oh, she hoped he wouldn't throw up.

The other couples were introduced, and they applauded, then Jenna asked the judges what they were looking for.

Marco pointed to the dance couples. "You know what I want to see? Amazing dancing."

John nodded. "Give me some technique, please."

Cynthia smiled. "Remember, we know you're not pros, and while you might feel nervous, the most important thing you can do is just enjoy it."

Dear Lord, help us to enjoy this.

LUC HAD NEVER BEEN SO nervous in his life. Even going for a shoot-out goal in the playoffs had never made him feel so tense. And he couldn't let Bailey down. She'd worked so hard with him, but he knew he wasn't anywhere near the caliber of some of the other celebrities he'd seen. Seriously, who thought it a level playing field to include singers who were used to dancing on stage or in music videos? He'd seen their performances during rehearsals. How were they considered amateurs? He could only hope a few poor souls would pity-vote him through. Bailey had tried her best, and knowing her routine was classy and elegant, he hoped his performance might be okay, provided he nailed the lift.

The lift. How had she thought him up to doing that? He was still getting used to the stupid shoes, and now he was dressed like James Bond in this suit, while she looked so pretty in her white dress it almost made his eyes hurt.

Bailey wanted them to tell the story, and apparently the story they were supposed to tell was of two lovers, and her white dress was supposed to represent a wedding dress. He sure hoped people didn't get ideas, although he knew he couldn't really be responsible for what people might think. Her dress was beautiful, but she was even more so, especially when she did that graceful split thing in the air when he lifted her. He clenched and released his fingers, as nausea swirled inside. Everything would probably go okay as long as he nailed the lift.

They returned out the back, and he was sorely tempted to do the lift one more time. "Hey Bailey, do you think we should practice the lift again?"

"Are you still worried?" she asked.

"I'm not confident."

She winced, then glanced around. "Look, there's a space there. We probably have time."

They moved into position, she counted in then softly sang the words of the section he was nervous about. "It had to be you, wonderful you, it had to be you, two three four, one two three four."

Here, where the trumpets would come in, was where he'd swing her around, then she'd pause, and he'd crouch, and she put a knee on his hip then go over his back while he clutched the backs of her thighs. It had looked insane the first time she'd shown him, but when it worked, it looked so cool, and made him hungry to perfect it.

"You missed it," she said.

"Sorry. Try again?"

She nodded. "Okay, let's go from wonderful you, it had to be you, two three four, one two three four."

He grasped her underarms and swung her around, her skirts billowing like a parachute. But he had to count, and concentrate, to make sure he hit the moment when the trumpets changed. There!

He bent, she placed her knee in position and moved behind his neck, and then one, two, three, and she was over. Awesome!

"What are you two doing over here?" an assistant hissed.

"Just practicing," Luc said.

"There's no time. You're on next."

"Feel better now?" Bailey asked.

"Yeah." He smiled at her. "We've got this."

She nodded. "Just remember, it's supposed to be fun. So have fun, okay?"

He nodded, rolled his shoulders, popped his neck.

"What are you doing?"

"This is how I prepare for game day just before I go on the ice."

"Okay then. Let's go crush the opposition."

"I thought we were going to smoke them? That sounds more dancy, especially considering the smoke machine they've got."

"Now," the floor manager pointed to them. "You two are on."

Bailey squeezed his hand, then drew him onto the dance floor. "Let's do this."

He swallowed. He might be used to bright lights and crowds, yet the churning in his stomach was nothing like what he'd experienced before. But he couldn't think about any of that. He could only think about Bailey. About the hours and hours she'd committed to helping him look good. This moment was for her. *Lord, help me.* He realized he probably should've prayed with her beforehand, but maybe they could do that next time. If there was a next time.

The studio hushed, the music started, the piano tinkling, then she tapped him on the shoulder and he turned around.

This first part was easy, just a walk across the dance floor, or glide as she had said, with that slow, slow, quick, quick step movement she had drummed into him. Then he held her hand, and she did a spin, and he caught the way she big-smiled at him, which reminded him to smile back. This was supposed to be fun, remember?

His trepidation eased a bit as they did another sequence of slow, slow, quick, quick steps, then a third line before another spin, which was when the music changed into the trumpet section. He clutched her underarms and began the spin. He was feeling dizzy, but he had to concentrate. He had to get this lift right. He lowered, she put her knee into his hip and moved over onto his back, just like they'd practiced minutes ago.

He grasped her legs, but his hands were slippery or something, and instead of hoisting her onto his shoulders, she slipped, sliding down his back while he frantically tried to grab her legs to stop her hitting the deck. Somehow, somehow, she slid from his back in a tangle of white skirts, before she turned and faced him, gritting out a "Luc!" which got his attention, and his feet automatically moved into the sequence they'd rehearsed for hours.

But the feeling of failure sang through the rest of the song, and his smile felt as phony as a pink unicorn. He completed the final move, a spin that sent her to the corner of the floor as she beamed at the camera while he hurried to draw her up again. He held her in an arched back pose while he drew his arm behind him, before the final plinks of the piano saw them swiftly reverse sides and he dipped her at the end.

He was breathing hard, and she smiled up at him, one arm outstretched, the other hand around his neck.

"You did good, Luc."

He shook his head, pulling her upright. "I messed up."

"Hey." She hugged him, like what seemed to be the norm here, and while he was glad the dance had finished, he was still conscious that his performance needed to go on. He had to pretend he didn't mind screwing up, that he hadn't wrecked things for Bailey. He'd never forgive himself if his clumsiness was the reason they exited tonight. She needed to get to the third round for her money.

"Come on."

Jenna, the main host, drew them into position in front of the judges' box, as the crowd continued their applause. He knew that wasn't real, either. He'd seen the warm-up guys before, and knew their job was to make it sound like the celebrities had danced better than they had.

"Wow, Luc Blanchard. What a dance. How do you feel?" Jenna poked the microphone in front of him.

He bent down. "Relieved?" That was safe enough, right?

Jenna laughed. "Relieved it's over or that you didn't drop her?"

"Can I say both?"

Bailey wrapped her arm around his middle and squeezed. That's right. He was supposed to bring perky fun to the situation. He slapped on a grin.

"Okay, well, let's hear what the judges have to say. Over to you, Marco."

His stomach tensed. *Please Lord, let them be kind. For Bailey's sake.*

"Ah, well, Luc Blanchard. I have to say you cut quite a dashing figure in that suit."

Okay, well, that was nice enough.

"You moved across the floor reasonably well, but you need to work on your posture. You need to tuck in that big butt—"

Yeah, good luck with that. He didn't lead his team in squats at training camp for nothing.

"—and work on your frame and upper body. Sometimes

your shoulders are going in one direction, your hips in quite another."

He didn't know what that meant, but hopefully Bailey did. If they stuck around for next time.

"The lift was a disaster, darling, but I liked the physicality you brought. Hopefully the viewers liked that too so we can see more next time."

"I agree," Cynthia said. "You're a powerful, strongly built, good-looking man, you've got so much potential. I would like you to engage in the story a little more and work on your musicality. Listen to the song every day and feel it so you can work on your timing."

Luc nodded. He had so much to work on. Maybe it would be better to get eliminated and not have to go through this.

John read from his notes then glanced up. "Hands like spades, my boy. Hands like spades. If there's one thing I cannot tolerate it is hands that are splayed like little garden forks. And there was little connection, little rise and fall in the steps, your progression across the floor is supposed to be a glide, not a walk. You're supposed to be light on your feet, and I have to admit that I didn't see anything of the swing and sway that epitomizes the foxtrot. You're a big man, but you should be projecting elegance. Bailey, if he survives this round, then I really want you to work on that, and focusing on what strengths he has. There might not be many—"

Ouch. The crowd booed.

"—but I'm sure they're in there somewhere, okay Bailey, dear?"

Bailey nodded, and Luc felt so bad.

"We won't talk about the lift. It's obvious it did not go as planned. Wouldn't you agree?"

So much for not talking about it. Luc nodded. "We worked so hard at it. We even nailed it just before."

"You did?"

Bailey's honey-blonde head bobbed up and down. He wrapped an arm around her. He'd disappointed her so much.

"Well, I don't know about you," Jenna said, "But I think we'd all like to see the lift. Who's with me?"

"Do it, and that's an extra point from me," Cynthia said.

Oh no. Now he really needed to get it right.

"Come on." Bailey pivoted, her smile soft. "You've got this."

He sucked in a breath, then nodded, and amid cheers and applause they moved to the dance floor.

"Ready?" Bailey asked. He nodded. "It had to be you, two three four, one two three four."

He grasped her in the spin hold, then completed the maneuver as he should've done in the actual dance, with Bailey flying up over his shoulders and then down in a flow of white feathery skirts, exactly where she should've landed in their actual routine. Thank goodness it had worked this time.

As the cheers rang louder, Bailey hugged him close. "See? You nailed it."

He nodded, his face pressed close to hers, as the judges clapped their sympathy claps, and Jenna released them to the skybox where Peter, Jenna's cohost, waited.

Peter smiled at them. "Ready to hear your scores?"

Nope. He pasted on a smile and nodded anyway. "Bring it."

Marco held up his paddle. "Three."

Ouch. He kept smiling.

"Four."

That was better.

"Two."

How humiliating. Poor Bailey.

She hugged him again, then Peter turned to them, the cameraman right behind him. "Well, Luc Blanchard, I'm guessing nine out of thirty isn't the score line you'd like to see."

He tugged Bailey closer. He needed her close. Needed to feel her nearness, that she wasn't too upset with him. "Look, I'm frustrated that I didn't nail the lift, especially because poor Bailey here has worked my butt off this week."

"Not enough butt, it seems," the cheeky cohost said.

He winced. "I never expected this to be so demanding. But Bailey here is amazing. I really hope viewers will vote for us so they can see how great she is."

"Well, viewers, you know what to do. When the voting opens up, make sure you vote for Luc."

He smiled, tilting his head to Bailey, as he waved at the camera.

"And that's a cut."

The cameras fell, as did his smile. And he prayed this wasn't the cut that meant the end.

CHAPTER 9

"I'm so sorry," Luc said as soon as they were backstage and able to grab a moment's privacy again. Around them, production assistants raced around barking orders as the remaining couples prepared to dance. "I'm really bad, Bails."

She smiled at his using the diminutive of her name, like her family and close friends did. "Hey, it's okay. Judging from what we saw the others do, you're not too bad." They were supposed to go to the green room where they could relax and watch the other couples on the TV monitors, but she sensed she needed to say this without others overhearing. "Remember, there are still four contestants to go, so you're in with a chance."

"We're equal bottom, Bailey. Man. I never meant to make you look so bad."

"I know. And look, the lift wasn't perfect, but you just have to keep a smile on your dial. This might be a competition, but it's supposed to be for fun. Are you having fun at all?"

"It was fun seeing you come out in that floaty white dress."

She picked up the skirt and held it out. "It's almost too pretty, isn't it?"

He glanced at the dress then back at her. Lifted his hand as if he was going to touch her, then dropped it. Visibly swallowed. "Suits the music."

"See? I told you. They do this for a reason, and they want you to act a certain way, so viewers engage with the story."

He shook his head. "I hate to think what story they're going to run with now."

"Well, I sure hope it's not going to be a professional athlete who feels sorry for himself." She added a smile to soothe her harsh words.

"Wow. Gosh, you're tough."

"Sergeant Bailey, remember?"

"You won't let me forget."

"Exactly. And when we're back next week, you're going to show everyone just how much you've improved." And she was going to make *sure* he had nailed the routine. This whole situation was supposed to be about him, not her. The pro dancer had to help the celebrity, not just with his moves but with his confidence as well.

"You know it."

"Now that's what I want to hear. Remember, they haven't done the voting yet, and you're in with a good shot."

"What do you mean?"

She leaned closer, and tugged down his head. "You have two major advantages. One, you're a hockey player that people know. Simply the fact that you play hockey will be enough for some people to vote for you, because it's part of that story, remember? People won't expect you to do well, so they want to see you again, whether it's to mess up or improve."

"That's not exactly filling me with confidence."

Clearly she needed to work on that. "The point is, they'll likely want to see you return, so they're more likely to vote for you."

"And the second point?"

"Your charity. Everyone knows someone who's been touched by cancer, so if you can keep the focus on the good work your charity does then people will want to support you, so that's a real advantage right there."

"You forgot the third advantage."

"What's that?"

He smiled. "I've got you."

Her heart skipped a beat or two. She patted his bristly cheek, as she worked to calm down. No. This was not the time to misread things or get swept up in emotion. They were still on display. This was only week one for goodness' sake.

She grabbed his hand. "Come on. We better join the others."

He nodded, and she saw how Coco looked at her. "Give me a moment."

She hurried to Coco. "Good luck tonight."

"You two were cute, I think viewers will definitely see the chemistry."

"Please." Bailey rolled her eyes. "There is no chemistry."

"I disagree," Jason said, Coco's actor partner. "And I wouldn't be surprised if you knock out the author or the one-hit wonder."

Coco nodded, and whispered, "They may say it's about the votes, but the network knows who's going to be the bigger drawcard, and let's just say it ain't eighties pop music nobody remembers. They know what this country loves, and babe, you've got him."

Oh. She smiled, wished them well again, then returned to Luc's side.

"What was that about?"

"Coco and Jason think we're in with a chance."

He sighed. "I'd never forgive myself if we went out the first round."

"It's a dancing competition, Luc. Someone has to go."

"As long as it's not us, I'm okay with that." He grimaced. "My mom wanted to come, but I put her off and said we'd be back next week."

"What?"

"I know. So I'm praying hard that we'll make it through, otherwise she'll never let me live it down."

"Oh my goodness, Luc. You should've said something. I'd like to meet her."

"And she'd like to meet you."

She shivered, but whether it was from his intense look, or the sudden sweet smile he offered her, she didn't know. She only knew that she was even more motivated now to do well. Because if they didn't make it through…

"AND THE VOTES ARE IN, and here we are with tonight's bottom three. Kate and Miguel, Luc and Bailey, and Harry and Olivia."

Bailey squeezed Luc's hand harder. Funny how a mere hour ago she'd been so blithe and comfortable, but now she was sweating more than she ever recalled.

"And now, in no particular order, our first couple safe tonight is…" A drumroll filled the studio.

She glanced up at Luc, who tugged her closer to himself, as if he thought he could protect her from what would come next. Could ten minutes of voting offset the equal bottom score?

"Kate and Miguel!"

There was a squeal from the author, who clearly hadn't expected to dance on, and Bailey plastered on her smile as she congratulated her, even as her insides plummeted. Oh no. If the author, who had earned the equal lowest score, had managed to survive, surely that had to mean their names were on the chopping block.

She glanced up at Luc, who smiled at her. "Hey. It's okay."

She nodded. Five thousand dollars was still better than none, and would go some way to paying off her debts. And now, having had a bit of national exposure, maybe she'd get a few more dance enrollments.

"Which leaves us with our final two contestants. Luc Blanchard and partner Bailey, and Harry Stynes and his partner Olivia."

Hockey versus eighties pop. Would people assume that Luc was safe and not vote? She glanced up at him, he smiled back, and her heart eased. She'd really like to see him do well, for his own sake as much as hers.

"And our final couple, safe from elimination tonight, and going through to next week, is…"

She winced.

"Luc and Bailey!"

"Yes!" Luc swept her up in a huge hug.

She might've squealed a little, too, as she hugged him hard. "I'm so proud of you."

He kissed her cheek, and she froze, then pulled back, turning without acknowledging his kiss as she went to commiserate with Harry and Olivia. Olivia had been part of the pros since the series began five years ago, so it was a shock to have her leave so soon.

They were hurried off the dance floor, leaving Harry and Olivia to receive the judges' final remarks before they danced their exit dance.

As soon as she made it backstage Coco wrapped her in a hug. "I knew you'd make it!"

"I was starting to have my doubts there for a moment."

"Really?" Luc asked her. "You looked calm enough."

"You know that saying about a duck that's calm on top but madly paddling underneath?" She tapped her chest.

"That's been me all week, too," Luc said to Coco.

Except he hadn't exactly projected calm. Not that she was going to point that out.

"Now, we go out there again in a moment, then you need to

brace yourselves for the postshow interviews." Coco pointed to Bailey. "And don't forget to get your choreography for next week."

So many things to remember.

She glanced at the clock. "Our flight leaves at 10.30PM."

"They'll make sure you interview first then. Although why you're returning to Winnipeg I don't know. You'd save a lot of time if you stayed in TO."

Bailey pointed to Luc, who seemed to notice. "Hey, I've got some hockey stuff this week, but maybe we could stay if we're still around after next week. Which is what dance, remind me?"

"We've got jive."

He nodded. "Well, if we make it through that round, maybe we can hang here. I could see my folks more easily, and you could meet them."

"Um…" She glanced at Coco, whose fake-lashed eyes were wide.

"Hey, you two do you, okay?" Coco leaned close and whispered in Bailey's ear, "But let's just say that most pros don't meet the celeb's families."

Oh. Good to know.

"Um, okay then." She faced Luc as Coco smirked and moved away. "We better get back to it."

"What did she say?" Luc asked.

"Nothing to worry about. I think she was happy for us." Coco was pleased they'd made it through, but was there a warning in her whispered comment?

THE POSTSHOW PROVED to be another kind of performance, one where she worked hard to alleviate any potential suspicion from Coco or any producers as she and Luc mingled and answered questions from the media.

As expected, Luc was popular, and her cheeks were getting

sore by the time ESPN appeared. It wasn't Hannah interviewing, but one of the Toronto-based sports reporters who Hannah had said was nice, according to Poppy.

The woman flicked her hair as she talked to Luc, before facing Bailey.

"Bailey Donovan, you must be thrilled with how things have gone tonight."

Bailey smiled. She needed to be careful. Whatever she said now would frame how viewers saw him, and she didn't want to portray him in a way that would be perceived negatively. "Oh, look, we've danced a lot better in rehearsals, so it's a shame we couldn't execute the lift as we wanted. But I thought he did very well for the rest of the routine. Luc is definitely trying hard, and I think it's wonderful to see someone stepping out of their comfort zone and trying something new, especially when it's for such a good cause. And full props to him for doing this." She placed a hand on his chest. "Luc might be tough on the ice, but he's a real sweetheart, and passionate about doing whatever it takes to make a difference in other people's lives. I really hope people vote to keep him around so you can see what other moves this man has."

"Aww. Sounds like you have a fan there, Luc."

He smiled down at her. "I hope so. I'm a huge fan of hers."

HE PROBABLY SHOULDN'T HAVE SAID that quite like that on national TV. He had a feeling that the Bible study Messenger chat was gonna explode with stupid love heart emojis and other dumb things. But he couldn't help it. Bailey had stuck her hand on his chest, and though she'd done it many times before, this time it felt personal, like she was protecting him or something. Which made him feel even more vulnerable and appreciative for her.

"Care to elaborate, Luc?"

He shrugged. "I can't help it. I love working with her. She's always so bubbly, never in a bad mood, and always knows just what to say to bring me up when I'm feeling flat, or in my head about things. I'm really blessed to have her in my life. She's everything you could ever want."

Bailey glanced up at him, and he knew her well enough by now to know that smile was fake.

He'd obviously said something wrong. And he needed to make it up to her. Quick. "I just want to do well for Bailey's sake, especially as it's her first season. I don't want her to go out too soon, know what I mean?"

"I understand." The reporter winked at the camera. "And I'm sure all those viewers out there do, too. Hear that? If you want to see what other moves Luc Blanchard has, be sure to vote for him next week and keep this man on his dancing toes."

Bailey's grin fell as the camera cut away, the reporter thanking them then moving to the next couple. "How are you feeling?" she asked Luc.

"I wasn't joking before. I am so relieved. I never meant to fumble that."

"Hey, it's in the past, so let it go. We all make mistakes sometimes, don't we? I should've rehearsed that more, and—"

"No." He grasped her upper arms. "You've been amazing. That was all my fault. And seriously, I now can almost understand why you like dancing so much."

She mock-gasped. "You can?"

He glanced around the room, still filled with the buzz and adrenaline. "It's the high of a performance, like in hockey. Which reminds me, you need to come skate with me sometime."

"Maybe."

"Definitely." He smiled. He might even suggest it to Ella this week. That could be more fun than watching him fail to nail his dance moves.

She shrugged. "Well, right now we need to get to the airport and start thinking about our routine for next week."

He joined her in moving to the dressing rooms. "Have you had any thoughts?"

"Not really. I've been so focused on this."

He nodded. "I can't get over how intense this week has been, especially these last four days. How on earth are we gonna get enough practice when we have to be back here on Thursday night?"

"We're doing the jive, so in some ways, that's a little more straightforward."

"Any crazy lifts I need to be worried about?"

She smiled. "Are you worried you're not strong enough?"

"You know, I haven't told my trainer, but I've actually lost weight this week."

"So *that's* why you keep ordering all that food," she teased.

"Hey, I have training camp at the start of September, and I need to be at my baseline fitness for that."

She touched his stomach. "I'm sure there are abs under here somewhere."

"Do you want to see them?"

"It sounds like the female judge does." She smirked. "Maybe you'll have to get us an extra point or two by whipping off your shirt."

He shook his head. "Or maybe I'll just have to work more on my dancing. But hey, I was serious before. If we do make it through this next round, then I could make sure that I'm based here in TO for an extra week."

"Only one extra week?" Her forehead furrowed. "Aren't you wanting to try to make the final?"

Shoot. He'd forgotten that she needed to make the final to make even more money. And after all she'd done for him, he couldn't stand to disappoint her. Not again. Guess he was going to have to man up and try a little harder for a little longer. "Of course we're aiming for the final."

She smiled up at him, and his heartstrings eased. He'd do anything to make her smile like that at him again.

Dude, that was frickin' awesome.

You got more moves than I thought.

She is one hot tamale.

Luc grinned as he read the comments on his social media post from his teammates, plus a few from people he knew across the league. Maybe he hadn't looked as much of an idiot as he thought he had.

He glanced at where Bailey slept, her head on his shoulder, as they flew back home. Maybe he should rearrange his schedule to make sure he wasn't wasting so much time on flights. She must be exhausted, especially as he bet she didn't go home after rehearsals and crash like he did. With all her planning and prepping it seemed she always had more work to do.

But while moving to TO for however many weeks made a lot of sense in cutting down travel time, it also meant they couldn't do this, couldn't spend more time in each other's company where they weren't being filmed or having their every move scrutinized. The last flight out of Toronto had been half full, the people onboard not realizing the dude in the sweats and cap with the chick in the hoodie were the ones who'd been dancing across their TV screens only a few hours before.

This, being with her incognito, felt like they were a secret couple, especially when she'd gotten so tired she'd simply used his shoulder as a pillow. He liked these moments with her. It felt sweet. And she was fast becoming a kind of sweet addiction for him. Moving elsewhere and losing this time together, filling it with more rehearsals and the possibility of more eyes on them, like family or friends or fans, felt like they wouldn't have the chance to relax and just be. Where they could joke, or be silent. Where they could probe about each other's families and pasts, or keep it light and talk movie or music tastes. He got to know her more in these times together than when she was in drill sergeant mode, and his brain was turning to mush as he tried to remember steps and moves.

His heart twisted. From what he was getting to know of her, she was fast becoming one of his favorite people.

He hadn't been joking before. Bailey was a huge blessing in his life. He hadn't realized how often negativity and defeatist talk crept in. After years in the pros he should be past that by now. But put him in a new situation where he floundered and it was obvious that some habits might be pasted over with peppy clichés but hadn't truly died. And while he might have been a Christian for a while now and knew he was supposed to speak life, sometimes his mouth still didn't obey. So to have someone who constantly saw the bright side, who cheered him on in her bubbly way, was really special.

He peeked across at her. Reached to tug up his jacket that he'd placed across her when she'd first fallen asleep. He didn't want her to get cold. He'd be okay—he had muscle stores for days—but she was a little thing and might catch a cold, especially in a plane.

His phone buzzed again. He glanced at it, saw the Bible study group chat had come to life. He exhaled heavily. Here went nothing…

He opened the chat, and was instantly met with a dozen emojis from the guys, with everything from red dancing dress lady to John Travolta and Patrick Swayze memes, to hearts-eyes emojis and more. He rolled his eyes, but a smile crept out anyway, as he finally tapped out a reply.

Thanks for voting, guys. Don't know who I owe but pretty sure it's your votes that kept my dancing dreams alive.

He smirked, just knowing the other guys would be laughing their socks off at that comment.

Sure enough, Ryan answered not ten seconds later. *I have never seen anything more beautiful than that performance in my life.*

We won't tell Sylvie you said that, he replied.

That scored a laughing-face emoji from Chris and Jai, both of whom were on the west coast and had probably watched the episode with their wives.

Chris started typing. *Had Zac Parotti here for dinner and a show tonight. Your show, ha ha. I think he's personally funding half of BC's votes to see you make it to the final.*

Awesome. Luc tapped back: *I didn't think dance was his thing but okay.*

The man's been asking some interesting questions, so you could pray he sees the light.

Whoa. Seriously? Zac Parotti was like the west coast's version of Brent Karlsson, an All-Star player with a similar high-end range of skills. Zac was pretty much responsible for Vancouver winning their most recent Stanley Cup, earning the Stanley Cup MVP award in the process, and even prior to that, had endorsements and a profile that was movie star-worthy. If the man was actually seeking God...

Are you for real? Mike asked.

One hundred percent, Chris replied.

Wow. Ryan.

Awesome! Jai.

Amazing. Mike.

Don't you guys believe that God really does work in the hearts of all men to draw people to themselves? Chris asked.

Hmm. When put like that, maybe it was easier to believe that God would be sought by the poor rather than those who didn't obviously need Him, like those with looks, charm, and cash.

Praying for you, dude, Luc typed.

And for you, Chris instantly replied. *You better watch yourself, else you'll be the next of us to settle down.*

Whoa. He did not say that. He glanced at where Bailey slept, her long hair splayed across his arm. He picked up a soft strand, rubbing it between his fingers. Could she feel that? Should he stop? What would she say if she knew what these guys were saying about them?

She's a professional, he reminded them.

That didn't stop you looking at her like she was deep dish pizza. Jai.

He winced. Deep dish might be his favorite thing whenever he visited Chicago, where Jai hailed from. Exactly how had he looked at Bailey? He probably should sit with her and watch the tape of tonight's performance, just like he did in hockey, learning where he could improve, what he shouldn't have done, or what he shouldn't have said.

A still from tonight appeared in the chat, courtesy of Ryan. It showed Luc looking down at Bailey with a small smile on his face as she looked up at him with her usual sparkly smile. Beneath the pic, Ryan had written *"I'm really blessed to have her in my life."*

Wait—had Luc actually said that?

She's everything you could ever want, Chris added.

Oh. Man. Now he remembered. That had been when Bailey had looked up at him, and he'd wondered if she was annoyed, and he'd tried to make amends by saying just how special and wonderful she was.

But Bailey *was* really special. Beautiful, positive, and kind. And somehow, he didn't mind his friends' teasing, as it was just another case of him teetering from that place that he'd thought he'd always known.

The non-dancer, who now liked dancing. A little bit, at least.

The happy-being-single dude, who now wanted more. A lot more.

He peeked back at Bailey, tempted, *so* tempted, to touch her cheek, to know the softness of her skin.

His heart expanded, then contracted.

But what if what he said was true, and she was such a professional that she never wanted to know him? What if he was simply a job to her, and once this was done, they'd never see each other again?

The plane hit a patch of turbulence, which bounced her against his shoulder, jerking her awake. She blinked up at him, her dark lashes less long than those crazy Bambi ones she'd been wearing during tonight's show. He liked this version of her more, and he bet part of the reason she'd gone unrecognized was because she'd washed off most of the heavy TV makeup. Even normal Bailey was usually made up beautifully, and he'd rarely got the chance to see her without a mask. This version of Bailey was softer, more real, more unguarded and natural.

"Hey."

"Did I fall asleep?"

He nodded.

"On you? I'm so sorry."

"It's okay."

"Is this your jacket?" She moved to tug it off, give it back.

He pressed a hand on hers, stilling her movement. "Keep it. I don't want you to get cold."

She blinked a heavy-lidded blink, and smiled. "You're so sweet."

No, he wasn't. But she was. And he'd do anything to make her realize that he'd do all in his power to protect and comfort her.

Including making sure he'd get the lifts right in the jive.

CHAPTER 10

"*O*kay, now the jive. What do you know about it?" Bailey tilted her head slightly at where the cameras were filming them. Rehearsals stopped for no man, even if their arrival back home so late—so early, actually, it being almost one when they got home this morning—had seen a delayed start until eleven, instead of their usual nine AM. Ella had understood, but still wanted footage, even though Bailey still felt a little too slug-like. Thank goodness Luc had arrived with coffees made by Max today. She might even have to schedule an extra coffee break as well. She didn't think she'd manage travelling like this next week. But for now, the show must go on.

Luc drained his coffee and placed the to-go cup down near the mirror. "So, this may surprise you, but I actually looked up some of the dances we might do."

"No!"

"Yes!"

She laughed. Oh, she liked it when he was fun like this. Probably liked it a little too much, but anyway. "So, tell me what you know."

"Okay, so it looks kind of fun, it's fast-paced, with lots of kicking."

She clapped her hands. "Exactly!" The jive was pretty technical, but maybe this week would be easier than she thought.

"Have we got a theme or something?"

"Not really. Well, I took on board what some of the judges were saying about looking for your strengths. So, I thought maybe we could try to do something like what you might do on the ice."

"You mean like beat people up?"

He did that?

"Whoa, no. I never do that." He winked. "Not much anyway."

Okay. That was a surprising revelation she hadn't expected today. Luc didn't really hurt people, did he? Maybe she should follow Poppy's advice and watch some of his previous games. The fact he might hurt people was a disconcerting twist on what she'd thought she'd known about the man. "Well, I'd sort of imagined something more like an old-fashioned ice rink, or roller rink, I suppose, complete with mirror ball. You could start in the middle of the floor, clicking your fingers as the music starts, you know, to prove your musicality, then spinning around when I come on, which is when we'd start the dance."

He nodded, arms folded, but his face didn't hold protest.

She felt an internal ping of relief. "And I know you want a redemption round with a lift, so I thought we might try to add one or two in. They're not hard." She quickly demonstrated, bending her knees, explaining how if he bent his knees at the same time, she could propel herself up using the momentum as she held his hand, and he could direct her body into a new position. "See how easy that is?"

They did it a few more times, then she got him to hold her in what she called a trapeze grip as he spun her around before gently lowering her to the floor. "We might not do that spin this week, but we definitely could use it for the waltz the week after."

"I hope so. That felt amazing."

She smiled, her heart snagging at the soft expression on his face as he studied her. Almost like he wanted to absorb her features forever, like he liked her or something.

What was she thinking? Hadn't he told his friends he didn't want a relationship with her? She really needed to get a grip and stay professional. She glanced across at Ella and the guys. She couldn't give any impression that they were more than dance pro and celebrity.

Maybe Luc thought the same for he coughed. "Yeah, those lifts are three thousand times easier than what we did last week," he said.

"Right? They're pretty fun, provided you can keep up because it's so fast."

"I hear a challenge there, Sergeant."

Good.

"So, do we have more modern music?"

"How do you feel about The Weeknd?"

"He's Canadian, so that's a plus."

"You know the song 'Blinding Lights'?"

It was like a switch was flicked and he became animated. "Yeah, that's a cool one."

"Okay. So, imagine a dark room, lasers, spotlights, and you, dressed in suspenders, black pants, white shirt—"

"No suit?" he asked with a hopeful look.

"No suit."

He fist-pumped.

"But maybe slicked-back hair, pulled back in a ponytail."

"Ugh. Man-buns have never been my thing."

"Don't look like that. Come on, you're playing a part, remember? Anyway, you could wear a fedora—"

"A what?"

"A snappy-looking hat. Tilted over one side of your face. Like you're a cool dude."

"Are you saying I'm not cool?"

She bit back a laugh. "Like the coolest dude you know."

"Like Zac Parotti?"

"Who?"

He laughed, the big bellowing sound causing her to smile. He looked at the cameras and smiled. "I like this one. She's a keeper."

"Come on." She gently slapped his arm. "Stop worrying about what you're going to wear."

"Do I need to worry about what you're going to wear?"

She shook her head. She'd seen the sketch of her outfit, and she didn't think he'd mind it. "There's no big billowy skirt for you to get tangled in this time."

He bit his lip for a moment, and she regretted reminding him of last night's fail. Resolve dug deeper to make sure he was confident. Which would only come from practice.

"We need to get dancing. Now this dance means you really have to work on your musicality. You need to feel the rhythm, and hit the beats. Which means listening to the song lots of times so you know where to come in. But before we can do that, we need to get to work on all those kicks, and flicks, and your fast footwork. So, are you ready?"

"Bring it."

So she did.

SHE WAS close to puffing by the time they'd finished, but his cardio was pretty good, his stamina impressive, as he'd barely broken a sweat. "I can't believe I'm puffing and you look like you've just gone for a stroll."

"I go running every morning." He half-smiled. "Maybe you should come sometime."

Blessed coolness trickled down her throat as she guzzled her water. "I know it doesn't look like it at the moment, but I get enough fitness from leading classes here. I occasionally go to Pilates, but I don't go to the gym and I *definitely* don't need to run."

"You're missing out."

"I really don't think I am."

He clicked his fingers. "But you are missing out on something."

"What's that?"

"The greatest sport on earth."

"You mean ballet?"

He snorted, and the cameras drew near again. "Ballet isn't a sport."

"Yes, it is. Ballerinas are just as much athletes as you are."

"Come on. It's not a sport. There aren't any goals or score lines."

"Um, excuse me, but ballet is both a sport *and* an art form. The preparation elite ballerinas undergo is similar to anything you do, and requires similar levels of physical exertion, difficult skills, and long, long hours of discipline."

"Yeah, but there's no team or competition—"

"There is." She stepped closer, enjoying this sparring of words. "We might not have a scoreboard you can read, but there's plenty of competition to get into the best schools and perform the lead roles and be known as the best. In fact, ballet is so physically demanding that a study ranked ballet as the number one most physically and mentally demanding activity there is. Did you know that?"

"Really?"

She nodded, arms crossed. "So there."

His mouth puckered into a little smile. "What are we, twelve?"

"Look, I just hate it when people think ballet isn't a legiti-mate sport." She turned around and pointed to her back. "See my muscles? They didn't get there by accident."

She spun back around, and she saw how he swallowed. Her leotard might have a low back with its twist-back detail and open cutouts, but it was way more modest than some of the outfits some of the other dancers had worn yesterday. But maybe he wasn't used to noticing a woman's back. "Was there anything else?"

He scuffed the floor with his dance shoe. There'd been no complaints about wearing them today.

"What is it?"

He glanced up. "Can you ice-skate?"

"No, no, no! This is such a dumb idea!"

He laughed, holding onto Bailey's hands. "Come on. You can trust me. I'm not going to let you fall."

He followed her glance at where Ella and the guys were filming, this little adventure on the ice "exactly what we love to see" as Ella had said.

He hoped it would prove to be, that he wouldn't drop Bailey. She might have poise for miles on the dance floor, but she hadn't yet managed to figure out how to balance on skates. And the fact that she hadn't, that she was stumbling at something he felt was as natural as breathing, made him feel a little better about his failings on the dance floor.

The jive was kicking his butt. His *big* butt, thanks Marco. But here, when he and the ice were almost as one, was a lot better.

He held Bailey's hands, using his upper body strength to boost hers, and said, "Look up at me." She tentatively did, her eyes finding, holding his. "You can trust me."

She gulped, and the moment suddenly morphed into another of those weird ones where he and she seemed to connect more deeply, and a wave of something indescribable seemed to pass between them. He was almost tempted to try to dance with her out here, to do one of those spins they'd prac-ticed that looked so cool on the dance floor, like ice dancers did at the Olympics, but her fears about falling and maybe twisting something made him pause. He didn't want to break his promise to her.

Anyway, it was enough that she was close, almost in his arms as he skated backwards around the practice facility the team used. Their usual arena had reverted back to use as a concert venue, which meant this was the best place he could find relative privacy on a summer's evening in Winnipeg.

"Want to have another try?" he asked.

"I just don't want to fall."

"How about I skate you to the side, then hold your hand. I promise, I won't let anything happen to you."

"Promise?"

He nodded, throat dry.

He skated her to the boards, and she grasped it tight, then squeezed his right hand in her left. "Now, push with your right leg, imagine you're gliding along the dance floor, and I'm Marco. 'I want you to be light on your feet, let's see you gliding, Bailey,'" he said in a terrible Italian accent that drew her smile. "Hey, that's it."

She glanced down and wobbled. "Luc!"

"I got you. You're safe. Don't look down. Look ahead. That's what you're always telling me, right? No looking down or at my feet."

She exhaled shakily. "I'm glad to know that some of what I've said is sinking in."

"You'd be surprised at just how much."

Bailey peeked at him, and he shook his head. "Uh-uh. Straight ahead."

She obeyed.

He swallowed a snicker at her scared look. If he was a wussy man, he'd call that look adorable. "Am I allowed to say I'm kinda surprised a local gal has never learned to skate?"

"No."

He didn't bother to hide the laughter this time.

"Don't laugh at me. I don't laugh at you, do I?"

"Oh, you do, Bails. All the time."

Her smile poked out. "That's because you're funny."

He was? "Do you mean that in a good way, or like you think I'm weird?"

Her lips pulled wider, and she opened her mouth—

"Don't answer that."

She giggled, the sound warming his heart. "In a good way. Honestly, for such a tough guy, you seem awfully insecure sometimes."

"I'm not insecure," he insisted. "I just really want to know what other people think of me *all* the time."

She smiled, then peeked at him again. "Well, I think you're pretty great."

Her words walloped his chest, and before he knew it, he'd slipped, his backside pounding the ice. "Ow!"

She grabbed hold of the boards, laughing.

"It's not funny," he complained, rubbing his backside. He hadn't planned on falling, and these jeans held none of the protective elements he usually wore on the ice.

"I'm sorry," she said, looking anything but. She held out a hand. "Do you need help getting up?"

He was so tempted to "accidentally" pull her down into his arms. He looked at her hand, then back up at her, saw the way her eyes widened, then she dropped her hand and tried to move backwards. "Luc, don't..."

"Luc?"

Luc's stomach tensed. He recognized that voice. He peeked over his shoulder and quickly scrambled to his feet as Sean Hart skated closer.

After a few harder-than-necessary backslaps hello, Luc glanced at Bailey, who held a nervous smile. "Hey Bailey. This is Sean, who I used to play with. Sean, this is Bailey Donovan."

Sean's eyes widened and he grinned. "Your dance partner, huh? Well, hello Bailey." His gaze trickled down her snug pink sweater and slender legs encased in jeans.

Luc clenched his hands, and moved to place a protective arm around her. "We're just taking a break from rehearsals."

"Is that so? Didn't look like all you were doing."

Bailey nestled closer to Luc's side, and murmured, "Um, if you want to talk with him, I'm totally okay with that."

"You don't want to skate anymore?"

She winced. "You know I appreciate this, but I really can't skate without you."

"Maybe you just need a better teacher," Sean said.

Luc took Bailey's hands. "Sorry, she's with me, and we still have work to do."

"We do?" she murmured.

"One hundred percent," he muttered back.

No way did she need to spend a second longer in the company of the man the team had privately called Casanova. The man had more notches on his bedpost than Luc had hot dinners. His involvement in the betting scandal last year had apparently also seen his name linked to a few even less savory things, including rumors of violence against a prostitute. Luc had had a few run-ins with Sean before, and as the man didn't fit the family culture the team was striving for, it'd been good to see him go.

"Catch you around," Luc said. Like hopefully never.

"Keep practicing, dude. You look like you need it."

"Wow," Bailey said, as Luc drew her away. "He doesn't like you much, does he?"

"Sean and I always had differences of opinions about how to treat other people."

"Let me guess. You called him out for how he treated women."

He glanced at her quickly. "You could tell?"

"Please. I wasn't born yesterday. It might surprise you to learn this but some dancers can have narcissistic qualities."

"No way!"

"Way." She grinned.

He couldn't help it. That smile pummeled straight into his chest, and made him do crazy things. So he scooped her up in both arms, to her shriek of laughter, which instantly drew every eye to them. Including Ella's, who stopped what looked like an interview with Sean to focus on them. So he did what he'd wanted to do earlier, spinning around with Bailey in his arms, her arm around his neck, her chest pressed close to his, then slowly lowering her to the ice again.

She fanned herself. "Oh my goodness, Luc. You need to warn a girl before doing something like that."

"Would you have said yes?"

"Probably not."

"Are you glad I did?"

Her lips puckered, and he wished they were somewhere private where he could learn if that was a signal for a kiss. "Maybe."

He grinned, his heart thudding with happiness. "You want to try that spin move we practiced earlier out here on the ice?"

"No! I can't even skate in a straight line properly, let alone do something like that."

"You just need to hold onto me. Like I said, I won't let you fall."

She bit her lip, and he could tell she was considering it. And she looked up at him. "Do you promise?"

"I care about you, Bails. I'll always take good care of you."

She looked deep into his eyes, then finally nodded. He held

her hand, drawing her away from the boards, then clasped both of her hands together in both of his. "Trust me?"

"Yes," she whispered.

He smiled, then slowly spun with her forearms in the trapeze grip she'd taught him. He built up speed until she gasped and slipped, one leg off the ice, then two, her grip sliding until she was holding onto his hands for dear life. But other than it being on ice, it was exactly as they'd practiced: him holding her, her beautiful hair splaying out, and Luc feeling that strange sense of power and joy at the center of it all. He slowed, then before they lost too much momentum, lowered her gently so she slid slowly near the boards.

Applause broke out behind him, and he glanced back to see Ella and Sean watching, the cameras on them still. He grinned, then skated to collect Bailey, who was flapping a hand at her cheeks, her broad grin saying she'd enjoyed that as much as he had. "You okay down there?"

"Apart from my tush getting cold."

"We can't have that now, can we?" He stretched out a hand and gracefully pulled her up. Then he gestured to their little audience. "Do you think you can manage a bow?"

"Maybe."

He held her firm as she curtsied while he took a bow.

Then he helped her to the side, holding her hand as they found the guards and put them on. "Was that fun?"

"So fun." Her cheeks were glowing, her eyes sparkling. "I was so tired before but this has been amazing. Thanks for bringing me here."

"Now we just have to get you to a game one day."

"Maybe."

He leaned closer. "Definitely."

She patted his chest. "We'll see."

He wrapped her hand in his, keeping it firm against his chest. "What would it take for you to say yes?"

She tilted her head. Then smiled.

"What?"

"You mean apart from winning the final?"

"Bribery and corruption, huh?"

"I prefer to call it motivation to do well."

"Hey, I know all about that. I've seen the stash of chocolate treats you keep for the kids in your studio. I still think it's unfair you haven't offered one to me."

"To bribe you?"

He smiled, drawing closer still. "I prefer to call it motivation to do well."

She laughed. "Well, if winning the final is too hard to get me to a game, maybe we could aim for something a little more achievable."

"Like what?" Would them intentionally spending time together in a non-rehearsal way count as a date? Did this count as a date? He'd give anything to get to know this woman more. To spend more time in her company. "You name it, and I'm there."

In the echo of that, he had a funny realization that he'd said something very similar not too long ago. And look what had happened since.

"A movie," she said.

"You want to watch a movie with me?" That had to count as a date, right?

She nodded. "Get through to the next round, and we'll watch a movie, and I'll come to one of your games."

He held out his hand. "Put it there. You got yourself a deal."

She took his hand, her small hand looking absurdly small in his large rough one.

"I can't wait. When and where?"

Her smile grew. "If we get through next week's round, then I'll tell you. How is that for motivation?"

He grinned. "Perfect."

CHAPTER 11

Toronto

It was funny how the nerves still ate, even though she'd been here before. Maybe that was the knowledge that Luc's family were out there in the studio audience and she was meeting them after tonight's performance. She'd asked her family to wait until next week, provided they got through. At least she had a far greater confidence that Luc would get the steps right tonight, and if he did what he'd done during rehearsals, then they were in with a good shot.

"How are you feeling?" Coco asked, as they waited in the wings to take their positions for the show's opening pro performance.

"Slightly more confident than last week." She slid a hand down her satin skirt. "I'm grateful that I'm wearing something shorter tonight."

"Hmm. I bet Luc is too." Coco winked.

"What?"

"Come on. Everyone could see from the way that man keeps

looking at you in rehearsals these past few days that he's halfway to being in love."

"What?"

"You don't think so?"

"No. He's not that way at all." Her chest tweaked at the lie. Okay, so maybe there'd been a time or two when she'd thought he liked her a little more than as a friend, but she hadn't encouraged it. Well, apart from saying that almost-flirty-sounding thing about watching a movie together. And smiling and laughing so much with him. None of that had been wise. Besides, "We have contracts forbidding that kind of thing."

"Yeah, but it doesn't mean it doesn't happen. People usually just keep things on the down-low until the show is over. And I get that he might not be used to women with your kind of sweet and bubbly personality, so maybe that's part of it too. I'm just saying, you need to be careful."

Coco went on to share a scandalous story about a dance pro and an actress that twisted Bailey's heart. She could understand how easy it was for two people spending so much time together, touching and holding each other, in each other's personal spaces, even breathing each other's air, to develop feelings simply based on proximity, not on anything real. That had happened before, when she'd realized it was only one-sided on her part, and she'd determined after Mark had made her feel like a fool that she'd not leave her heart unguarded again.

But Luc with his funny mix of vulnerability and kindness had somehow tiptoed around that, to the point that seeing him was fast becoming the highlight of her day. She enjoyed practicing with him because she enjoyed him. He seemed like a genuinely nice guy. And all the hand-holding and hugs of this hothouse of a dance environment only seemed to force feelings to grow faster. But what would happen when this show was over, and they went back to hockey star and dance nobody? He was in this for his own motivations, just like her. He wanted to prove himself as captain-worthy material, while she'd agreed to do this for the money. It wasn't real. She needed to remember that.

She nodded. "Thanks for the reminder."

She snuck a look at where Luc stood with the other celebrities, waiting, watching. He gave her a thumbs-up, which she acknowledged with a nod and a smaller-than-usual smile. She didn't want to change who she was, but Coco's words had put a damper on tonight. Maybe meeting his family wasn't such a great idea after all.

The assistant pointed to the stage as the music of the show filled the studio. She sucked in a breath, knowing she had to focus. She might have to support her celebrity in his dances, but now was about supporting herself. A pro dancer's contract depended on so many factors, not least of which was her celebrity's popularity and technical ability. Conversations with Coco and Miguel and some of the others in recent days had revealed how some pros had been cut due to factors beyond their control. A celebrity could be immensely popular, but their lack of dancing prowess or technical skills was sometimes seen as a reflection on the skills of the pro dancer, resulting in some pros' contracts not being renewed. Others had been forced into retirement, thanks to ageing and unwanted curves. "Nobody wants to see a thicker dancer," Miguel had said at last night's group dinner at the hotel. "This show is supposed to be aspirational, showing what can happen if you dance the heck out of your body, and we all know the camera adds ten pounds."

She'd put down the dessert she'd been about to consume, knowing only too well that while there were some things she couldn't control, like whether Luc remembered his steps, there were other things she definitely could, like what she ate or how much. So, if she wanted to continue, then she needed to hit all her cues, execute all her routines perfectly, and pray that Luc's performance was enough to see them make it through.

They were sent onto the stage, the lights dimmed, the crowd hushed. Then the music began, and she snapped into her role. Precise movements. Controlled arms. Sexy sway. Then she partnered up with Miguel as they did the 1950s-themed dance moves that would showcase tonight's jive, rumba, and paso doble.

She grinned, settling into the rhythms of the dance, kicking, flicking, careful to keep her movements defined and clean. Tonight's little motivational talk had only doubled her efforts to prove herself, to prove to others that she was strictly a professional, that there was nothing to worry about for anyone. And she'd do so—

Ow! Her foot collided with Miguel's—a joint mistake—but after a "sorry!" she instantly pasted her smile back on. See what happened when she wasn't paying attention? She finished the routine, her sitting on Miguel's knee, arm around his neck, as she pointed her aching toe to the ceiling. She could feel the animosity coming off him.

But he also had to pretend nothing was wrong, and thanks to the fact Miguel was opening the show, she had no time to say anything but a quick "I'm so sorry, I didn't see you there" to him as they departed backstage.

Coco found her in the dressing room, where they were helped out of their costumes and prepped for their celebrity dance outfits. "What happened? Miguel was fuming."

"It was my mistake." Her stomach grew queasy as she described her mishap.

Coco winced. "Don't let him get to you. He's always snarky with those he blames for getting things wrong. But we're professionals, and as they say, the show must go on."

The trepidation about tonight's performance trebled as her dress was zipped up, and her makeup and hairstyle refreshed. But no. She wasn't dancing with Miguel, but with Luc. She had to focus on him, focus on doing all she could to help him feel confident and sure. They were dancing last, which meant after their introductions at the start she'd have over an hour to keep him calm. Which also meant over an hour of trying to act strictly professionally with him, and not stirring up unnecessary feelings. *Lord, help me focus.*

She hurried back to the wings, finding Luc, who held out his hand then slowly twirled her as he smiled. "Looking good, Bails."

"Thanks." She released his hand, gesturing to his costume. "I'm loving the hat."

"Apparently it's called a fedora."

"Is it now?"

Oh, it was too easy to banter like this. She needed to stop. She dimmed her smile back.

He nudged her. "What is it?"

She shook her head, they were due on…

"Now!" hissed the assistant beside the curtain, pointing at them.

Bailey pasted on a big smile as she tugged Luc to the stage, while the announcer said, "Please welcome Luc Blanchard, and his partner Bailey."

The lights and camera and swell of applause at their entry accompanied them to their position on the stairs this week, the producers judging Luc's height wouldn't hide anyone standing behind them.

She stood, ramrod-straight, smile fixed, wondering where in the crowd his family sat. Luc's hand was on her waist, and through the nude mesh she could feel his hand was already sweaty. Her toe throbbed from where she'd accidentally hit Miguel, and she hoped his wasn't worse. Still, stuff happened, and she'd apologize more thoroughly later, and pray he wouldn't hold it against her. And thank God that because Miguel was on first and their act was last there'd be reduced time to talk with each other.

They were released, then she returned with Luc backstage, as her toe complained. Still, a dancer couldn't protest, and she knew if she took her shoe off now there'd be no way she could get it on later. She'd just need to toughen up—and pop an ibuprofen or two if it got worse.

"Are you okay?" Luc asked her.

"Yep!" She needed to hide her pain, not give him a second's worry. "How are you feeling?"

"Better than last week, but still nervous."

She straightened his collar, as the temptation grew to run her hands down his shirt and feel those muscles underneath. She stepped away. Put her hands behind her back. "Did you want to run through anything again? Going last means we have time."

"Could we? I don't want to seem needy, but if we've got time that would help."

She nodded, and ignoring the music that signaled the start of the author's dance with Miguel, she slowly walked her way to the corner, doing her best to not limp like she wanted. *Lord, please let it not be a broken toe.*

"Are you sure you're okay?"

She nodded, looking around for one of the ever-present bottles of water. She grabbed one, sipped it, then smiled. "Okay, let's see what you've got."

"You're not going to dance with me?"

"I will, after I see if you remember the moves." And after her toe calmed its fiery roar.

He grinned. "Is this more of your motivation? I haven't forgotten about the movie, you know."

Darn. The movie. Why had she suggested such a thing? She knew exactly why. Because she'd started to succumb to his charm, and thought that he might even enjoy the opposites-attract underdog story of her favorite movie, ever. She'd have to find a way to make it seem less date-like. She couldn't afford for anyone—Luc or producers—to get ideas. Well, none more than what she'd already given.

"But first you have to get through tonight. So let's see what you've got, big guy." She perched on a stool and watched as he began his introduction, clicking his fingers for two beats, not the four as she'd originally planned, but tweaked during rehearsals. Then he spun around, in a skater move like he'd done on the ice last Monday, then skidded forward like he was skating to where she'd meet him.

He looked lost for a second when she didn't join him, but she simply called "Keep going."

The job of a performer was exactly that. Keep going, even when you messed up, and missed a cue or a word or a note. Redos weren't possible with live TV, and part of the challenge was being able to sell the performance even when you knew you'd made a mistake. He was used to that anyway, so he'd said in Wednesday's rehearsal, when she'd first had him go through this alone. He'd explained how hockey had the potential for all kinds of errors, from turnovers to icing to missed checks and missed shots and goals. That was one way training an athlete was helpful, they knew how to press through adversity.

Just like she would. With her sore heart and aching toe.

"You nailed it!"

Bailey wrapped her arms around him as the studio's cheers filled the room.

He grinned, swinging her around, then settling her on the floor. "We got through, baby." Her eyes widened at that last word which had slipped out, honest. "I mean, Sergeant Bailey."

She pressed her lips together, and shifted slightly away. "That's better."

But her shifting away wasn't. He grabbed her hand as they

joined the other couples safe from elimination, and got hugs from Coco and her actor dude. He wished Jason wasn't so handsome and kept his hugs to himself.

Miguel and the author lady were eliminated, which wasn't a surprise as anyone could see Miguel was limping like a sore loser.

He'd scowled at Bailey when they'd passed before, and she'd rushed over and said "I'm so sorry."

Miguel had muttered something back which caused Bailey to stiffen, which instantly raised Luc's own hackles. It was funny how after dancing with her so much he was getting used to what her body said when she wasn't talking. For a moment he could swear that she was frightened. Luc had wrapped an arm around her, which she'd left there for a moment, before shrugging it off in a move he suspected she hoped he wouldn't notice.

But he had. He noticed all kinds of things about her. And something had been off all night, even though their dance had gotten solid sixes, and was the third best of the night. So surely she should be happy they'd gotten through. She'd get her next five thousand dollars now, wouldn't she? She'd have to be happy about that, just as he was happy about the fact this now meant he'd get to go on a movie date with her. He couldn't wait.

He followed her to the green room, where the reporters were ready to pounce. Ugh, this. He'd forgotten about this. The cameras in his face, the fact he'd have to pretend he was glad to talk about himself. This was all part of the performance, so Bailey had said, and Coco and the producers had made clear.

"Congratulations, Luc!" a reporter from ET said. "The judges really seemed to like your connection this week, as well as commenting on your fancy footwork tonight."

Luc slung an arm around Bailey's shoulder. She was looking as sparkly and happy as ever. And not just because of the silver bling in her short dress. "It's all due to Bailey here."

"And what do you say to that, Bailey?"

Bailey tilted her head into his chest. "I think Luc forgets what skills he brings from his work on the ice."

"Yes, we saw the highlights package earlier. You took Bailey ice-skating, huh?"

Luc nodded. "It was a lot of fun to show her some of my world after being in hers so much lately. I can't wait to get her to a game one day."

Bailey stiffened. His heart froze, and he didn't hear the next question. Didn't she want to do that anymore? Just what had happened to her tonight?

"Luc? What do you have to say to that?"

"Sorry. Could you repeat the question?"

The reporter's smile grew strained. "I'm just wondering how far you think you two can go in this competition?"

"In this competition? All the way." He flexed, which drew the reporter's laugh.

"And dare we ask, out of this competition?" The reporter winked.

Luc's mouth dried, and he quickly glanced down at Bailey. Her smile had dropped, and she looked down at the floor. "Out of this competition?" Luc repeated slowly. He had to say something, and no way was he going to say anything that would embarrass poor Bailey. "I think it's safe to say..." *Lord? What do I say?* The answer shot to him like a bolt of lightning. "Nothing."

The reporter laughed, and Luc relaxed. But Bailey still seemed tense, even though he knew she was trying her best to keep smiling.

They soon finished that interview, then were immediately pounced on for another, then a third, so it was getting late by the time they finally finished and he could meet his folks.

"Hey," he grabbed Bailey's hand. "Are you ready to meet my parents?"

She closed her eyes, and winced. "I just need to go get changed."

"Oh, but Mom really wanted to see us in our costumes. It won't take long, I promise."

She studied him then nodded, and he took her hand and hurried her from the room to where his folks waited.

"Lucas!" His mom opened her arms and he stepped into them, drawing her up into his hug, which pulled her off the ground. "Oh, you were so good."

"Hello, Mr. Blanchard," Bailey said while Luc hugged his mom.

"Mom, Dad, this is Bailey Donovan." He wrapped his arm around her waist. "Bails, this is Simon and Valentienne Blanchard."

"It's lovely to meet you both."

His dad was still holding Bailey's hand like he was starstruck. "Dad," Luc said.

His mom muscled past and drew Bailey in for her own hug. "You're so pretty, aren't you?"

Bailey shot him a panicked look as she was smothered in his mom's arms. Luc laughed and drew her back. "Yes, she is. And modest, so don't go saying that too often, otherwise you'll get Sergeant Bailey instead of the sweet thing you're seeing now."

His mom looked down at Bailey's dress. "I can see why he likes you so much."

Luc's neck heated. "Mom."

Bailey laughed, and he sighed with relief. That was what he'd missed. She'd barely laughed tonight. And an evening without her laughter was like a night sky with no stars. Something had been wrong before, he just knew it.

Bailey gracefully stepped back. "You'll have to excuse me. I need to change."

"You mean you don't wear that out?" his dad asked.

Luc cleared his throat. "We'll be back in a moment, then we'll go have dinner like I promised."

"Are you coming, Bailey?" his mom asked.

"Oh! I, um, didn't want to intrude, so I thought I'd go with my friend Coco—"

"You're not intruding," Luc said.

His mom nodded. "We want you there."

Bailey's smile wavered, then she nodded, her smile drooping before she hitched it up. His heart fell. Didn't she want to come? Granted, his mom was a little forward, and his dad had been a bit weird, but they were his folks, and the fact she might not want to spend time with them—with him—hurt.

"It was really nice to meet you," Bailey said, not looking at him.

"Hey, before you go, can we get a photo with you?"

"Of course!"

They gathered close for a selfie, which he took, seeing his arm was longest, then Coco walked past and offered to take a few more. He was conscious of Bailey's slender frame as he wrapped his arm around her, her hair tickling his nose.

"I think you'll find some there that should do." Coco handed back his phone and he thanked her. But as he was looking through the photos—yep, just as he'd hoped, Bailey looked perfect with his family—he stepped on Bailey's toe.

She gasped, wincing, wobbling as she drew her foot up.

"Oh, Bails, I'm so sorry!"

She shook her head, shut her eyes, but he saw a tear leak onto her cheek.

He glanced at his folks. "How about I join you at the restaurant as soon as I can?"

They nodded, and told Bailey they'd enjoyed meeting her, to which she nodded in reply, bright and happy, until he held her arm and pivoted her to the dressing room. "Hey, I really am sorry."

She bent over, her nose wrinkling, then a producer appeared. "Bailey?"

Bailey instantly straightened, smiling bright. "Hey Erin."

"Everything okay here?"

Bailey shot him a look and he knew he had to step in. "We're good. Bailey was just showing me how faint she gets when she's not fed enough."

Erin frowned. "Didn't you eat at lunch?"

Bailey nodded, but Luc knew he still had to do more. "I know this will surprise you, but she actually eats more than me."

"As long as she can fit into those costumes and she's not throwing it straight back up that's fine with me."

Erin winked, but Bailey had paled, like there really was something wrong, more than a sore toe. He hurried to her, drawing her to a darker corner, holding her close, saying in a quiet voice so nobody else would hear, "Bails? What is it?"

She shook her head.

"No, don't try and deny it. What's wrong? Is it my folks? We don't have to eat with them if you don't want."

"They're really nice. It's not that."

"Did I hurt you before? I'm really sorry."

Another shake of her head. "Miguel and I collided in the pro dance, and I hurt my toe." She winced. "I really hope it's not broken."

"Bails! You should've got that checked out right away."

She nodded. "I know, but we needed to go over your dance, and—"

"You're more important than my dance. Come on. Let's get you undressed." He cringed. "Man, I really didn't mean that. I meant changed."

"I know." Her smile was a welcome beacon of light in a storm.

"Can you walk, or do you want me to carry you?"

"If you carry me there'll be all kinds of other questions, and I really don't want the producers thinking I can't do my job." She sighed. "They're probably already hearing that from Miguel, and I don't want them to fire me."

"They won't fire you," he scoffed. "Stuff happens, Bails, and you gotta dust yourself off and keep going. You're awesome," he encouraged. "Besides, everyone knows that you're the only reason we're going to round three. That's what you wanted, wasn't it?"

She nodded. "The money will help, that's for sure."

He blinked, as hurt swirled through his chest. The money. See? He knew this wasn't about him for her, but was about the money.

"Come on. Let's get you changed. You can hold onto me."

She clutched his hand, and he half-lifted her onto his back in a move for which the judges should give him a solid ten. He soon deposited her at the women's dressing room, where Coco met her. "You two still playing?" Coco asked, with her arched brow.

He ignored the insinuation, saying, in a quiet voice, "She's hurt her toe, but doesn't want the producers to know."

Coco's eyes widened and she nodded, and he hurried off to change, where he was met with a clearly upset Miguel.

"Your Bailey cost me the competition," he hissed.

"Pretty sure it was your low scores that did that."

"This was my year for the mirror ball."

Yeah, no. Obviously it wasn't. He ignored the rest of Miguel's words, stripping off his shirt, exchanging it for a fresh tee. He'd normally shower, but his parents were waiting, and he still really wanted to talk to Bailey. She'd been upset about more than a sore toe. He'd noticed that even before the pro dance opener. Was she worried about the rumors about them, like the ones implied by Coco, or voiced more directly, like the reporter?

They couldn't control what others said about them. That

was the price of fame. It was part of why he was careful to always tell the truth, to be honest and direct to the point of bluntness, because that way there was no having to second-guess what he said or did. That, and God wanted him to, as well. But maybe Bailey hadn't had her shell hardened by years of the spotlight, and maybe she worried about things like that.

He really needed to talk to her, and find out.

CHAPTER 12

"Oh my gosh, Bailey. You shouldn't have danced on that."

Bailey winced as Coco removed Bailey's tights. The dark gray surrounding her right big toe wasn't the first time she'd seen such a thing. "I'll ice it, and rest it as best I can."

Coco sighed. "You've got the waltz this week, right?"

"Yeah. That should be easier."

Coco grabbed Bailey's Uggs and gently slipped them on. "Are you coming home with me or going with him?"

No guesses who "him" was. She winced again.

"You don't have to go with him," Coco said. "Just tell me you're not thinking of flying back to Winnipeg."

The thought of her own bed drew longing, but she shook her head. "We agreed to stay here and rehearse this week." She winced. "And all I want to do is put ice on this and go to bed."

"And you can do that as soon as we get you back to my place." Coco frowned. "Unless lover boy…"

"Stop," Bailey begged. "Please stop. He's not, he can't be. We barely know each other. He certainly doesn't know the important stuff."

Like what Erin had alluded to before. Well, not alluded. Pretty much said outright. Bailey had worked so hard since Mark's rejection, and she didn't throw up like that anymore. But that season in her life, the season that had ultimately pirouetted her into a new career, had shaped her, and while she'd worked so hard to leave it behind, it didn't take much to question things again. Like everything that had happened tonight. Oh, she hoped Luc wouldn't be out there, being all kind and concerned. She might really cry then. And if the producers saw her cry, then what might happen?

Already she'd had the lead choreographer express his disappointment with her mistake in the pro dance earlier. That, along with Miguel's death stares, had really rocked her confidence. She knew she needed to shake it off, but some days were a lot easier to do that than others. And everything that had happened tonight—the misstep, the rumors about her and Luc, his parents meeting her like she and Luc were a couple, Erin's unwitting reference to bulimia—had made her feel so fragile she might crack at any moment. And the sunshiny persona would fall to reveal the woman who was trying so hard to make up for past mistakes.

The glitter costume was hung up, exchanged for her sweats and a top warm enough for the night's cool temperatures. Her Uggs provided welcome softness, even if her toe still throbbed. Thoughts of Coco's apartment beckoned, a shower, bed, quiet, sleep, and maybe more ibuprofen.

Then she exited. And found Luc waiting at the door.

"How are you feeling?" he asked quickly.

"Fine. Well, my toe is really sore, so I'm going to go ice it and lie down."

"Where? At the hotel?"

"Coco's," she reminded him.

"Oh." His shoulders drooped, like her answer disappointed him.

That's right. His parents. "I'm sorry I can't spend time with your folks, but please tell them I enjoyed meeting them."

He nodded. "Will you, um," he glanced around, then added more softly, "still be able to dance next weekend?"

She nodded. She had to. She'd had another look at her contract and it seemed to say that she actually had to dance at the third round, not just get to it. Not dancing next weekend would be the equivalent of exiting in round two, so yes. "We've got the waltz." And she would dance it, if it killed her.

He glanced at her, then down at his feet, then back at her. "Can I, uh, help you with your bags or anything?"

Oh. "Um, sure."

She hobbled back inside to where Coco was still talking with Michelle, one of the other dancers. Coco glanced at her then nodded. "Catch you later, Mish. My girl Bailey needs me."

She sure did. Coco mightn't be a Christian, but she knew this scene way better than Poppy or any of Bailey's other close dance friends. And having someone to guide her through the labyrinth of emotions would be helpful right now.

They exited the dressing room, and Luc straightened from the pillar where he'd been standing, talking on his phone. He ended the call.

"You're still here?" Coco asked him.

"As you can see." He bowed, in a graceful movement Bailey bet he wouldn't have been able to do a few weeks ago.

Her chest squeezed. Was it really just such a short time they'd known each other?

"Hey Coco, would you mind if I talk to Bails for a moment?"

"How long is this moment, hmm?" Coco put her hand on her hip, her gaze swiveling from Luc to Bailey then back again. "I thought you had parents to see."

"I do. But I also have to see Bails as well. In private."

Coco sighed. "Bails, do you want to speak to him, or come home with me?"

The little kid inside might want to run away, but the adult had to stay. "I'll talk with him."

"Want me to wait?"

Bailey shook her head. "You know these tough hockey players, once they start talking there's no shutting them up."

As expected, Coco laughed, but as she hugged her goodbye, Bailey caught the look of hurt on Luc's face.

Oh. She hadn't meant to do that. She moved to him, held his arm. "I'm sorry."

He lifted a shoulder. "You don't have to stay if you don't want."

"I do want." And she suddenly did. More than icing her sore toe, more than sleep. She wanted to wipe that look of dismay from his eyes, and let him know she cared for him. "But your parents?"

"They can wait. You're more important."

Her shock at his postponing his parents faded in the sweetness of his last three words. She'd sensed that, that she was important to him. Which again showed why they needed to have a real conversation about real things, and clearly define boundaries before their next dance, the Viennese Waltz, blurred things again. If people thought their moves before had chemistry, wait until the most romantic dance of all put them in a spin.

They moved outside and he held her bags in one hand, her waist in the other. She caught how some producers looked at her, the way one of the singers eyed her askance, but nobody said anything. He found a taxi, he mentioned a restaurant, and her heart sank. "Are we going to see your parents?"

"We're speaking to them for five minutes tops, promise." He shot her a look.

She cringed. "I don't know why I said that to Coco before. But I was joking."

"Yeah, well," he sighed, and her heart filled with fresh regret, "so was I. We're talking five hours, not minutes."

"Luc!" She slapped his arm, laughing, and he grinned at her.

"That's what I like to hear. I missed hearing you laugh tonight."

And just like that, the mood in the taxi tilted back to serious again.

"Five minutes, I promise. And I won't ever break my word to you, Bailey."

She nodded. She knew that. They mightn't have known each other long, but she knew he would keep his promises. There was a core of goodness in this man, something her heart yearned for.

He picked up her hand, studying it, like it was made of porcelain, then the taxi slowed and stopped. Luc asked the driver to stay, with her bags, for which he'd get a sizable tip later, and they got out and entered the building.

He spoke to the maître d', and they were immediately shown to a booth.

"Lucas, oh, and Bailey. I'm so glad to see you again! Although you don't look quite so glamorous now, do you?"

"Hello Mrs. Blanchard. Mr. Blanchard."

A volley of French flowed between parents and son, and Bailey recognized certain words, but not enough to follow too closely. She shouldn't be surprised Luc spoke French, he was from Quebec after all, but the French they spoke was different to what she'd picked up while dancing in France. Her gaze dropped to the table, where they'd started their meals, and she wondered why Luc had brought her here.

Then the maître d' returned with two boxes and Luc thanked him, kissed his mom on the cheek and hugged his dad, which seemed reason for her to do likewise, then Luc paid, and they returned to the taxi and her waiting bags, not five minutes later.

"How long was that?" he asked the driver.

"Four minutes, forty-two seconds."

Luc shot her a smirk, and she laughed. "Okay, Mister I Can Do Pithy Conversations With My Parents, where to now?"

"I prefer Mister I Keep My Promises, but okay." He glanced at her. "You need to eat, so do I. So we're going to eat, and talk, and you're going to get your foot seen to."

"But where?"

"You'll see."

A minute later, they'd pulled up out the front of a tall apartment building not too far from Lake Ontario. "Who lives here?"

He grabbed her bags, and steadied her as she exited the vehicle. "My friend Dan Walton and his wife Sarah. They're in Muskoka right now, at his cottage, and I called him and asked if we could stay."

Her stomach tensed. "You don't mean staying here together?"

He keyed in a code, the door opened, and they moved to the elevators and got in. "I've called a doctor who does home visits to come check your toe, then you're either going to Coco's or resting here if the doc says not to move, while I go stay back at the hotel."

"You've called a doctor?"

He shrugged. "You're an athlete. You need your toe to work. And I understand you didn't want the show's producers to know, so this way you get to avoid that, get to avoid people seeing you in public or any weird questions if we were seen going to the hotel together, and we can talk privately, and you can just relax."

Her eyes filled. The elevator's doors opened, but he didn't move, watching her. "Did I do the wrong thing?"

She shook her head. The fact he was so considerate made her heart sore. "You're so sweet."

His lips twitched. "Yeah, that's what they call me on the ice."

She smiled, they exited the elevator, and he escorted her a

short way down the hall. Then he pressed another key code and the door unlocked, and he held it open for her.

"Now where...? There." Luc switched on lights. "There you go."

"Wow."

She glanced around the room. Spacious, decorated with a mix of masculine leather and more feminine touches, like the vase of roses sitting on a side table. A large photograph sat on the mantelpiece showing Dan looking deep into his wife's eyes on their wedding day. Her heart clenched. "I can't believe your friends are doing this for me."

"Dan's a good guy. Sarah's gold, too." He half-smiled. "She's a singer."

"Really? Has she sung anything I'd know?"

"If you know a group called Heartsong Collective, then yeah. She's written songs for them."

"I like their music."

He shrugged. "They play her songs in my church. It's good stuff."

She limped to the window, and looked down as a few lights from other apartments showed. See, there was so much to learn. Like where he went to church. Why hadn't they had that conversation yet?

"Bails, come sit down." He pointed to the dining table where he'd placed their boxes of food. "The doc has messaged that she's on her way, and it'll be easier if you've eaten before."

She nodded, settling at the glass dining table. "What's for dinner?"

"A bit of everything. I wasn't sure what you'd like, so there's everything from pasta to salad and steak and fries and cheese and fruit."

"Where's the salad and fruit?"

"You gotta eat more than rabbit food, okay?"

"Yes, Doc."

"I mean it. Protein is important."

"Fine. Give me some cheese as well."

"And carbs."

"I don't do well with carbs."

He eyed her seriously.

"But I'll have a few mouthfuls, okay?"

He nodded, his smile poking out.

They ate, gratitude filling her as she savored the still-hot meal, and it wasn't long before she'd finished. "I still can't get over you doing this for me."

"Like I said. I care about you, Bailey."

His intense look drew a shiver inside.

Then his phone buzzed, and he answered it. The doctor, judging from Luc's side of the conversation. He pushed his plate away. Glanced at her. "I'll be back. The doc's here."

She nodded, and wondered what else this most strange night might bring.

"Thanks again, Callie."

He shook hands with the petite doctor, Mike Vaughan's sister, another of tonight's surprises. They'd met at the January christening for Mike and Bree's twins, but he hadn't realized she worked at the emergency clinic he'd called. Last he'd heard she was supposed to be moving to Calgary, after working in Germany these past however many years. She and Bailey had had quite the conversation about European places during the examination.

"She needs to be careful not to bump it, which means you need to watch yourself with her, know what I mean?"

He didn't have to be Einstein to know what she meant. In all senses. "She's safe around me. How much do I owe you?"

"A ticket to next week's show?"

"Done." He didn't know if it could be done but he'd make it happen somehow. "Thanks again."

Callie nodded, yawned. "Don't stay up too late."

He nodded, not needing an interpreter to know what that meant, either.

He returned to sit with Bailey on the leather couch, her poor toe now bandaged with a professional's touch. How she'd managed to dance on it at all he didn't know. "How are you doing?"

"Better. That food was so good, and Callie was really nice. I feel so much better now I could almost fall asleep right here."

"You can stay in the guest room, Dan said."

"I could, but it looked like there was some baby stuff in there." Her nose wrinkled. "I might've accidentally found the spare room when I was looking for the bathroom before. Is his wife pregnant?"

"Not that I know." And not a question he was about to ask. He might pride himself on being direct but some things were so personal even he knew not to ask. A woman being pregnant was one of them. Far better to let that fall from the happy couple's mouths. Although, now he thought about it, he could see Dan wanting to start a family soon. He'd always said that. So the fact he hadn't said anything, if there was baby stuff but Sarah wasn't pregnant, meant maybe things hadn't gone the way they'd wanted.

"We should pray for them, huh?"

He studied her, fresh gratefulness for her insight filling his chest. Which only grew when she prayed aloud for God to "bless Dan and Sarah with favor, good health and a family. In Jesus's name, Amen".

"Amen," he echoed gruffly. "Thank you."

Her lips curved, and he knew a blinding desire to kiss her, that made him rear back. Point his face at the floor. Close his eyes and pray for strength. That he'd stay focused on what needed to be said and not expose his heart once and for all.

"So, um, what was it you wanted to say earlier?" she asked.

His gaze lifted. "You. You weren't okay tonight, and I want to know why."

"You know about my toe, and the fact I messed up my routine."

He shook his head. "It was before that. You were worried. And I can't help but feel like you were worried about me."

She blushed.

Okay, so it had been about him. "Have I done something wrong? If I have, you need to say so. But I don't do well without knowing." He sighed. "I'm probably too straightforward at times. Believe it or not I've been accused of being blunt a time or two."

"Really?"

"You're cute when you're sarcastic."

"Only when I'm sarcastic?"

"Yep. The rest of the time you're so pretty it almost makes it hard to look at you."

See? More overshare right there.

Her eyes were so wide, they rivaled the fancy blue drinking glasses he'd found in Dan's kitchen.

"I didn't mean to say that," he mumbled.

"That you think I'm pretty?"

He sighed. He could see potential for this conversation to go way wrong.

She sat up a bit, her foot slipping off the cushion, and he shifted to place it on his lap.

"What are you doing?"

He barely knew. "You need to be careful."

She gestured between them. "We do."

He knew what she meant. And suddenly knew the main reason for her concern. "It *is* me, isn't it?"

She slowly nodded. "Look, I know it's a completely different world to what you're used to, but believe it or not, I'm finding it hard too. I… I haven't danced with a partner like this for years, and it's bringing back memories of how easy it is to get, um, caught up in things, in emotions, that happen simply because we're in each other's company so much. And with all the things that people are saying, it's hard to not start wondering if maybe some of it is, uh, maybe true."

"That I like you."

"Yes," she whispered.

Which meant she probably didn't like him the same way. Which wasn't awkward or anything. All his years of directness sure hadn't prepared him for the depths of discomfort of this kind of conversation. He exhaled, then glanced up at her. "I'm sorry I've made things harder for you."

"It's okay."

"Is it?" he pressed. "I'm serious. If you need me to fake an injury or something, and withdraw from the competition, then I will if that makes it easier for you."

She hunched over, covering her face with her hands.

His heart knotted. "Bails? What is it? What can I do?"

She shook her head. "I know I'm tired, and everything tonight has been such a lot, but it's this constant niceness you keep showing me that I don't know what to do with. I don't know how to cope with you right now."

He was pretty sure the crack of pain inside was akin to what a heart felt like when it broke. He swallowed. Tried to speak. Produced only air. Took a swig of water and forced it past the boulders lining his throat. "I get it." He cleared his throat, praying the wobbly rasp would stay away. "I'm sorry things are awkward. I'll call them tomorrow and say I had an emergency and need to quit." He managed a broken-sounding laugh. "That'll give you time to heal anyway."

"No!"

He peered at her. "No?"

Her fingers dropped down, sliding past her nose, then her lips, in a slow reveal. "You can't quit. We need to dance the next round."

For a moment, his hopes had soared, then they death-spiraled again. "Because you need your five grand."

"No. I mean, yes, I do, but that's not why." She sat forward. Winced. "Oh, I'm so tired I don't even know if this is making sense, but I want you to dance. I want us to dance. It's just... I don't trust myself to dance and not develop feelings for my partner again."

"Again?" He held his breath. Surely "again" meant she felt something for him?

"Okay, I'm just going to say this and hope it makes sense. I'm sure my meds are messing with my brain and I don't know if it will sound right, but bear with me, okay?"

He nodded, unwilling to say anything that might stem the honesty pouring from her.

"When I was dancing ballet in Europe, I had a partner called Mark, and I fell hard for him. But then when I tried to say something he shut me down, and basically called me fat."

His chest heated. "You're not fat. You're perfect." With just enough curves to steal his breath, mess with his senses and intrude into his dreams.

She was shaking her head. "I... I developed an eating disorder because of him."

His breath hitched. He slipped his fingers between hers.

"It was really hard to break free from. It didn't ever get so bad that I needed hospitalization, but I did need therapy. And ultimately I left the professional ballet world because it wasn't healthy for me. I wanted to run a dance school where people came from all walks of life, who could feel good about themselves, regardless of what their body shape was like. I came back from Europe because of that, and, um, some other things, and got back into ballroom, which I'd always loved, and I'd kept in touch with Coco since we first met in our early dance days, and anyway…" She shook her head.

He squeezed her fingers, gently.

"And anyway, it shows how easy I've found it to depend on a guy for how I see myself. And I like you, Luc." She peeked up, met his gaze in one scared yet sacred moment. "I feel like I could *really* like you. And that frightens me, because I can't go down that road again. And you keep being so nice and kind to me, that I don't know how to shut that off and make this just work and not make it personal."

"Are you saying…?" He swallowed. "Are you saying that you like me more than as a friend?"

Her forehead wrinkled as she lifted her long white throat to the ceiling. "I could."

Only could?

Her shoulders slumped. "I actually already do."

Her eyes might be red-rimmed, her nose sure was, but she'd never looked more beautiful than now. "I feel the same way," he confessed.

Her gaze caught his in another of those soul-tugging moments. Then she sighed. "And I shouldn't, because I don't want to have these emotions, especially when there's all this speculation around us. I don't know how to manage this."

"I know what you mean."

Her lips lifted in a half-smile. "So what do we do?"

He knew what he'd like to do. But he'd promised God—and Callie—that he wouldn't. So he'd play this cool. And, actually… "We pray. Ask God for wisdom and direction. If we make it to the final, that's another two weeks away? Three?"

She nodded. "Three."

"So this is a job. We're friends, and if we keep things cool, then when we reach the end, we see if we still feel this way. That way we're not breaking any rules. We'll just be compartmentalizing, like what I have to do on game days."

"Are you saying the next three weeks are like game days?" Her smile flashed. "I like your confidence."

He nodded. He was pretty sure he wouldn't make it to the final, but miracles happened. As did pity votes. "Then when it's over, we explore this. If you still want to."

She pointed a finger at him. "Don't go thinking this is an excuse to bomb the next round."

"Don't you go thinking that either."

She laughed, his favorite sound.

Then she grew serious. "So, uh, what are we going to tell people when they ask?"

"Simple. That we're friends, and we enjoy each other's company, and like hanging out together. And if people want to draw their own conclusions, well, we can't help that, can we?"

"My friend Poppy said we should do something like that, get people wondering, so they vote to keep you, so they can see you in the romantic or sexy dances."

His mouth dried. "There are, um, sexy dances?"

"Some of the Latin dances are a little sexy, yes. But nothing you need to worry about. Or your mom."

"Look, I'm just going to put this out there, that if you need to do some sexy choreography, I'm probably going to be okay with that."

Her lips half-curved. "I'll keep that in mind."

"So that's not this week?"

She shook her head. "This week is the waltz. It's quite romantic, so brace yourself for that."

"But not wussy?"

"Nope. I'm pretty sure I can make you still look strong."

"With more cool lifts?"

"Absolutely."

"Are there cool lifts in the sexy dances?"

"There can be. If you make it that far."

"I'll be making it. Don't you worry."

She nodded, eyeing him. "And you're okay with telling people that we're just friends?"

"One hundred percent. Because we'd just be telling the truth, right?"

"That there's nothing going on."

He dipped his chin, even as his heart beat in anticipation. There was nothing going on.

Yet.

CHAPTER 13

The Viennese Waltz was a dance that was all about the romance. Big dresses, soft movements, twirls and dips, and everything expected by anyone who had ever watched *Beauty and the Beast*. She'd been tempted by that theme, then thought Luc might not appreciate the connotations of that, or that it mightn't be tough enough for him, so she'd requested a song change to something more fitting. But she hoped he'd like it.

Many of the adults who signed up for dance classes came specifically to learn the waltz, usually for a wedding, usually as the bride and groom. She'd taught so many classes over the years that she knew what needed to be done. And Luc was improving. His steps even had some grace to them, and he was nailing the rise and fall. It did help that this was an easier dance than the last two, that the main thing he needed to concentrate on was his frame, keeping his upper body upright and looking as graceful as he could.

It also really helped that they'd had that conversation, that he knew more about her, and she knew more about his thoughts towards her, and that whatever happened with the dancing there was the potential for something exciting in their future.

It put extra bounce in her day, even in a new hired studio in Toronto, even as Bailey admitted to the producers about her toe, even as Ella and the guys filmed their every interaction, poking questions at them to find out the truth about their relationship. The fact that there could be a relationship in three weeks—next week, if this didn't go well—made her smile, and the fact Luc was happy to hang out with her, laughing, talking about anything and everything, like when they waited for their coffee while people took pics on their phones, also seemed to draw them closer. It was like a secret that only they shared. Even if Poppy and Bailey's own family were busy messaging her and asking for the truth about what was going on.

"I can't believe this!" her mother squealed on the phone. "When were you going to tell me about your boyfriend?"

"He's not my boyfriend, Mom."

Yet, Luc mouthed, smirking from across the dining table at Coco's.

She rolled her eyes at him. He'd joined her and Coco for a meal tonight, before she finally watched that movie with him. She'd wondered whether Jason should join them too, had even murmured something along those lines to Coco, but Coco had said that he was learning lines to audition for a Hallmark movie with Ainsley Beckett. She preferred this anyway. Coco loved this film as much as Bailey, and there was something special about introducing her favorite movie to the person who'd fast become one of her favorite people. How funny to think she hadn't known Luc a month ago.

"Well, I want to meet him," her mother continued. "Can we come watch you this weekend?"

"Sure. They have tickets that can be reserved for family members."

Coco nodded. "Be good to see your folks again."

"Coco is here, and she said she's looking forward to seeing you."

"Oh, wonderful! And how is your foot? We've been praying since you sent the prayer request."

In the family group chat. "Thanks, Mom. It's actually been okay today. I kept off it, had to teach the waltz while sitting down mostly." She wasn't sure how that would translate on-screen in Ella's package. "But it really helps that it's an easier dance, and Luc is getting much better at the rise and fall."

"You should tell him he should practice that one-two-three movement wherever he walks this week."

She laughed. Luc looked up, smiling, and she repeated what her mom had said. He winced.

"Yeah, I'm sensing he's pretty eager to do that when he meets some of his hockey guys later this week."

Apparently, his folks weren't the only ones wanting to meet her. Dan and Sarah, and Mike and Bree, were also eager. Along with her parents and Poppy, and Dr. Callie, there should be quite the contingent of supporters in the audience this week.

"Tell him to remember his frame."

"I will." Her mom had worked as a dance instructor back in the day, before retiring to raise her family. She'd been so excited when Bailey's dance dreams had taken her overseas, and had never really understood why Bailey had quit ballet. That was probably because Bailey had never really told her the full story, like she had with Luc. He really had danced past her guard to get that admission from her. After Bailey had quit chasing her ballet dreams, Bailey's dance studio was some compensation for her mom, and now her appearance on national TV was likely up there with Bailey dancing at Covent Garden with The Royal Ballet. If only her grandmother and sister could see her now. Her heart tensed. She wondered what Chrissy would think if she had watched the show. And what her father thought. He'd never been a fan of men with tattoos, and Luc had plenty.

"And we want to meet him."

"You will. And don't worry, I'll send you all the information, okay? If you arrive on Saturday, or even Friday, we'll have on-site rehearsals most of the day, but we could do dinner maybe." If she could juggle that with what Luc had tentatively arranged with his friends. She swallowed a smile. This couple-ness, without officially being a couple, was kind of fun.

"Okay, well, rest up. I suppose you're going to have to actually dance with him soon?"

"The plan is to do that tomorrow. But I'll be taking it easy, don't you worry."

"Throw a few more lifts in there, get him to do the work."

"There will be a few lifts. It'll give his muscles a good workout. Which is good, because he's getting soft."

"Come on," Luc protested, as Coco and her mom laughed.

"Love you, Bails."

"Love you, too, Mom. I'm glad you're coming this weekend."

Luc studied her as she ended the call. "What day do they arrive?"

"I need to figure the tickets out first, then let them know and they'll arrange it from there. But she wants to meet you."

"Sounds like a busy weekend," Coco said, as Bailey gingerly made her way to the living area.

Coco knew their plans as Bailey had deemed it wisest to have her friend privy to the truth about their relationship, especially if she was going to be living in Coco's apartment until Bailey's time in the competition was over. Coco thought it sweet, but also wise, given their contracts. And Bailey didn't mind the fact that Coco could act as a chaperone, not only because it helped aid their story that there was nothing going on—yet—but because having a third party around when they were together was a good reminder to keep this strictly platonic. Which also reminded her…

"Are you ready to watch this movie now?" she asked him.

"So ready." He glanced at where Coco was settling on the couch nearby. "Um, is she...?" he asked softly.

"Watching it too? Yep. It's her favorite as well."

"Oh. Okay. Um, can I hold your hand while we watch this?"

"Would you normally hold hands with a friend of yours while you watched a movie?"

Coco laughed, and got the TV ready.

"Yeah, no."

"I guess that's your answer." She smiled at him, pulled the blanket around herself, and positioned her injured foot on the cushion on top of the coffee table, and slurped her green juice.

"Wow." Luc exhaled heavily. "Did you know she was such a hard taskmaster?" he asked Coco.

"She looks all sweet and nice, but she's a real hard horse's butt, right?"

"I was going to go with Sergeant Bailey, but that's pretty close."

Bailey threw a cushion at him, and he snickered. "Now, I need to let you know that you're not allowed to talk in this movie," she warned him. "It's my favorite, and if you watch it, you'll understand why."

"Mm-hmm. That Sergeant Bailey thing?" Coco said. "It'll really come out if you talk, so just follow orders, Corporal."

"Yes, ma'am."

Coco's big screen filled with the image of red curtains scrolling open, then the gold lettering appeared, as the well-loved music filled the room.

"No way," she thought she heard Luc say.

"Quiet in the back," Coco commanded.

Then the images of dancers appeared, then the exquisite music composed by Strauss continued, and Bailey sighed with happiness. Then smiled as Luc straightened as the beautiful scenes on the screen paused and reverted to mock-documentary style. "Huh?"

Clearly he had never watched a film like this before.

She peeked at Coco, who smiled back. This was a satire, but not everyone understood that in their first viewing, and she loved the fact that the film structure messed with people. She loved so much about this movie, not least the fact that it might be Australian but it resonated with ballroom dancers around the world. And though it had dated a little, so much remained true. Dance culture, ballroom culture, still had relevance beyond the dance world, which was why dance remained a constant on screens, whether in movies or on TV shows like hers.

"I recognize that song," he murmured.

"Are you talking?" Coco asked, eyes still on the screen.

"Nope," Luc said.

The on-screen dancing continued, the love story twisting through scenes not too far removed from her own experience. Her heart clenched in the memory of Mark telling her the dance was "pretend" and not real. The ugly duckling's transformation to beautiful swan was not dissimilar to Luc's own transformation on the dance floor.

She had read that the director had attended ballroom lessons when he was a kid and knew this world well, which was why it felt so authentic, even though it was set a world away. The nature of dance was that many dancers could be international, and she knew that the US version of *Dancing with the Stars* had employed numbers of Australian, English, and European dance pros. Dancers had to make a living one way or another, and while there might be some variations in the language, the language of dance tended to remain the same.

She snuck a peek at Luc, who was frowning at the scene where the paso doble was being taught, the strong man's dance, full of fire and energy.

He peeked at her. "Is this what we're doing?"

"Only if they give it to us."

"Shh!" Coco said.

She smiled at Luc, and he reached across and she held his hand. Maybe friends could do so, after all.

~

"THAT FILM WAS THE WEIRDEST," Luc complained, smiling as Bailey rolled her eyes.

"Just because it didn't have any flying superheroes in it, or blood and gore," she scoffed.

"Which film?" Sarah Walton asked.

They'd booked out a private room of one of Toronto's top restaurants, as it seemed half the Bible study group had gathered to watch him dance in person this weekend. Maybe they were all here because they didn't trust him to make it to next week, but he had a good feeling about this one. He and Bailey had performed the waltz together only a few times thanks to her sore toe, but he knew this performance would be gold. Not just because of her stunning costume—a pale pink gown with sparkly bits in it that caught the light while he was back to wearing a dumb suit—but he knew the lifts would work and look amazing. Especially if he nailed the last one, their most dramatic one yet, which deserved a ten just for sheer audacity.

This week's song was an older one, "Iris", by The Goo Goo Dolls, the rhythm perfect for the three-quarter time he had started to nail. He was confident this would be their highest-scoring dance yet, and secretly hoped they might earn their first seven, or even an eight.

Bailey told Sarah, and Sarah's jaw sagged. "I can't *believe* you don't love that movie. It's one of my favorites too, and not just because I'm Australian. What is wrong with you?"

"He's a guy," said Poppy James, Franklin's youngest sister, rolling her eyes.

"Hey, don't go assuming all guys only do guns and gore,"

Bree said. "I happen to know there are some men seated here who even watch Jane Austen movies."

Luc snickered as Mike groaned. "It was once, babe. And you weren't feeling well at the time."

"I think once counts, am I right, ladies?" Bree winked.

Gladness filled his chest to see Bree back to her perky self, after her illness with her last pregnancy. Apparently this visit to Toronto was one of her and Mike's first real weekends away since the twins' birth.

"For sure." Sarah chuckled, casting a look at her husband.

"Honey, no." Dan shook his head.

"Don't you want people to know what a proud Canadian you are?" Sarah's animation was not dissimilar to Bailey's. "I would think it should be mandatory viewing for everyone in this country."

"Let me guess: you made him watch *Anne of Green Gables*," Bree said.

"The real one, from the 1980s, I hope," Poppy said.

"Of course. And look." Sarah did a hand gesture like a model on a giveaway show. "He even survived."

"How long was that movie?" Luc asked Dan.

Dan held up three fingers, which triggered laughter around the table.

"He's obviously the most committed man here." Sarah smiled at Bree. "Unless your Austen movie was the five-hour BBC production of *Pride and Prejudice*."

Five hours? Just the thought of watching a chick flick for that long was enough to make him bust out in hives.

As the women swapped stories about their favorite films, he took the chance to talk with the guys, while his parents small-talked with Bailey's. The fact they'd all come to support them meant a lot.

"So, let me get this right: you and her are not a thing," Mike said in an undertone.

"Nope." Not yet.

"Did everything work out okay with the doctor?"

Luc nodded. Pointed to Mike's sister. "Meet the doctor."

"Callie? I wondered why she was here," Mike said.

"She was on call, and stepped in—"

"After you stepped on Bailey's foot," Dan said.

"She's still in pain, but she'll be okay. The medics on set at least know now, so that's something."

"I'm glad it worked out okay."

"Amen." Thank goodness things were working out okay. The producers had assured Bailey she didn't need to worry about being fired, either, which had added extra spring to her step. "Thanks so much for letting us use your place." Luc fist-bumped Dan.

"Sarah appreciated the flowers you left there."

"It really helped to have somewhere private to go."

"Private, huh? Is there something I need to know here?" Mike asked.

"Nope." But Luc filled him in anyway. No need to have the man guessing.

Mike nodded. "So, you dance tomorrow, then what, if you get through you're still staying here to rehearse?"

"It's easier than travelling back to Winnipeg. We did that the first weeks and it was really tiring, so we're sticking around here. It's been much easier to get to rehearsals and do some other stuff as well." Like interviews. And make the most of the big smoke and do tourist things while blending into the crowds. With both of them in civilian clothes, unmade-up, they could almost pass as ordinary folk. Well, she couldn't, because Bailey had a sparkly-like quality about her, pretty enough that she often got second glances, even with no makeup on. The fact she liked him still blew his mind.

"And then what?" Dan studied him. "Are you back to hockey training?"

Luc nodded. "They said they're planning to save the official captain announcement until training camp, so if all goes well, I'll be back into peak fitness by then."

"Bree was saying how a lot of these celebrities really shred the kilos with all the dancing they do on these shows." Mike eyed him. "You're looking a little leaner."

"It's insane how much cardio there is in this. After the jive we did last week, I swear I dropped two kilos just doing that."

"You need to be careful then. What's your trainer saying?" Dan asked.

"He said as long as I work on muscle mass and do weights I should be okay. But man, I get so hungry all the time."

"Must be all those lifts you keep boasting about."

Luc grinned. "I know that I might've mocked a few things about dancing and stuff in the past, so don't tell anyone, but I'm really starting to enjoy this."

"Bailey!" Dan waved.

"Don't." Luc dragged his hand down.

"What is it?" Bailey asked.

"Nothing," Luc said. Man, why did everyone have to watch their little interactions, like it was amusing? Seriously, these people needed to get a life or something. He peeked at her dad. He didn't look too amused. He'd seen the way Bailey's straitlaced dad had curled his lip when he'd seen Luc's tatts earlier. Clearly the man hadn't jumped onboard the Luc Blanchard fan train. He sure hoped his own folks weren't making things worse.

Dan shot Luc a smirk then called to Bailey. "Do you think Luc's enjoying dancing now? Enquiring minds want to know."

Her gaze fell on Luc, soft and lovely, warming his heart. "I hope so. Because I would hate to think he's going through all this and hating it."

"Oh, I'm pretty sure the man isn't hating it," her dad said, with a double raised eyebrow lift at Luc.

He swallowed, straightened, conscious he should be making more of an effort with her parents so they'd approve of him. "Look, I don't want anyone to take this the wrong way, but," he sighed, noting Bailey's concern, "I really think I like the waltz the best of all."

There was a new wave of tease and applause, along with a few "Awws" from some of the ladies. But he barely noticed, his heart full of Bailey's soft gaze on his, her smile for him. It was all he could focus on.

Until he heard Poppy's voice murmur, "Just wait until he gets to do the tango."

CHAPTER 14

*M*onday morning Bailey entered the studio and found Ella and the crew waiting. "Oh! Are we late?"

"Nope. We're just early." Ella grinned. "We figured you two might be running a little behind time after celebrating last night."

Bailey smiled up at Luc. "You did so well."

"Two eights, Bails. Two! I was praying for one, but we got two!"

The highlight of last night: when John, the technical judge, had said Luc's rise and fall had looked effortless and her choreography was amazing. Well, that, and when their last lift had worked, ending in the dramatic fish dive used by ballet dancers in everything from *The Nutcracker* to *Sleeping Beauty*, where she ended with her nose mere centimeters from the floor. She was very glad that had worked. That Luc's promise to never let her fall had held true.

"I was so relieved," she admitted. And relieved to see her bank balance had increased substantially this morning. "Especially after barely dancing together last week."

"Well, you looked beautiful. Like you were wearing a pink cloud filled with diamonds. Don't you agree, Luc?"

Bailey glanced at him, catching his proud look. "She always looks beautiful, but yeah, I think that was your best look yet."

Aww. She placed her hand over her heart, but his words touched her. She had thought she looked her nicest, too. "The costume and makeup crew did a fantastic job."

"Right? The way they get those costumes whipped up, and yet they still allow for movement? I've been involved with this production for a few years now, but I'm always impressed. So how is your toe this morning?" Ella asked.

"It's still attached." She kicked off her scuff and showed them, and as expected, they grimaced.

"You're so hard-core," Ella said.

"Really hard-core," Luc agreed.

Gladness heated her chest. It felt good to impress the tough hockey man in this way. She'd felt that same approval when he'd introduced her to his friends on the weekend. She'd enjoyed meeting them and discovering how normal and easygoing they all were, and she'd thought his meeting her family had gone smoothly too. She wasn't sure if he'd won her dad's approval— her father was a little more conservative about full-sleeve tattoos than some—but Luc's forthrightness seemed to win them over. Which still felt weird. Like they were a couple but not quite yet. Still, having knocked out the football player last night, and with a samba to perform this week, they'd see whether they could make it to the following week's final.

"So," she faced Luc, "this week we do the samba."

"Let me guess; this is one of the Latin ones, right?"

"You're so smart!"

"You're so sarcastic," he mocked back, drawing her smile. Then he winked. "Is this one of the sexy ones?"

She winced. She was glad her folks had been here for her beautiful gown ensemble. Dad would have a fit if he saw what the producers had picked out for her to wear this week. It was definitely her most revealing one yet, basically a green and orange rhinestone bikini top and the tiniest skirt that seemed to consist mostly of green feathers. Apparently they wanted her to amp up the sexy moves as well. Awesome. "Look, have you ever seen the scantily-clad women who do the carnival parades in Brazil?"

"Not in person."

"But you know what I mean?" He nodded. "Well, that's like a traditional samba. We're doing a version of that, so think short skirts, lots of hip action and wiggling, tight dance formations. It's pretty technical too."

"Have we got lifts?"

"Not as many as you'd like. Maybe one or two."

"What do I wear?"

"I kind of feel like this needs to be your week for slicked-back hair and for showing off your abs."

He grimaced.

"Look, if we're going to get through to the finals then we need to give the viewers something special. And I'm not above using ab appeal to get some votes."

"You're so shallow."

"Apparently I am."

"I love it."

Her chest constricted, and she turned away, exhaling slowly. He loved it. Not her. It was too soon to talk like that. And he wouldn't say something like that when they were being filmed. Would he?

She sucked down some water, hoping it might pour sense to her brain. "Okay, are you ready to get started?"

"Are you dancing with me, or are you resting that toe?"

She wrinkled her nose. "Look, as much as I would like to demonstrate the steps with you, after yesterday, I think I'm better off resting if that's okay."

"Whatever you need is fine with me."

What she needed was a cold shower, and not just because Toronto's muggy heat was making her sweat when it was barely ten in the morning. How was she supposed to keep her cool when Luc would be wiggling his hips at her all day? Maybe she would be better off standing up so she didn't have to focus on that.

"On second thoughts, let's give it a go here. Now turn to the mirror, and I want you to wiggle."

"Wiggle?"

She nodded. "Pivot from side to side, but let the action come from your hips and not your shoulders."

She swallowed a smile as he tried. "Okay. Not thrusting but shifting. This dance really works the hip flexors, and the back, and your hammies, so you'll likely feel a little sore at the end."

"Awesome."

She chuckled. "Come on. Shake that thing."

"This big butt?"

"You're gonna have to forgive Marco one day."

"One day. Not *to*-day."

"Come on. Back to it. It's time to focus. Let's samba, baby!"

SUNDAY

For a couple who weren't a couple—yet—a samba was not a great dance. She should've tweaked it more, maybe toned down some of the movements to make sure he got it, but despite his impressive abs on show in that open shirt, she could tell they weren't going to score well tonight.

Luc's rhythm was off, and as she grasped his hand and did her-back-to-his-front samba shadow reverse rolls—one of the characteristic movements in this dance—she could sense his timing was behind by a half-beat, like he'd been stunned by her outfit and hadn't quite caught up yet. It was revealing, and she really didn't like how these spangled straps kept trying to slide off her shoulders.

Maybe it was more of a sexy dance than she'd realized. But it wasn't like he hadn't seen her abs before, or that he hadn't touched her bare waist. Maybe he was struggling with some of the moves because they'd admitted to wanting a relationship one day. He'd complained earlier this week in practice when she'd slid her hand to his hip then to his upper thigh. He'd thought that too sexy. She wondered what he'd say if they made it to next week and did the tango as they'd been allocated.

Still, the bounce and intricate rhythms, along with the high energy and performance, were things he needed to nail if they were to get through. He just needed to shift his head, so she could do this high kick as they'd planned. In three, two, one. "Now."

He swerved, and she kicked high as his head shimmied away. She just missed his ear, then she swiveled to face the front to go into a whisk step then a splits lift sequence. He went to grasp her upper arms, missing, grabbing the top of her dress instead, right where the spangles were.

Time slowed, the spangled straps snapping, flinging off like a diamond whip as she completed the movement. No! But the show had to go on, including the last promenade sequence followed by a triple pirouette where she *really* hoped the fashion tape was working. This was a family-friendly show after all. She only had to complete the last spin, move into the last dip, then the jump and dive. *Please Lord, let him catch me!* A half-beat of wrong timing could lead to a bloody nose. She spun, saw his concentration as she jumped, and dived, and he caught her, mere inches from slamming into the floor. She glanced down. Her chest was still covered with fabric. And partly by his fingers. Oh no. That would *definitely* be a bad look. Although it could've been worse. Thank goodness the tape still worked.

The music ended, and he swung her up, hugging her, his face in her neck. "I'm so sorry. I don't know what happened there."

She shook her head. "It's okay. It's over." She hugged him harder. And unless there was a spectacular fail from one of the remaining couples, they'd just danced their last dance.

～

"Luc, darling," Marco sighed and shook his head, "I hate to say this, because last week I was so impressed by your improvement, but tonight, my friend, I really think it showed that it's time to hang up your dancing shoes and get back to your skates."

Luc winced, as his grip on Bailey's hand tightened. He knew he'd failed her, that she wouldn't get her ten thousand bucks for making next week's final. He'd tried, but ever since the wiggling exercise of day one of samba rehearsals he'd struggled. Struggled not to want to take this further. Struggled with wondering if she meant it when her hand had wandered to his hip. Struggled even more when he'd seen her in her costume that left so little to the imagination. He knew she had to choreograph according to the theme, but her movements were so distracting. Of course, it would be so much easier if they were married and she could wiggle like that for him in the privacy of their own home. His heart clenched.

"I don't know where your head was at but it didn't seem to be here tonight. Your musicality was all over the place, you missed your beats, you had poor Bailey trying to carry you along. Hats off to you Bailey, but I think we all know tonight you've reached the end."

Luc winced, catching Bailey's nod and shrug of resignation. Good news: they could be a couple now. Bad news: he'd disappointed her.

"Oh, now, let's not get too hasty," Cynthia said. "I'm prepared to add an extra point simply for the suave slicked-back hair that made you look very handsome. And another point for the shirt-lessness. Thank you very much for that, Luc."

He grimaced. Good to see double standards in ogling wasn't a thing. Still, an extra point meant the humiliation of a spray tan was almost worth it. No way would he ever admit to the guys he'd done *that*.

"And Bailey," Cynthia continued, "I just want to commend you for pushing through, even with that wardrobe malfunction. I know how hard that can be, and I'm glad it didn't get any worse."

So was he. Poor Bails.

"Look, I can appreciate what Bailey was trying to do with that routine," John said, "but I'm afraid I agree with Marco here. There's only so much one can do with a lump of dead wood—"

The crowd booed. Wait. He was talking about Luc?

"—and I fear that Bailey has done her best, but I'm afraid there'll be no more crafting anything from poor Luc."

Bailey hung her head.

"I'm really sorry, Bails."

She nodded, lifting her chin.

Jenna shoved the microphone in their faces. "Have you got anything you'd like to say, Luc?"

He glanced at Bailey. He could tell from the way her smile had no sparkle that she was really disappointed. But it didn't have to be the end. They might be receiving low scores, but there was still the public vote to try and win over.

He picked up Bailey's hand and kissed it. She froze, as if wondering what he was doing. He might be wondering that himself, too, but right now, although he might be going rogue, this felt like the moment to try and win the public support. And if his abs couldn't do it, then he'd do whatever else it took. "I'm pretty sure everybody knows that the fact I'm standing up here at all is all due to Bailey's hard work. She's a rock star, and I love dancing with her, and I'd love the chance to dance one more time. At least to leave you all with a better impression than what I gave tonight."

"Are you saying you've got more moves left in the tank?"

He slapped his chest twice and pointed as he looked straight down the camera. "I've got more moves. And I'd love your vote to show you what I've got."

"That sounds like a plea to stay," Jenna said, to the crowd's cheers. "Well, if you want to see Luc shake that thing with Bailey one more time, viewers you know what you have to do. So when the lines open, make sure you're voting. Okay, let's give it up one more time for Luc Blanchard and Bailey Donovan."

He smiled, waved, and walked off, clutching Bailey's hand as they moved up the stairs to the skybox. She let go, readjusting her top, retying her spangled straps around her neck. "Bails, I'm sorry. I didn't mean to grab you there."

"Like I said back in week one, stuff happens."

But it shouldn't have happened like that. Not on national TV. He could bet what her father would say. He'd likely want to get a gun and shoot him. As for what his teammates would be saying, what they *would* say as soon as he faced them after this… He'd had a few show up unexpectedly tonight. Which was awesome. Not.

They now had to join Peter in the skybox, and he and Bailey pasted on instant grins.

"Luc and Bailey, not the performance you were hoping for, especially when you're so close to finals now."

Luc bent closer to Peter's microphone. "You're right. I'd hate to miss the finals because I messed up. Bailey is amazing, and I'd love you all to see what she's got planned for me for next week's dance."

"Two dances next week, if you get there of course."

Two? Bailey hadn't said anything. He glanced at her quickly.

Judging from her expression that she quickly smoothed into a smile, maybe she hadn't known.

"Alright, well. We've heard the judges' comments. Now it's time to get their scores."

He wrapped his arm around her, hugging her close.

"Five."

"Four."

"Three."

"Thunderbirds are go," he muttered. As would he be. Going, that was.

"Well," Jenna said from down on the dance floor, "that gives a final total of twelve, which puts Luc at the bottom of the leaderboard with only one couple to go."

He hugged her. "I'm really sorry, Bails."

She shook her head, as Peter commiserated. "It's okay."

No, it wasn't. As the camera cut to the break he flashed open his shirt a little more and winked. Cynthia had seemed to like his open shirt. Man, he was shallow.

"You can stop doing that," Bailey murmured.

"What? I'm trying to get the votes."

She looked defeated.

"Bails?"

She descended the stairs to get a drink of water. "Look, I'm sorry the choreography was too hard."

"It wasn't that. It was just a little too sexy." For him to keep things platonic and professional, that is.

She glanced up at him. "I'm really sorry."

"It wasn't you. Well, I suppose it was your choreography, but you were just following what the producers wanted, right?"

She nodded. "My dad won't be happy."

Luc winced. No, he wouldn't. He bet from some angles it might've even looked like Luc had grabbed Bailey's chest. Which he hadn't. Just the top of her top when he'd missed the catch. After he'd accidentally snapped her strap and sent it whipping away. At least he'd still caught her at the end, and she hadn't kissed the floor.

She sighed.

"What?"

"I forgot until Peter mentioned it that in the final each couple is supposed to do two dances. We'd been allocated a contemporary."

"What's that?"

"A freestyle kind of dance, where you can basically pick your own music and moves, which means you can do the ones that showcase your strengths."

Like his lifts. "That sounds fun. So, what's the other one?"

"The tango."

No way. "Is that the really sexy one?"

She nodded.

Man. Now he *really* wanted the votes so they could get through.

"The producers thought a James Bond theme would be fun, which apparently means amping up the appeal for the viewer."

"I like James Bond. Even though the dude always seemed to go through too many women."

"Yeah, well, I think they were wanting me as your Bond girl, which would've meant some moves where my mom might've had to cover my dad's eyes."

"He doesn't like the sexy stuff, huh?"

"I think he struggles seeing his little girl do stuff like that. Ballet wasn't the same as ballroom, in that regard." She sighed. "I have to admit, it's kind of weird being a Christian on this kind of show and trying to be sexy without being *too* sexy if you know what I mean."

Oh, he knew what she meant. Which was why he hadn't coped with her hand on his hip. If they got any sexier next week he might combust on stage. Then the votes would come in. Or there'd be calls to ban him from dancing ever again.

"Let's just wait and see what happens with this last dance."

But he knew Miranda, the country singer, would get through. He'd seen them during rehearsals, during their show-and-tell performance, and he knew they'd be okay. Their quickstep to a Supremes song was fun, although he was really glad to not have to do such a high energy dance again. He probably did need to be careful not to lose much more weight.

He joined the other couples, watching Miranda do her moves, knowing she had a jump that was pretty spectacular, that they'd nailed in every rehearsal. His heart was tight with regret at his failures, and he peeked at Bailey again. Was there some way he and she could keep dancing? Doing this show had opened his eyes to so many things, and he didn't want to leave yet. *Lord? Is there any way—?*

"Oh!"

A collective gasp filled the room, and his gaze jerked back to the floor, where Miranda had just fallen with a resounding smack.

"Ow." He winced, felt Bailey's shudder next to him.

At least he'd never dropped her—and he wasn't even the professional.

The singer was peeled off the floor by her partner, Tim, but the blood made it obvious the dance had to end, and they waited, hoping, praying she'd be okay.

"You guys might still have a chance," Coco murmured from beside them. "Although Miranda may get a big sympathy vote."

Was it wrong to hope she didn't?

They waited as the medics checked Miranda, then pronounced her okay, which drew a big sigh of relief from the studio audience and within the green room. Then the judges' scores were read out, and sure enough, Miranda and Tim had scored three points more than Luc. He sighed. He had no idea whether the judges' votes were worth that much of a difference compared to the public vote, but it would be interesting to see.

The voting lines were opened, and they had a quick touch-up of makeup and Bailey got an emergency re-stitch of her costume, while the production assistants raced around. Then they were called to the stage, the four couples remaining, and he gripped Bailey's hand.

"Our first couple safe tonight, and through to next week's final is Jason and his partner Coco."

No surprises there. He joined the applause for the couple who truly were the best tonight. He fully expected them to win the whole thing.

"Our next couple safe from elimination is… Fiona and Dominic."

That was hardly surprising. The actress was also an influencer with a rabid support base.

"Which leaves our bottom two couples: Luc and Bailey, and Miranda and Tim, who suffered that very unfortunate slip in the last few moments of their routine. Can I have both couples join me down here please."

Luc held Bailey's hand and carefully drew her to stand beside Jenna.

"Luc and Miranda, can I say it's been a real pleasure to have you both join us, and I'm very sorry that tonight we have to say goodbye to one of you." There was a pause, and Jenna looked at her notes, glanced at Luc then at Miranda, then nodded, as the deep tones of the drumroll filled the room. "And now, with the tightest margin we've had in years, the scores have been tallied, the votes have been added in, and I'm very sorry to say, the couple that is leaving us tonight… is…"

Luc hung his head. How he wished…

"—Miranda and Tim!"

Huh?

The crowd erupted. Then Bailey was hugging him, jumping into his arms as she screamed. "We made it!"

"What?"

"We're through to the final!"

They were?

He glanced at the other couple, who weren't looking too hot, and he shook their hands, avoiding kissing Miranda's cheek which he figured was probably still sore from before. Then while Jenna was closing the show, he pulled Bailey into a corner, one arm around her waist, one cradling her head as he bent to kiss her—

Whoa.

He pulled back at the last minute, her eyes wide with shock. "Luc, people are watching."

Oh. Shoot. So they were. He kissed her cheek instead, savoring her nearness, then drew her into a close hug, her body flush against his. And as his hands slid down her back to those tiny feathers near her butt, he could feel how the song they were supposed to dance to before was made for people who hugged like this.

"Ah, excuse me for interrupting."

He broke away, pivoting to see the stage was now filled with reporters. Dang. Who would have seen that? He sure hoped her father hadn't.

"Luc Blanchard. Looks like you and Bailey are really relieved to be getting through to next week's final."

He swallowed. Man, he could do with a cold shower about now. Or maybe a bucketload of ice. He nodded at the ET reporter. "I don't know if I can ever express how grateful I am for people's votes. I know I let Bailey down, and I really want to make it up to her next week."

"Rumor has it that you're hoping it's a sexy dance, am I right?" She winked. "Looks like you were getting some moves in just now. Care to comment, Bailey?"

Bailey grinned, but Luc could tell her smile wasn't really real. "I, um…"

"Yeah, it's true," Luc said.

The reporter's eyes widened.

"I mean about me hoping it's a tango or rumba or something cool like that. Tonight was a bit quick for me, so I'm hoping I can slay with some boss moves next week."

"I see. Care to comment on the other? Are you hoping for some boss moves off the dance floor as well?"

"Look, as we've been saying all week, we've become really good friends and we are enjoying hanging out together. People can read into that what they want. Bailey is a professional and I'm just doing what Bailey wants me to do."

"And do you care to respond to that, Bailey?"

Bailey's smile was tight. "Not at this time, no."

The interviews continued, but his energy was flagging, and so, apparently, was hers. He'd expected his accidental after-show-end move to get some interest, but hadn't expected this much.

"Luc, you seemed so relieved like you wanted to kiss Bailey," the *Toronto Life* female reporter said.

"It's a shock for sure. But like I said before, I know Bailey deserves a shot at showing everyone what she's got. If she can make this hunk of dead wood dance, then she can work miracles for anyone."

"Well, I have to say hunk is right," another reporter said. "Can I hear an 'Amen', ladies? Now, can we be expecting more costumes like this next week?"

"You'll have to wait and see." Luc grinned at the camera.

The interviews went on, then it was time for the postshow party at an upmarket restaurant.

"We don't do this all the time," Coco said, as they walked to the private room. "Only for those couples who make it through to the final."

And he and Bailey were one of them. He felt so giddy he could almost collapse. Somehow, somehow, by God's good grace they'd made it this far. He grabbed Bailey and drew her to an alcove. "Can I say again how grateful I am for you? We're going to the final, Bailey. Are you excited?" He really thought she'd look more excited than this. "You get more money, too, now, don't you?"

She nodded, her gaze not meeting his.

"What's wrong?"

She shook her head.

"No, don't do that thing where you pretend nothing is wrong. I want to know. I need to know. I thought you'd be more excited but you look like I've done something wrong again."

"You tried to kiss me, Luc, on national TV."

"I was excited. And hey, I know going through means we can't kiss yet, but I forgot myself for a moment."

"I know." She placed a hand on his shirt. "I just am a little concerned about how others might see it."

"They might think we're dating, and that's a good thing, right? That's what Poppy suggested, wasn't it? That if they think we are dating, they're more likely to want to vote for us and see us through."

She nodded. "I know that, but it's not the general public I'm concerned about."

"Then who? The producers?"

"My dad."

Oh. Her father. Who had looked at him askance last week. His guts tensed. How was he going to explain the accidental dress grab and almost-kiss to her father?

CHAPTER 15

She'd thought through Luc's comments a thousand times, but still couldn't figure out what she could've done better. And now, she had to create a contemporary routine and a sexy but not *too* sexy tango, and do her best to sell them as a couple, all without making her dad upset.

Her parents had called after last night's performance. And while her mom had been pleased and had understood about the dress mishap and Luc's clumsy moments, her dad, as suspected, had not. She hadn't shared what he said, with either Luc, or with Coco. That he was disappointed in Luc, disappointed in her, hated to see his daughter dressed like that, dancing those moves on national television like that...

And now she didn't know what to do. Coco was no help, she was fully focused on making her own routine as powerful as it could be, which was fair enough. Poppy, too, had her own ideas, considering how it had basically looked like Luc had groped her on TV.

"He didn't," Bailey insisted during their phone call. "He touched my décolletage, not anything lower. Anyway, it was an accident."

"Yeah, he tried to kiss you. We all saw that."

She'd closed her eyes. "Isn't that what you suggested? That we should somehow sell the idea that we are a couple, that that would get votes?"

"I know I said the audience will eat up the idea of a show-mance, but you need to be careful. I don't want to see you ending up hurt," Poppy said.

"But I'm not. We've talked about this. As soon as the show is done, then we're going to go out."

"For real?"

"Yeah. He likes me, Poppy, and I like him."

"But just be careful, okay? Remember what happened last time."

With Mark. When she'd lost herself in trying to please a man.

"He's a Christian, Poppy. He's not going to ask me to do stuff that's inappropriate."

"You and I both know not all Christian guys practice what they preach."

But she knew Luc was different. He'd always been respectful, kept his word.

She shook it off. Told herself to focus. With two dances to perform at the final so she could get her ten grand and clear her debt, they had no time to lose.

Ella and the crew arrived at the studio, and she said hello. Then Luc arrived, dressed in a tight black tee and pants, looking no worse for wear despite their one AM departures from the celebrations at the restaurant. Maybe it was because he'd already had a few sips from one of the coffees he held, before giving her the other to-go cup.

"Hey Bailey. How'd you sleep?"

The gravelly tone in his voice made her wonder what he looked like first thing in the morning. Whether he wore PJs or— Stop! *God, forgive me.* She needed to be careful. This was exactly what had happened before, letting her imagination go where it shouldn't. She took a giant slug of coffee, then started sputtering.

"Hey, don't drink it all at once." He gently patted her on the back. "Are you okay?"

She glanced across. Ella had the boys filming. Of course she did. She straightened. Coughed out the last of it, then forced a smile. *Focus!* "I'm okay now. I was so excited last night I don't think I slept as much as I could, but this is helping." She sipped. "Thanks."

"It's almost as good as Max's at the Coffee Haus in the Peg." He winked, as if aware of this shameless promotion. Max hadn't minded Bailey's leave of absence, nor Luc's plugs, some of which had made it on TV.

"You two getting started anytime soon or have we got time to grab one of those ourselves?" Ella called.

"Nope. We're starting." *Lord, help me focus.*

She clapped her hands. Luc smiled, and her heart fluttered some more. *Stop it!* "Okay, now we're into the final"—the final! —"we have to perform two dances. And those are the contemporary and the tango."

His eyes lit at that last, his lips twisting to a smile that sent a shiver to her bones.

"And that means we need to work extra hard this week to nail both performances. But the good news is the contemporary is pretty open to what we want. Remember, it's about telling a story. Of course, it will need to be guided by the music we pick."

"We get to pick this time?"

"It's more like a choice between two songs chosen for us. So I'm going to leave that to you. The first song is a modern version of 'Wonderful Life' by Smith & Burrows, the second is 'Midnight' by Coldplay."

"I don't mind some Coldplay."

"Well, have a listen to both songs, and you tell me what you can see the songs saying, and how you think we can interpret that in dance."

"You're not choreographing?"

"I have some ideas for both pieces, but I figured you should choose the song you like more, especially as I know you're so worried about looking tough."

He shrugged, but yeah, the little smile there suggested he didn't mind her tease.

"Okay, so here's the first one." She pressed play, gave him her phone.

It was obvious from the way his brow furrowed that he wasn't a huge fan. "The guy is singing about how wonderful life is, but he sounds depressed."

"I think the word you're looking for is moody."

"Yeah, depressed."

He should really talk to her therapist if he didn't know the difference. "I like it, but the decision is yours. So have a listen to the second song here." Coldplay's "Midnight". It had plenty of drama, and would be more accessible to audiences who'd be more familiar with the wash of sound.

"Yeah, definitely this one." Luc handed back her phone.

"Okay. So, for this dance, the most important thing is to tell the story, which means finding a narrative, and from what I've seen in these shows, they often like the celebrity to show a little of their personal history in this kind of dance."

"I don't have a story."

"Everyone has a story."

He shrugged. "I can't think of anything apart from you and me and how we met, and I'm not comfortable sharing my private life like that."

Her heart glowed. This man was trustworthy. "But you could share about the reason you chose this charity."

"You mean my mom getting sick?"

"Maybe more how you found hope in that moment. I don't

in any way want to exploit that, but I think you'll find it resonates with so many people, especially if it's told from your point of view."

He sighed. Glanced at Ella and crew. "If I do this, then I'd like to show how this pointed me to God."

The backs of Bailey's eyes heated, and she swallowed a ball of emotion, as she hugged him. "We can do that." She fanned her face. "Wow, I'm getting all emotional here."

"Luc?" Ella called. "Want to do your to-camera piece about this?"

"Not really." He sighed, glanced at Bailey, who nodded. "But okay."

Bailey listened, hungry to hear details about this crucial time of his life. And as he shared about his mom's unexpected diagnosis, the fear in him that had led him to find hope in God, she inwardly wept for the broken boy inside the tough man, and praised God He used all manner of things to bring people to Himself. She squeezed his hand as his voice grew raspy, and shot him a quick smile when he glanced her way, and prayed that his words would touch hearts.

"And that's why I said yes to this show so I can encourage others who are struggling, to know there's always hope that can be found in God."

"And, cut. Wow, Luc. I think I'm tearing up here, too." Ella said. "That's gold."

"I still want to check with my mom that it's okay to do this."

"Mind if we film and use that too?"

"You can only use any of this if she says it's okay."

As Luc called his mom, Bailey reflected on his story, and how best to demonstrate such a journey through movement. She had some ideas, but hearing his thoughts would make things so much more powerful.

"Thanks, Ma, love you."

Oh, she loved a man who loved his mom.

He glanced at Bailey. "She says hi, too."

"Hi Mrs. Blanchard," she called.

Luc smiled, then shook his head. "No, Ma, she can't talk. We've got rehearsals. I'll call you later." He placed down his phone, and smiled wryly at Ella. "You got your yes."

"Fabulous!"

Bailey studied him. "Are you okay? Do you need a moment?"

He rubbed a hand over his face, through his hair. "I did not expect that this morning."

"Welcome to the world of dance where anything can happen."

"Nice line, Bailey," Ella said.

Bailey glanced across, and sure enough, Ben and Tony were still filming.

Luc's lips curved then he pushed his shoulders back. "So, now you know my story. What's next?"

Okay, back to business. "Well, seeing this is the final, I figure we should incorporate some of your best moves, and because it's quite emotional, I figure we might even try some ballet moves."

"We're doing ballet?"

"You want to look tough, right? Ballet dancers are among the toughest."

"What'll I be wearing?"

"Not a tutu, so don't worry."

He wiped his brow.

"Probably an open shirt again."

"Woot!" called Ella.

"So shallow," Luc murmured, his lips flicked up in resignation.

"Now, contemporary is all about capturing the emotion, trying to show what the song inspires within and showing that physically. Have you looked at the words of this song?"

"Not really."

She opened her phone. Showed the lyrics. "See, it's about finding hope in the darkness, leaving a light on, being a light to someone else. Which is perfect for your story."

He nodded. "Like you are to me."

Her heart caught. "Or like God can be for us."

"Yeah, I like that. But how do we show that in dance?"

"You'll see."

THEY WORKED ALL DAY. She figured spending today learning this until he'd nailed it would give room for working on the far more technical tango tomorrow. And she was asking a lot from him, asking him to dig deep and find the emotions, to be vulnerable. It helped that he was already a little familiar with the music, could see how it could translate to movement that would be fluid and lead to a lift at the end where she pointed her toes—they'd both have bare feet— as he held her high, her gauzy cream skirt flowing down. Thank God her toe had healed so quickly. This routine was probably leaning more towards ballet than contemporary, but she was glad to have this chance to show him what this emotional part of dance involved. With the lighting she'd suggest—dark at the start, with spots, then a gradual lightening of the stage as they reached for the "star" and the heavens—it would look powerful and effective.

"Now, at the end. I think you should see if you can manage that with one arm."

He flexed. "I've got this, babe."

"We'll see."

He smiled, a smile that quickly faded when she told him where to place his hand.

"You want me to put my hand where?"

"It's a body, Luc. We've gone through this before. I've had guys lift me there before. Put your hand there, then lift me up. If you can," she added with sassy tease.

Okay, then. He clasped her high in her inner thigh, and hoisted her in a wobbly move.

"Yeah, not perfect. Try again."

After a few more attempts they put that with the prior choreography, then, when that flowed, added it into the whole. The end effect in the mirror was strong and powerful, the reach to the heavens something she hoped all those watching would recognize as a stretch to God, the ultimate light and hope. She'd pray so, anyway.

They ran through the routine several more times, each time seeing it become more smooth and polished. By dinnertime that night she was confident he'd have it. Which meant that they could work on their tango tomorrow. She shivered.

"You okay there, Bailey?"

He was always so solicitous. "Yeah, just thinking through the routine. We've almost got it."

"Want to run through it one more time?" Ella and the crew had already left.

"Are you sure your muscles can take it?" She might've gone overboard with the lifts with this routine.

"I hear a challenge."

"I just don't want you to suffer an injury."

"Let's go one more time. Then we get to tango tomorrow, right?"

She swallowed. "One more time."

She moved to lie on the floor. He was positioned just above her, braced in a plank pose, an inch lower and they'd be touching, and the music was cued. This song, like all the others, was edited to be shorter than normal, although because it was the final the song would go longer than the usual ninety seconds.

She stared up at him, his eyes on hers, sharing breath, even as they both held ruthlessly still. The music began, and they rolled in opposite directions to upright positions, reaching in synchronized movements for the star that was their prop, then she straddled over his back in the first lift, then slid through his legs before he gripped her hands and took her into a spin. As the song's ooh-aahs began, Luc held her up in a jackknife lift then hoisted her into a straddle press, before they mirrored each other in a series of steps that brought them together then apart. Luc held her in a starfish spin, then a ballet-like attitude as she leaped and stretched in each movement trying to demonstrate the progression from despair to the hope found from reaching for the light. The routine finished with his one-arm lift as she arched above, leg outstretched, one arm behind, the other reaching forward, parallel with his, toward the light above.

By the time they finished, she was puffing, as was he. "What did you think, boss?"

"That was beautiful."

He drew closer, his hand slipping to her waist, but she couldn't go there, not even for a simple hug. It was getting late, and the tango she'd prepared, as per the "make it sexy" instructions from the producers, would be enough challenge for her self-control this week.

He pulled away. "Is everything okay?"

She nodded, avoiding his gaze. "I just have a lot to think about."

"Yeah, two dances. But this one was good, right?"

"You were great. No, there's no need to worry. I think if we do it once or twice a day until rehearsals, we'll have it sorted."

"And we're going to do the tango the rest of the time?" He smiled. "Call me crazy, but I've heard it takes two to tango."

She slapped his chest lightly, pushing him away. "Don't go getting ideas. This is a family-friendly show, remember?"

"Can you tell me what the music is? That way I can listen to it."

"Sure. We had the option of a traditional piece, but knowing how insecure you are," she smiled teasingly, "I thought maybe we'd go with my ultimate favorite song to choreograph to.

'Black and Gold' by Sam Sparro has a great groove, and I love the meaning behind the song. At first it sounds like a piece about evolution, but I read that the guy who wrote it was the son of a church minister, and he grew up as a Christian. So what he's actually saying is if God isn't there, then life is all just a bunch of matter, that life is meaningless. So while our theme is James Bond, this music will still point to God." Even if some of the moves might not. Oh well.

"That sounds great. I can't wait."

"You'll have to. Until tomorrow."

"Bring it on."

WHEN HE'D ASKED her to bring it on yesterday, he hadn't actually realized just what she'd be bringing. And while the music might point to God, he wasn't feeling saintly as she slid her hands down him while standing behind. According to the production notes, he'd be wearing a James Bond-like suit, while she was wearing a gold dress as his Bond girl. She'd slide her hands down his front in time to the music, then spin under his leg while he'd pretend to look for her, and she'd arch away. His search for his Bond girl was another hint at man's search for God, although he wasn't sure how clear that would be in this dance.

After that, they'd then start the proper tango sequence, legs in and out in precise movements. Already in practice he'd accidentally kicked her once, and she'd trodden on his toe when he hadn't moved as quickly as he should. And while he was filled with regret at kicking her, she'd waved it off, reminding him their bodies were but tools of the trade. At least he hadn't stepped on her toe again, which seemed to be better. And at least in this routine they were wearing shoes.

Their moves echoed some of the words, with movements

that suggested swimming and walking, stars and more. Bailey's tango included some fun lifts, and she kept reminding him that the tango was all about looking strong, confident, with sharp angles and a sense of strength and fight for dominance. He enjoyed watching various examples of other performances, and could understand why people thought this dance was sexy. He just hoped her dad wouldn't be too concerned. He seemed way more conservative than most Christians he'd met.

Whatever. Luc enjoyed their dance, even though there was something bittersweet knowing this was the last dance he'd be doing with her. His favorite part of their routine was near the end, when she'd leap backwards into his arms, he'd catch her, then spin her around to finish with her facing him with their hands clasped high above their heads, his face tilted until they touched noses. James Bond hadn't dominated his girl; they were partners, equal. He understood the story being told now, but was sorely tempted to turn the nose touch into something more. But he couldn't. Not with Ella and her posse standing guard. He'd just have to wait until Sunday.

They finally finished, and Ella and the crew left, and he took another drink. "Did you want to rehearse the contemporary again?"

"Oh, good idea. Yes, we should."

"Want to get something to eat first?"

Her nose wrinkled. "I think I'd rather eat after. I don't like dancing on a full stomach."

She had zero stomach to begin with, her abs more impressive than his. For a moment he wondered how much her previous eating disorder had affected her, whether it still did, but he'd seen her eat food. He should probably talk with her and to her therapist and see how he could support her. Ballet wasn't the only sport where athletes abused their bodies, which was why he'd made it his personal mission to make sure she ate well. After all, she had to keep her strength up. "Grab a snack then, and we'll do the dance, then I'll take you out for dinner."

"Okay."

It was fun switching up the intensity of the tango with the more languid movements of the contemporary. To feel almost effortless as they worked to create poetry with their bodies working together. At least, that's what it seemed like to him. Bailey was still noticing details, finding things to fine-tune. She wondered aloud whether the starting sequence was too much for a family-friendly show, and he'd assured her it was fine.

"It's not like we're rolling across the floor in each other's arms."

Her eyes widened, and part of him was tempted to ask her to tweak the dance and include that. But she was already conscious of their nearness. Just as he was.

"I think my dad would have a heart attack if that happened."

"Is he really that concerned?"

Her gaze left his. "Let's just say he had some friends contact him about the samba, and when I spoke to him, he was not amused."

Luc winced. "I'm sorry. Did you explain the dress thing was an accident?"

"Of course I did, but my father has always been a little funny about things like that. My costume probably didn't help either."

"It sounds like this week's costumes will be more tame." She had a white floaty number for Midnight, and a gold slinky dress with a thigh-high split for the other.

"At least there's less chance of a wardrobe malfunction." She winced. "Did I tell you the wardrobe assistants were so apologetic?"

No, she hadn't. There were a few secrets this woman kept. But that was part of his reasoning in taking her out for dinner. He loved everything that he knew so far, and wanted to get to know more about this beautiful woman who fascinated him. It seemed weird to think there was a time not so long ago when he hadn't known her at all.

After a few more tweaks they completed the rehearsal, then took a cab to a quiet restaurant Dan had mentioned as having good seafood. But Luc hadn't shared his plans with anyone. He wanted now to be between them, without observers. And just like other times when they'd gone out in their hoodies, nobody recognized him or her.

Which meant they could relax. Could laugh and smile, and he could stare across the candle and drink in her beautiful eyes. They might not have kissed yet, but it would be soon. Like, maybe Sunday. The second the show finished.

He broke the connection, glancing down at his plate of seafood ravioli. He'd normally be bulking up at this time of year, getting in the reserves needed before the hockey season began. Despite what Luc had said to Dan a week or so ago, he didn't think his trainer would be too impressed by how much Luc was shredding. Next week he'd go back to Winnipeg, back to real life, and this would be over. His stomach tightened. How could he lose this?

"Luc? Are you okay?"

He loved her sweet concern. Loved how she always looked out for others. Loved her bright and enthusiastic joy and playfulness. Loved that she loved God. In every way they seemed a great match. And he was itching to get to Sunday night—after the final performance—and finally show her all that lived in his heart.

"What are you thinking about?"

"You." His gaze lowered to her mouth then up again. "Wondering what we'll do when this show is done."

She nodded. "I can't believe that this time next week we'll be back at home."

"And figuring out how we'll make this work."

She bit her lip. "How *are* we going to make this work?"

"Like this," he said. "Spending time together. You still promised to come to one of my games, remember?"

"Only one," she teased.

"The first of many."

She smiled. "We'll see."

Oh, he loved this sweet tease of hers. Loved her smile, and the way it seemed to light sparkles in her eyes. "You're so beautiful," he blurted.

"Luc."

"What?"

"Why did you have to say that here?"

"Where would you prefer me to say it?"

She studied him, a smile tweaking her lips, and he exhaled heavily. It still seemed amazing that someone like her seemed to enjoy hanging out with him. And though it might make him sound egotistical, he really wanted to know why.

"One day, very soon, like maybe Sunday, I'm going to tell you, and the rest of the world, exactly how I feel."

Her smile widened. "And how is that?"

"Uh-uh. Don't go getting ahead of things now. You'll have to wait for Sunday."

"Can't wait."

He exhaled heavily again. Oh, this was going to be a very long few days.

CHAPTER 16

Sunday

It was time for the final show. Around her all the noise and activity continued, echoing the tumult within. She had to be the professional that others thought she was, to focus, to get in the zone. First, she had the pro dance opener, a longer, more elaborate effort than usual, as it was the last for the season, so they'd have to give the audience something to remember. Fiona would dance first, then Bailey would dance the contemporary with Luc, followed by Coco, Fiona's second dance, then Bailey and Luc would have their tango. She glanced around, wondering where Luc was. She might be the pro, but her nerves calmed when he was around, like his faith and bigness could scare off any foes.

She stretched, and rose, almost meeting Miguel's foot as he did his own pirouette.

"Sorry. Didn't see you there," he muttered.

Her words to him from three weeks ago. Good to see the pro didn't hold grudges. "No problem." On her side at least. Coco had said the man was vindictive, and she'd noticed he wasn't as obliging as he'd been in those first couple of weeks.

She shifted away. Miguel wasn't partnered with her in the pro dance at all tonight, and she saw no reason to stay near him now. She moved closer to where Coco was warming up. Everyone was tipping Coco and her famous actor partner to win, which was totally deserved. Jason and Coco had been consistent all season, unlike her and Luc, with their rises and falls. A hysterical giggle burst out, and she forced herself to focus.

"What's so funny?" Coco asked, her knees flat on the floor in a butterfly stretch.

"I was just thinking about this season, about Luc's rises and falls these past weeks."

Coco snickered. "The man is certainly a surprise package. Bet you're hoping he finishes on a rise tonight, huh?"

She nodded, sucking down water.

"So what's next after this?"

"We go back home. He's got hockey, I've got the dance studio to run."

"I know that. But I mean with the two of you." Those last three words she said in a lowered voice.

The two of you. What *would* happen once they were back in the real world? "I don't know. I guess we figure out if this has enough legs to stand, or whether this was just a..." She shrugged.

"Office romance?"

Bailey winced. "That sounds so corny."

"You know it's not the first time that's happened. That's why you're here after all."

Because of the married celebrity who'd had a fling with his equally married dance partner.

"Look, I hope for your sake you can keep it going. He does seem to really be into you. And I don't know if you have noticed, but he never looks at any other woman apart from you. It doesn't matter what she's wearing, he's a gentleman in that way. But when he looks at you it's with this mix of hunger and adoration."

Her insides tensed. She'd seen that look too. Which made her wonder just how deep his feelings ran.

"You need to figure out what you are going to do," Coco said, "because I think you'll find that the producers will want you back again next year."

"Really?"

"Uh-huh. They want dancers that the audience can connect with, and you and Luc have been doing really well with your social media posts and promoting the show. And I think that between that and the fact you're a newbie who has taken your celeb to the final in your first year, they're gonna be really impressed and want you back again."

"I hadn't really thought beyond this season."

Coco did another stretch. "Well, you should. I know you have your studio, and you could still keep that open, like lots of the other dancers here do. This show doesn't pay all the bills."

"I'll definitely think about it if they ask."

Coco shrugged. "You could live with me again next year, if you're not living with him by then."

"You mean Luc? I wouldn't live with him. We... no. We're, um, Christians, and don't do that."

"Wow. So all those hot routines are the product of your fevered imagination, then, huh?"

"The producers wanted me to spice things up. So I've tried."

But judging from the way Coco was looking at her, maybe Bailey had tried too hard.

"Has it been too much?"

"Hey, don't sweat it," Coco assured. "You've had your moments, but your dances and outfits have been more modest than most."

Like Coco's own. But somehow, Bailey wasn't sure this would reassure her father who'd be watching tonight's performance from the studio audience, along with Luc's parents and his friends and teammates. The nerves rolling through her stomach trebled.

"Bails."

She peeked over her shoulder, saw Luc beckon to her. She jumped up and hugged him. Then leaned back. "Oh, I like this." She stroked his white shirt, opened ready for their introduction.

"I like this." He eyed her appreciatively, the silver dress the same as from the opening promotions all those weeks ago.

"You're going to be amazing."

"So are you."

He stroked her cheek, and she was tempted to lean into his hand, but already the sounds of movement and noise from the crowd outside suggested she needed to get ready.

"I better go."

"Praying for you," he murmured, before pressing a kiss to her palm.

She pressed her hand to her heart, saw his smile widen, then he waved goodbye as an assistant asked what he was doing here.

Okay, refocus. But that moment of seeing him had helped ground her. She just had to get through this number, then the next, and the one after that, and then this would be over.

"Okay everyone. Take your places."

She was partnered with Tim, who had been Miranda's pro partner before they had been voted out. "Ready?"

She nodded. This opener was high energy, with everything from cha-cha to salsa and disco, and she knew she had to bring the vivacious personality viewers liked, such as full hair tosses and looking into the camera, winking and pointing at the viewers at home, so that they'd be reminded to vote for Luc and her.

They danced until the music ended, held their pose for three seconds as scripted, then she was released to find Luc who was standing at the top of the stage. She joined him as he was introduced, doing a twirl then leaning into him as the cheers filled the audience. She could see his family, and hers, and a few more of his friends. Her smile broadened. Dad couldn't complain about any of that. Yet.

She hitched her smile up higher, then she and Luc were released to go change for their first number. They were dancing second for both dances, and tonight's important final voting would occur while the already-eliminated couples had their chance to strut their favorite dances one more time. The dances were longer, too, around the two to two-and-a-half minutes mark, allowing for more time between each set for costume and makeup and styling.

A short time later, she was dressed in her soft, ethereal-looking ensemble for "Midnight". Then she found Luc backstage, who had shed his other shirt for this open number that held its own silver-strewn sparkle. "Are you ready?"

He nodded. She moved to join the others, but he stayed her by holding her hand. "But hey, before we go out, I think we need to pray."

Oh, he was a good man. "Yes, please."

"Hey Lord," Luc said aloud, "Thanks that You are with us, help us do our best. For Your sake. Amen."

"Amen." She hugged him, and caught Miguel's sneer from across the room.

Whatever. God was with them. And this next moment was about showing all the viewers that there was light and hope to be found by reaching up to find God.

ONE DANCE DOWN. The tango to go.

Luc's nerves might have made their presence felt this morning, but since his to-camera piece about his mom and finding hope in God—Ella hadn't left that out—he'd felt peace fall. This dance wasn't really about him, after all. Then they'd gotten the contemporary done, and received such glowing reports from the judges, and equal top scores—including tens from Cynthia and Marco, with the judges enthusing about everything from his emotional connection to his improvement and Bailey's ballerina form—that he really settled into the night.

Now he had the tango, which was probably his favorite dance he'd done, the one in which he felt most comfortable, and his last chance to really be the character he'd been persuaded to play by his team's management all those weeks ago. The man whose slick moves transcended the ice.

He squeezed Bailey's hand, and she smiled up at him, her gold dress slinky but not too revealing, her hair pulled back in a tight bun in a huge contrast to the previous dance where it had been all loose.

She looked serious, ready for business, and he knew his sharp suit—designed so he could still move with ease—made him look fierce too.

"Are you ready?" the assistant asked, as the cheering suggested Fiona's performance was now done.

Bailey looked up at him, and he nodded, kissing her hand. "Let's go slay."

She laughed, and his heart eased. "James Bond, eat your heart out."

He grinned, and they moved into position. During this week's camera blocking rehearsal, they'd tweaked things so they'd start on the platform, giving viewers better access to seeing Bailey's initial moves. It meant a few adjustments to the stage, including a runway over the steps so they could tango their way down, but they'd managed in rehearsals just fine. Besides, nothing was going to wreck this. He had the same feeling about this as when he entered the zone or state of flow in hockey when he sensed where other players were and just knew his team were about to score. This tango would go well.

"Okay."

Jenna was talking to the audience, and they smiled and waved at the camera as their week's rehearsal package was played. He'd already had his little "I can't believe I'm in the final" promotional video played, and he knew this package would go a little longer, showcasing his ineptness at the beginning and building to some of his better moments on the dance floor. And considering all the interest in them, all the questions about their relationship status, he knew people would be analyzing this for clues about whether this was a "showmance" as he'd heard it called, or something more genuine. Well, he hoped there wouldn't be any more questions after tonight.

"Ready?"

He nodded, tugging his dinner jacket down, as Bailey moved behind him. Then they were announced again to more cheering, and he waited, his heart thudding at the hush, before the opening electronic beats of their music grew louder through the studio.

He closed his eyes, then the first synthesizer sound saw her hands cover his eyes, before they slid down to his face to his chest in time with the broken chord. He opened his eyes, looked to the right then the left, which was when she slipped around on his right hip and slid through his legs before reappearing on his left. Then she arched away as he reached for her, before he grabbed her hand and spun her up into the tango hold as the words began.

They traversed the platform onto the main dance floor, their movements crisp, sure, as precise as when they'd practiced this routine the fifty times or so this week. A shimmy to represent a fish, the high kicks for walking, then some lifts and spins that were the crowd-pleasers, before they came together again in a similar move to the samba, their arms held straight up, her back to his front as they rotated their hips side to side. He didn't care who saw them. This moment was about pleasing Bailey and getting everything right. They might not win—anyone could see Coco and Jason were the best—but Luc was giving everything.

He pulled her into another lift, drawing up her knee behind his neck which turned into a cartwheel across his back, before she hooked her knee over his and slid down. They stepped around, one more lift, another shimmy, then another progression of tango movements Bailey had insisted were necessary, then the last spin, like their ice-dancer move on the ice weeks ago. He drew her up and lifted her onto his hip, before she slid down as the words "next to you" were sung, one hand on his chest, the other holding his other hand as he dipped her low, then the last bar saw her snap upright again with their arms held high, her nose touching his, their breath heaving in and out, her lips a touch away.

The crowd was screaming, he knew he'd hit every beat, and as Bailey's eyes shone up at him, he lowered a fraction further and touched her lips with his, grazing then possessing them more fully in the sweetest moment of his life. She was softness, sweetness, a delicious concoction he only wanted to drink more of.

Until he felt her shock, then lowered their hands so he could hold her more closely, ending the kiss as the noise from the crowd said they'd finally seen what they'd come to see.

"Luc!" Her eyes were so wide.

"Bails." He kissed her cheek and hugged her, picking her up off the floor and twirling with her, hugging her close to his heart, wishing he could keep her there forever.

She pulled from his grasp, sliding to the floor. Then stroked his cheek and smiled up at him. "That was perfect."

His steps or the kiss?

But there was no time to find out as Jenna was gesturing

them near, fanning herself. "Oh my goodness you two. Is it getting hot in here or what?"

The audience cheered. He didn't think the kiss was that hot. He'd save that type of kiss for when Bailey was expecting one. Which he hoped would be as soon as they left here tonight. If not before. But now it didn't matter that their relationship was out in the open.

"Wow, Luc Blanchard, when you said you had moves, we weren't expecting that, were we? But maybe we were hoping, am I right?" she asked the crowd.

The audience whooped more loudly.

Sweat trickled down his back. He hoped Bailey was okay. She might be smiling big, but he'd seen how good she was at pretending.

"So, let's throw to the judges. Marco, what do you think about that performance?"

"If we're talking about the kiss then I'd say it's about time! Bailey is one hot tamale and Luc, you might be the man of ice but you set this floor on fire tonight! Your best dance ever."

Really? He smiled as Bailey wrapped her arms around him and squeezed. He kissed her forehead.

"And you know I don't say that lightly. Not when your contemporary was so beautiful before. Wow. When I think back to your very first routine and now seeing what you've accomplished tonight, I applaud you Luc, and especially you Bailey. It's wonderful to see what this show can do."

He glanced down at Bailey, at her shining eyes sparkling up at him. Sure was.

"I have to agree with Marco," Cynthia said. "A really strong and sexy routine, and I totally bought the theme of James Bond seeking his golden Bond girl. And while I'm not always a fan of PDA on this show, I'd say you definitely knew when to bring it."

But that hadn't been why he'd kissed her. He'd done that spontaneously. He hoped Bailey knew that. He'd hate her to think he'd cheapen their first kiss out of some crass need for more votes. He hugged her tighter as Jenna poked the microphone in his face.

"Was that a rehearsed kiss?"

"Not at all." A man couldn't rehearse perfection.

Jenna nudged Bailey. "So, you had a surprise tonight?"

"Yes."

"Well, I guess this makes you an official couple. Let's hear what our final judge has to say about your final dance in this year's competition. Over to you, John."

He leaned back in his chair, not looking at his notes. "I could say a lot of things, like how good it was to see you nailed the technical elements, to say Bailey I have really loved your choreography this season and I hope you'll be coming back next year —"

Whoa. That was a possibility? She hadn't mentioned that to him.

"—to say that was everything I want to see when I see a tango, so well done, you two. But I'm not gonna say that. I'm just going to say this. That you, Luc, are what this show is all about. I know I've been hard on you in the past and called you a lump of wood and worse, but the transformation we've seen from someone who said he didn't dance to what we saw here tonight is exactly what dancing shows like *Dance Off Canada* are all about. So well done to you, well done to you Bailey, and whatever this is between you two," he waved a hand at them, "good luck with that too. But I hope you will be doing more dancing in your future, Luc. You need to. You're that good."

Wow. Words he'd never thought he'd hear John say.

"Any final words you wish to share, Luc?" Jenna asked.

"I'm a little overwhelmed, to be honest. And like I have said a million times before, I couldn't have done this without Bailey." He held up her hands. "She is the best. I'm so impressed by the talent and compassion and beauty of this woman. And I'm so, so grateful that I've had this chance to be with her and get to know her and get to know how good dancing is."

"Hear that everyone? You heard it here first, Luc Blanchard is a fan of dance!" Jenna winked. "And a fan of Bailey, too. Sorry ladies, looks like this man is off the market. And now you two had better skedaddle on up to the skybox and join the others up there."

He exhaled, pressing a kiss to Bailey's hand, then pointed and waved at his family and friends as they hurried past them to the stairs. Then they were swooped on by Fiona and the other previously eliminated contestants, save for Coco and Jason, who were dancing last, as Peter struggled to push past and thrust the microphone in their face.

"Wow, Luc, Bailey, that was some performance, eh? Way to finish on a high."

"I'm so glad we got the chance to dance one last time," Luc said. "I told you I had moves left in me."

"You certainly did. That kiss at the end? Call the fire brigade. Whew!"

That wasn't what he'd meant, but okay.

"Are you ready for the judges' scores?"

"Bring it." He smiled down at Bailey. It didn't matter what the scores were. He'd won no matter what. And judging from the way she gazed back up at him, she felt the same.

He suddenly had an almost overwhelming urge to steal her away for some privacy so they could continue what he'd started before.

"And now, for our judges' scores." Jenna pivoted to face the judges.

"Ten."

"Ten."

"Ten."

Three tens? Bailey jumped up in his arms, and he squeezed

her tight, swooping in for another kiss, before realizing Peter's microphone was there, and they were still on TV.

"Sorry to interrupt, you two, but you must be happy with those scores."

"I never dreamed I'd get a ten from John," Luc admitted.

"Anything you'd like to say, Bailey?"

"I'm really grateful for this whole experience, and have been very blessed to have Luc as my partner. Thank you everyone who has been voting for us. You're the best!"

"Oh, I think they're thinking you guys are pretty close to that. But we still have one more dance to go. Can Jason and Coco bring a scorcher in their final dance tonight? Stick around and find out."

Luc grinned at the camera, and waved, as the music pumping through the studio got all the contestants vibing. He was happy to simply hold Bailey close and kiss her cheek. He'd done all he could, the rest was up to the public. Not that he cared if they won. As far as he was concerned, they were already winners, this feeling the equivalent of winning Lord Stanley's Cup and the jackpot combined.

She didn't need to win. But she also kind of did. Because winning would mean a guaranteed invitation to next year's show, even if she wasn't sure what all the ramifications of that would mean. Coco had won once before, and said it wasn't the weekly earnings the pros made, but the endorsement opportunities that opened up. Something she'd never had to think about before, back when she was a ballet corps member, or running a little studio in Winnipeg. What would the bank manager say now?

Sweat slicked her palms, and she subtly wiped them on her skirt as she peered out into the audience, spotting Luc's parents sitting next to hers, while Mike and Bree, Poppy and Franklin James, and Franklin's new wife Hannah, and a few of Luc's other friends, sat nearby. Her big smile widened. What would happen if they did win? Would Luc kiss her again? Anticipation made her heart shimmy.

Luc's arm slid around her waist as she wondered again what would happen when they returned to Winnipeg. He'd already mentioned he needed to head straight into prepping for next month's training camp, then he'd start his preseason games at the end of September. The schedule had been released, and she knew he'd be super busy, what with his commitments to work, especially when he was officially announced as their new captain. Was this a short-lived bubble of fun thanks to forced proximity, or would they be able to sustain a real relationship?

Jenna took to the stage again. "Wow, wasn't it great to see all of this year's couples dancing one last time? Let's give it up for all of this year's contestants."

A wave of applause and cheering filled the room.

"And now, the votes have been tallied and we're about to see who is crowned this year's winner of *Dance Off Canada*. Tonight's performances have seen a record number of votes which, remember, makes up half of the points when added to the judges' scores. And now, and this *is* in particular order, can we get a drumroll as we get ready to find out who has come third in this year's *Dance Off Canada* competition."

The booming drums filled the room, as she clutched Luc's hand.

"And in third place, let's give it up for… Fiona and Dominic."

What? Bailey smile-commiserated, her chest growing so tight she might have another wardrobe malfunction. They were still in with a shot at the mirror ball.

She glanced up at Luc. "I'm so proud of you, whatever happens."

He leaned down, and kissed her forehead. "You're my winner, no matter what."

Aww. She wrapped both arms around his waist, and he tucked his chin over her head, as Jenna was passed the envelope.

"And now, in the closest scores we've ever seen, your winner for *Dance Off Canada* is…"

The drumroll grew louder, and seemed to stretch abnormally long, while her breathing slowed until she could hear an echo in each drumbeat.

"...Jason and Coco! Which means Luc and Bailey are runners-up. Congratulations, guys!"

Bailey turned to Coco, kissing both her cheeks before doing the same to Jason, then turning to Luc and hugging him. He picked her up, nuzzling his face in her neck as she shut her eyes and clung to him. He'd never let her fall. And regardless of what happened in their future, she sensed he never would.

The cheering continued behind them, and she knew she had to compose herself and look happy for the crowds at home. And she was. But the competitive spirit inside that had fueled her need to succeed sang a small song of disappointment. Still, it was best to not look that way at least.

She smiled, leaning against Luc's chest as he wrapped both arms around her, as Jason and Coco squealed and gold confetti dropped from the rafters. She peered up, and Luc gazed down at her, his hand catching hers. Then, in a move that would've shocked the week one version of Luc, he was tugging her to the dance floor to join the other couples who were dancing, and they were sashaying around the room, laughing. It really didn't matter that they'd lost. They'd actually won. She'd pushed past so many of her insecurities, as had Luc, and dance was the winner.

Luc spun her, and then she was dancing with Marco, who complimented her, then, in a scene that could've come straight from her favorite movie, the floor was soon filled with other special guests, and she was hugged by the other contestants, then her parents, then Luc's parents.

"Oh, Lucas." His mom pulled him down and kissed both his cheeks. "That dance you dedicated to me was so beautiful. And Bailey." She clasped her tight. "I don't know what to say except thank you."

"You're more than welcome."

Luc blew his mom a kiss, just as he had after the contemporary performance, and they were engulfed by Poppy and his friends.

"I can't believe it!" Poppy screamed over the noise. "You came second! That's incredible."

"Nice job, you two. Loved the meaning of your first dance, and you definitely brought the Bond themes for the second." Franklin introduced Hannah to Bailey. "Remember how this man complained about dancing at our wedding, hon? This all feels so hard to believe."

Hannah nodded. "I loved everything about that. I wish I'd known you before, Bailey, so we could've gained some tips before our wedding back in June."

"It's never too late to start."

"Obviously," a dark blond man said, whom she'd never met in person before but recognized from a long-ago video call. He drew forward a tattooed magenta-haired woman. "I'm Ryan, this is Sylvie. I can't thank you enough for making a liar out of Luc."

"I beg your pardon?"

Mike Vaughan nodded. "For as long as I've known the man he's been allergic to anything that has any degree of romance. Then you come along and boom, he's a changed man."

"Kissing her on national TV!" Ryan high-fived Mike, as Franklin laughed.

Sylvie smiled. "If you two are a couple then brace yourself. This crew is wild."

"And she doesn't know the half of it." Another guy, she half-recognized from the video call from ages ago, shook her hand. "I'm Chris, remember? Thanks for putting a smile on Luc's dial. The whole crew thanks you."

"You're, um, welcome?"

He laughed, and slapped Luc on the back, as she was swallowed up by the "crew".

This crew. His Bible study friends. But did Luc's kiss mean they really were a couple publicly now? She'd love to get a chance to ask him privately, instead of wondering herself as others wondered aloud.

"Hey, congratulations, honey." Her mom again. "You were amazing. And Luc—where is he?" She peered around, then waved as Luc drew near. "Oh, Luc, congratulations. I was just saying how you did so well."

"Thanks, Mrs. Donovan." He nodded to her dad. "Sir."

Her father's smile was small, and she had a horrible suspicion he hadn't liked the dances she'd done. Or Luc's kiss. But there was no time to wonder further, as they were forced to attend interviews, with more reporters shoving microphones in their faces.

"Luc and Bailey. Congratulations." The reporter from ET again. "What a wonderful couple of dances to end your time on the show. Ooh la la! Now Luc, the question everyone at home is dying to know, can you tell us more about that final moment—that kiss!—was it planned?"

An excellent question. Bailey turned to face him.

Luc shrugged, smiled. "Let's just say that I'm an artist. I was in the moment, so I kissed her."

So he hadn't planned it. Okay.

"From everything we've seen in those packages and in those dances, you two share an incredible chemistry, and can't seem to keep your hands off each other. Is there truth to the rumors you two are a couple now?"

"We, ah," he glanced at her. "Maybe. You'll have to see."

"You two would make such a cute couple."

"Thanks."

"Bailey, did you have anything you'd like to say? You've certainly had a memorable first season. Are you hoping for more?"

"That depends on so many factors. It would be nice to have the opportunity to do something like this again, but I don't know if I could have a better partner."

"Oh, you two are so cute! Now Luc, now the show has finished, how would you sum up your experience?"

Luc turned to Bailey. "So much fun. I'm so incredibly grateful to have had this opportunity, to have met this woman. She's the best, and after spending the last six weeks together, I don't know how I'll cope not being with her every day."

"Well, you're both from Winnipeg, so I'm sure you can make that work out. A little easier than if one of you was based here in Toronto, right?"

So true. But what would that mean if she was asked to do a second season?

THE WRAP PARTY went on for longer than some Cup winner celebrations, or so Chris and Diana Thomas said. There might be a lot in this dance world Luc still didn't know about, but dancers sure could throw good parties. But maybe that was because of the company with his friends and family around.

"You were robbed, man." Chris slung an arm around his shoulders. "Robbed. You were the best couple out there tonight. Even the judges agreed."

Half a point. Not that it mattered. He felt like a winner even if the public had voted for the actor.

"They were on fire," Ryan said. "But you were on fire more."

Luc shrugged. "It was all Bailey."

He glanced around, but couldn't see her, the space too full of heaving bodies.

"She's pretty cute." Ryan wrapped an arm around Sylvie.

"Like a peppy cheerleader," Sylvie added. "But a sexy one."

Yeah, that. "It wasn't too much, was it? Everyone keeps going on about it, but I didn't think the routines were too spicy compared to the other couples."

"Look, I think most people understand it's an entertainment show, that what you're doing is not necessarily who you are. Like, you're not strutting around thinking you're James Bond, are you?"

"You clearly don't know the man very well, Sylvie," Ryan said. "He does that all the time."

Luc sighed and shook his head. "I think I liked you more when you had less to say."

Ryan laughed. "See? It's obviously getting under his skin."

He needed to steer this conversation back to where he'd get answers. "So that's a no, then?"

"To being too sexy? You were fine," Ryan assured.

But judging from Bailey's dad's expression as he drew into view, he might not agree. "Luc."

"Sir." He introduced Wayne Donovan to his friends, who seemed to sense the awkwardness here, and soon exited, apart from Ryan, who hooked an eyebrow as if asking if Luc wanted him to stay. Luc shook his head. Whatever Wayne wanted to say was likely something the others definitely didn't need to hear.

"Have you got a moment, Luc?"

"Sure."

Bailey's dad motioned him to a quieter corner. Luc glanced around for Bailey but she remained unseen. Nerves rippled along his veins. What would Wayne say about the fact that Luc had kissed his daughter on national TV? "I, er, hope you enjoyed the show, sir."

Judging from that narrowing of eyes, the man definitely hadn't liked all he'd seen.

"You know that's what this is, right?" Wayne said.

"I'm sorry. I don't follow."

"It's a *show*. It's not real."

"I beg your pardon?"

"You and her. You've spent so much time together doing this dancing show, but you haven't been in the real world. Now you're going to be in the real world and you're going to see that this was nothing more than two people spending too much time too close together."

"Sir, I disa—"

"Let me finish." Wayne sighed. "I know Bailey far better than you, and I know she puts her heart and soul into everything she does. I can't say this to her, but I can to you and will admit I'm disappointed that she chose to wear some of those costumes, and did some of those moves." He shook his head. "My wife tells me that it's only a performance, that it's not real, and both her and Bailey have assured me that you did not manhandle my daughter last week, despite what the cameras, and various friends of mine, said."

"Of course not, sir." Wow. Sounded like the man needed new friends. "I missed the hold, and caught the top of her dress, but that was all. I didn't touch, er, anything else. I promise."

"It didn't look like that."

"Well, sir, like you said. It's a show, not everything you see is real."

"I would hope not. Especially not when you were almost lying on top of her in that first dance tonight, then kissing her at the end of the second like you thought it was real."

Luc pinched his lips together.

"So, is what we saw real?" Wayne pressed. "Let me tell you that you may think it is, but I don't think it'll last. She's twenty-four, Luc."

"Twenty-four?"

"You're what, thirty-one?"

"Next year," he mumbled.

"You might think I'm overprotective, but if you knew what had happened to my girls, you would be too."

"Your girls?"

"Bailey's sister. She married someone like you, and he beat her, and he's now in jail."

Whoa. Why hadn't Bailey ever mentioned that? Maybe he and her weren't as close as he'd thought.

"Perhaps that has made me overprotective," Wayne continued, "but I worry about my girls, and don't want them getting involved with people who will hurt them."

"Sir, I know it's easy to look at my ink and think I'm something that I'm not, but I assure you I'm a good guy."

"Well, you would say that."

"No, I am. I'm a Christian. I can give you my pastor's phone number, and you can check with the guys I do Bible study with. There's quite a few of them here tonight. And I want you to know that I'd never disrespect your daughter."

"Those maneuvers on the dance floor suggested quite the opposite."

Now probably wasn't the time to say Bailey was the one who'd choreographed them. "I plan to keep seeing her once this is done," Luc said. "I'm sorry if you disapprove, and I don't want to do anything that upsets her relationship with you, but I care for her a lot." Cared for? That was such a lame expression for the depth of his feelings, feelings that he thought ran awfully close to love. "She might be only twenty-four, but she is an adult. And she's been making adult decisions—"

Wayne sniffed. Okay, that probably wasn't the best way he could've expressed that.

"—and she's been working so hard. And you know she's doing all of this because she's trying to save her business."

"She is?" Wayne's forehead wrinkled. "Why, what's happened?"

Luc clasped the back of his head. It seemed Bailey was

perhaps a little too good at keeping secrets. Which made him wonder what else she wasn't telling him. Still, her father should know the reason she'd done the show. Maybe he was speaking out of turn, but, "I really think you should talk with her. But let's just say whoever advised her about the financial operations of her studio didn't do a great job. She's been losing money, and had to take this gig to pay her debts."

Wayne's eyes narrowed, and Luc suddenly had a sinking feeling about just who had advised her. "Sir, my father runs a small business advisory company and—"

"So you think that gives you license to advise everyone else, do you?" Wayne crossed his arms.

Uh-oh. Looked like Luc had just scored an own goal. "You should probably talk to her about this."

"Are you now trying to tell me she's acting like this for the money, and not for you?"

His heart stabbed. What if she was? What if her father was right and she was only caught up in the emotions of the moment? Hadn't she admitted she'd done that before? What if, once out in the real world, she realized she didn't want this at all?

Luc swallowed. Cleared his throat. "I can't answer that. Again, that's something you should talk to her about."

"You don't know her, Luc. You might think you do, but you've been in this bubble and have no real clue. And you might think you have feelings for her, but I suspect we both know those feelings won't last. And you'll break her heart, and her mother and I will have to pick up the pieces, just like we had to do with her sister."

Luc shook his head. "I won't hurt her."

"You say that now, but I know you will."

"Dad?"

Luc turned, pushing past his frustration to find a smile for Bailey as she tucked herself close to his side.

"What are you two doing talking over here? Come on, everybody is enjoying themselves and you both look so serious."

"Sorry, Bails." He was sorely tempted to kiss her again, right in front of her dad, just to stake his claim. But that wasn't fair or right or kind, so he let her lead him back to the crowd, offering a nod to Wayne. "Thanks for the chat, sir."

"I'll be watching you, Luc."

His stomach dipped. And no doubt hoping he'd fail.

Before he could get swept into other people's conversations, he had to have an important one with her, so he drew her aside and pivoted to face her.

"Is everything okay with you and my dad?"

"Yeah." It would be. He hoped. He'd pray. "How about you? How are you doing? Is this crazy enough for you yet?"

"It's so amazing. The whole night has been amazing. I'm sure I'll be tired as anything tomorrow, but at least we can sleep on the plane, right?"

He nodded. They'd fly back tomorrow afternoon, then the real fun would begin. Him with prepping for hockey, her back to her studio. And they'd see if Wayne was right and whether this was a bubble or was something real. His heart tensed. "Bails, about before, I just wanted to make sure you were okay about that kiss."

The sunshine in her face faded, and she nibbled her lip. "It took me by surprise, that's all."

"So you didn't mind?" He had to know. Especially after her dad had sown seeds of doubt about whether this could work.

"I don't mind if… if this means we really are a couple now."

"Of course we're a couple."

"Really?"

"One hundred percent."

Joy lit her face, and she jumped into his arms, and he automatically caught her. Then she smiled and leaned close, and her eyelids drifted closed, and her mouth was on his, in an innocent fairytale kiss worthy of that pink dress she'd worn for their waltz. Then her lips firmed, tentatively exploring. He wrapped both arms around her more firmly and let her continue, then kissed her back in a way that would make her feel in no way uncertain about his feelings. Her hands dug into his hair and her lips slowly parted and he was sorely tempted to deepen things, but knew they were too new, and this was hardly the place for that kind of kissing.

He ended the kiss in a series of three pecks and caught his breath, and she leaned her forehead against his, their noses touching. No. Wayne was wrong. This was real, this would last. It had to. He was never not living without this woman in his life. Especially knowing he'd be forever missing out on the best kisses of his life.

"So Bails, does that answer your question?"

Her smile shimmered joy through his soul. "Yes."

He had to kiss her again, then, conscious that with her in his arms like this, her gold dress with its split was probably revealing more than it needed to, he gently lowered her without breaking the kiss in a graceful move worthy of a ten.

She pulled away, sighed, and smiled up at him. "Look who's got all the moves."

"I've had a great teacher."

Bailey laughed, and he smiled at his favorite sound. "Does this mean we're Instagram official now?" she asked.

"Only if we post something to Instagram. Which means we better do that."

She touched her hair which she'd taken out of its tight hold. "Do I look—?"

"Perfect? Of course you do. You look great. Come here." He tucked her close, stuck his phone on selfie mode and snapped a few pictures of them, then asked her to choose. She did, and he sent it to her number. "Let's post it when we're at the airport tomorrow."

"You mean today." She pointed to the clock.

He glanced across the hushed room, to see all eyes on them. Judges, contestants, crew, his friends, hers, his folks and her parents.

And sure enough, Bailey's dad was frowning at him.

CHAPTER 18

Winnipeg
Tuesday

"Oh my gosh, Poppy. This is insane." Bailey leaned back in her chair in the studio's tiny office, the emails she had to respond to numbering in the hundreds. *Hundreds.* She'd already done a quick delete of the obvious spam ones, but there were so many enquiries for dance lessons, from little kids wanting to learn, to adults inspired to return to dance or finally take up lessons as a long-held dream. Overwhelmed didn't begin to cover it. Amid all the lesson enquiries had even been a few sponsorship opportunities from local—and national—businesses, as well as all the comments on the studio's social media platforms. Even her YouTube channel had hit the magic number of subscribers to finally earn money. "I don't know how you've managed these past weeks."

Poppy stretched. "I'm really glad you're back now. I was keeping on top of things before, but it's just been hectic since Sunday night."

So many phone calls. So many interviews. She and Luc had

returned yesterday and since then she'd barely seen him, apart from a bunch of interviews this morning, before he'd had to rush off again. He'd been swallowed up in hockey prep, stuff with his training and his team, and she'd been caught in the maelstrom of the studio, and discussing with Poppy how they were going to go forward now her name—and her studio—had national attention. Even their waiting lists had waiting lists, and trying to juggle all of this, along with the usual business stuff she'd put on hold for the past six weeks, was exhausting.

"What are we going to do?"

Poppy studied her. "I think a lot depends on what you want to do about next season."

Next season. Her heart tensed. Joanne Mascieski had told her on Sunday night that *Dance Off*'s production wanted her back for next year, and possibly a spin-off tour that would take in a bunch of the major cities across Canada and northern US. It was a dream to even be considered for such an opportunity, especially after only one season, but Joanne had told her that Bailey had been the most talked about dance pro this season, and they wanted to capitalize on that while they could. "And you should be doing all you can to make the most of it as well," Joanne had advised.

Coco had agreed. "Come on, it'd be so fun having you dance with me again."

"But the studio—"

"Get Poppy or your mom to run it."

"But Luc—"

"He's an adult. He'll have work he needs to do, so you don't need to factor him into anything."

But part of her felt like she did. And the fact she didn't know how to express this to him, that they'd barely had a chance to talk since Sunday night, made it feel like the conversation was getting bigger than it needed to be. And now she had exposure to this world, she wondered just how much she would cope. She might've given Luc some confidence in his dancing, but he'd also given her confidence in things as well. She'd always wondered if part of the reason she had failed at ballet was because she'd been too soft. She might be competitive, but she wasn't ruthless, and didn't possess the hard edge as so many pros did. And while she considered Coco a good friend, even Coco held an edge that Bailey wasn't sure she ever wanted to possess.

"Bails?" Poppy asked.

"I still don't know. I could only do that if I had someone I could trust to run the studio here."

"What about your mom? She could probably run things okay."

But asking her mom to run things was a bit like returning to live at home. Bailey might be close to twenty-five, but sometimes it felt like her parents still weren't ready to let her go. Which was understandable, considering what had happened to her sister, but sometimes their help felt a little too much like smothering. And after all the debt issues, she also couldn't help but wonder if some of her dad's financial advice hadn't been so sound, after all. And knowing her mom was always inclined to bow to his wishes over hers, such as giving up dancing when Chrissy was born, she didn't think her studio would be as safe as it would be in Poppy's hands.

"Mom hasn't taught professionally for years," she said instead, "and we both know I trust you, and that you can obviously do this standing on your head. But I don't want to interrupt your own plans, especially with what you were doing at the Calgary dance school."

Poppy shrugged. "I don't think my boss would miss me. I think Melissa has me there more because of my brother's name than because she values me."

Bailey winced. Franklin was nice, but she now understood how being associated with a famous hockey player might influence how others saw her. Hence all the emails needing attention.

"So, are you saying you'd be happy to stay working here?"

"I told Melissa that I'd need six weeks, and she was glad as that was most of the summer, when enrollments dropped anyway. But if you want me to stay then I can."

"Oh, God bless you. I'd *love* for you to stay." As much for Poppy's sensible head as her dance skills. Things were so chaotic she barely trusted herself to make wise decisions anymore.

"Have you talked to Luc about this?"

"No. He's been so busy. I've barely seen him since yesterday." And the second-guessing had started as soon as he'd kissed her goodbye after dropping her home after the airport. Was this real, or had this just been a romantic bubble for a few weeks? He might've said they were a couple, but she would've thought he'd contact her by now at least. The fact he hadn't made her wonder just where this was going.

"You need to make the best decision for you," Poppy said. "And I know you might think you love him, but just be wise, okay?"

Love him? She hadn't said those words, and he hadn't said them to her either. And really, how could anyone know they truly loved someone after the intense pressure of those few weeks? He might know a few things about her, but she didn't know too much about him.

Her phone buzzed, and she looked at it. Unknown number. There'd been so many of these lately. "Hello, this is Bailey."

"Bailey, this is Stella Jones from the *Winnipeg Post*. I'm confirming an interview with you and Luc Blanchard tomorrow at ten at your studio."

"Um, I beg your pardon?"

"Did Luc not tell you? I was in touch with him and he said he'd talk with you."

"Well"—*he hasn't*, she didn't say—"I'm sure we can make that happen. What time was it at the studio tomorrow?" She motioned to Poppy.

"Ten."

"Ten," she repeated, eyeing Poppy, who glanced at the calendar and nodded. "Okay, see you then."

"Great."

The call ended, and she sighed.

"What's happened?"

"I've got an interview here with Luc tomorrow, apparently, which he didn't tell me about."

"Maybe this will be a good chance for you two to sort a few things out."

Like what a relationship would look like. In the real world. Because it sure didn't feel very real right now.

She glanced at her phone. She could call him. She *should* call him. So she did. And got his voicemail. Which she hung up on, not knowing how to say what she wanted without sounding pathetic. She then toyed with how to word a message that didn't sound too needy, but the phone rang again. Another unknown number.

"Hello, this is Bailey."

"Bailey," a male voice asked, "do you teach adult classes?"

"I do. What style of dance are you interested in?"

He described a style she definitely did not teach, thank you very much, and quickly ended the call, her fingers shaking.

"What is it?" Poppy asked.

She shook her head. "Just another nuisance call."

Coco had said to expect a few of those, along with random people wanting to slide into her DMs, which was why she was wary with some of the unknown numbers pouring in. But she couldn't afford to ignore all of them. Like, literally could not afford to ignore them, as some of the unknown numbers had proved to be endorsers and local businesses that had wanted to partner with her for greater exposure. Coco had advised that Bailey find herself a publicist, but even that felt ridiculous, like she was one of the celebrities she'd been paid to dance with. She wasn't. She was just plain Bailey, even if others seemed to see her differently now.

"I can talk to Hannah about finding you an agent or someone to help with that if you like," Poppy offered. "She knows way too much about the need to screen calls and deal with the weirdos out there."

Bailey had learned a little more in recent weeks about Hannah's situation, and some of the challenges associated with being a female sports reporter. How insane were people to throw food at a woman who was simply doing her job? "Maybe. I don't know. My head is in a whirl, and we haven't even sorted out our schedules going forward."

"Then let's do this. You've got time to do the other stuff later."

She nodded, and they started compiling the enrollment forms that had come online from the basic website she'd created four years ago. Even the website needed updating, but she didn't have the time or energy or skills to update it, let alone the money. Thank God—and she did, every day—that the debt outstanding at the bank had been paid, but she still needed to repay Poppy, and expanding like they were doing required more financial outlay. They could run back-to-back classes from eight to seven, six days a week and still not fit in all of the applicants. And while that was a good problem to have, Coco had once again advised that Bailey needed to get on top of things now in order to capitalize on this wave of show-induced recognition and enthusiasm, before people forgot her name. She probably should've been doing this while on the show, but had instead been caught up in all that was going on with the show and their routines. And with Luc.

Luc. Her heart tensed. She glanced at her phone again,

picked it up to text him, when an image flashed across her screen. She gasped, then flung it away.

"Bails?" Poppy picked up her phone.

"Don't look at it," she pleaded.

"What is it?"

Something gratuitous. Something she'd certainly not seen before. Something she'd bet good Christian girl Poppy hadn't either. "Maybe you should contact Hannah, after all."

"Bails." Poppy glanced at the screen, then her face stiffened. "Unbelievable."

"Just delete it."

"No." Poppy held up Bailey's phone. "You need to report this to the police."

The police? She closed her eyes. *Lord, help me.*

"And yeah, it's been crazy."

Pastor Josiah Abrahams nodded. The Chicago-based pastor had started this online Bible study with Jai and a few of the others, like Mike, Dan and Brent, a number of years ago. Josiah didn't join as much as he used to, but was always available to provide spiritual counsel along the way. His vacation with family in Florida had meant he'd not been privy to as much of what had been happening in Luc's world as the others, not until he'd watched the finals, so it had been good to fill him in a little now.

"How were your coaches?" Mike asked.

"Mostly okay. The social media team was happy to see my improved numbers, anyway."

"Not surprising, considering all you've been posting lately," Ryan said, smirking.

The video group chat was kind of weird. He'd been in the room with most of these guys only a few days ago, but here he was again, talking about himself yet again. He'd never talked as much about himself as he had in the past forty-eight hours.

This celebrity stuff was exhausting, and almost enough to make him question whether he should've agreed to the captaincy. But the coaching staff had seemed pleased when he'd showed up, after rushing through three interviews with Bailey in the morning. Apart from the strength and conditioning coach, who'd been more than a little alarmed at the weight Luc had lost.

"This ain't good," he'd said, tapping Luc's leaner frame. "You might've done okay with keeping up your cardio, but you need to get the muscle back, and you've only got four weeks until training camp."

"I'll do it."

He was given strict protocols: weights sessions alternating with days including both speed and mobility, with only Sundays as his day of rest. Combined with the extra media and team and organizational stuff he had to do, he'd barely had a moment to think, let alone see how he could touch base with Bailey.

He glanced at his phone, itching to call her. He kind of felt like there was something he was supposed to say, but the past two days had been a blur, and it had slipped through the cracks of utmost importance. He'd barely seen her, or spoken to her since their dance on Sunday night. She'd slept most of the plane trip home, and knowing he'd see her this week he hadn't thought he should wake her.

"So, what's next with her?" Jai asked.

"With Bailey? I don't know."

"Is she going to do another season?" Mike asked. "Bree said she saw the producer talking with her on Sunday."

She had? Man. Now he really needed to talk with her. "She hasn't said anything to me yet."

"Okay, well, I'm sure you'll get the time soon."

"Nothing to be sure of there. My trainer has got me working

hard to make up for the past few weeks. That show was good for my cardio, but not so great for my strength, so I've got to build the muscle mass again."

"Yeah, seeing you throw Bailey around doesn't give that impression."

"She weighs next to nothing, and you know a lot of that is because of momentum and stuff, right?"

Judging from those blank expressions they hadn't. Judging from Chris's smirk, he knew what was coming, so he had to get in quick. "Actually, no, she weighs a ton, and I tried to convince the trainer of that but he wasn't buying. So there you go. Hey Chris, I know this will be hard to believe, but I'm actually getting tired of talking about myself. I want to hear what's going on with Zac Parotti."

"Zac Parotti?" Josiah asked. "Last season's MVP of the Stanley Cup playoffs? Why, what's going on with him?"

"Last we heard he was having real conversations with Chris about God," Mike said.

Chris shrugged. "Keep praying. The man still seems open."

"I still can't believe it," Ryan said. "Like, the man has everything."

Luc nodded. Skills, money, looks. "Has he got a girlfriend?"

Ryan laughed.

"What?"

"Ah, it's just so funny hearing you ask something like that. You, the man who always, *always* complained about hearing us talk about relationship stuff, and now you're as bad as Mike and Jai."

"Hey!" Mike and Jai protested, while Chris and Josiah snickered.

"Look, we just know that a man who finds a wife finds a good thing," Mike said.

"Amen," Jai said.

A wife? Luc coughed. "It's a bit early for a wife. I think you need to focus your energy on Ryan here."

That shut Ryan up quick, as he coughed. "Anyway, moving right along, I don't think Chris answered the question."

"About whether Zac has a girlfriend? I know he's had a few in the past, but I don't think he's looking."

"A man can have a lot of success but still miss what's really important," Josiah said.

Chris nodded. "I think that's what he's found recently. He was definitely the biggest factor in us winning the Cup but he's still feeling a little empty. Not that he's said it quite like that, but that's the impression I'm getting."

"He needs God to fill that emptiness."

Luc leaned back in his seat. "Well, we're praying."

"And we'll be praying for you too," Josiah said. "It sounds like there's a lot going on in your world right now."

"So much."

"And we'll be praying for Bailey too, huh?" Ryan said.

"Go for it." Luc crossed his arms.

"Does anyone else think Luc is looking a little defensive?" Jai teased.

"I'm not feeling defensive," Luc said, then caught the joke as the others laughed.

Okay, maybe he was feeling a *little* defensive. It seemed like there were an awful lot of jokes being made at his expense. Not that he'd ever done anything to deserve it. He rolled his eyes at himself. Yeah, right.

"Bree says to tell Bailey she says hi," Mike said.

"I thought she'd be able to tell her herself seeing they followed each other on Instagram," he snarked.

"It's not the same as the message being passed on in person, so she says."

No. Messaging someone never was. "Fine, I'll pass it on."

"Yeah, say hi from me and Sylvie too," Ryan said, grinning.

"And Diana and me," Chris added.

"And I've never met her, but Gloria loved her dances in the final and I'm sure she'd love to pass on her good wishes to your young lady too," Josiah said.

"Ditto from Allie and moi," Jai said.

"I love how you all seem to like her more than me," Luc grumbled.

"There's a reason for that. She's much nicer than you," Chris teased.

"And much prettier," Bree's voice sang in the background.

"That's for sure," he said, thoughts spinning to her smile. His heart clenched. And he now couldn't wait to see her tomorrow.

Tomorrow! "Hey guys, sorry I can't stay for the study. I just remembered something I need to do."

"A Bailey something?"

"Yep. Hey, good to see you Josiah. Catch you next time."

He switched off his laptop and grimaced. He so should've spoken to Bailey before now. But life was so busy and he was caught in such a whirl that he barely knew what to do. He pressed her number, but she didn't pick up. Then sent her a message, but it got no reply. And he wondered whether she was okay, or if, like him, busyness was consuming her life, too.

CHAPTER 19

"And now, let's finish with our hands raised up high, like we're reaching for the stars."

Bailey demonstrated, smiling as the little girls obeyed. "Now turn around in a circle, then feet together in first position." She waited until they were all finished. "Now step to the right," she showed them, "tuck your left foot behind as you curtsy, then do the other side, as we say Thank You."

"Thank You," the little girls chorused.

The studio's door opened, and her heart tightened, but no, it was only one of the tiny tots' moms. She kept her smile dialed wide, as the little girls chattered, and she thanked them—and their parents—for their support these past few weeks.

"It must feel weird being back," one of the dance moms said.

She nodded. "It certainly does."

It was an even weirder feeling knowing she had a target on her back. The nameless goons out there who sent her pictures of body parts and other tawdry requests were part of the price of fame, so Coco, Hannah, and the nice police detective she'd spoken to had said. But while her phone was now in the hands of the police, and they'd begun a criminal harassment file and asked her to keep a record of all such encounters as more evidence, it didn't help as she continued to feel the sting of injustice. How could her success be tainted by some stupid people? How could her phone number, which she needed for her business, be held to ransom by such cruelty? She prayed the police would find them soon.

She listened as various parents offered their opinions on her dances, and her costumes, and most often, Luc, and just what a hunk of spunk he'd turned out to be. She nodded politely, deflecting some of the more personal questions as she wondered whether they'd be here when he finally appeared. The nine o'clock Wednesday class had been at maximum capacity today. No guesses why.

She glanced at Poppy, who seemed to understand the need to intervene, allowing Bailey to excuse herself to quickly change from her ballerina costume. It was off with the pink tights and leotard and a pale pink sheer skirt, something the little girls all liked her to wear, to something more appropriate for the interview with Stella from the *Post*.

She really hoped she could see Luc before Stella arrived, as there was so much to say. It was crazy after spending so much time together in recent weeks that she physically *ached* to see him. And while she understood he was busy, she still thought he'd want to know some of what had been hitting the fan in her world.

The last of the tiny tots disappeared, and she returned to see Stella had arrived and was speaking to Poppy. There was still no sign of Luc.

Okay, then. Time to adult up and push past her fragile emotions. "Hi Stella. I'm Bailey."

"Bailey, so nice to meet you."

They exchanged pleasantries, and Bailey gestured her to the seats on the side where the *Dance Off* crew had sat just a few weeks ago. How bizarre to think so much had happened in such a short time.

"So, Bailey, how are you feeling after all that's happened? Your head must be spinning."

"There's definitely been a lot to take in," she admitted.

"And while I've got you, before Luc arrives, anything you care to share, woman to woman, about him?"

"Um, not really. He's a hard worker, and I know he surprised himself with how good he got in just a few weeks."

"He obviously had a very good teacher," Stella said.

"Obviously." She half-smiled, so Stella knew she wasn't taking herself too seriously.

"And now you're going out with him, so everyone is saying."

"Are they?"

"That's definitely what that kiss suggested on Sunday night's finale. And all the pictures that have been posted of you two holding hands or hugging. Are you suggesting otherwise?"

She'd be suggesting they reschedule this interview—or postpone it indefinitely—if Stella didn't change topics soon. But she couldn't afford to tick off the local media. She wished Luc would hurry up. *Lord, what do I say?*

The words appeared. "I think I'd rather save that topic for when Luc is here." She smiled, willing the woman to accept it.

Stella's forehead creased, then smoothed as she nodded. "I'm sure there is a lot you're working through."

Bailey nodded, pressing her lips together, as she studied her leopard dance shoes. They were new, a gift from a local dance supplier, and a little more "extra" than her usual dance attire. But she liked how they made her feel more assertive, and after last night's confidence-stealing situation at the Police Service, she wanted every bit of assurance boost she could get. If only Luc was here.

"So, I don't know why Luc is late," Stella said, "but I suppose we can get started. How about we start with an easy one. Can you tell me about how you first got into dance?"

"Sure."

Bailey shared about her mother's passion for dancing, her childhood learning the usual ballet, tap and jazz before ballroom stole her attention as a preteen. Then it had been a battle between ballet and ballroom, before a ballet scholarship had won out, which had later seen her travel and dance in France, Germany, and England.

"And what brought you back?" Stella asked.

"I had some health challenges, and it soon became clear it was time to return," her heart panged, "and my family were glad to have me back." *So* glad. She still remembered her parents clinging to her at a time of great grief.

Stella shook her head. "I find it interesting that you could train for so many years only to give it up."

Bailey shrugged. "Sometimes these things are out of your control." Like illness because a man she liked called her heavy. Or dancing masters who refused to give her lead roles. Or family pain that tugged her home. "Anyway, when I was back here, I realized how much I wanted to pass on my love of dance, so I opened the studio four years ago with my good friend Poppy James." She smiled at Poppy, who waved.

Stella nodded to Poppy. "And I understand that you're the youngest sister of Franklin James?"

"Yes."

"He plays for Calgary, right?"

Bailey caught Poppy's slightly exasperated look, as she pressed her lips together. "That's right."

"And you—sorry, Bailey, but Poppy is interesting, too—I understand you grew up on a ranch with its own movie set."

"You've certainly done your homework. Yep, it's the Three Creek Ranch. They've filmed some of the *As the Heart Draws* series there, which is something *Dance Off*'s winner, Jason

Streetley, once acted in." Poppy rose. "Is there anything else? I have some work to do."

"No, thanks. That's great. Actually, can I get a quick photo of you? Maybe the two of you together?"

"Sure."

They got a picture taken of them, then Poppy exited to the office, and Stella asked Bailey to continue. "So, you and Poppy opened the studio? You must've been very young."

"Yes." Young and foolish, some might say. "But we loved working together, and loved teaching, and because we had a range of experience it meant we could offer a wide variety of classes."

"I see. And the call-up to *Dance Off*?"

"I've been friends with Coco Flintoff since our earliest dance days, and then she moved more into theatrical performance while I went to Europe and later opened my studio here, but we always stayed in touch. When she heard there was a Winnipeg-based celebrity she recommended me for the job, as it meant we could start training straight away."

"I see. Well, that's most interesting. Now, I wonder where your boyfriend is?"

She shrugged, not biting, as she wondered that too.

"Can't say or don't want to say?" Stella teased.

Just then the door opened and Luc walked in.

Her chest grew tight, and she knew an overwhelming desire to cry, but she blinked it back, conscious Stella was watching closely. Bailey stood, smiling as he drew nearer. "Luc, this is Stella Jones from the *Winnipeg Post*."

"We talked on the phone," Stella said, shaking his hand. "Thanks for coming."

"Sorry I'm late. I had a meeting with the GM and couldn't get away." He glanced at Bailey, but she could only smile briefly before glancing down, before realizing how that must look to Stella, and fixing her attention her way instead.

Why she felt awkward around him, when she'd been doing so many interviews with him in recent times, she couldn't explain. Except she really needed him to hold her, for him to notice that she needed him, and the fact this woman was here while she had an urgent need for his hug felt too difficult to explain. And maybe that made her as immature as one of her tiny tots but she couldn't help it. The fact he'd barely acknowledged her in the past few days, especially when she'd really needed him, made her want to cry.

"Bailey?"

Luc's deep voice sparked fresh tears, and she shook her head. "Excuse me a minute."

She hurried to the washrooms, bracing her hands on the edge of the metal sink, and stared at her reflection. Good. Red eyes hadn't made an appearance yet. She needed to get it together. She'd managed the rest of her life without leaning on a man, so why had she let herself fall so fast?

She sucked in a deep breath, smiled at her reflection. She was a performer. A pro. She could do this. Her shoulders straightened, and she drew comfort from her excellent posture, something which always gave an edge, or so her many dancing instructors had said.

She exited the bathroom only to startle at the sight of Luc, arms folded, leaning against the opposite wall.

"Bails."

No. She wasn't going to lose it. Not with a reporter out there wanting every juicy bit of gossip. "I can't, Luc."

"Can't what?"

"Whatever you want to do or say, I just can't right now."

"I told her I needed to speak with you."

"If you do, then I'll cry, and I don't want that. Please, let's just do the interview, and talk after. Okay?"

He nodded, and she returned to her seat, and smiled. She'd fake it until she made it to the end.

HAD HE DONE SOMETHING WRONG? Bailey was hardly her usual sunny self. She'd barely looked at him, and he had a funny feeling he was somehow responsible, but he didn't know exactly why. He studied his shoes as the reporter asked another question. He hoped she would finish this interview soon, because he had another meeting at twelve, and already he was burning to hurry this up and talk to Bailey properly. They'd be squeezed for time as it was.

"Luc?"

"Sorry, could you please repeat the question?"

"I asked which was your favorite dance during the show."

"The tango."

Stella smiled. "I'm going to guess that's because of the special ending?"

"Sure." He wasn't about to tell her it was the dance that made him feel most alive.

"And Bailey wanted us to wait until you were here before answering this question. Can you tell us about the rumors that you two are now a couple?"

Luc glanced at Bailey. She glanced away, her fixed smile on Stella like she didn't want to look at him. Why didn't she? Why hadn't she answered this question? Hadn't they discussed this already? "Yes, we are."

He reached across and grasped Bailey's hand and squeezed it, doing his best to reassure. Something had happened, and he needed to know. Now. He cleared his throat. "I'm sorry, especially as I was late today, but I'm really slammed with stuff at the moment. Is there anything else you need us for, or can we take a few pics and be done?"

"Oh! Well, I suppose I can call you if there's anything else I need you to clarify. But yes, a few pictures would be nice. Perhaps the two of you striking a pose?"

"Sure." Anything to get this done so he could talk to Bailey. He turned to her. Tipped her chin up. "Bails? What do you suggest?"

"Whatever you like," she murmured.

What he'd like was a kiss or hug, but he settled for a pose that showed the drama of their waltz, where he held her in one of those dramatic lifts that had scored so well with the judges. Stella wanted another, which they obliged, then a third, which he did not, as he was fast getting the impression this reporter was out for whatever she could get, and the longer they did this the more apparent it was that Bailey needed her to leave.

"Well, thanks, Stella. It was nice to meet you. You'll let us know if there's anything else you need, right?"

"Thanks. I'll call you. I have your numbers."

Bailey coughed. "I have a new phone, so maybe call him instead."

So that's why she hadn't responded to his calls. Okay. "Thanks again, Stella." He studied her, his arm around Bailey as he waited for his unsubtle request to sink in.

"Good luck you two," Stella replied, gathering her things, then exiting with a final wave.

He counted one, two, three, then Bailey turned to him. "Oh, Luc."

He folded her into his chest, as she shuddered, and his shirt grew wet. Whoa. "Bails? What's happened?"

She shook her head, sniffling, and he caught sight of Poppy James standing at the office door. He made a "What's wrong?" gesture at her, and Poppy grimaced, then drew close, and placed a hand on Bailey's back.

"Bails? You need to tell him."

"You tell him," Bailey rasped.

"Okay." Poppy sighed. "Bailey got sent some gross images, and has had a bunch of idiots make all kinds of rude comments.

She's taken her phone to the police which is why they still have it, just in case you've tried to call her recently."

"I did, I have." He bent to see Bailey. He'd never seen her cry like this before, and the sight ripped at his heart. "Bails, I'm so sorry I wasn't here for you. I wish I'd known."

"I know you've been busy, and I didn't want to get in the way of all you had to do."

"Hey." He glanced at Poppy, and tried to gesture for her to scram without saying it. He appreciated her, but right now needed a moment alone with his girl.

Poppy smirked and sashayed back to the office, earning herself a thank-you bouquet later, and he picked Bailey up and hugged her closer to his chest. "Bails, you're safe. You're okay. I'm here, and I'll never let anything bad happen to you."

Except it already had. He grimaced. Then stroked her soft, soft hair, as her breathing calmed. A desperate desire to say three words he'd never told another woman gathered in his mouth. He swallowed. He was so bad at this boyfriend stuff, but knew he could've—should've—done better. "I'm so sorry I haven't been around much. I promise I'll do better."

She lifted a tearstained face, and swiped at her tears. "Oh, Luc. It's not you."

"Are you sure? I'm not great at knowing what you need, but if you tell me, I'll do my best to help."

She crumpled, her arms around his shoulders. "That's all I really need."

Okay, then. He hugged her, silently praying for her to know peace, as her breath shuddered.

"I don't even know why I'm so upset. I think it's just everything feels so much. Too much. It's crazy to think that when we were doing the show things actually felt a lot easier, and now it's all so overwhelming."

"What's overwhelming you?"

"The business. There have been so many applications and

students, and offers to partner with us pouring in, we can't keep up."

"Isn't that a good thing?"

"Yes," she wailed, then laughed.

It was a pale version of the laughter he loved so much, but it was a start, and a thousand percent better than her tears.

"It *is* a good thing, and I shouldn't complain. It's just we've been overwhelmed with trying to figure out how to go forward and what classes to have, and then I have to redo the website and then there are all these creepy people out there."

Yeah, that. His hands clenched, and he forced himself to calm. She didn't need him getting furious about the weirdos. Besides, "The police are handling that now, aren't they?"

"Yes. But my phone number is the one associated with the business, so I hate to think that some idiots out there are stopping potential clients or opportunities."

Like Joanne calling about Bailey returning next season. But now was not the time to talk about that. "The people who really want you will figure out other ways to be in touch. And the police will likely find out soon who has done this, so I'm sure it won't be long until you're back to normal."

"But that's the thing." She pulled away, looked up at him seriously, as he cradled her waist. "I don't know if there is a normal anymore. We can't go back to being unknown. I'm always going to be the dance pro who danced with Luc Blanchard."

He knew exactly what she meant. The level of interest in his life was something he'd never expected. He wondered if people like Zac Parotti ever figured out how to manage success. "Well, if it makes you feel any better, I'm always going to be known as the celebrity who was lucky enough to dance with Bailey Donovan."

She laughed then, a real laugh, her smile shining in her eyes this time, not just in her lips. He slid his hands up her back, to her neck, to her cheeks, and lowered his face. "I've really missed you."

"I've missed you too," she whispered.

And he lowered his face for a kiss.

Long, golden, as perfect as a sunset over the sea, his stomach swooped and sang as her arms stole up his back. This wasn't a kiss witnessed by millions. Wasn't witnessed by anyone, he hoped. He cradled her face in his hands and kissed her more deeply, until she drew back with a gasp.

"Sorry." She drew in a deep breath, then pointed to her nose. "Clogged-up nose. I couldn't breathe."

He smiled. "We need to go out on a real date soon, huh?"

"That'd be good."

"I know life is frantic at the moment, but if you let me know when works best for you, I'll make it work." Somehow.

"But you're so busy."

"I'll make it work," he repeated. "You're my priority."

Her face softened. "Really?"

"Yep." He hugged her close again, murmured in her ear, "I'd much rather spend time with you than my teammates or trainer."

She laughed as he'd hoped. "Then you should be sure to do something about that."

"Dinner. My place tonight."

He didn't know where those words came from. Had no idea what his apartment looked like, or what time his last appointment finished. But as she stroked his face, her look close to adoration, he found he didn't care.

He hadn't been joking. Bailey was his priority, and he'd do whatever it took to show that she'd never need to doubt that again.

CHAPTER 20

$\mathcal{A}$fter spending the rest of the day wrangling children and wrestling applications into potential classes, it felt good to leave the studio and return home and change into jeans and a pretty top. She'd said she could catch an Uber, but Luc had insisted on picking her up, saying he had zero desire for random people to know where either of them lived, and he'd much rather have the opportunity to spend time with her anyway. So she'd waited, watching out the window for his shiny black pickup, smiling as he parked in the no-stopping zone.

"Don't be out too late, otherwise I'll come hunt you down," Poppy warned.

"Yes, Mom." She rolled her eyes, blew Poppy a kiss, and scampered down the stairs. She probably should contact her parents again, see if they wanted to catch up for lunch this weekend. Which was a dumb question, as they always did. But maybe it would be a chance to help them get to know Luc more.

She reached his vehicle just as Luc was getting out.

"You beat me."

She smiled. "I'm competitive, or so some people tell me."

"I happen to like competitive." He opened her door, waited until she was settled, then gently closed it.

She snapped in her seat belt, and noticed a few people had stopped to stare. Was a wave inappropriate? Or would that simply clue them into where she lived? Best to not invite more strangers to dig too deeply into her world.

Luc rejoined the traffic. Peak hour had picked up lately, as summer vacations drew to a close. It reminded her that school would resume shortly, that his preseason would begin soon, and once again she teetered at the edge of spiraling into doubts and confusion. Then his hand found hers, and she grasped it like she would a lifeline, her fears settling, like he'd prayed for her. She exhaled.

"You feeling better now?"

"Yes. Did you just pray for me?"

"Yes."

She squeezed his hand, emotion clogging her throat. Oh, he was a good man.

He drove to a different neighborhood, not too many blocks away, but still within walking distance of the Coffee Haus café. "So this is where you are," she said, craning her neck to look at the high-rise, as he slowed then turned into an underground parking garage.

"This is home sweet home."

A few minutes later she was standing in the lobby of his tenth-floor apartment. Cream, hardwood floors, the place would have looked cold except for the amazing view. Even from here she could see the full-length glass at the end of the hall showcasing a view of the city as it stretched to the horizon. And at this time of evening, with the lights showing, and the last rays of sunset, "It's beautiful."

He shrugged, placing his keys in a black bowl, then gestured her to the living room. "It's not far from the arena and I like the fact you can see the river from the balcony. I can get to the river easily." He shot her a look. "That's where I go running most days. You know, in case you're interested."

"Mmm, I'm interested, but not in running so much."

"Yeah?" He drew closer, a smile on his face like he enjoyed this banter. "What are you more interested in?"

She wrapped her hands around his neck, and smiled up at him, and whispered, "Dinner."

He laughed, and swooped in for a kiss, which soon grew a little hungry, and she had to place one hand on his chest. "Careful. We can't do dessert first."

"Haven't you heard the saying, 'life is short, so eat dessert first'?" he murmured against her lips.

"No. And," she gently pushed him away, "I think you should feed me. Before I get hangry."

"I can't actually imagine you as angry, let alone hangry. I've never seen you eat too much."

"Dancers can't. A moment on the lips, forever on the hips, or so they say."

"I've always wondered who this 'they' are. They seem to have a lot of opinions that are wrong."

Or sometimes right, too. There was a reason she'd gotten a little fanatical about her eating over the years. A reason why so many of her teachers had always been careful about portion control.

She blinked, shifted closer to the window, as the final rays of sunset tinted the sky in hues of peach and gold. Her breath hitched as Luc drew close, then wrapped his arms around her, his front to her back, as they watched the sky together, saw the lights of the Legislative Building flicker on. She leaned against him, thankful to have this small pocket of calm in the midst of stress and strife.

"What are you thinking about?" he murmured.

She wrapped her hand over his. "How faint I'm going to be if I don't eat soon."

She felt the rumble of his laughter drift from his chest through her. She closed her eyes. Was there a nicer feeling than being held like this?

"Well, we can't have that, can we? What do you want to eat?"

"Anything."

"Indian?"

"You know how to cook Indian?"

"I know how to order it."

She laughed, and he showed her a takeout menu, she picked her two favorites, and he ordered.

"So, I figure we've got maybe ten minutes before the doorbell rings, and I have to go let them in. We could spend that time looking at the view, or we could explore some more dessert from before…"

She swiveled and faced the window. "Yeah, the view is looking good."

"It sure is."

From that husky tone in his voice, she knew he wasn't talking about outside. And when his lips found her cheek, then slid down her jaw to her throat, she knew she couldn't cope with much more. She grabbed his hand, and arched away, and did a spin under his arm as he laughed and tried to keep up. "Don't make me make you drop and give me twenty," she warned. "I'm not that kind of girl."

He offered tweaked lips of chagrin. "I'm not that kind of guy, but I find it way too easy to forget when I'm with you."

"I know exactly what you mean."

They stared at each other for a long moment, then he exhaled heavily. "This is a whole different thing to when we were on set, huh?"

She nodded, "It's not like when there were dozens of eyes on us."

He pulled her close, leaned his forehead on hers. "I meant it before. I'm not going to let you fall. Whether it's in a dance lift, or something else. You're safe with me."

"I know," she whispered. She *knew*.

Luc might sometimes wrestle with desire, but he was honorable. And she could trust him. A good, good man.

"Man." He blew out a breath.

"What?"

"Oh, nothing."

"No, what is it?"

He pressed a kiss to her palm. "Isn't it funny how we can think we know the answers, but until we live someone else's experience, we really have no clue?"

"Whose experience are you thinking of?"

He winced. "Ryan. Him and Sylvie were a thing before she was a Christian, and I might've got on him about getting carried away, and now I know how easy it is."

"Oh no."

"What's wrong?"

"Are you telling me you're not perfect?"

His lips twitched. "I guess I am."

She sighed. "That's just as well."

"Because?"

"Because I'm not perfect, either."

"Oh, come on. You're *pretty* close to perfect." He held out his fingers a quarter inch.

She chuckled. "I really like you, Luc Blanchard."

"That's just as well."

"Because?"

"Because I really lo-ike you too."

H᷈ saw how her eyes widened, as if she'd caught his near slip. But would it be a slip of the tongue to speak what his heart had been saying? He loved her, but saying that would take this relationship far deeper than mere kissing seemed to. At least, that was his experience. He might've kissed plenty of women—more—back in pre-saved days, but he'd never loved them. Not like this.

Maybe it was that he'd seen his friends dig deeper into what a real relationship was, or the fact that God had been working in his heart to show what real love was, but he knew this deep care and protectiveness was far more powerful than the desire he'd felt for other women in the past. Far deeper even than the desire he felt for Bailey. He might've mocked his friends for talking in the group chat about relationships so much, but he could now see how finding the right girl provided sustenance for life. More than a smile or a laugh it was like having a partner, someone who was on your side, no matter what. And the past couple of months had showed that Bailey was like the ultimate partner he'd want in life.

His doorbell buzzed, shaking him from his moment.

"That sounds like dinner is here. Want to come with, or hang here?"

"Of course I'm coming with you."

He held her hand as they took the elevator to the foyer, and met the delivery person at the door. He tipped them, having paid on the phone before, then five minutes later they were eating in his apartment.

This, sharing a meal, was nice. He could see them sharing plenty more. Dinners, lunches, breakfasts. Here, at hers, at restaurants, wherever.

"So, how did you go with the rest of your day? You were stressed before about the studio and things."

She swallowed the last of her butter chicken, and pushed her plate away. "Poppy and I have pretty much sorted out most of the classes now. We might need an assistant to do some of the paperwork though. And find someone who can help upgrade the website."

He motioned to the curry, and she shook her head, so he ate the rest of it, as he chewed on her dilemma. He had some friends, some connections who could probably help with both. But she wouldn't like a handout, he knew that much from spending time with her. "I can ask around if you like."

"Only if they're cheap."

"You don't want cheap if it means it won't work properly."

"I want the price I can afford."

He drank his water. "You mentioned before about people wanting to partner with you. Were any of those tech companies? I'm sure there's a company out there who'd like to work with a famous dance studio, or at least offer a deep discount for the privilege of being associated with you."

"Really?"

"Really."

"Wow. You're probably right. I haven't even had a chance to look at all the emails yet, so maybe there is."

"And if not, I can put some feelers out, see if people at the club know people who know people, but only if you want."

"Thank you." She reached across the table and grasped his hand. "I really appreciate that."

"I live to serve."

"Which is what will make you a good captain." She sipped her water. "How did your team things go today?"

"It went. I have more press and have to arrange a few team things later in the summer. And every day between now and the preseason, I have to work on building back my muscles."

"Too much dancing knocked it out of you, huh?"

He stared into her eyes. "I wouldn't have missed it for the world."

She smiled, and his heart took flight. How strange to think they lived in the same city, that she'd even worked at his favorite coffee shop, but they had never met until *Dance Off* brought them together. He shivered. It was almost scary to think they hadn't met. "Hey, what church do you go to?"

She told him. "I've gone with my parents to theirs for years."

He swallowed. Maybe this was a big call, and likely wouldn't win him favor with the parents, but he still had to ask the question. "How would you feel about coming with me to mine?"

"With you?"

He told her where and when his church met, and a bit about the style of service, and she agreed to go.

"As long as your parents won't be put out if you're not there."

Her lashes lowered, then lifted. "I normally have lunch with them on Sunday though. It… it would be nice if you came with me. If you wanted to, of course."

"Of course I want," he said. Well, of course he wanted to be with her. He suspected her parents might not be so eager for him to tag along. Her mom might be okay, but he thought her father would be glad if Luc's relationship with Bailey had ended with the show.

"So, Sunday, huh?"

"Three days away. Or is it four?"

"It's too far away, whatever it is, that's for sure."

"Are you saying you want to see me before then?" she asked playfully.

"I definitely want to see you before then."

"And have more dessert?"

He exhaled heavily. "Don't tempt me."

CHAPTER 21

"Thank you for inviting me to your home," Luc said to Bailey's parents, as her stomach knotted. She might've spent their last two dinner dates assuring Luc they'd welcome him, but her words had been more hope than truth. Her mom was fine, she seemed a big fan of Luc. But Dad, well...

She studied her father as he watched Luc interact with her mom, that heavy pull to his mouth suggesting he didn't like what he saw. Dad had never liked tattoos, and it had been part of the reason he'd said he hadn't coped well with Chrissy's husband. That, and Jed's violent streak, which hadn't revealed itself until too late.

Her heart sorrowed for her sister, for the estrangement that distance and unforgiveness had put between them. Chrissy wouldn't be here today, although yesterday her mom had dropped the bombshell that Rhett and Cindy would. As Bailey hadn't seen Rhett in forever that'd be great. Cindy, well, that was up to her how things progressed. But as Rhett was a hockey fan, she figured he'd at least cope with today.

Her father turned, spotting her, and his face noticeably

relaxed. He held out his arms and hugged her. "How's my little girl?"

"I'm good." The dates squeezed around Luc's and her busy schedules had helped them delve deeper into knowing each other. And the kissing had been the cherry on top. "Really good."

"And how was that church you went to today?"

The way he said this, like with a sneered inflection, drew Luc's attention. Bailey smiled, and like she'd said to Luc after the service, "It was different, but I enjoyed it." She swallowed, but knew she had to own her brave. "And I'd like to go again."

"You know you're welcome anytime," Luc said, his voice soft.

She nodded. She did. Although she suspected once his busy game schedule started, there'd be far less opportunities to attend with him, and the place felt so big and bright and new that she wondered if she'd get lost. That was exactly the reason Luc said he enjoyed going, as he could come late and sit in the back and escape without drawing much attention. But she'd felt the life there, even though she'd missed the traditions of her parents' older church. There was much to be said for both expressions of worship.

"Well, we're just waiting on Rhett and Cindy. They should be here any moment," Mom said.

"Rhett and Cindy?" Luc asked Bailey.

"My brother and his wife." She pointed to the mantelpiece where a series of family photos were gathered in silver frames. The most recent family picture had her parents positioned in the center, Rhett and Cindy to one side of her mom, while Bailey stood next to her father. They'd all been grinning at the camera, except Cindy whose smile had seemed forced.

Luc shot her a smile. "You look so pretty." He glanced at the next photo, a much older one which included Chrissy, but not Jed. Photos of him had been expunged from the house the second they'd learned of his betrayal. He motioned to the picture. "Who is this?"

She moved to his side, and said in a softer voice, "That's my older sister, Chrissy."

"She's not around?"

"It's, ah, complicated." She shot a look at her father.

"She lives in Florida now," Dad said. "With a man who isn't her husband."

"She's married?" Luc asked.

"Was," she murmured. Her father might've despised Jed, but he'd not understood why Chrissy had divorced her husband, saying divorce was against God's law. Then, when she'd found a new man, her father's values had seen him raise objections against remarriage, which had been enough for Chrissy to declare she was done with such conservative prejudice and would go live with a man she'd met on the internet. Some days Bailey suspected her father had never really gotten over the shock, and this was why he was so protective of her.

She lowered her head. Her sister might've been older, and much of this had happened when Bailey had lived overseas, but she wondered what her life would be like if she hadn't left. Chrissy had always encouraged Bailey to chase her dancing dreams, and together with Gran and Mom they'd been enough to persuade Dad to let Bailey leave for France as soon as she'd finished school aged seventeen.

But when the truth about Chrissy's marriage saw Jed jailed, and the other pieces of Bailey's life crumbled, Bailey had sought the safe space of home. Her parents' home. Her parents' church. Her parents' influence in the studio that she'd started with her portion from her grandparents' will. She'd had adventures, and since that time of initial regrouping, had struck out to live with Poppy, then on her own, then stepped into the *Dance Off* show. But still, the cords of familial obligation and responsibility pulled tight, something especially obvious whenever she visited home. She suspected Luc might think she stayed too close to the family nest, but being close to her family was part of who she was.

The sound of a car outside drew her mom to the window, then she clapped her hands, and rushed outside, her dad following soon after. Bailey caught Luc's half-smile—yes, she might possess a few of her mother's attributes—and she moved to his side, holding his hand. "Don't worry," she murmured. "Rhett is nice, and Cindy, well, she can be too."

He chuckled, and she winced, realizing what she'd said, but it was only the truth. Nobody knew what weather Cindy would bring when she came, her temperature as variable as a spring day. But the fact they hadn't attended the show's tapings—Bailey had messaged Rhett with the invitation to come, but he couldn't spare time from work—meant it was likely Cindy would be holding some resentment, as past experience had proved.

A moment later, the door opened, and Bailey hurried to her brother, encasing him a hug. "Hi Rhett."

"Hey, it's the celebrity."

Who—? Oh, he meant her. She squeezed him tighter. "It's good to see you."

"You too, Bailey Rose."

"Rose, huh?" Luc murmured, his lips tilting up on one side.

She shrugged, returning her attention to her brother.

"I'm really sorry I couldn't make it to your gig. But Cin and I watched it every night, didn't we honey?"

Bailey turned to her sister-in-law, their lean-in-quick-back-pat a maneuver perfected over the past four years, ever since she'd returned from Europe and discovered that just as her brother-in-law was going to jail, her brother had got himself engaged. "Hi Cindy."

"Bailey." She nodded to Luc. "So, you're the truck, huh?"

Bailey wrapped an arm around him, her heart tumbling. When Cindy said things like that Bailey was never sure if she meant to be rude or just had no filter, all of which made her feel uncertain. She hoped Luc wouldn't be put off.

Luc held out a hand. "I usually go by Luc, but I've been called a truck a few times, too."

She wanted to cheer as he shook a stunned Cindy's hand, then Rhett's. "Good to meet you."

"You, wow. Like, this is kind of awesome meeting you," Rhett stuttered.

Luc snickered softly, and she realized he must be used to similar interactions with awestruck fans. "And it's great to meet more of Bailey's family."

"Are you two actually going out?" Cindy said. "You kissed her, but I was sure you only did that for the ratings."

Wow. Bailey fixed her smile in place. Apparently for today's lunch Cindy had brought winter.

"Actually, yeah. We're going out." Luc kissed Bailey's cheek. "I'm so grateful I met her. She's just the best, isn't she?" he said to Cindy.

Cindy's upturned lip spoke volumes. "Hashtag grateful and blessed," she snarked before dragging Rhett off to the open concept kitchen where her mom was fixing a salad.

Luc swiveled to meet Bailey's gaze, his upraised brows and mouthed "Wow" concurring with what she'd thought. "Is she always like that?"

"Not usually as bad as that, but who knows? The day is young."

He bent his head and murmured, "How long are we staying for?"

"Let me guess. You want to get straight to dessert."

"Always."

She laughed, which drew her mom and Rhett's smiles, and her dad and Cindy's frowns. Surely the rest of the day could only improve.

~

"Oh my gosh. Luc, I'm so sorry."

He reached across his vehicle's center console and held Bailey's hand. "It's okay."

"It's not okay. I cannot believe she spoke like that to you."

Cindy was, in the words of his mom, "a piece of work", but saying so to Bailey right now wouldn't help the situation. Judging from the way Wayne had eyed him, he didn't like Luc much either. But again, pointing that out wouldn't help the situation.

"I don't know what you think of my family," Bailey murmured.

"Your mom and Rhett seem to like me, so that's something."

"They do. Mom is a big fan, and I think you've officially made Rhett's year."

Luc chuckled. Rhett might be in his late twenties, but he'd seemed more excited than some of the kids Luc met at preseason family days. "He works hard at the pharmacy, huh?"

"He works too hard, but Cindy likes nice things."

"She doesn't work?"

"She has a photography business she never does much with."

"I see."

Some of the players he knew had wives or girlfriends like that. The classic trophy wife who existed more to look good than contribute meaningfully in any way. And maybe that sounded judgy, but when he saw how some of those women treated his workmates, hearing their complaints about the travel and times away, despite knowing that his teammates worked their butts off, risking injury to collect a paycheck, yeah, he wasn't sympathetic to their cause. A woman who worked hard herself, who made few demands, yet obviously valued family, was much more his speed. He glanced across, picked up Bailey's hand and kissed it.

"What's that for?"

"Being brave enough to take me today."

"I hope you enjoyed some of it."

"Of course I did." Seeing her world, some of what had shaped her, was fascinating. And in the course of that, learning more about the dynamics of the Donovan family spiked a sliver of concern. Bailey was close to her family—anyone could see that—but how much did she place her sense of value and worth on what they said? He'd noticed the way she shut down when Cindy started sharing her opinions. Maybe it was politeness, but it seemed the whole Donovan clan just pretended that Rhett's wife was pleasant, when her behavior should've been called out. If it was his house he would've done that, and had been sorely tempted to pull her down a peg or six, but respect for Bailey and her mom had kept his lips zipped.

Then there was Bailey's dad, with his prodding and poking and glances at Luc's arms like he didn't know how a sweet girl could fall for a guy like him. He sighed.

"What is it?"

"Does your dad have a problem with tattoos?"

"You've noticed that, huh?"

Like someone noticed an ambulance screeching by with its lights on and siren blaring.

"You know that picture of Chrissy, and what he said before? She married a man who had ink like you, and Dad was never a fan." She sighed. "So now, I'm afraid he feels the same about anyone who sports similar things."

He half-smiled at her use of "sports."

"What?"

"I love some of these words you use like 'sports'."

She shrugged. "I think I picked it up when I was in England." She squeezed his hand. "Let me guess: you love it because it's 'sports'."

"That's it exactly," he drawled.

"You're fun."

"You're funner."

"Aw, now who's pulling out the fun words?"

He steered to her street, and found a park, reversing into the street parking with ease.

"Want to come up?"

"Is Poppy there?"

"Probably. Does that make it a yay or a nay?"

Maybe this would be a good chance to find out a little more about the business. Bailey's dad certainly hadn't appreciated his questions earlier. "Definitely a yay."

She snickered, and he smiled, racing around the vehicle to get her door. He loved this, this looking after her, helping her out, making her feel special. Well, he hoped she felt special, that the flowers and dates had been something she enjoyed. She'd seemed to, even enjoying meeting Travis and his girlfriend Molly last night at dinner. His best friend on the team had given a huge thumbs-up whenever Bailey was talking with Molly, and he'd loved drawing her into his world.

Upstairs, her space seemed as pretty and dainty as everything else about this woman, and probably made his modern place feel really cold and sterile. There were art posters labelled with Paris and Cologne, photos of Bailey and Poppy in costume, including that dramatic one of Bailey in a white tutu which he'd first been sent by *Dance Off* in one of their many emails. Trinkets and girly things he'd always rolled his eyes over, but because they belonged to her, he was intrigued.

"I like your space," he said, looking around. "Suits you to a T."

"Speaking of, would you like a cup of tea? Or are you more of a coffee man?"

He shot her a look, then she seemed to remember where they'd first bumped into each other. Literally.

"I might not read minds but I can read that face," Poppy said from the kitchenette. "How do you have it?"

"Strong and black. Thanks, Poppy."

"I'll help," Bailey said.

"No, you sit right there," Poppy commanded. "I know you're an English breakfast tea girl on a Sunday afternoon."

"You are?" Luc asked Bailey. "Why don't I know this?"

"Because every Sunday afternoon we've been slammed for time. Until now." She sighed, cradling his hand in hers. "Can you believe the final was only a week ago?"

"It seems like another world." So weird. The intensity of those rehearsals and flights and attention, followed by his return and the rush of media and hockey and training. It was like he'd been sucked into a whirlpool and near drowning, and finally spat out on a beach with gentle waves, and he could breathe. Could see the horizon. Could see a future. Where he and Bailey shared lives, and a house, and a—

Whoa. He wasn't going *there*. Not even in his head. Thoughts needed taking captive. Now.

"Here you go." Poppy deposited a tray with Bailey's cup of tea and a small French press of dark coffee on the table and a mug that said "Dance is Life!"

"Sure is," he said, gesturing to it.

Poppy laughed. "Wow, I love how dance can transform people's lives, don't you?"

He kissed Bailey's hand. "I'm a convert."

"Okay. Well, that sounds like my cue to go and—"

"You don't have to leave," he said. "I actually wanted to ask you both some questions about the business."

"The studio?"

He nodded. "If that's okay."

"Sure." Bailey tucked up her knees on the couch. "What do you want to know?"

He had to tread carefully here. He didn't want to upset her, or Poppy, or have more of his questions come back to Wayne. "I'm just curious about how two young women managed to fund something like that in the middle of a major city."

"That's easy enough," Poppy said, as Bailey said at the same time, "Sure."

"You go," Bailey said.

Poppy waved her off. "It's your story."

Bailey shrugged. "Okay. Well, as you might've gathered from today, our family had a bit of a tumultuous time. Around the same time that my sister's husband was arrested for domestic violence, my surviving grandparents both got sick, and both died within the space of two months."

"I'm so sorry," he murmured.

"It was a shock. Especially as my mother's mom had always supported my dancing dream. Gran was the one who encouraged my mom to dance, and she'd given me money to go to Europe to study there."

"Would that we all had grandmothers who could afford to do that," Poppy teased.

He pointed at her. "This coming from the woman whose family have their own movie set."

"Right?"

Bailey's chuckle broke through the poignancy of the moment, and he again sensed the depth of affection between these two.

"So, anyway, when she died, two months after Granddad, she left me her car and some money. It was earmarked for further study or to start a dance studio, so that's what I did."

"And this was all while your brother is getting engaged and brother-in-law was going to jail, huh?"

She nodded. "I think part of the reason Cindy gets annoyed with me is because she thought our family was wealthier than we are, and then a big chunk of my grandmother's estate came to me instead of them."

"Your brother wasn't annoyed?"

"He's the most lovely, generous man, and understood why Gran did what she did."

"He seemed that way," Luc agreed. Wanting to hush over strain and keep the peace, a lot like Bailey did too.

Poppy sipped her tea. "It's always been a mystery to me how those two paired up."

"Opposites can attract, I've heard." Luc kissed Bailey's hand, as Poppy snickered.

Bailey's smile grew wistful. "I'm so grateful for my family, and the fact they've supported me with my dancing, and with going overseas. I wouldn't have been able to do that without them, and definitely couldn't have started the studio without Gran's money. Nor without Poppy's contribution."

"See, that's what I wanted to ask." He turned to Poppy. "So you put in money too?"

"I put in five grand from my savings, so I was always the minority partner."

"And now the debt is paid we can repay you soon too," Bailey said.

"One day, no rush." Poppy's head tilted. "But why all the questions about money?"

Because he wanted to know how much Bailey's dad had been involved in setting it up. "I, um, just wondered, as I wasn't sure who was the financial brains behind the business. And I haven't heard either of you say you've studied that kind of thing."

"Mom used to have a studio, and Dad advised her," Bailey said. "Now he advises me. He's a member of the finance board at church, and has always been willing to help with financial things."

Luc kept his lips clamped as he nodded. Just as he suspected.

"Then your mom's studio closed." Poppy stared at him. "Right Bailey?"

Bailey nodded, but Poppy's unsettling stare at Luc kneaded fresh concern. "Can I ask why?"

Bailey shrugged. "It was before I was born, but Mom always said it was because she wanted to concentrate on us kids when we were young."

Clearly a question he should ask Bailey's mom. Delicately, perhaps.

"But I don't really want to talk about that. It's all okay. I've paid off the debt except what's owed to Poppy so we're now nearly up-to-date. So, who wants another tea or coffee?"

He and Poppy declined, which saw Bailey move to the kitchen.

As soon as Bailey exited, he murmured, "Do you have some concerns about it?"

"Look, Wayne might be ultra straitlaced about a bunch of things, but he is a nice guy, and I don't want to speak badly about him," Poppy said in a low voice.

"But?"

She sighed. "But, let's just say he's not as clever as he thinks he is. I think the reason Bailey's grandmother left the money directly to Bailey was to make sure Wayne didn't get his hands on it. He might not be too smart with money, but Bailey just adores him."

He knew that. Bailey might be independent in some ways, but in others she still seemed like Daddy's little girl. And while he loved that they were a close family, he also could understand some of Cindy's frustrations in trying to break into such a close-knit unit.

"So why haven't you said something, especially if you've invested five grand of your own money?"

"Do you know how hard it is to even remotely criticize her family?"

He was getting a fairly good idea.

"What are you two talking about?" Bailey asked on her return.

He might be all about honesty, but now didn't feel the right time to deep dive into financial questions. "I was about to tell you both that I've got a lead on a website designer who's prepared to offer a significant discount." Well, it would seem so, because Luc would subsidize it.

"Are you serious?"

When he nodded, Bailey clapped her hands, her action so reminiscent of her mother's it made him smile again. "Oh my goodness! That's awesome. When can we meet him?"

"It's a her, actually. She lives in Ontario, and does a lot of work remotely, but is excellent. And she's a Christian, so I think she understands the need to keep things affordable for your students."

He gave the name, and Bailey kissed his cheek. "I really appreciate that. Thank you."

Poppy nodded. "You're really proving yourself as excellent boyfriend material, aren't you?"

"Hashtag grateful and blessed," he deadpanned.

Bailey snickered, and Poppy looked bemused. "Clearly there's something going on here that I don't know about, but okay." Poppy rose. "Now I'm going to leave you two to it. Unless, of course, another viewing of *Dance Off* is on the menu."

Bailey turned to him. "Have you seen all our dances put together?"

"Not together, no."

"Ooh, well, just you wait, mister."

He glanced at Poppy, who shrugged and reclaimed her seat,

and he watched the package of their dances from the previous weeks, the high points, the lows, the moments where he'd stumbled, and those where their connection was so obvious it was like the studio could erupt in flames. And as he watched himself improve from stumbling baboon to someone more suave and risk-taking, he wondered exactly how to tell Bailey she needed to stand up to her father and fire him from his role with the finances at her dance studio.

CHAPTER 22

"... *A*nd that's why we need to be careful with our arabesques."

Morgan nodded, as her mother waved from the studio's glass door. "Looks like your mom is here."

"Thanks, Miss Bailey."

"You're always very welcome."

The teenager completed her curtsy goodbye then moved to the side to change her shoes as her mom entered, gesturing like she wanted to have a private word.

Bailey smiled. "Hi Jane. Morgan is doing so well. I think she'll be ready to start her Grade five RAD ballet exams soon."

"Oh, it's so wonderful to think after all she's overcome that she might finally step into her dream."

Bailey's gaze fell on Morgan, whose dad had died in a car accident that had caused significant injuries to the girl, and made her question whether she'd ever dance again. Bailey hadn't charged Morgan's mom standard rates for the past year, insisting an anonymous donor had heard about her situation and paid. The anonymous donor was Bailey, and perhaps her grandmother who was probably watching down from heaven, and who Bailey figured would more than approve. "I remember what it was like."

"And now look at you." Jane glanced around the studio, then placed a hand on her heart. "I don't know if you get told this enough, but thank you for helping children like my Morgan. The other schools were all so expensive, but to know she can come here and receive top-class training, it really means so much."

"It's what I love to do."

"And we can tell. The other parents and I often say how lucky we are to have you."

Bailey blinked back emotion. "You're so sweet."

"Now I know it seems greedy, especially as you're no doubt full to the brim of new students after your TV show, but will you still have time for more private lessons like this?"

"Morgan is a priority for me." She'd make it work. Somehow.

"I know she enjoys the classes with the other girls, but she always says she gets more out of the solo time." Jane leaned closer. "Personally, I think it's because she's hoping to see your boyfriend, but then, aren't we all?"

Bailey chuckled. It had been a little obvious the number of people who wanted to check him out. She was still fielding questions most days about her TV dance partner. "He's been busy with hockey."

"But never too busy for you, I'm sure."

She shrugged. While he was plenty busy, with everything from hospital visits to cancer fundraising dinners, he'd made a serious effort these past weeks, making time among his schedule to invite her to meet some of his friends and team-mates. She enjoyed seeing this part of his world, and couldn't wait to watch his first game in a few weeks, a preseason matchup against Vancouver which would see her meet Chris Thomas again. Apparently she and Poppy would have seats in the WAG section, where the wives and girlfriends and families hung out. She was excited to meet some more of them.

Her phone—freshly returned from the police as they continued their investigations—rang, and she noticed it was the bank. Odd. Why would they be calling so late in the day? It was past their usual close of day. "I'm sorry. I need to take this call."

She waved a hand at Morgan and moved to the office, as Poppy stretched, readying for her tap class with the preteen boys. She closed the door and sank onto her chair. "Hello? Mr. Mitsom?"

"Bailey, I'm glad I caught you. Look, we need to have you make an appointment and discuss a few more things."

"I'm sorry, but why?"

"There are a few other matters that need attention. Look, can I pencil you in for tomorrow, say two PM?"

She glanced at her schedule. "I'm sorry, I'm booked all day."

"How about the next at, say, five?"

"Same thing, I'm sorry. Would the following day work?"

"That's the weekend, and I don't work Saturdays."

Lucky him. "Can't you just tell me over the phone?"

"I'm afraid it's not our policy to discuss these, er, kinds of matters except in person."

"What about an email?"

"An email is not in person, is it?"

No. "Okay, look, I'll try to juggle things and make it on Friday. Five did you say?"

"Yes. Thank you. See you then."

She hung up, then sat back in her chair. What on earth was wrong? She flicked open her computer, saw where Dad's accountancy software kept track of income and expenditure. Everything seemed to be fine, and with all the interest in classes, they even seemed to have a small profit for once.

Her memory flicked back to that odd conversation with Luc, where he'd been angling to find out more about the studio's finances. She kept meaning to ask him, but then his news, or her news, or his kisses always stole such thoughts away. There was so much going on these days she could barely keep up.

These past weeks she and Luc had squeezed in dates around Luc's training, his new commitments to the team, which seemed to involve plenty of media, plus new corporate sponsorship too. He'd been gifted a car by a local car dealership, and surprised her by driving up in a silver luxury SUV. Then there was a clothing endorsement from a Canada-wide suit company, like people were finally recognizing him for the kind of player he'd always aimed to be. He was humble about it, genuinely surprised, and she knew it was likely to tick Cindy off even more, but what was a man to do?

And what was a woman to do, when she was being gifted similar things? The clothing company that provided Luc's game-day suits were also sponsoring her wardrobe. Of course, the price was a mention or two on their social media, but it was nice to showcase people who were willing to sponsor them.

Even now, several weeks after the final, she was still being recognized. The harassing emails and phone calls had eased, perhaps due in part to the week when she'd been without her phone, the automatic forwarding to a new number confusing a few potential students. Nothing could be done about that, her phone had been returned, the perpetrator still not found, and the police said the number came from a burner phone. At least the studio was moving on.

The sounds of tapping and thud-thumps reverberated across the floor as she continued working on more paperwork. If the enrollments stayed steady, and Poppy was to stay, maybe they would have to expand to a bigger studio with separate dance spaces. This place was good, but the office was really too small, and her apartment hardly had room for the equipment and boxes of spare shoes she liked to keep on hand. The apartment might just be big enough to fit her and Poppy, but whenever

Luc visited it seemed to visibly shrink in size. She probably needed to investigate another studio space, but again, that raised the question of what that would mean for people like Morgan, whose single mother was working as hard as she could to help her daughter live her dream. Going out into the cheaper suburbs might allow more dance space, but there was no way that she could help students like Morgan as they'd really struggle to get there. Maybe she could investigate if there was an upcoming vacancy on another space in this building. But for that to happen, they'd really need to get their money issues with the bank sorted.

It was getting late by the time Poppy's tap class finished, and she and Poppy soon got caught discussing various room options. Running classes concurrently would bring in more income, thus offsetting the initial outlay. And surely the time to strike was now, so they could capitalize on the momentum of the show, and make the most of it while they were still getting attention?

Tap tap.

Bailey jumped, head swiveling to the door. "Oh! I didn't know you were there!"

Luc leaned against the doorframe. "You two looked completely out of it. I could've been a serial killer and you wouldn't have known."

"Thank you for that wonderful picture," Poppy said, as Bailey lifted her cheek for Luc to kiss, before he took a seat on several boxes of spare paper.

"It's getting late." His forehead melded into a slight frown. "How do you manage when it's dark? What's your security like here?"

"We have a camera." Bailey pointed to the room's corner. "And there's one at the building's entrance."

"But don't you ever worry about people trespassing? The front door is always unlocked every time I've come here."

"You don't think people want to hurt us, do you?" Poppy asked.

A beat. "No."

But his hesitation was enough to tense Bailey's stomach. "You do you think that, don't you?"

"Look, last I heard the police never found out who the phone call was from, right?"

She nodded.

"So yeah, I think you should be careful. At least have the two of you here on-site at all times."

"We always do. And we have an emergency app on our phone so if there's any issue we just press that and it alerts our folks that something is wrong."

He winced. "Look, no offense, but Poppy's parents won't be able to do much, seeing they're in Calgary. And I hate to say it, babe," he said, looking at Bailey, "but I don't know what your parents would be able to do in a hurry either."

Her chest tightened. "They can call the police, that's what they can do."

"So why isn't it hooked up to 911?"

Poppy glanced at her, they both shrugged. "I guess because it's never been an issue."

"But now might be a good time to take your safety seriously."

"Fine." Who knew that Luc would be so protective? Honestly, sometimes it was like he was vying with her dad in the overprotectiveness stakes. She opened the app, plugged in 911, then showed it to him. "Happy?"

He glanced at it, then her. "I'd be happier if you added my number there too."

"So you can come and whack them with a hockey stick?"

"I'd do that if I needed." His serious glance shifted to Poppy. "Just as I'm sure Franklin would appreciate me doing the same for you."

Part of Bailey thrilled that he was so intense about this. But part of her heard her father's voice complaining as she half-joked, "Hockey is such a violent sport."

"Just wait until you watch a game. Then you'll understand why people love it so much." He half-smiled, but the intensity was still there. "So, have you both added my number yet?"

"You want me to do so as well?" Poppy asked.

"I consider Franklin as one of my brothers, so that makes me yours too. So yeah, put me in."

They did, then he rose. "So, are you almost finished here? Can we go?"

"You two enjoy your date, while I eat at home alone." Poppy mock-sighed.

Bailey shot Luc a glance, he half-lifted a shoulder like he knew what she was going to ask. She loved how their time dancing together meant she was so cued into his non-verbal communications. "You'd be welcome to join us."

"Thanks, you're sweet, but I don't want to be a third wheel. I've got my Lean Cuisine for one, and a good scroll of my Dream Match app might help me find the man of my dreams."

Maybe it would. Maybe it wouldn't. But as she switched off lights and locked up, and they walked Poppy to her car and said goodbye, her fingers tangled in Luc's as she wondered about the mysteries of how God brought people together. She leaned into his side.

"What is it?"

"You. Well, you and me. I'm constantly amazed at how God brings people together."

"Like two opposites like us, huh?"

"We're not that opposite. Both Christians, and—"

"Both athletes."

She smiled. "Both extremely witty."

"For sure. And both trying to make the world a better place."

Her heart grew soft. His work in recent weeks, shining a light on cancer, visiting local hospitals and partnering with a food drive, certainly made that claim true. "You're so sweet and thoughtful, aren't you?"

"Yep, that's me."

His dry tone made her chuckle, which drew his smile, as he gathered her close.

"Speaking of being thoughtful, I can't help but think about you, like nearly all the time."

"Only nearly?" she teased.

"Sometimes I sleep. But even then I dream of a certain ballerina with the most beautiful eyes, whose laughter always makes me smile." He bent down and kissed her.

"Luc, people are looking," she protested, as he stole another kiss.

"Let them look. We've kissed on national TV."

And seeing he didn't mind such an overt example of PDA, she decided to go with it too. And thanked God that He knew what He was doing in bringing this man into her life.

"So, who's ready for preseason?" Jai asked.

Luc clasped his head and rocked back on his chair as the others in the video chat answered. "Can't wait."

"Bring it on."

"We're gonna crush you guys," Chris said to Luc, the remembrance of his words all those weeks ago drawing his smile.

"You're gonna try and everyone is gonna watch you fail."

"Ooh, the new captain sounds feisty." Franklin laughed. "I should tell Hannah that words are being exchanged and a smackdown is a'comin'."

"Speaking nothing but the truth here," Luc drawled.

"Same," Chris said.

"Well, all eyes will be on Winnipeg for that game, won't they?" Mike said.

"How is Bailey with it all?" Ryan asked.

"She's saying the right things. She's met a few of the guys and their wives now, met Coach Frantzen, and it's all gone well."

"It's gonna be fun to see how she handles seeing the real Luc, instead of the soft dude who likes to waltz on ice."

"Please." He rolled his eyes, shaking his head as the others laughed at Ryan's comment. "There's nothing soft here." He flexed.

"Looks like someone's been training hard lately," Jai said.

"Someone needed to. Man, I've been sore. The dancing stuff was great for my cardio, but my strength and conditioning trainer has had me working so hard."

As the other guys shared some of their preseason training routines and targets, his mind flicked back to Ryan's earlier comment. Bailey was excited to see him play. She fit into his world so well, her bright and sunny personality the perfect balance to his bouts of focused intensity. Some of his teammates had noticed, with the goalie, Nate Campbell, commenting to Bailey at dinner last night how Luc was smiling a lot more these days. Which was true. He was. Even if he was still wrestling with how to talk to her about the business side of her dance studio.

Truth be told, he figured Poppy should've said something ages ago, but he understood how the lines of friendship made things blurry sometimes, which made it hard to speak openly when you didn't want to hurt someone's feelings. And this conversation, one that involved her father no less, was ripe for all kinds of miscommunication and offense. He'd been enjoying this time with Bailey too much to willingly burst this cozy bubble. But the fact he wasn't being himself and open and honest made him itchy inside with nerves. When he'd overheard Bailey and Poppy talk yesterday about expanding the business it only upped the ante in making him extra wary. He needed to say something soon. If only he knew what to say.

"So, what are everyone's prayer requests?"

The guys shared, and when it was Luc's turn, he knew he needed help. "Look, I need some wisdom about a conversation I need to have with Bailey."

"What kind of conversation?" Chris asked, winking.

"Not that kind of conversation. No, it's about her dad."

"You need to have a conversation with her dad?" Mike asked.

He nodded. Maybe he should just go direct to the source. That was one way of knowing more about what was going on. And Bailey needn't know and wouldn't get upset with him for poking his nose in where it wasn't exactly wanted.

At the extended silence, he looked up at the screen to see the guys were staring at him. And he suddenly realized just what his words might mean. "Hey, no. Calm that farm down. It's nothing to do with that. It's way, *way* too soon to be talking like that."

"I'm sure we don't know what you mean." Franklin grinned, as the others chirped and teased.

"Just pray I have wisdom. It's got the potential to get messy, and things are so good with her I don't want to blow it up."

That instantly calmed them down, and they nodded.

Then he remembered. "Oh, and they still haven't found the person who was sending her creepy messages, so please pray he's found soon, too."

Franklin nodded. "Thanks for keeping an eye on Poppy."

"Anytime. She's family, right?"

"We all are," Ryan said.

Family. A close family. Like the one with secrets that he wanted to be part of.

CHAPTER 23

The slap of sticks on ice, the cries of "Here, here" and "Hey" filled her ears as the scent of hot dogs and beer filled her nostrils. This was a world away from the refined concert halls and performance spaces she had danced in. But while this scene was so unfamiliar, it still held an excitement not unlike what she'd known when she'd performed on stage. Not that it was her turn to shine, but watching Luc, with his deft turns and spins, the very physicality he demonstrated as he crunched the opposition into walls, made her tense, anxious, and literally sitting on the edge of her seat.

"Come on, Bails, relax." Poppy tugged her back. "You won't make a good impression if you fall off your chair."

That drew the laugh of Molly, Travis's girlfriend, who had insisted Bailey and Poppy sit with her. "That's true. Have you seen how many times the camera has panned up here tonight?"

It had been a few, but she thought that was normal.

But apparently not. Nothing about tonight felt normal for her. And she could suddenly understand why Luc had felt so lost when thrust into the dancing world. Dance was a whole different field to this, and hockey's rough-and-tumble was far removed from the grace and elegance which filled her world.

Molly nudged her. "Don't worry. He's doing well."

She nodded. "There's just so much to get used to. And I've never really known much about hockey."

"Oh we know. You should've heard Travis laugh when you said that on TV."

She winced. "I hope I didn't embarrass Luc."

"Embarrass Luc? You? Girl, you transformed a bear into a prince, and you gotta be proud of that. Nobody knew Luc had those moves in him."

"Luc included," she agreed.

"And don't tell anyone, but I think it's inspired Travis to get lessons for when we finally get married."

"Really?"

Molly nodded.

Poppy leaned across. "I happen to know a local dance studio that might be able to help you with that."

"Is that so?" Molly grinned.

Bailey's attention returned to the ice as a portion of heavy rock blared. "Why is there music?"

"It's a time-out," Poppy said, pointing to the side. "Ice over glass, which means Vancouver gets a penalty, and Zac Parotti goes to the penalty box and is off the ice for two minutes."

"He's the really good one, right?"

"He's hot," Poppy agreed.

"And single, so I heard," Molly added, winking. "But it was careless, so it means Winnipeg has an advantage with an extra man on ice."

Bailey so didn't understand all this new terminology, but was doing her best to keep up. She plucked the edge of her brand-new Blanchard jersey with nervous fingers. The music cut abruptly as the play resumed.

Luc had the puck, and was skating to the opposite end where

Chris Thomas guarded the goal. Chris looked huge padded up in his goalie getup, but she guessed he needed it to protect him from all the missiles of flying pucks and sticks and elbows and sharp skates.

Her breath suspended, as Luc's number 34 passed to Travis who passed it back to him, then he shot and scored.

"Whoo!" Poppy and Molly stood, cheering, clapping, and Bailey stood too, clapping as Luc skated around the back of the goal and was patted on the back by his teammates as another rock classic blared through the sound system.

As Chris sucked down a drink, she noticed Luc glance up at them, and she waved, smiling, and he grinned and pointed her way, before skating to the side and doing a bunch of high fives with his teammates.

"Aww." Poppy hugged her. "Someone out there must be in love to dedicate the very first goal of the team's season to you."

"Preseason," Molly corrected. "But yeah."

The song abruptly cut off, and play resumed with another scuffle in the center that was apparently called a face-off.

Molly offered them more popcorn. "So that was Luc's goal song? Nice."

One thing she'd never thought she'd do: help her boyfriend select a song that would be played each time he scored a goal. The classic by Elton John might contain the team's name, and be an obvious choice, but she'd wondered whether it would sound tough enough for this crowd. Clearly, from the way the crowd had sung along, they approved.

"Come on, make some noise!"

The organ did its own little number, and the announcer revved up the crowd with a series of chants. The atmosphere was exciting, the fans were in a good mood, and she was so glad to be with people who helped her understand the game a little more.

The play continued, and she peered at where Luc sat,

watching the game intensely. The action moved closer to Winnipeg's end, and Zac Parotti, the number forty stitched on his back, skated closer then smacked it into the back of the net.

There was no goal song for him, simply a red flashing light and an announcement over the loudspeakers that drew a collective boo, apart from a few brave Vancouver fans who stood and cheered before being told to shut up.

She laughed, the parochial fans so committed she could understand why this sport got so much funding and sponsorship. And maybe she hadn't realized before just what a big deal Luc actually was, especially after the recent announcement that he was captain. She'd noticed on their dates how many people gravitated to him, wanting pictures, handshakes, and a quick chat. He was always polite, though reserved sometimes, unless it was with little kids. She wondered if his reticence might be due to the *Dance Off* show, but now she realized it was because he was constantly being swamped with hockey questions. Which maybe made her a little bit naive, but how was she to know just how big a deal hockey was?

He came back on the ice, and Poppy nudged her, pointing him out. A Vancouver player pushed him, and he skated past, eyes fixed on the puck.

"Uh-oh," Molly said.

"What's wrong?"

"That's Logan Johansen. He's always been mouthy, and it looks like he's trying to get under Luc's skin."

"Oh." Nerves rippled, her stomach tensing, as she wondered what they'd say to try to get Luc to snap. Something about his dancing? Something about her? She hated to think she might be the reason anyone would mock Luc.

"Luc's a big boy," Poppy said, "and he knows how to keep his temper."

"He's gonna have to," Molly said, "especially now he's captain."

"Although sometimes the captain has to stand up for what's right."

"Yeah, but he's hardly going to get in a fight anymore, is he?"

"A fight?" Bailey asked.

"Come on," Molly said. "Surely you've heard the joke about going to a fight and a hockey game breaking out?"

Would they believe her if she said, "No?"

Molly laughed. "Oh, I love that we have a hockey virgin here. And love even more that you're dating the captain. That must mess with his head so much."

"Look, I'm trying. I'm here, aren't I?"

"And he appreciates it. You know he does," Poppy encouraged.

"That's right. And just like you got to teach him lots of things about dance, so he now gets to teach you lots about hockey."

She nodded, her eyes on the game. Some days it felt like she and he were too much opposites, and Molly's words just reinforced that. She would try harder, would try and learn the game, but finding time to do so felt impossible, especially given the recent interview with the bank.

When she'd finally called in, Mr. Mitsom had pointed out that there were still some discrepancies, then he'd asked about the loan repayments and extra fees.

"But I don't understand. How can there be issues?" Her dad had always assured her that things were paid on time.

Mr. Mitsom sighed. "It seems that some have been missed."

Missed? She'd been tempted to call up her father straight away. But when she'd left, a reminder on her phone to wish Chrissy a happy birthday had stolen her attention, and she remembered why she didn't make waves, why she wouldn't upset her dad, especially not on that day when he and Mom would only be too aware of their eldest child who lived so far away. Since then, she'd kind of forgotten. But still, she'd do so soon. When she found the right words to say.

"Bails?" Poppy nudged her again.

"Sorry, did you say something?"

"Molly and I are getting some food. Want anything?"

"Um, no. I'm okay." If she ate anything else processed she might be sick. Eating clean had helped her overcome some of her food issues in the past. She needed to be careful not to trigger things again.

Instead, she watched the ice get swept clean by the people on skates with what looked like brooms. She hunched forward, elbows on jean-clad knees—the arena was cold—and her ponytail swung to tickle her chin. Around her conversations continued, and every so often she heard Luc's name being mentioned by a trio of men in the section next door who liked their beers and their swearing as they offered their opinions freely.

"Blanchard is looking good so far."

She smiled. She thought he looked very good indeed.

"Can't believe he went on that show."

Her breath hitched as a pithy commentary went on, involving lots of four-letter words she never used, describing Luc, her, and just what some of those dance moves implied. She cringed, wondering how many others thought the same, before reminding herself that their words didn't have to define her.

"Yeah? Well I think he's pretty ballsy, not caring about what anyone thinks."

That was more like it. She glanced across at that speaker, smiled.

He noticed her, straightening, then nudged his friend. "It's her. Blanchard's dance chick."

Oh. Maybe she shouldn't have smiled. She peered at her phone, pretending to message someone, when her name was called. "Bailey."

She peered up. The three men were still staring at her. "Um, hi?"

"You made him soft," the biggest one said.

"Excuse me?"

He shook his head. "He never used to smile on the ice, he was always mean, and now he's smiling."

"I'm sure he's only smiling because he enjoys the game."

"Or enjoying the action later, huh?"

She blinked, her cheeks burning with embarrassment, but her tongue had knots in it and she didn't know what to say, so she looked at her phone as the screen blurred.

"Whoa, what did we miss?" Poppy said, with a scowl at the men that suggested she'd missed nothing.

"Were those jokers harassing you?" Molly asked. "I can ask security to kick them out," she said, in a louder voice that drew the men's scowls but made them shut up and look away.

She exhaled, accepting the cup of popcorn that Poppy handed to her, despite not requesting anything. Surely doing something would be better than thinking over what those men had just said.

"Are you okay?" Poppy asked quietly.

"Yep. I just don't want Luc copping any criticism because they think I'm to blame."

"Well, you can't help what other people say. That's on them. But it's on you to not let it sink into your heart, so don't let it, okay?"

She nodded. Easier said than done.

Molly pointed to the big screen that Bailey had learned was called a jumbotron. "Hey, it looks like they're gonna be miking Luc up for this next period."

"Really?"

Molly slurped her Coke. "It's always kind of fun to hear how they talk to each other on the ice, and Luc's a safe one, as he doesn't say those words that scare little kids or grandmothers."

Or girlfriends.

"And you'll probably see that the opposition won't be mouthing off as much now either."

Poppy nodded. "Yeah. They don't want to have their words recorded."

Bailey hoped so, for Luc's sake. Was it silly for her to be worried about him? But the men's comments before had prickled awareness that while Luc might've got the biggest cheer when he was introduced on the ice tonight, others had a different opinion.

She watched more intently this time, noting when Luc won his face-offs, he yelled, "Hey, hey!" for the puck to be sent his way. His "Good try" when Travis missed, his encouragement to his teammates, all wrapped around her heart.

A good man. One whose actions she hoped would prove to her father he was worthy of her. That there was nothing to worry about. That her father had no need to fear a repeat of Jed and Chrissy's situation, that his tattoos didn't automatically equate with a temper or a violent streak. And she prayed he wouldn't get into a fight.

As they moved back through the tunnel to the ice for the third period, Luc did his best to stay focused on what they had to do. They were tied 2-2, so now it was all about getting pucks on the net, which was exactly what he would aim to do. Focus on that. Lead his men. Not think about the pretty woman he loved who was wearing the jersey he'd got her with his number on it. He would do anything he could to try and make her proud, but he needed to stay in the game and help his team win.

He skated to the center dot and bent, ready for the puck drop, anticipation making him twitchy. He won it from Johansen, sending the puck to Travis. It might only be the first game in the preseason, but already there was chemistry between them. These first few games were about getting regular-season ready after a long summer off, and already he could feel his legs tiring. Coach Frantzen was tweaking the lines and mixing combinations, seeking those which would prove more offensive and score the goals that would help Winnipeg get off to a good start in the regular season. Score enough goals early on in the regular season, and later, when everyone's batteries were running low, there wouldn't be such a need to grind out enough wins to get to the playoffs. That was the coaching staff's strategy, and it made sense to Luc, so he'd do all he could to support Coach Frantzen's vision.

Johansen clipped Luc with his shoulder as he skated past, but the refs didn't notice, so he skated on.

He'd expected the jibes to resume after he was de-microphoned for this period, when people couldn't hear what was being said. Johansen was dirty, and it seemed grossly unfair to much of the hockey world that a known agitator who loved to pick a fight had a Cup ring while Luc and others didn't. Still, he'd be doing all he could to rectify that this year.

Knowing that Vancouver had a need to prove their win last year wasn't a fluke, it wasn't surprising that they were coming hard out of the gate. Zac Parotti skated close, and Luc weaved away, puck on his stick as he shot at Vancouver's goalie. The puck bounced off the pipes with a loud ping.

"Too bad," Chris smirked.

Luc pointed at him. "So sad." Then he skated off with a smile. He probably should rein those in. People weren't used to seeing him smile on the ice. He'd always been a little more intense than some, and he didn't want to give the opposition any more excuse to call him weak.

Judging from the words being tossed around tonight, plenty of them had opinions about his dancing, most of them bad, although a few, like Zac Parotti, understood he'd done it for his mom.

He skated back to the dot and took the face-off, this time losing as Johansen passed to Parotti and down to the blue line.

Luc skated fast and stole the puck and changed direction, when Johansen appeared on his left. Luc swerved, and slammed him into the side with a nice hip-check, which sent Johansen to the ice and drew thunderous cheers from the crowd. Yeah, that was more like it. Tough Luc was back. There'd be no more questions over his masculinity after—

Johansen's stick slapped his midsection, and Luc automatically grabbed it as Logan started talking, spewing words about Luc, about Bailey, about Luc's mom.

He ignored it, ignored it, but the guy kept jawing, about Bailey, about her dance costumes, his every word and smirk like a flame to an oilcan. Luc's temper rose, but he wouldn't bite. He *wouldn't* bite.

Johansen's eyes narrowed. "Yeah, I'd tap that too."

Luc wheeled to face him, dropped his stick, and threw off the gloves, and swung a fist. His knuckles collected the dude on his jaw and he fell down. Luc fell on top of him, pounding him, pounding him, as Johansen tried to hit back. Then the zebras skated in and tried to separate them, all while Johansen kept spewing his garbage.

A few moments later Luc skated to the penalty box, sat, and removed his helmet, and sucked down a drink. A five-minute minor on his first game as captain. Awesome. Would everyone know he was easy to target, that they only need to mention Bailey and he'd explode? And here she was watching, at her first-ever game. He leaned forward, scrubbing his face. What would she think of him?

Another thought hit him, harder than Logan's punch. What would her father think of him now?

CHAPTER 24

*B*ailey felt shaky. It didn't matter how many times Poppy or Molly tried to tell her it was normal, that standing up for himself and his teammates was something Luc was respected for, seeing Luc lose his cool was shocking. She watched the rest of the game on tenterhooks, super tempted to gnaw her nails, despite the recent mani-pedi with Poppy when they'd celebrated the first check from her YouTube channel earnings. Luc had also scored an assist, which apparently meant he earned something called a Gordie Howe hat trick, when a player scored a goal, an assist, and had a fight. The first two were okay, but she wished he hadn't had the last. For his sake, because she dreaded what had been said to make him snarl like that, as much as for what it would mean about her father.

She exhaled slowly. Dad would freak out. And it wouldn't matter what she said, he'd likely tell her to avoid Luc, like he'd been hinting for weeks now. Luc was too big, too ruthless, too tattooed, too fierce, too different. But still a stubborn thought refused to bend. The same stubborn thought that had refused to listen when her father had suggested she put her grandmother's will money into a trust he'd set up.

"Come on. Let's go find him."

She followed Molly and Poppy to the room where the family members waited until the players were released. This felt awkward, like there were so many eyes on her, and nerves gnawed as she wondered what she'd say.

Perky Bailey she could not be. Not yet. She didn't know how to reconcile this side of him, of this sport he loved passionately, with the man she thought she knew. The one who called himself a Christian, who had prayed with her, who had tenderly cared for her when she'd wept. Maybe she didn't know this man as well as she thought she did.

The door opened, and a few players trickled in. Some she recognized, like Nate Campbell, the goalie. Most she didn't, although she might've met them before. Then Molly's partner arrived and kissed her, and he nodded to Bailey. "He'll be out soon."

She nodded, her mouth too dry to speak.

"Want me to stay?" Poppy asked.

Bailey nodded again.

"Hey, you don't need to look so worried. He's tough, and to be honest, he probably needed to do that to set the boundaries so people won't call him soft."

Soft. Like those drunk men had done. She exhaled. "I wish people knew how unsoft dance is."

"I don't think we'll ever be able to change some people's minds." Poppy shrugged.

Probably not.

The door opened, and at the sight of Luc, she squeezed Poppy's hand, then released it, moving tentatively to him.

The hard slant to his face softened, as he smiled. "Hey you."

"Congratulations on your win."

"Thanks." His lips pulled to one side. "It was pretty scrappy."

"Speaking of scrappy." She touched the cut on his cheek and he winced. "Are you okay?"

"Totally okay. Seeing you is the icing on my day."

"Isn't icing something that happens in the game?"

"Look who's been paying attention."

"I tried."

He smiled, more fully now, then drew her near, bending his face as if to kiss her, when he noticed Poppy. "Hey Poppy."

"Good game. Good fight. You looked like you won. The game and the fight."

He shrugged. "It wasn't the plan, but these things happen." He turned to Bailey. "I'm sorry that happened on your first game."

"It's okay," she murmured.

"Is it?"

She nodded. It would be. It would have to be, if they were going to stick together.

If? That it was even a question shocked her, and she hugged him. He pressed a kiss to her hair, then nodded. "So, we're all going back to yours?"

She nodded. It was what they'd agreed on. She and Poppy would Uber to the arena, and he'd drive them home.

"Actually, if it's all the same with you, I might Uber back," Poppy said.

He shook his head. "It'll take forever on game night. I'll drive you."

"Yeah, but I think you and Bails need some time alone."

He nodded, but said, "I'll drive you both home then we can talk there or somewhere else."

Five minutes later she and Poppy were sitting in his vehicle as he finished talking to a member of staff. "Bails, you need to not make a mountain out of this," Poppy warned.

"Has Franklin been in a fight?"

"A few. Not as many as Luc, I imagine, but then part of Luc's role has always been to stand up for his teammates. It's why the team like him, and probably why the staff made him captain. They know he's passionate about the game and his team."

"Won't they be upset that the new captain was fighting in his first game?"

"It probably wasn't ideal, but we don't know what was said. And from what Franklin has said in the past, it's probably not something you want to know."

Bailey swallowed. That sounded like Poppy thought it had been over something to do with Bailey.

"Just remember that fighting is pretty close to inevitable for anyone who has been playing a few years."

"But he's a Christian."

"And he still is. Salvation isn't dependent on whether a man punches or not."

True. She sucked in a breath. "I still can't—"

"I know. And you need to let it go. If he wants to explain himself, then okay. But he might not. I know Franklin has always felt a little embarrassed that he got goaded into something."

She sighed. There was so much about this sport she'd never thought to know.

Luc appeared, and Poppy gave the conversational zest needed, while Bailey did her best to appear okay. But when Poppy exited, and Luc shifted to study her, she knew he'd noticed her less-than-peppy attitude.

"Bails."

That tender note in his voice drew emotion, and she blinked hard to keep it away.

"Hey, it's okay." He grasped her hand.

"I'm sorry. I should be all cheerleader-like, right? But I'm just trying to wrap my head around this."

"I get it. It's a lot."

"Why did you do it?"

"The fight, you mean?" He sighed. "I shouldn't have. It was

dumb, especially when it's basically an exhibition game which ultimately doesn't mean a thing. But I felt like I needed to draw a line, especially as we play Vancouver a lot, and I wanted to let Johansen know I won't stand for that. I wasn't going to let anyone disrespect anyone I care about."

"Did he say something mean about me?"

He winced. "I really didn't mean to imply that."

"So it's true. Well, in that case..."

He glanced quickly at her.

"Good."

"Good?"

Her chin lifted. "I appreciate you standing up for me."

"Thank you for understanding." He picked up her hand and kissed it. "I'm sorry for worrying you. The team weren't too happy, but I think they understand now." He shot her a wry look. "I won't be doing that anytime again soon."

"I hope not. I want you in one piece. But hey, at least you won."

He chuckled. "I love the fact you care about that."

"It must be that competitive thing, right?"

"Right."

He leaned closer and kissed her, and suddenly it didn't matter about the fight, or her father, or anything else at all. All that mattered was this was a good man, who wanted to stand up for those he cared about.

"No. I don't like it. I really think you need to keep away from him. He's violent."

Bailey studied her parents across the dining table as Sunday's lunch grew cold. Luc was away this weekend, and she had attended her parents' church this morning, then joined them for a meal as per usual. She pressed her lips together. She should've known this was an excuse for her father to dump on

Luc. And there was never a better time than when the man wasn't here to defend himself.

"I can't give my blessing to a man who is prone to violence. I just won't."

"But that's what Luc does, Dad. He protects people. He never lets me down. I can always count on him."

"But he's so different to you. He's not your type."

"Dad, no. Please stop."

"But Bailey, we care about you."

"And so does he!"

She peeked at her mom, but her mother's head was bowed, as if she too had had this conversation with her father and knew the outcome. Some days when Dad got on his high horse about things there was no reasoning with him. She glanced around the room, the kitchen cabinets with their diamond glass showcasing Mom's porcelain collection. Everything the same. Dad with his prejudice, Mom with her silence, the quiet enabler.

She dropped her head. Was it disrespectful to think of her parents in this way?

"We just want you to be safe," her father said.

"I know you do," she murmured.

Memories of Jed and Chrissy, of the bruises her sister had worn, flared into consciousness. She understood her father's concerns, really she did, but, "Luc isn't the same as Jed."

"But his tattoos—"

"Dad, stop sounding so prejudiced. Do you seriously think tattoos mean he's not a Christian?"

"Well, no."

"But?" She pressed.

"But perhaps he's not walking as close to God as I'd like to think my daughter would require in a man with whom she's in a relationship," he replied stiffly.

"How do you know how close Luc is to God? Have you ever asked him? Or just judged him from afar?"

"I don't understand all this hostility, Bailey."

"I'm not hostile, Dad. I'm simply trying to defend the man when he's not here to defend himself."

She paused, realizing again that attacking people when they weren't there was what her father had often done. Her family was way too good at playing games and passive aggression, acting or speaking one way while meaning another. All her life she'd been taught to suppress negative feelings, instead of openly addressing them. Her family's need to avoid conflict had reached gold medal levels in recent years, after Chrissy's marriage breakdown had led Dad to try to maintain some semblance of control. And she and Rhett enabled him, as much as anything her mom had done.

She pushed back her chair. "I'm afraid I need to leave. I've got some paperwork to do."

"On the Sabbath?"

She swallowed. Trying to explain that God's grace extended to people who worked on Sundays was probably a step too far for her dad today. The concept that God might love tattooed people was probably enough for one day. "I'm sorry." Was saying sorry when she wasn't simply being polite or just a lie?

"But you haven't had dessert," her mother complained.

She swallowed. No, she hadn't. "Thanks, but I'm not hungry." Not for this kind of dessert, anyway. She couldn't wait for Luc to return.

THE ROAD TRIP to Saint Paul and Chicago proved a useful trip to school his emotions. Being away from Winnipeg—Bailey— helped him refocus on what he was meant to do. Play well, inspire his team, lead by example. He didn't want anyone getting sloppy or undisciplined or letting teams goad them, like what had happened with Johansen in the Vancouver game last week. And though Minnesota's Mitch Reilly liked to intimidate with his big presence, checking Luc into the boards, then muttering that Luc should've quickstepped faster, the words had ignited his sense of humor, and he'd decided to play along too. Which was why he used as many dance puns as he could in his press conference after.

"So, Luc, tell us what's ignited this new passion on the ice. Has it got anything to do with a new passion off the ice?"

"I'm gonna guess from that comment you're talking about the lift you've seen in my recent games. I guess it's no secret that I've been in a spin these past few months, and I'm glad that my fancy footwork is paying off."

That scored a few laughs, and he kept his own amusement locked behind flat lips, turning to the next reporter. Hannah Wade. Hannah James now, Franklin's wife, and Poppy's sister-in-law.

"Luc, I'd like to concentrate on the score-line tonight."

"I appreciate that."

Her lips quirked, like she was as tired as he was of some of these other reporters poking around his love life. "Three wins on the trot—"

"The foxtrot?"

"If you're the fox."

"Ba dum tish."

She smiled. "Tell us how it feels to be the captain and what you're doing to inspire your team to play hard each time."

"I think everyone knows that I consider this a true honor. I'm working doubly hard to maintain focus and lead by example. I'm aiming to have the most shots on goal per game, if not the most goals, and I expect all the boys to want the same."

"Except for Campbell," she joked.

"Except for Soup"—the goalie—"that's right."

"And would you care to comment on that fight in that game against Vancouver?"

"Nope." But knowing this would only lead to more speculation, he figured it was best to clear the air. "You know, it's no secret that I've been someone who's brought some grit and aggression in the past. But it's also no secret that I've long been someone who stands up to injustice, and when smart-butts like Johansen want to have a go at me for doing something for charity, I really think it says something about the weakness of their character. And I can't help but notice that Johansen wasn't the dude asked to dance on national TV. I'm gonna guess he was just sore about not being asked. I guess we'll know that for certain if he tries anything like that again."

This earned a round of laughs, and a nod of appreciation from Hannah. Nothing like calling a man out in a way that would make him look cheap if he went after Luc again. And that might just serve as a warning to anyone else to not push him, otherwise he just might say something similar.

He clenched then relaxed his fingers. He couldn't wait to return and see Bailey again.

"It's so good to hold you."

"It's so good to be held by you." His grip tightened, then she squeaked. "Although maybe not *that* tight."

"Sorry, babe. I forgot." He relaxed, but didn't let go.

The lights of the Peg glimmered through the window, the sun setting as he drank her in, highlighting the warm bronze and red strands in her hair. He didn't want to move from this position. Like, ever. She was the perfect height, the perfect shape, had the perfect scent, the right amount of curves and length. He loved everything about her. Everything.

He drew back. "You want dessert?" She tipped her lips up invitingly, so it was only polite to obey her request. But his kiss soon grew a little hungry, which made him draw reluctantly away.

"I think I want too much dessert."

She laughed, and there it was, that easing in his soul again.

"Then you better sit down over there, and I sit down over here—"

"Or I could just sit next to you on the sofa and we could hold hands and watch the sun set."

"You'll behave yourself?"

"Yes, ma'am."

Her smile revived memories of their dance rehearsals, and she seemed to think that too, as her amusement softened, and she traced his jaw with her hand. "I miss all those dance practices with you."

"Maybe we should do some more sometime." Or maybe he could find an excuse for a team function involving dance that he'd label an exercise in team building, team bonding, or whatever.

"When I watched the game with Molly she mentioned that she and Travis might be interested in dance lessons for their wedding."

"He popped the question?"

"I don't think so. But I get the feeling she hopes it'll be soon."

"Well, look who's just dived into the deep end with the team's girlfriends."

"It was really good to sit with her and Poppy. They both explained the game pretty well."

"So, do you think you might enjoy it one day?"

Her nose wrinkled, and his heart fell. "Maybe not as much as someone I know enjoys doing the tango."

He chuckled. "I gotta admit, the tango is up there. At least if I get to do it with you."

He drew her legs over his knees. "So, what else has been happening? I know it's only been a few days, but I feel like it's been so much longer. So tell me everything. How's the business? How are your folks? What's news?"

Her face blanked for a second, so he knew she had news. But the fact she didn't light up and tell him suggested it wasn't good. "Bails? What's going on?"

She shook her head. Sighed.

"What is it?"

"I went to my folks after church on Sunday. Their church, not yours. I'd rather go to yours when you're there."

He nodded. He understood. It was big. "And?"

She sighed. "Dad warned me about you. Again."

"Again?"

She stretched, then inched closer, tucking her head next to his. "I'm so sorry. He's so judgmental, and still hasn't got over that fight."

He exhaled silently. He should've refrained, been the bigger man, even if what he'd done had stopped the aggression against his team. "I'm sorry."

"And that's the other thing. I realized last weekend how often I don't actually say what I mean when I'm around them."

He nodded, but couldn't verbalize that. Not yet anyway. The door to her self-revelation had to crack a little wider before he threw any truth bombs in there. "You love your parents and don't want to hurt them."

"Exactly. And yet, sometimes I wonder if it's not helping if I don't say what I really mean. Although I did manage to tell Dad to stop."

"Stop? You mean with the business?"

She blinked, her brow furrowing. "No, I mean about you."

He kissed her brow, hoping she'd hurry past that slip of the tongue. "What did you tell him? That I kiss so divinely you want to kiss me all the days of your life?"

"Yeah, that." She rolled her eyes, as a smile played around her lips. "I think my dad would explode if I said something like that."

"Best to not tell him that then. Not yet, anyway," he added, without thinking.

"Not yet?" She sat up, turning to face him in a lateral crunch his trainer would applaud.

"I mean, one day you'll probably need to tell him how much you adore me, and that you want to spend forever with me." Just like he did with her.

Her eyes were wide, and he realized how much of his own heart he'd just opened for her to see, so quickly added, "But that's a one-day thing."

"Definitely a one-day thing," she agreed, settling beside him again. "I honestly think Dad would have a stroke if I was to say that. Not when he wanted me to end things with you."

His heart sank. "Wow. I didn't think he disliked me that much."

"It's not you. I think it's more the thought of you. He doesn't really know you yet."

"Well, there's a way to change that. Why not invite them here? We could have dinner together. You could even invite Rhett and that happy wife of his."

"Cindy."

"That's the one."

"Are you serious?"

He was serious about a future with her. Which meant getting to know the family of the woman he loved. "Maybe they could come watch a game."

"Rhett would totally be okay with that."

"Then let's make it so."

CHAPTER 25

*T*his was such a bad idea. Bailey touched up her lipstick in Luc's ensuite bathroom and eyed her reflection. Tonight was supposed to be a chance for her family to get to know him better, but instead it had been a debacle. She'd thought the game starting at three on a Saturday would be perfect for her parents who didn't like to stay up too late. But here they were, at eight PM, and her father had barely looked at Luc all night, let alone thanked him for the tickets, or tonight's meal. And Cindy was being Catwoman tonight, snarky about everything from the food served at the game to the meal Luc had arranged tonight. She wouldn't blame Luc if he left Bailey because he thought her family just too hard.

"Bailey?"

Speaking of the she-devil.

"Oh. Here you are." Cindy's gaze met her in the mirror. "Right next to his bedroom. What a surprise."

What? "Um, I'm here because you were in the other bathroom, and I…" Her words faltered as Cindy pried open the mirrored cabinet. "What are you doing?"

"Just looking." She closed it, shrugging. "It'd be helpful to know if the man is on drugs, don't you think?"

"I beg your pardon?"

"Well, you don't want someone marrying into the family who is on drugs, now do you?"

Was Cindy on drugs herself? This seemed surreal. "He's not on drugs."

"He must be on something. Everyone's talking about how different he is this season. Unless, he's on..." She turned and eyed Bailey, and arched a brow.

Words drained away, her confidence, already wavering during the game, sinking to a new low. She turned then plowed into a big chest.

Luc steadied her, but didn't move. "If you mean to suggest that we're involved sexually, you're wrong."

"Okay." Cindy flipped her hair behind her shoulder.

"And," Luc's voice could turn flowers into stones, "you owe Bailey an apology for insinuating such a thing."

"Did I insinuate? Or did you just hear what everyone else is thinking?"

Bailey's breath hitched, and she felt how Luc stiffened as Cindy smiled and sauntered out. Clearly he was as shocked by her sister-in-law's behavior as she was, but as host he didn't want to kick her out. "I'm so sorry."

"You don't need to apologize, Bails."

She still felt like she did.

"She doesn't like you, does she?" he murmured.

"I don't know what I ever did to make her hate me so much."

"Can I kick her out?" he asked hopefully.

But that wasn't the way to build bridges. "Maybe we can pray her out," she said instead.

"Like ask God for an emergency phone call?"

"Something like that."

But it didn't take an emergency phone call, just a couple of her father's barely hidden yawns before he said stiffly that they needed to leave soon because they had an early church service to get to tomorrow.

She caught the relief on Luc's face, which twisted her heart, before he hid it with a polite nod of understanding. Her heart grew sore. Perhaps this was impossible, and they'd never bridge the divide. At least Luc had tried.

"Before we go," her father eyed Luc, "I wanted to ask how old you are."

"Dad."

"No, it's only reasonable that the man should tell us. If Luc wishes to be in a relationship with my daughter then I have a right to know."

"I'll be thirty-one next year," Luc said evenly. "We had this conversation already, Wayne."

They had?

"Thirty-one?" Cindy nudged Rhett. "He's even older than you."

Bailey swallowed. She could see how her dad might have fresh concerns about that.

"Well, you certainly don't act your age, do you?"

"Dad!"

"No, it's only right that he should know that one doesn't expect a thirty-year-old man to fight like in that last game."

Bailey closed her eyes, and prayed that she and Luc could disappear. Actually…

She pushed to her feet. "I need to go." She glanced at Luc, whose stony face had barely changed expression since the bathroom. "Would you mind taking me home?"

He peered up at her, his expression unreadable, glanced at the table, then nodded. He rose. "Please excuse me. You're welcome to stay—"

"Oh, but we could take you, Bailey," her mom said.

Her parents could, but right now she wanted to be as far away from them as Luc probably wished to be. "No, I need Luc."

He dipped his chin. "As I was saying, if you'd like to stay, you're very welcome to. Otherwise, you're welcome to leave. Just close the door behind you."

"Bye sis." Rhett hugged her.

Bailey glanced at Cindy but couldn't even manage a smile for her.

She air-kissed her parents, then after Luc made his farewells, she tugged his hand as they hurried to the elevator. As soon as they were inside, she hugged him. "I'm so sorry. That was so bad."

"It wasn't what I hoped for."

The whole night hadn't been. The 4-1 loss to Vancouver had been a little embarrassing, even if Zac Parotti had proved his A-game skills. At least that mean guy from last time had kept his mouth shut from what she could see, and there'd been no scuffles like the previous game. Her father had still found plenty to complain about, with everything from the volume of the music to the language of fans to the smell of beer.

She hugged Luc harder. "Let's not do that again in a hurry."

"For sure."

She sighed. "Are you sure you don't mind leaving them there alone?" She cringed but had to tell him. "You know that Cindy was looking through your bathroom cupboards? I think she wanted to know if you're on drugs."

"I know. I heard her."

Then he'd heard everything else that had been said. "I'm so sorry."

"Bails, it's not your fault."

But it felt like it was. They drove past the Coffee Haus and he soon pulled up at her apartment. She invited him upstairs, which he reluctantly agreed to. Maybe there was some way to salvage the evening. Like with more dessert.

THIS HAD BEEN A BAD IDEA. Playing pretend with Bailey was doing his head in. He couldn't do it anymore. He nodded to Poppy, their ever-accommodating chaperone, who looked up from reading on the sofa as they entered the living area.

"You're home early. And judging from those faces it didn't go too well."

He shot Poppy a look. Her nose wrinkled. "That bad, huh?"

"Maybe I'm tired, but yeah. It felt like a waste of time."

Bailey's gasp drew his attention, and he reached to hold her hand. "I didn't mean it to sound like that, but you have to admit that was painful."

"It wasn't that bad."

"It was. Come on, Bailey, just be honest for once. You said as much in the elevator."

"But…" She glanced at Poppy.

He released her hand. "What? Do you think Poppy doesn't know that your family has issues?"

"Excuse me?"

"Look, I know we all have issues, I'm not saying I don't. But come on, that was crazy. My folks might not be Christians, but you can sure as heck know they wouldn't be grilling you on being too young for me."

He caught Poppy's wide-eyed look and filled in the gaps. "Wayne asked me how old I was, again, and not"—he cut off Bailey—"in a way that was nice."

Poppy winced, then winced again as Bailey glanced at her.

"What is it?" Bailey asked her.

A heavy sigh escaped Poppy. "I've known your folks for years, and Bailey, I'm sorry, but I know what Luc means."

Bailey faced him, her brow knit. "What *do* you mean?"

He hated that hurt look on Bailey's face, knowing he'd put it there, knowing this conversation wasn't going to be easy. He slumped back in the overstuffed armchair. "Bails, I guess I'm just a little confused."

"About?"

"You. You're a boss in the dance world. I've seen you manage people and wrangle little kids and do all manner of things, but when you're around your dad it's like you second-guess yourself."

"You're just saying that because of what my dad said."

"Yeah, of course I am." He rolled his eyes. "Come on, Bailey. When you're with them you shrink back. I'm sorry, but your family don't do honesty much, do they? You keep secrets from each other, and you paste a smile on your face like you don't mind when someone hurts you."

"What do you mean?"

"Every time that Cindy creature opens her mouth you just take it. She deliberately says stuff to annoy you and you just let it slide."

Her mouth sagged. "I like to think that's called turning the other cheek. Perhaps you could try it sometime."

Frustration grew. He swallowed and prayed for calm. "There's a difference between turning the other cheek and naively faking it and pretending it doesn't exist and hoping it goes away."

She gasped. "I can't believe you said that."

"Someone has to." He glanced at Poppy. "I know you and Poppy have been friends for years, but even she doesn't always tell you the truth."

Bailey glanced at Poppy. "What haven't you been saying?"

Poppy glanced at Luc, then back at Bailey, then sighed. "Thanks a lot, Luc."

"You're welcome." Hey, if she'd been friends with Bailey for years he had no problem throwing her under the bus when she should've spoken up years ago.

"Poppy?" Bailey asked.

Poppy sighed. "I just didn't know how to say this."

"Say what?"

Poppy glanced at him, her eyes narrowed, her mouth now a flat line.

So he shrugged. "Bails, Poppy and I are concerned that your dad is mismanaging your accounts."

"What? How dare—?"

"Whoa, before you get upset, I'm not saying your dad has done anything wrong or illegal, just that—"

"Have you and Poppy been talking about this?" Bailey interrupted.

He sat back and shot Poppy a look. When she looked at him, he folded his arms. This was on her. As he'd said before, she should have spoken up way before this.

Poppy sighed. "Look, Bails, I never wanted to hurt you, but yeah, I've had some concerns about your dad and, well, how capable he is with managing the books."

"What do you mean? He's done it for years, and you've never said anything before."

"I'm so sorry," Poppy said. "It was never my intention to hurt you, but I have to side with Luc. I have concerns."

"But he's a member of the church's finance board," Bailey exclaimed.

"Is he the church treasurer?" Luc asked.

"Well, no. They have an accountant, I think."

"So he doesn't have any role that has a legal position?"

"No, but—"

"He's not trained as an accountant, is he?"

"You know he's not. I don't understand what you're getting at."

He rolled his shoulders, his neck tendons popping. "I've mentioned before that my dad's job is in small business strategic planning and he's seen countless times when people have been taken advantage of by someone they trust. And I don't want that to happen to you."

"But my dad isn't taking advantage of me."

"Have you spoken with the bank lately?"

Her gaze lowered.

"Bailey?" Poppy asked.

He pressed his lips together. So that was another secret she'd kept.

"I… I kind of forgot. But yes, Mr. Mitsom has had some concerns." She glanced at Poppy. "Apparently there are some fees that haven't been paid…" She pushed her face in her hands.

He shifted beside her, wrapped an arm around her. "Bails, you don't need to keep your dad on in that role. But you do need to be honest with him."

"I don't know what to say."

"Easy. Say, 'Dad, I've decided'," he shot a look at Poppy, "actually, say 'Poppy and I have decided we need a business accountant to run our books. Thank you for your help over the years but now we're growing so much we need more assistance'."

"I couldn't say that. I can't hurt him."

"If you don't, you continue to hurt your business. Especially if you want to grow and have a new building or more space. You're not going to get that if you're letting money slip through your fingers." He grimaced. "You probably need an audit, and then get a professional business accountant to help you. I can make some suggestions."

"I bet you can," she muttered.

"Bails," Poppy pleaded. "Hear Luc out. He's only trying to help."

Bailey shook her head.

Poppy glanced at him then back at her. "I think it's a good idea to get an audit done. Then you'll know for sure and we can confront him if that's the case."

"I can't believe we're even talking like this," Bailey murmured. "How can I know who a good auditor is?"

"I have connections," Luc said.

"Of course you do." Bailey rolled her eyes.

"Hey, you're welcome to go find your own people to do that, but I can ask my dad, or those associated with the team and they can recommend people they trust."

"Look," she turned to him, "I appreciate that you are trying to help, but this is not something you need to get involved in."

"But I care about you. I want to help."

"So does my dad."

"But what if what he's doing is not actually helping anymore?"

She stared at him, eyes wide. "I can't believe you're saying that. My dad *loves* me."

So did he. But now wasn't the time to say that. "And you love him, I get that."

"Of *course* I love him. And I'd never do anything to hurt him. Especially not after Chrissy abandoned the family."

So this was the heart of the issue. He glanced at Poppy. She grimaced. Great. So no help there. He swallowed his own sigh. "Are you telling me that you want to keep the peace with your folks because of what happened to your sister?"

Bailey lowered her head.

"You can't keep pandering to him, Bails," he said as gently as he could. "You can't keep pretending everything is okay when it's not. You need to be honest. Sooner or later you have to stand on your own two feet."

"I do. I have."

"Honey." He shifted to grasp her hands. "Please don't be mad. I'm trying to help."

She pulled free. "They're my family. Who have known me a lot longer than you have. Who do you think you are?"

He swallowed. Clearly, this was not going well.

"They love me," Bailey continued.

"I love you."

She froze.

He was aware of Poppy quietly exiting the room. "I love you, Bails," he repeated.

She pushed her head in her hands. "Why do you always have to do that?"

"Say I love you?"

"Yes! First you kiss me for the first time on national TV, then you tell me you love me—while we're arguing?"

He sighed. He knew he should've kept his mouth shut. Still, honesty begged to be spoken. "I'm sorry. I thought that might be something you'd like to hear. I didn't realize there was a protocol about it."

From the look in her eyes, that was the path best left untaken.

Man. "I'm sorry, Bails. I shouldn't have—"

"Can you please leave? I'm really tired."

So was he. But this wasn't how he could let today's fail of a day end. "Bailey, no. We should talk."

She shook her head, fake-yawned, not looking at him. "I've got church tomorrow."

So did he. Which meant he had one last chance to be with her before the next road trip separated them for a week. "What time do you want me to pick you up?"

"You don't need to." She stood. "I'll be going with my parents." Then she exited the room.

She was such a child. She'd known that as she'd argued with Luc last weekend, part of her wanting to stop, while something else spurred her on. She'd known so much of what he'd said was true, but hadn't wanted to face it. Like he'd said, she might be bold on the dance floor, and able to whip a non-dancing hockey player into a Patrick Swayze wannabe, but she couldn't speak honestly with her parents or whip her own feelings into the right shape. And now he'd left on a weeklong road trip and she wouldn't have the chance to speak to him face-to-face and deal with the strain that had crept up between them.

Her shoulders slumped as a few raindrops spattered on the office's window. There was so much she needed to say to him, so much to confess. Like *Dance Off*'s official offer for her to be part of another season, and the tour. She couldn't keep hiding things simply because she was worried he mightn't like it. That was no way to be real in a relationship.

Luc might've departed on a road trip for warmer climes, but his words hadn't left, rising and falling like waves on the sea. He'd been right, and she'd denied it. And she knew she needed

God's help to push past the years that had shaped her into being this way.

She leaned her head against the glass and closed her eyes. "Lord, I'm so sorry. I need Your help but I barely know what to ask. You know my family all like to tiptoe around the truth, but it's not healthy, is it?"

Today's morning Bible reading came to mind. Jesus cracking the whip at the sellers in the Temple. Some might view Jesus as meek and mild but there had been times when He'd been as bold as a lion. And while she could be bold in some areas, other areas—other people—had always made her second-guess what was right. How could she honor her parents and call out her father?

"Lord, give me wisdom to know what to say and when. And please bless Luc in all he's doing. Help him know I still care. Amen."

She probably didn't need to pray that last one though. She could always call him, or send a text, or—

"Bailey?"

Her mom's voice opened her eyes, and she turned to clasp her in a hug. "You're earlier than I thought you'd be."

"I finished my errands faster than I thought, and..." She peered at Bailey. "Honey? Is everything okay?"

She straightened at her mother's voice. Pasted a smile on her—but no. Wasn't this more of the pretending that Luc had said she often did? Maybe it was time to speak openly, honestly, and not just about right now but what had gone on before too.

"Actually, Mom, no."

Her mom blinked, her automatic response whenever bad news dared pass the lips of her child, then she went into phase two: nervous hovering. "What is it? What's wrong?"

Bailey blew out a breath. If they were going to have this conversation, they needed to be somewhere they could be businesslike, and not get caught in sidetracks and emotion.

"Mom, I would really like to ask you a few things, but not here."

"Then where?"

"Can we—?" No, that was more of the same waffling type of conversation she'd always used. She needed to be honest, be direct, speak the truth. "I would like to go to the Coffee Haus."

"Where you used to work?"

"Exactly. I haven't been there for a while, but you know the coffee is good."

"Then sure."

She motioned to Poppy who was leading a gentle Pilates class for older ladies and walked with her mom the few blocks to the café. Max was behind the coffee machine, and welcomed her with a half-smile. "It's our celebrity."

Bailey introduced her mom, placed her order, and went to pay, but Max waved off her card. "I saw all the mentions, and I might've boasted a few times about how you two met here, so I feel like it's only fair that you benefit from me benefitting off you."

"God bless you."

Max looked startled for a moment, unsurprising as Bailey had never really owned her faith with the staff here before. But even that was something she should've done long ago. Regrets chased her. She offered a smile, less big and fake, smaller but more genuine, and gestured for her mom to take a place on the comfy couch. This conversation was bound to get uncomfortable, so they might as well find what softness they could.

"What's wrong, Bailey?"

Lord, please help me be honest. She swallowed. "I had an argument with Luc after we left you on Saturday night."

"You never said anything on Sunday."

Because she'd been trained to not tell the truth. But even that was a cop-out. She was nearly twenty-five, for goodness' sake. It was time to stop acting like a child. "I didn't say anything on Sunday because I get the feeling that Dad doesn't like Luc."

"Oh, darling, that's not true."

Bailey eyed her mother. "Isn't it?"

"You know he's concerned about you."

"Do you like Luc?" She could high-five herself at being so bold.

"Of course I do."

Her shoulders relaxed. But she needed to press on, say this while courage remained. "His tattoos don't bother you? You're not worried about him being too old?"

"Of course I'm not worried. He's a lovely man, and very generous, too."

"He was generous, but did you know that nobody in our family said thank you to him?"

"That can't be right."

"Maybe Rhett said something, but I didn't hear him or anyone else say thank you for the tickets to the game or the dinner at his house."

"Well, that might be because you both left so abruptly."

"I had to leave and get Luc away from Dad. He wouldn't stop picking on him."

"Your father is just a little overprotective sometimes."

"Yeah, well, I'm not coping with it, Mom. And I know I should've said something about this long ago, but I... I guess I wanted to keep the peace because I was worried about you and Dad when everything happened with Chrissy. But now I can't do this anymore."

"What do you mean?"

"I love Luc." Just saying that out loud set her heart ablaze. But fresh regret poured in. She should be saying that for the first time to Luc, not to her mother about him.

"And?"

"I want him in my life, in my future. But I feel like Dad

doesn't, and I want to know why." No, she had to be more direct than that. "I want your help to understand why, and I want your help to bring Dad around so he'll accept Luc into the family one day."

Her mother's eyes widened. "Are you saying he's proposed?"

"No. But I suspect he never will if I don't learn to stand up and start saying what I really think instead of walking around on eggshells trying not to upset you and Dad."

"I truly don't understand where all this is coming from."

Max placed their coffees on the table in front of them. Bailey thanked Max, offering a tight smile, which dropped as soon as Max left. "Luc is worried that Dad isn't doing a good job with the studio's finances. The bank has been asking questions, and something Poppy said recently made me wonder again what happened to your dance studio and why you quit teaching."

"You know I wanted to stay home with you."

"I know that's what you've said. But is it actually true?" Bailey sipped her chai. "I'm sorry, Mom, if this comes across too blunt, but I feel like our family has always tiptoed around the truth, when we would've been better off speaking up loud and proud."

Max glanced her way, but no, not that kind of proud. She focused on her mother, who was staring at her coffee with a contemplative brow.

"You want the truth?" Her mother sighed. "Well, I feel as though your father has always felt like he had something to prove. As you know, my parents were well-off, and while they welcomed Wayne into the family, they soon learned that he didn't have quite the same touch as my father did when it came to investments. Your father is a good man, but a little inclined to seeing things his own way, and always felt a little snubbed when they wouldn't take his well-meaning advice. I'll admit I've found it challenging at times, but thought it best to keep the peace. And yes, I gave up the dance studio because you three were so young, but I also did it because your father was not as clever with the finances as he thought he was."

Bailey gasped. "But you didn't say anything when he offered to help me."

"I didn't know how much he was involved. I'm sorry."

Bailey sank into the corner of the sofa, glad for the surrounds that tamped emotion, that helped force her to say what needed to be said. "I wish I'd known this. I have to get a business accountant and probably an audit as it seems like Dad hasn't been paying some of the bank fees or repayments on time."

"Oh, Bailey." Her mother winced. "I'm so sorry."

This was what happened when people didn't tell the truth. Cover-ups became lies. Lies held a kind of darkness that could only be dispelled by speaking the truth. Truth that needed to be spoken to break the shackles from the past. And not just about the dance studio's finances. "You know I left my ballet course in England because I had an eating disorder."

Mom's breath hitched. "Oh my goodness. Really?"

Bailey nodded, weight lifting. "I saw a therapist which really helped, and I haven't relapsed for four years now. I still check in with her occasionally."

"Oh, honey." Her mom hugged her. "I wish I'd known."

Well, now she did. Truth-telling was addictive. So, in for a penny... "I think Cindy hates me. She acts like such a witch sometimes."

"Oh Bailey." A beat. "She does, doesn't she?"

Her mild-mannered mother agreeing sent a sparkle of laughter through her. "I try so hard with her, but it's like nothing I do makes a difference."

"I know."

She sighed. "I wish Chrissy would contact us again."

"So do I."

"We should message her."

"We should."

"No, right now. We should message her."

"But your father—"

"Is wrong, Mom. He's not acting like the prodigal son's father but the older brother."

"Oh, Bailey, now that's… that's actually true."

Bailey was thankful that her mother was proving to be a safe space, but she should be sharing these truths with those who needed to hear it. Starting with her older sister, whom—apart from that recent birthday message which had received no reply —she hadn't touched base with in far too long. As far as it depended on her, she'd make the effort and extend a hand of grace. To her sister, and to Cindy.

She tapped out a message to Chrissy: *I love you, I miss you, I hope we can talk soon.*

That was enough, she hoped. She pressed send. "We'll have to pray God opens Dad's heart again."

"I've been praying that for years," her mother admitted, which drew Bailey's hug.

Keeping the peace was important, but not when it was at the expense of real love. Honoring others didn't mean sweeping the truth under carpets. Being honest meant being real, at times raw, but respectful, and came not from emotion but from love.

Which reminded her to message Luc: *I'm so sorry for how I left things with you the other day. You were right. I was wrong. Please forgive me. I can't wait to see you again as there's something I need to say to you. In person.*

LUC GLANCED AT HIS PHONE, his heart twisting as he read her words, then placed it down again, as the Bible study guys' banter washed around him. He could barely tune in, was only here because he knew there'd be questions if he didn't show, but everything in the past few days since his argument with Bailey seemed to drift past. Like Mike had shared in their brief Bible discussion, God was his only anchor, sure and certain.

"Luc?" Mike asked. "Is everything okay?"

"Sorry. I've been a bit distracted. What were you saying?"

But before Mike could say anything, Chris joined the chat, his grin bursting from the screen.

"Whoa. Someone looks like he's got something to say," Ryan said.

"That's because someone does."

"So, what is it?"

Chris shook his head. "Not what is it, but who."

"Huh?"

Chris gestured to someone off-screen, then a familiar face wearing a baseball cap that said Canucks joined Chris's screen.

No. Way.

Ryan whistled. "No way."

"Big fat way," Chris smirked.

"Zac?" Mike lifted a hand. "Hey, good to see you, man."

Zac nodded, but clearly looked uncomfortable.

"Sorry, but Chris, can you elaborate?"

"I would've thought you guys would've figured this out. Meet the newest member of the Northwest Ice Online Bible study."

"Whoa. Zac? You're joining us?" Ryan asked.

"Are you really a Christian?" Jai asked.

Phrased like that it sounded too close to something Bailey's dad might say, forcing Luc to speak up. "You're welcome here, Zac. And hey, it doesn't matter if you've been a Christian ten minutes or ten years or are still seeking God, we're glad to have you and you're welcome anytime."

"Amen," Franklin said.

"Thanks." Zac nodded.

"Well said," Mike messaged Luc privately in the chat box.

"So, care to fill us in?" Ryan asked.

Chris glanced at Zac, who still seemed as much as of a deer-in-headlights as when Luc first competed on *Dance Off*.

Zac shrugged. "Chris has been yammering at me for months, and I thought I'd come along."

"He's a yammerer, for sure," Luc said, which earned a wry twist of lips from Zac and a round of laughter from the others.

"So, what's the deal, man?" Ryan asked. "Like, don't get me wrong, but you seem to be in a zone above some of us mere mortals."

"Speak for yourself, Ryan."

Ryan ignored Jai's tease. "No, I'm just curious as I've never really heard or seen any kind of faith mentioned with you before."

"Hey, that sounds a little pointed," Chris interrupted. "Maybe it's better if we share about our own experiences before expecting him to do the same."

Zac nodded, and the guys began to share.

"I've been a Christian all my life, and have found God to be my rock, especially in recent years when Bree got really sick," Mike said.

"I didn't grow up as a Christian but had a friend in school help me find the light," Jai said.

"I was similar to Jai," Luc admitted. "I didn't know anything much about God until my twenties, when my mom got sick, and then I found hope in God. Now I trust Him and know He's the most important thing in my life."

He ducked his head as Franklin and Ryan shared, his own words convicting him. If he really was trusting God, then surely he had to trust Him with the mess that was Bailey and her parents? *Hey God, I give it to You. Have Your way.*

Silence filled the screen, and he looked up. Zac shrugged. "I, um, I don't know, maybe it'll make me sound like an arrogant tool, but I've been searching for greater meaning for a while now. I've had a bunch of people in the past point to stuff but it didn't really fill me. And then Chris started talking to me about Jesus, and it made a lot of sense, and I guess I want to know more about this."

Luc nodded. So it didn't sound like the dude had prayed the prayer and crossed over into faith and following Jesus yet. "That's cool. We might be weird, but we're not as weird as some out there."

"I knew you were weird, especially with all that dancing stuff," Zac said, which sparked laughter, and Chris's comment of "True, that."

"Hey, it takes a real man to put on dancing shoes. Anyway, I'm not as weird as Chris."

Zac half-smiled as Chris protested, then shrugged. "But Chris was weird in a way that let me know he cared. So I suppose I just want to know more about… about this God stuff."

"We're glad you're here," Mike said. "What's the point in having the hope and joy in life if we never share that with others?"

"Exactly," Jai agreed. "You'll find we talk through Bible passages, discuss their relevance, and share about what's happening in our lives. Then we pray, and Chris and Luc tease people, and we try to support each other however we can. I think of these guys as like my brothers."

Franklin nodded. "And it extends to our families as well. My sister is in Winnipeg and Luc is keeping an eye on her, so it's nice to know this extends beyond a video call."

Zac nodded. "Cool."

"Speaking of that," Chris said, "How are things going with Bailey's weirdo admirer?" He nudged Zac. "She's Luc's dancer girlfriend, you know from that show? And she's got a stalker or something like that. We've been praying the police find him soon."

Luc's heart tensed. "Still no word."

"That sucks," Zac said.

He nodded. "Big time." But the word "stalker" seemed lodged in his heart, like a stubborn splinter. There might be strain between them, but he needed to talk to her. Pronto. And now he was itching to get home. He glanced at the time. There was still time to call her.

"Oh, and Zac, just a warning," Ryan said. "If you're going to hang around us, you need to know that Luc might look really mean, but he's actually a huge fan of all kinds of girly things."

"Like dancing?" Zac said, with a small smile.

Luc folded his arms, stuffed down a smile. "Don't knock it until you try it."

"And I heard his favorite movie is *Barbie*," Mike razzed.

"And his favorite color is pink," Jai said.

"Is that so?" Zac asked.

"For sure," Luc deadpanned.

Zac grinned. "In that case, I'll send a grand to your cancer charity if you wear a pink suit to your next game."

"Five and you've got a deal." What was he saying? He didn't own a pink suit.

"Now this I want to see." Chris smirked.

"Just make sure your boy there pays up and you will."

"Bring it on." Chris clapped his hands together, and again Luc was reminded to call Bailey.

So with a "Good to have you here" at Zac, and a "keep praying for her" for the rest, Luc ended the video call and called Bailey.

Her phone rang, once, twice, then, "Luc?"

"Bails." He closed his eyes. "I'm sorry about the other day."

"No, you don't have anything to be sorry for. I'm the one who flew off the handle. And what's worse is I knew it at the time, but I did it anyway."

"I don't like arguing with you."

"I don't like it either." She sighed. "And the problem is, I don't know how to argue well, because my family, I mean me, well, we—I have always dealt with disagreements by sweeping them under the carpet. So while I don't like how this feels, I almost feel like it's good for me, because it means I'm being honest for once."

That couldn't have been easy to admit to. He silently thanked God. "I'm really proud of you, Bails."

"Thanks, I'm proud of me too. But Luc, I need to tell you about some other things."

He braced, shoving his face in one hand, his too-long hair flopping over his face. It was way past lettuce, more like cauliflower leaves these days. "What is it?"

"Joanne asked me to join the show again next year."

"She did? That's awesome. Congratulations."

"Do… do you mean that?"

"Of course I do. I don't say things I don't mean, Bails. I'm really happy for you. You deserve it."

"But it would mean me being away for a couple of months or so. I'd be away from you."

His heart warmed. "Then if it's the same time of year then maybe I can come too. Dan Walton has a camp in Muskoka he's always inviting us to help out at. I could go there for a few days, and explore the city with you whenever you were free."

"You'd do that?"

"Absolutely I would." His heart trickled with excitement. He could get some training in, or fly to see his folks, then spend every night on dates with her. "Just don't go getting too tangled in the tango, if you know what I mean."

She laughed. "Well, while I'm being honest, I should tell you that they've also asked me to consider being involved in a dance pro tour in January next year."

More time apart. But this wasn't about him. "They had to ask you because you're the best."

"Oh, Luc. You're sweet."

No, he wasn't. But he was trying to be kinder, to let God's grace soften his tough heart. "I really appreciate you being honest with me. Please keep saying what you mean."

"I'm going to try harder," she admitted. "And I'm also trying to be more honest with my family."

She was?

"I talked with my mom today. We both got pretty honest about things. And it felt good, really good. I even contacted Chrissy again."

"I'm proud of you. That must've taken courage."

"It did. But I'm trying to be braver. You help me to be brave."

Her words, softly spoken, stole inside and clamped his throat. "I love you Bailey."

She sniffled, like she might be crying.

"Are you crying?"

"No."

Sure she wasn't. "Are you telling the truth?"

"No."

He laughed, and she did too, and at his favorite sound his heart eased for the first time in too long. "I miss you, Bails."

"I miss you, too. Just hurry home, okay?"

Home. To Winnipeg. And Bailey.

CHAPTER 27

"Okay ladies, now we're going to finish with your favorites: calf stretches."

Good-natured groans filled the studio. This adult ballet class consisted mostly of women in their forties and over, some of them had danced when they were younger, but some were raw beginners, which meant a range of exercises suitable for all. Fortunately, everyone here could do this last exercise, which began the cooldown component of their class.

"Please take your position at the barre, and remember, this is good for your calves."

She pressed play on the music, and the first sixteen beats began as they rose and lowered on their left leg. The barre wobbled a little as some of the ladies used it to hoist themselves up rather than let their feet and ankles do the work.

"Don't forget this exercise is targeting your calves, so there's no need to grip the barre so hard. Some of you who are more experienced should see if you can do it by holding on with just one finger."

After counting to sixteen, they swapped feet, and did the same again. By now, some of the women liked to complain, but she encouraged them on. The biggest challenge was this next part, when they'd be doing thirty-two calf raises on already fatigued muscles.

She swallowed a smile as the usual ones complained, her mind flicking back to when she'd danced in France, when their teachers would work them so hard she'd sob for hours at home, with feet that were blistered so much she used to soak them in methylated spirits to harden her blisters into calluses. Now *that* was pain.

The music concluded, which saw a bunch of relieved sighs, then they stretched, doing a roll down until their hands were flat on the floor for the supple ones, or ankles or knees depending on their flexibility. Then the class concluded with the traditional side curtsy, followed by the other side, then they were released.

Bailey chatted briefly, but with a new client consultation coming up soon, she didn't change from her pointe shoes, or linger as she might normally, instead gently encouraging them to move on by getting out the spray bottle of disinfectant and wiping down the barre, the cleaning seeming to remind the lingerers to go.

She cleaned, wondering about her next client. S. Zampa hadn't filled out much information, just their age and that they were female, but had booked for a consult. She hoped it wouldn't take long. Luc was due to get home from his road trip soon and she couldn't wait to see him. She had her outfit picked out, and was due to the hair salon as soon as this was done. Tonight was going to be special. She was finally going to say those three words she knew he needed to hear.

Now that school had returned, and their classes were up and running, she and Poppy were working harder than ever. It wasn't just the teaching either, but coming up with new content they shared on Bailey's YouTube channel. The sharing of *Dance Off* videos had run its course, so to capitalize on their subscribers they'd decided to release one new instructional video on a particular style of dance each week. Sometimes it was a full dance, sometimes it was just a sequence from a particular style, but seeing there were so many styles to choose from with everything from ballet to tango, tap and jazz, it meant they had content for years to come. And the five-minute videos were pretty raw, especially in contrast to the *Dance Off* professional videos, but people seemed to enjoy them, and enjoy the interactions between her and Poppy, even though many of the comments asked to see more of Luc and Bailey dancing together.

Turning off comments on her Instagram had helped stop some of the more lewd suggestions, and she'd increased the privacy settings around her social media. Their glossy new website wasn't shy about featuring Bailey's *Dance Off* connections. All of this was exactly what Coco said she should be doing, but chasing likes and shares and subscribers and such things felt a little artificial. Especially when all she really wanted in her world was God, time with Luc, and dancing.

"Are you all good here?" Poppy asked, as she shut the door to the office.

Bailey nodded. "I just have one more potential client who's running late."

"Want me to stay?"

"You have to get ready for your date, right?"

Poppy grinned, and did a little twirl. "I do, but I'm happy to wait."

Their safety system saw both of them stay at the studio until the last class was done, allowing for safe passage to their vehicles, especially during Winnipeg's early dark nights. But this client was a woman, and Poppy had a date for the first time in forever, so who was she to hold her up? "It's okay. This is just an initial consult, not a dance, so I'll be fine. I'll be home soon, anyway."

"Okay, well, be safe," Poppy warned.

Bailey nodded, and held up her phone. "I've got the app ready to be activated. But don't worry about me. I'll be fine. Now have fun!"

"He seems really nice," Poppy gushed.

"You be safe, too."

Poppy saluted and departed, and the studio fell silent.

Bailey stretched, swaying, closing her eyes as she waited for the client. She'd give Ms. Zampa ten more minutes, then she'd need to leave. It was already ten past their agreed-upon start time. She smiled, remembering the times when Luc would come to rehearse, and everything felt so strange. Now, he was like her favorite sweater, comfy, his arms around her like a cozy blanket, sure and strong, able to withstand the winds and chills of life. Hugging him was her favorite thing, apart from kissing, of course. Or dancing like they used to, his body close to hers, his gaze intense, like he wanted to—

Nope. She wouldn't think like that. She needed to see him, to say in person what tears had stopped her saying on the phone. She couldn't *wait* to see him tonight.

"Ahem."

"Oh!" Her eyes flew open, then she stumbled slightly. "Can… can I help you?"

The man wasn't her client. And she had the funniest feeling she'd seen him somewhere before.

He smiled, then she recognized him. The man at the rink all those weeks ago. When Luc had taken her skating and she'd wondered about the dynamic between the two men. What was he doing here?

She picked up her phone, checked the time. "I'm sorry, but I have an appointment with someone."

"I think you'll find that person is me."

"You? Are you…" she squinted at the screen. "Are you S. Zampa?"

He nodded.

Funny. She didn't recall that name at all. And, "You don't look like a woman to me."

"I'm glad you can tell the difference."

His smile took on an edge that made her insides roil. That's right. Luc had said this man had been involved in some immoral things. He advanced, and she fought the temptation to back away. She'd taught some surly teens hip-hop back in the day, and she'd learned it never paid to let them see her intimidated. But what she'd give for some of Luc's size and heft about now.

She arched an eyebrow. "I think you need to leave."

"I think," he drew closer still, "you need to dance with me."

That was it. She stabbed her phone's emergency button, and lifted her chin. "I need you to leave."

"No. I made an appointment. I'm going to get what I came for."

"Which is?"

"You."

Chills rippled up her spine as he reached to touch her. She drew back. "You need to keep your hands away."

"Who says?"

"I do." *Lord, help me out here. I need Your protection!*

"Well, that doesn't mean much."

She stepped away again, their strange dance something she hoped the security camera was recording. Dad had paid that bill, right? "I don't understand why you are here, but I need you to leave. Now." She put steel into that last word.

"Oh, look who is trying to be a tough girl. Did you speak like that to Luc?"

"Excuse me?"

"You know, your dancing partner. Everyone's favorite, Luc Blanchard." He sneered.

"Have you got a problem with him?"

"You could say that. Especially seeing he got me fired from the team."

"For what? Harassing women?" she dared.

"It's not harassing when they're dressed like that," he pointed to her leotard with its back cutouts, "and basically begging for it."

Where was Poppy? Oh, she wished Luc was nearer, and not just getting back from the airport! Surely someone should have got the message by now! She had to keep the conversation going until Poppy arrived. Maybe God would give her some wisdom to know what to do.

"I don't know what you're talking about, but I need to leave." She moved to the door, but before she could hurry out he grabbed her arm. "Let go of me."

"No. I want Luc to know how it feels when something you love is gone."

"Excuse me?" Her heart thudded with fear. She could smell the alcohol on his breath. "This is ridiculous. I don't even know you."

"Yes, you do. He introduced us, remember?"

She wrenched free. "Now get out, before I call the police." They should be on their way, anyway.

"No." He grabbed her again. "You can teach me to dance the way you taught him."

"No." She pulled away, slapping his hand as he reached for her chest. "Get away from me!" She followed this up with a solid kick to his groin.

He swore and hunched over, wincing, and she fled, knowing the pointe shoe would have to hurt. She'd almost reached the door when he grabbed her, something dark filled his face, then he slapped her and she fell to the floor. He straddled her, pawing at her chest as she screamed, and slapped him, scratching his face as he swore and threatened and she cried and kneed him and did her best to roll him off. But he was too big, too strong, too heavy, too much, and—"Lord, help me!"

She heard a yell, her vision blurring as she caught a glimpse of a face then a booted foot, heard a high-pitched yelp, as pain, exquisite pain, rocked her face and she blacked out.

"BAILEY! BAILEY!" Luc tried to shake her awake but she didn't move. He glanced at where Sean Hart lay out cold, as sirens blared. Footsteps rushed down the hall and he braced, but no, it was only Poppy, who must've got the same emergency call that had hauled his big butt here, where he'd seen Hart assaulting poor Bailey.

Poppy's shriek was like a wild animal's. "Is she alive?"

"Yes, but unconscious."

Some guy he'd never met entered, glanced at Poppy, glanced at Luc, then staggered to a stop. "Whoa. You're Luc Blanchard, right?"

Luc ignored him. "Have you called the police?"

"That's them now."

A groan stole his attention to his ex-teammate lying in the corner. "Poppy, come here, check on Bailey. I need to make sure that"—he said a non-Bailey's-dad-approved word— "doesn't go anywhere."

Poppy nodded, wiping her face, smearing her makeup, while her date, whoever he was, drew out his phone, then took a pic of him and one of Bailey.

"What do you think you're doing?" Luc yelled.

Poppy stared, horrified, from her position on the floor. "Devon? What on earth—?"

Luc hurried over to him, snatched his phone and threw it across the room where it smashed into a hundred pieces. No *way* was anyone ever going to post about this. What a sick—

"Hey!"

Sean rolled, groaning, and Luc was sorely tempted to kick him where it would make it impossible to procreate, when the police arrived, followed by the paramedics.

"You, hold it right there."

Luc put up his hands. "This man tried to rape my girlfriend." His voice shook. "I got here and kicked him off." His throat closed. "Please, help her. She's unconscious, and—"

"Who are you?"

He told them—"you're Luc Blanchard?"—and Poppy shared what she knew, including the date who'd tried to take a photo which accounted for the smashed phone.

"He destroyed my phone! I don't care how famous he is, he's gonna have to pay."

The next moments were a blur as Luc answered more questions, tried to recall specific details, tried to think how this would play out. But he had zero experience with anything like this, only knew that somehow he needed to let the club know that their new captain had got into a fight and police were involved.

He called Bailey's mom, his coach, his agent, his mom, and Mike Vaughan. He needed people who would pray, who'd help him and Bailey, and needed news of this contained. How on earth was anyone going to trust a man potentially accused of assault—with leading the team, with Bailey?

Emotion clamped his throat, and he sank to his knees, hands over his mouth, as he watched Bailey being loaded onto a gurney. "Can I go with her?"

"Sorry. You need to come with us to the station."

IT WAS LATE when he made it to his apartment. Travis had collected him from the police station, and he'd been assured by

Poppy from the hospital that Bailey had woken and was fine, but couldn't see visitors.

He unlocked his door, threw down his keys, and stumbled to the bathroom, regrets chasing him inside. Why couldn't he have got there quicker? If he'd skipped the haircut which he'd done to look more professional he would've been there, could've protected her. Instead he'd failed. Let her fall. None of this would've happened if it wasn't for him. It was his fault.

He turned on the shower, catching a glimpse of himself in the bathroom mirror. The haggard cast to his face, the shadows, the blood that still spotted his shirt. Thank God none of that was Bailey's. He couldn't live with himself if that was so.

He stripped off his clothes, but barely noticed the water pummeling his shoulders as awful memories from the night bubbled like a toxic brew. Bailey, helpless. Evil, trying to steal. Her mom's scream. His coach's shock. The police interviews. The murmurs that he might face possible charges against Sean. His team wouldn't want him as captain. Bailey wouldn't want him when his presence in her life had put her life at risk. Her family who'd dealt with domestic violence in the past would only see his violence again and not that he'd just tried to save the woman he loved.

That he *loved*.

"Lord. We need some miracles." And he sank to his knees, his tears joining the water from above.

CHAPTER 28

*O*ords were funny things. They had the power to
hurt or heal. They had the power to strengthen
or steal. *I love you. Please forgive me. I'm sorry.*

The whispers of this trio of phrases rolled to her ears, in and
then out like the waves on the sand. *I love you. Please forgive me.
I'm sorry.*

She recognized the deep voice, but not the rasp, not the
wobble, not the break, like this man was in tears. She slowly
opened her eyes, saw gray light wash over a bowed dark head, a
man clutching her hand. Who?

Maybe she made a sound, for his muffled words ceased as he
looked at her, his dark eyes widening. "Bailey? Oh, thank You,
Jesus. Bails, do you recognize me?"

She squeezed his hand. "Luc."

Tears slipped from his eyes and her heart grew sore. "I'm so
sorry, baby. Please forgive me. I love you."

She tangled his fingers with hers. "I love you too."

He pressed his lips to her palm.

Her nose wrinkled at the smell of antiseptic, the white room,
the unfamiliar sights and sounds. "What's happened?"

His Adam's apple dipped as he swallowed. "You… you don't remember?"

She shook her head, then winced.

"Careful. The doc thinks you might've got a concussion."

From what?

Then it rushed back at her. The man. The attack. The way Luc had saved her. "You were there."

He nodded. "I got the alarm when I was on the way. I was going to surprise you and arrive earlier, but I didn't get there in time, and I'm so sorry."

"But you were there."

"But I would've been there earlier, and could've prevented it from happening."

"I had a class though, didn't I?" So much felt foggy still.

"Yeah, I know you said not to come too early because of that, but because our plane got back early, I figured I had time to stop and get my hair done, and I wanted to surprise you." He put a hand self-consciously though his newly shorn hair. The mullet was gone. "I shouldn't have done that. I should've been there."

"But you *were* there. You were there when I needed you the most."

His lips pressed together and he shook his head. "None of this would've happened if it wasn't for me. So it's my fault Sean attacked you."

"You can't know what's going to happen in the future, Luc. You're not responsible for what others do or think." She gestured for him to come nearer. Then she drew his head down and stroked his hair. "I like it," she murmured. "And you didn't lose your Samson strength, did you?"

He turned to face her, his cheek resting gently on her stomach. "I think I might've used one of your jive kicks on him."

"Aren't you glad you learned to dance?"

His lips twisted wryly. "I spoke to the police last night, and again this morning, and you don't need to worry about him. The police have him in custody."

She nodded, vague memories of giving statements to them last night piercing her mental fog.

"From what they've said this morning, between the footage on the video, his phone records, and his prior offences, there looks to be enough evidence to put him away for a long time. So you're safe."

"You've always kept me safe," she murmured. "You never once let me fall."

"I'll always try to save you," he whispered hoarsely, his dark eyes glistening like he was fighting back tears.

Her heart stirred with deep compassion. She stroked his hair. "And you? Are you okay?"

"Coach said the team management need to see me this morning, so I've asked the guys to pray. I'm guessing they don't want a captain involved in this kind of thing."

"You might be surprised. Who wouldn't want someone who stands up for what's right and does what he can to protect those he loves?"

He swiped at his eyes, then rasped, "I love you, Bails."

She smiled. "I love you, Luc."

He drew in a shaky breath, then lifted his head and moved closer, closer, his bristled jaw drawing nearer before he captured her lips in a kiss. The fog and pain disappeared as a sense of rightness, satisfaction, of coming home filled her, and her hand lifted to cradle his bruised cheek. Yearning for him made her long to deepen it, but he drew back, smiling, just as a nurse entered the room.

"Bailey, you're awake." She moved to the monitor and wrote something on a chart. "I'll tell your parents and friend that they're allowed to come in, if you like. They've all been very worried."

"I should go and get ready for this team meeting." Luc said.

"Your dad wasn't happy when I came late last night and insisted on staying, but the nurse was kind and snuck me in. She's a fan."

Her fingers tangled with his. "Of course she is. I'm a fan of yours too."

"No." He smiled. "She's a fan of yours. From the show."

A different nurse appeared, carrying a vase of roses, which she deposited on the window ledge along with half a dozen others. She glanced at their hands, smiled, then gestured to the roses. "Apparently these are from a Z. Parotti."

Luc snickered. "Of course they are."

"I haven't met him, have I?"

"I think you're going to."

He mentioned some other names, but she barely heard. So much love, from people she knew, and those whom she might one day. Then there was this man, his heart, his lips, his life ready to help her, to protect her, and help her be more brave. She reached for his hand, and gently squeezed. "I love you."

His face softened, and she thought he might try for another kiss, when noise drew her attention to the door.

"Bailey?"

"Mom."

Her mother rushed to her, her father not far behind, followed by Poppy, and she was clasped in hugs and rained with more tears. "Oh, honey. How are you feeling?"

"Like I've been hit by a truck." She caught Luc's wince, and grabbed his hand again. "I didn't mean you."

Her mother turned to Luc, and hugged him. "Luc, I can never thank you enough. From what the police say, Bailey owes you her life."

"I love her, Mrs. Donovan. And I once promised to never let her down. And I mean to keep that promise all my life."

Her mother glanced at Bailey, then back at him. "And I want you to know we're very sorry we haven't always treated you as we should have."

"I understand."

"You're a more gracious man than some," she murmured.

Like Bailey's father, who had barely looked at Luc since entering the room. Bailey's heart hurt.

Luc soon made his apologies for leaving, blew her a kiss, his exit pulling a plug on what remained of her energy, and she soon closed her eyes and fell back into sleep.

WHEN NEXT SHE awoke it was to see her father in the room, no one else. "Dad?"

He looked up from reading his Bible. He looked older these days. "You're awake. Thank You, Lord. How's your head feeling, sweetheart?"

"It hurts, but I think the meds they gave me before are helping." She pushed up against the pillows. "Where's Mom?"

"She's at the studio with Poppy, seeing the police are finished there now. They're covering your classes, as they figured that'd be easier than cancelling and giving all kinds of explanations."

"And Luc?"

"He's still at his meeting with the club." He swallowed. "The police told us what he did, that he saved your life. I… I haven't been fair to him, have I?"

She could lie and pretend in order to keep the peace, but those days were done. "No. Luc is a good man, and I love him. And I wish you'd learn to like him for my sake. And you know he only did that to protect me." She smiled. "He's obviously got as big a protective streak as you."

Her father shook his head, and her heart dropped. Did her father still resent Luc?

"I should've been the one to protect you, but I didn't know…" Her father's gaze met hers. "I didn't know about this stalker person. I wish you'd told me."

"I didn't realize it would escalate like that. I thought it was just a few random people and I didn't want to worry you and Mom."

"Because of my overprotective streak?"

In the quiet of the room with no one else here, perhaps this was the time to finally be honest. "Dad, I know you love me, but I am an adult. I'll be twenty-five next month. And sooner or later you're going to have to let me make my own decisions even if you don't like all of them."

"But honey—"

"No, Dad, please let me finish. See, I know you didn't like some of my costumes or routines with Luc. You know I was given my outfits and told by the producers to make my routines more sexy."

His nose wrinkled, and she realized that she'd never said that word aloud to her father before.

"And I'm sorry you were upset, but looking back on the experience I'm so glad I did it. You know they've asked me to do a second season?"

"That's exciting."

She nodded, then winced at the pain. "It is, but it means I'm going to have to put some new measures in place." She swallowed. "Especially with the business."

He frowned. "I don't understand."

Lord, help me to be honest. Help him to hear. "Poppy and I have been talking with the bank and we need a new accounting system to make sure things like fees and loan repayments get paid on time."

"I can try and learn a new program."

She reached to clasp his hand. "It's okay. We've talked to someone who can help us who deals with this kind of thing all the time. But thank you." There. That was kind and yet honest.

Her father nodded and looked down. "It's hard to get older, seeing your children live their own lives. I want to help my children, and you and your mother always had dance in common, but I haven't known what I can do. You know we've always just wanted to support you."

"You *do* support us. I know you love me, but sometimes what I need most is a hug and a listening ear."

She swallowed. This time of raw openness was so rare, it felt like God had opened this door to say what had been left unsaid for far too long. "I know both Rhett and I have felt supported by you, but I know that Chrissy would like that too."

His lips pressed together.

"She's hurting, Dad. She feels rejected by God and by us, and she'll never come back unless she knows we want her home." She motioned to his Bible. "She's the prodigal daughter, and just like the Father ran to welcome the lost son, so we need to run and hug her." Her eyes filled. "I miss her, Dad. I hate that she's not around anymore."

He squeezed her hand, but didn't say anything, and she prayed that what he read would change his heart.

A noise stole her attention to the door. Luc stood there with her mom, her mom's makeup smudged like she might've been crying. "Mom? Is everything okay?"

Luc wrapped an arm around her and gently escorted her to Bailey's father. Were her mom's tears because she'd overheard that exchange?

Bailey glanced up at Luc, and he reached to clasp her hand. "She'll be fine. Give her a minute," he murmured. "You're looking better."

She sighed. "I feel like I've been run over by a bus."

"Sometimes speaking the truth can be like that."

So he *had* heard her.

Luc's strength wrapped around her as he leaned down and gently hugged her. "I'm really proud of you, Bails."

She closed her eyes, clutched him tighter, savoring his nearness. "Don't let me fall back into fakeness."

"I'll keep you honest," he murmured.

"And you?" She drew back, glanced up at him. "How did your meeting go? Are you okay?"

His smile was crooked. "Never better."

"Really?"

He nodded. "The club is fine, the police have officially cleared me. It's all good, truly." His gaze was deep. "You can always trust me, Bails. I'll never lie to you."

She nodded, knowing this was true. Luc Blanchard might be tough and know how to use his fists, but she could trust him. Her protector, her best friend, her courage-giver, her number one cheerleader. The one whose presence cheered her heart most of all.

LUC GLANCED at the woman standing next to him, gnawing her nails. "Hey, it's gonna be okay."

"Why are you doing this?"

Admit that as soon as he'd heard Bailey's words to her father in the hospital room and seen the tears trickle down her mother's cheeks that he'd felt a solid *yes* in his spirit about what he could do? That he'd been so proud of her he'd determined then and there to make her deepest wish come true? "Because it's Bailey's birthday, and you'll be the best present." He shrugged. "And if it means she thinks I'm the best because I got her the best present, then I'm okay with that, too."

She laughed, the sound tinkling like Bailey's. "You're weird."

"Yes I am." He nudged her. "But you're weirder, doing this with some random guy you've never met before."

The amusement faded from her face. "Haven't you heard? That's what I do. I've always been the weird one."

"I think we can all be weird in our various ways. Which is just as well, right? Imagine if we were all plain vanilla."

The elevator stopped, and he led the way to his apartment.

"You're wrong, you know," she said. "About being random. I recognized your name. I watched you both on that dancing show. You and she were…"

He glanced at her, recognized the blinking back of tears. "That bad, huh?"

She laughed again, pushed his shoulder. "No, I was gonna say amazing, and that it was everything Gran and I hoped for, but now I won't."

"Fair enough."

She snickered. "I understand why she likes you."

"I've been told I can be very charming." He held out his arm. "And that I look great in a pink suit."

She grasped his arm, glancing up with nervous eyes that looked so much like Bailey's.

"It's okay. You've got this. And so does God," he added for good measure.

Her chin dipped, and nerves stole over him. It was one thing to plan this with Mrs. Donovan, quite another to enact this and hope all went as he'd prayed. Secret-keeping might have its issues but he hoped this one would count as a good surprise.

He opened the door, leaving her at the foyer and walked through various groups of chattering people and scores of pink helium balloons.

"What took you?" Bailey asked, from her chair—the leather chair that matched his that he'd bought so she could always feel at home here. "Let me guess, you got bailed up by fans wanting pics with you in that pink suit."

Yeah, there'd been a moment or two like that while he'd waited downstairs for the taxi to arrive. Zac's dare of a pink suit had seen Luc wear it on more than a few occasions. And because he was so secure in his masculinity, he'd even themed tonight's party around that very color. The room was filled with floral bouquets of that color, from everyone from his teammates to Ryan and Sylvie, Chris and Diana, and Dan and Sarah.

"Apparently the captain is supposed to be nice to fans. Who knew?"

"They like you a lot around here."

So they should. That's what a five-game winning streak should earn a man. He slapped his chest. "Hey, there's a lot to like about a sharp-dressed man."

"Didn't you get any ice cream?"

"Ice cream? Oh man. I forgot." He studied her, loving how comfortable and easy she looked sitting there, among her family and friends, like last month's attack was a distant memory. "But I did get you something better." He stepped to the foyer, and gestured his special guest forward.

Bailey's jaw dropped, then she squealed, and in a leap worthy of a ten she wrapped her arms around her sister, a hug which was soon joined by her mom, her brother, and her father, and plenty of tears. "I can't believe you're here!"

"Told you." He smirked at Chrissy, before moving to the kitchen island where Cindy sat near Poppy and Molly, who were both watching the reunion with "Aww" faces.

He cracked his knuckles and glanced at his mom. "See what they're like? So huggy. Man." He rolled his eyes and smiled.

"You need to marry that girl, Lucas. I want grandbabies."

He kissed her cheek. "You'll get 'em. One day, when it's the right time."

He glanced at Cindy, who had behaved herself so far but was now frowning.

He was tempted to go talk to Travis, but felt his hosting duties—and maybe God—prompt him to ask, "So, is there anything I can get you?" He motioned to the pink mocktail Sarah Walton had described as a "Fairy Floss Delight" when he'd messaged her and Bree about girly drinks they thought Bailey might like. "Need a refill?"

She shook her head.

He longed to go, but his feet had rooted to the ground. "Thanks for coming."

"You don't mean that."

"Hey." He touched her arm. "You are part of her family, and you know that's important to her."

She ducked her head.

"What is it?"

"It's not that easy, you know."

"What isn't?" Being accepted by them? Well, Wayne liked him enough now, apparently having swallowed his pride and finally heard Bailey's request to give Luc a chance. Luc and Rhett were tight, and he was pretty sure Bailey's mom was like his and saw a wedding next year. As for Chrissy, he hoped his actions in bringing her home meant she'd give him a chance, too.

"Having babies," Cindy whispered.

Oh. He glanced around, but everyone else was busy in other conversations. Looked like this was something God wanted him to step into. *Lord, You better help me here.* "I'm sorry." It was always good to start with the truth.

She shook her head. "I just want one. You know how hard it is to see everyone else achieving their dreams and I can't even get pregnant?"

The despair in her voice cracked the wall he'd had in place since she was so mean to Bailey. "Do you trust God?"

"I'm trying."

"I can't give you any answers, except if you're God's child, then you can always know He's got you in the palm of His hands and you can trust Him with your future. That whatever happens, it's ultimately going to be for good."

She ducked her head, blinking rapidly. He grasped her arm. "I'll be praying."

Her chin dipped, then she slid off the stool and took her drink to the window, staring out at the sunset. He prayed for her, his gaze slipping to Bailey as she wrapped her arms around his waist. "What was that about?"

"She's hurting, but I think we might've turned a corner."

She nodded, clasping his hand as they used to do for their dancing. "Thank you so much for bringing Chrissy here."

He spun her, then lowered her into a dip. "You're very welcome."

He pulled her upright, and her hands stole around his neck. "Best boyfriend ever."

"You know it." He pressed his lips to hers, happy to let the world fade in this moment of perfection.

"Luc, stop kissing her. We're going to be late," Poppy called.

"Late to what?" Bailey asked.

"To your party."

"But this is my party, isn't it?" She glanced up at Luc.

"This is the pre-party. The real one is at the studio, with all your kids."

"Really?" At his nod her jaw dropped. "Will there be dancing?"

"You betcha." His head tilted to Poppy. "She's been arguing with me all week about the best tunes."

"I can't believe it." Bailey's blue eyes lit with stars. "You're throwing a dance party for me?"

"Of course I am. You're worth it." He smiled. "And I love you."

"Aww!"

He shot a look at Molly and Poppy, both of whom were doing the chest pat and tilted head move. "What are you two looking at? Don't you have another party to get to?"

Poppy pointed her finger at him. "We're having a jive-off, just warning you."

"Bring it." He pointed to Travis and Rhett. "I hope you two are ready to learn some boss moves to do with your ladies."

"From you?" Bailey said, smiling up at him.

"Nah. I'm still a learner, but I'm happy to demonstrate a few moves with you, if that's okay with the birthday girl."

Her laughter rippled, his favorite sound. "One hundred percent."

He wrapped his arm around her, looked down into those shining eyes. "You and me. We're partners forever, right?"

She grinned. "They didn't know what they were doing when they put us together to dance all those months ago."

"But God did."

She nodded. "God definitely did."

And she leaned against him, offering her lips which he claimed in a kiss that sparkled light and hope and joy and a future shinier than any mirror ball.

THE END

Enjoyed this? Then make sure you check out *Faking the Shot*, book 4 in the Northwest Ice Christian hockey romance series

A NOTE FROM THE AUTHOR

Thank you for reading *Pointe, Shoots, and Scores,* the third book in the Northwest Ice romance series. I have long enjoyed *Dancing with the Stars*-type shows, so it was super fun to imagine how a tough hockey player like Luc would act when placed in his worst nightmare! As someone who grew up doing ballet, I was excited to get back into it recently, and to imagine how someone like Bailey would adjust to a new dream when her original plan fell through.

Huge thanks to Brooke Charpentier, director of Infused Dance and Infused Fitness, whose experiences as an interstate and international ballet professional and running a dance studio helped to colour some parts of this story. www.infusedfitness dance.com.au

~

Reviews help other readers find new-to-them authors, so if you can spare a moment to write a quick review at Goodreads / your place of purchase, I'd be very grateful.

Make sure you check out Zac and Ainsley's story in the next book in the Northwest Ice romance series, *Faking the Shot*.

If you enjoy Christian contemporary romance you may want to check out the books in the Original Six hockey romance series, a sweet & swoony, slightly sporty Christian contemporary romance series.

The Breakup Project
Love on Ice
Checked Impressions
Hearts and Goals
Big Apple Atonement
Muskoka Blue

Romance fans who enjoy small town life may also enjoy reading the Muskoka Romance series, that starts with *Muskoka Shores*.

I'd love for you to check out my other books and to sign up for my newsletter at www.carolynmillerauthor.com where you can be the first to learn all my book and contest news, and discover more behind-the-book details and photos. Newsletter subscribers can also get an exclusive bonus book free, so grab your copy of *Originally Yours* here.

If you're on Spotify and want to listen to some of the music that inspired this and other Northwest Ice novels, then please check out the Northwest Ice Spotify playlist.

ABOUT THE AUTHOR

Carolyn Miller lives in the beautiful Southern Highlands of New South Wales, Australia, with her husband and four children. A long-time lover of romance, especially that of Jane Austen, Georgette Heyer and LM Montgomery, Carolyn loves to write contemporary and historical romance that draws readers into fictional worlds that show the truth of God's grace in our lives.

To find out more about Carolyn's books, and to subscribe to her newsletter, please visit www.carolynmillerauthor.com

You can also connect with her at

ALSO BY CAROLYN MILLER

Contemporary:

<u>The Original Six hockey series</u>
The Breakup Project
Love on Ice
Checked Impressions
Hearts and Goals
Big Apple Atonement
Muskoka Blue

<u>Muskoka Romance series</u>
Muskoka Shores
Muskoka Christmas
Muskoka Hearts
Muskoka Spotlight
Muskoka Holiday Morsels
Muskoka Promise
Muskoka Miracle

<u>Northwest Ice hockey series</u>
Fire and Ice
The Love Penalty
Pointe, Shoots, and Scores
Faking the Shot

<u>Three Creeks Ranch Romance series</u>

A Cameo for a Cowgirl

A Valentine for a Vet

<u>Trinity Lakes collection</u>

Love Somebody Like You

Tangled Up in Love

Only You Can Love Me

<u>The Independence Islands series</u>

Restoring Fairhaven

Regaining Mercy

Reclaiming Hope

Rebuilding Hearts

Refining Josie

<u>Our House on Sycamore Street</u>

The Lost Daughter's Irishman

Historical:

<u>Regency Wallflowers</u>

Dusk's Darkest Shores

Midnight's Budding Morrow

Dawn's Untrodden Green

<u>Regency Brides: Legacy of Grace</u>

The Elusive Miss Ellison

The Captivating Lady Charlotte

The Dishonorable Miss DeLancey

<u>Regency Brides: Promise of Hope</u>

Winning Miss Winthrop

Miss Serena's Secret

The Making of Mrs Hale

<u>Regency Brides: Daughters of Aynsley</u>

A Hero for Miss Hatherleigh

Underestimating Miss Cecilia

Misleading Miss Verity

'Heaven and Nature Sing' from the Joy to the World Christmas
novella collection

'More than Gold' from

the Across the Shores novella collection

'Convincing the Circuit Preacher' from

The Courting the Country Preacher novella collection

www.ingramcontent.com/pod-product-compliance
Lightning Source LLC
Chambersburg PA
CBHW031309210726
48287CB00005B/1476